4-5-05

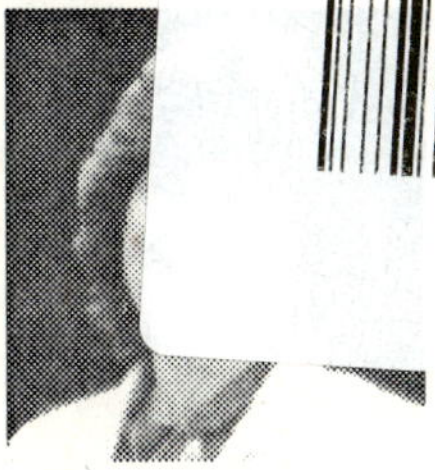

Rosie Ford was born in Haverfordwest, Pembrokeshire and lived in Whaley Bridge until 1974 before moving to Buxton, Derbyshire. She worked as a weaver at Goyt Mills until 1969. Married to John, she has four children – three sons and a daughter. When her last son left home to live in London she started writing children's stories. "The Moores of Bridgevale" is the sequel to "Weaver's Knot".

To Margaret
with love & Best Wishes

Rosie Ford
xx
x

THE MOORES OF BRIDGEVALE

BY

ROSIE FORD

Published 2005 by arima publishing

www.arimapublishing.com

ISBN 1-84549-017-7

Printed and bound in the United Kingdom

Typeset in Garamond 11/16

arima publishing
ASK House, Northgate Avenue
Bury St Edmunds, Suffolk IP32 6BB
t: (+44) 01284 700321

www.arimapublishing.com

This Book is dedicated to the memory of my father
William Francis Ford
6th August 1912 – 26th December 1982

The song has ended but the melody lingers on.

(Ye Carrie Du)

CHAPTER ONE

First Anniversary

A chill wind swept through the churchyard, it was a cold place, even at the height of summer. Lizzie arranged the buttercups and daisies in the old jam jar, the tears trickled down her cheeks, "Oh Camy" she whispered, "why did tha hav ta die? Why did ya leave me?" She had loved Camy so much and without her, life was unbearable. It had been one year today since that dreadful night when Mam had died, and herself and Joe and little Alex had heard the sobbing and running about, they had wondered what was going on, Mam must be poorly again, Lizzie wished they would be quiet and let her go to sleep. If Dad came home he would go bloody mad, all that racket, she hoped he wouldn't be drunk, she didn't like him very much but when he was drunk she was scared to death and hid under the covers and clung to Camy, but Camy hadn't come home that night. Her brothers had searched high and low for her, young Jim had been demented, pacing up and down the street, it was bad enough that Mam had died but for Camy, who cared so much for everyone, to go out and not come back home was unthinkable. She was never to come home again alive. Her body had lain in the parlour next to Sally's, two coffins side by side, two beautiful women taken so tragically, one in the prime of her life, with everything to live for but preferring not to. Lizzie remembered the dreadful screams coming from sisters Jean and Mary and Aunty Ada that morning, when Aggy ran to tell them about finding the bodies of Camy and Finton bobbing up and down in the weir. The whole neighbourhood had reeled with the shock, and the Moore household would never be the same again. They had been buried together, Ada adamant that Sally's son would not be laid to rest anywhere else, Ted and Ada had paid for the new plot and the simple headstone which read: "At Rest 21st June 1938, Sally Moore aged 41 Years. Also Cameo, beloved daughter aged 17 Years. Also Finton O'Grady, beloved son aged 25 years. So beautifully, but so briefly ours." It was so beautiful thought Lizzie, the dark marble with gold lettering. She loved to come here and feel close to Camy, her Camy. She looked down at the jam jar with the buttercups and daisies, "one day when I'm working I'll buy you red roses," she said every week. She meant it too; when she was able there would be three red roses every week as long as she lived. "I'm going home now Camy, ta-ra for now." She left the churchyard by the side entrance, she always liked to see the tombstones on the old part of the yard, the inscriptions always interested her, what she could read of them, which wasn't a lot but there were carvings of Angels and babies to see. Not many flowers in this part, probably because all the families had died out. There were many crypts too, she was a bit frightened of these and usually scuttled past quickly. From the top of the hill there was a magnificent view, fields and hedgerows and the rooftops and mill chimneys bathed in sunlight, the canal glinting and winding it's way down the valley from up there. Lizzie knew that Camy would always be watching over them all. The tears sprang to her eyes again when she remembered the funeral, that awful day. Everyone in the village was upset about the three deaths, no-one could believe that Sally Moore had an illegitimate son aged 25 years, she had never spoken about him even to her sister Ada, eh, it was a right old how d'ya do and no mistake. If that wasn't enough for the gossip-mongers, the father of the lad Finton was a bloody millionaire, his sister had stayed on to the funeral and offered "financial help" but Ada had turned it down, "we see to our own thank you very much I'm sure. The sooner Mrs Ernestine Lawson-Bloody Groves heads back to London the better for everyone," said Ada to herself. They had nothing at all in common these two formidable women, Ernestine with her furs, chauffeur, and Ada like a Galleon in full sail taking command like Bodicia. Ada had suffered badly by the deaths of her loved ones and she mourned them deeply, her life would never be the same again, but she had to take the family in hand and get on with life as best she could, no more cups of tea and a fag with our Sal, no more tittle tattle 'round the kitchen table, no mucky jokes or harmless chit chat, that was all over now. She would never see her beloved sister until the judgement day, then and only then would they be re-united. That day would be worth waiting for although not yet, she didn't want to leave Ted or the other kids just yet. She missed Camy too, that lovely young lass so much in love with her Finton, life had dealt them a bloody awful cruel blow. Ada cleared the image of their dead bodies out of her mind, sometimes the thought of it almost drove her mad.

Lizzie passed by the foundry where her dad and brothers worked, Big Jim wasn't any comfort for his children, and he spent all his time with Meg or Ginny at the pubs, coming home legless every night. He could be heard sobbing for Sally over and over again, it was pitiful to hear. He was still as bad tempered as ever, until Aunty Ada arrived then he would shut up and clear off to work. Lizzie decided to call on Sister Jean and see little Elizabeth Jean, she was one year old now and she was beautiful, everyone said she looked just like Cameo. Lizzie loved her very much and Sally Victoria too, she looked very much like Sal when she was a young lass, so Aunty Ada always said, and if that made her happy, what the hell? Hadn't everyone suffered enough, whatever they could use to cling to their loved and lost ones, was alright with all of the family.

Lizzie arrived at sister Jean's neat cottage and was made immediately welcome, "where 'ast bin our Lizzie?" enquired Jean, putting the kettle on the fire, "bin up'th' boneyard our Jean," she answered, Jean's eyes swam with tears, she didn't need reminding it was one year today since fate had dealt them that cruel, cruel blow. However, the daft way Lizzie had of talking about the Churchyard always made Jean smile. "Buttercups and daisies again I bet, eh Lizzie? Go upstairs an' bring baby down wilt tha?" she didn't need telling twice and galloped up the stairs two at a time, baby Elizabeth was standing up in her cot ready to be picked up and cuddled, she gurgled with delight at Lizzie and squealed with pleasure when she was whirled round the bedroom, round and round 'til Lizzie felt quite dizzy. Little Elizabeth didn't want to stop, she was ready for another go, but Lizzie had had enough so holding her tightly she went down the stairs to Jean who took over the baby to change her bottom and put on dry clothes. Lizzie then played with her for about an hour, it was good to watch them so happy together. Jean missed her sister Cameo badly still, she was always so loving and kind and Jean's heart ached to see her once more, just one more time, but she knew that could never be. It was a scary time too, there was always talk of war, and everyone said there would be war with Germany. Adolf Hitler was getting up everyone's nose and most folk were really afraid of what the future held for them and their families. She looked at baby Elizabeth and prayed that it wouldn't happen; she couldn't bear the thought of anything happening to her family. What would she do if Arthur were called up and had to go away and fight the enemy, "don't think about it Jean," she told herself, "don't think about it". She called to Lizzie, "come on our Liz, its time tha were goin' 'ome, Aunty will be waitin' fer thee."

"Aye, all reet Jean, I'll geroff now then, thanks fer th' tea an' cake," she said and kissing little Elizabeth Jean, she bade "ta-ra" to Jean, "see tha t'morra." They waved her off down the street.

Aunty Ada was preparing the tea for the rest of the family, "where ast bin Lizzie?" she asked, "it's gettin late," "sorry Aunty" said Lizzie, " I went t'see our Jean and little Elizabeth," then added, "I took some flowers up t'th' boneyard first," Ada smiled, "eh lass, y'do say such daft things." She didn't need reminding of that day last year, she closed her eyes and set her shoulders right, "best get on," she said "wash that lettuce Liz an' I'll cut up th' ham." The smell of it filled the house, a big ham boiled slowly all day, one of Ada's specials with lettuce and tomatoes and crusty bread and butter - it was grand. However, Jim Moore wouldn't appreciate it, he would wolf some down and be off to his watering hole to meet his floozies. Ada didn't care, she was always glad to see him go out, she never knew what to say to him anymore. She knew that Sally's death had hit him very hard, whatever else, he had loved her far more than they would ever know despite the way he had always treated her. Ada dished up the evening meal and they all sat round the large scrubbed table, Ada and Ted sat with them for most meals, you couldn't leave little ones to cope alone, they were well fed if nothing else, better dressed now that Ada was in command. They were hugged and kissed more now that Sally was gone, they had all loved their Mam very much but they missed Cameo more than they could say. Jim hadn't any patience with his children, they got on his nerves, he couldn't be bothered with them, they were Sal's job not his, he wanted to be free of them, that's why he went out every night to escape the house, the kids, Ada and Ted, to escape the ghost of Sal. He couldn't stand it without her, so he went out on the ale every night, get legless, then go back home with Meg or Ginny, sometimes with both of them, he'd never had so much sex in his life and he made the most of it. He would imagine himself with Sal and give her a right good seeing to, only to hear the moaning or squealing of Meg or Ginny. He would jump up and dress quickly and dash back home leaving his floozies to rant and rave at him, Jim didn't give a shit about them or what they thought of him, they were always ready to be shagged the very next night whatever happened. He would lie in the bed he had shared with Sal, aching for her, wanting her so bad it hurt like hell, he would remember her lithe slender body, her large ripe breasts, her belly flat and firm, long legs, her long hair falling down her back when she shook it free, "Oh Sal" he would call out and his body would be racked by sobs. He had never told her that he loved her because he knew that she had never loved him but no one could have loved any woman more than Jim loved Sal. Jim's mind would go back to the night that she had died, it was all the fault of that bastard son of hers, "hers and William's" he sneered, if it hadn't been for him Sal would still be here and Camy too, he didn't like Camy, he never had but she was good with the young ones. Sal had named her after the Cameo broach she always carried, even to the end it was clasped in her hand. Then the silly pair of buggers had gone and drowned themselves, what a pair of fools they were, thought Jim, and all that weepin' and bloody wailin' what a right pissin' palaver. Now he was without his Sal and had Ada to put up with, always watching him always seeing straight through him as though she could read his every thought, so Jim got out of the house as much as he possible could, anything to escape those eyes, that look, he'd christened her "Old Fartarse," she suffered badly with wind and was always dropping one here and there, she always looked embarrassed and would pretend it was the chair or the cupboard, whatever was handy, Jim would tell the men at work that she could play a tune on her arse anytime and they would roar with laughter. It was the only laugh Jim ever had these days. Everyone was talking about war and saying what they thought should be done to Adolf Hitler, Jim was sick of hearing about it, it got in the way of good drinking time and bawdy jokes which Jim loved, whenever anyone started on with it Jim would be off leaving the war mongers to get on with it. Visiting Meg or Ginny was always a pleasure, those two knew how to keep a man happy, true they were floozies but they were good hearted and meant well, give them a few Gins and you could have anything you wanted, the only thing Jim insisted on was that he was the only man in their lives, he would be off like shit off a shovel if they were handing it out elsewhere, couldn't do with sharing - all or nothing that was Jim Moore. He had been seeing Meg for a couple of years when Ginny had turned up broke, pissed and in need of a friend, Meg had taken her in hand and got her a room in the same house as herself. The owner lived away and as long as the rent was paid no questions were asked, mind you you had to be discreet, couldn't go about "shoutin' and ballin'" about what you were getting up to. Jim laughed to himself remembering how he sometimes had to hold his hand over their mouths when they were shrieking with delight at the height of their sexual activities. Meg was a little bit more reticent than Ginny, she was afraid of saying what she wanted to say fearing rejection, when Jim was full of ale he could be a stroppy bastard at the best of times. Not so Ginny, she would ask for more, urging Jim to greater heights telling him to suck her here, grope her there matching him thrust for thrust, she really was a very experienced young woman. Meg would mostly lie there letting Jim do whatever he wanted loving every moment of it, loving him too, always hoping he would ask her to marry him now that Sal was dead but he never did, he was a strange man Jim Moore, never showed any love for his wife until she dies then he always seems to be in some kind of torment shouting her name many times at the height of passion. Sometimes stopping altogether looking at her as if she was a stranger and just leaving without a word. Still, she didn't mind, one day perhaps she would belong to him, he would take her home, she would help to look after his children and spend her every night lying by his side, her plump little body shook with the thought of it, yes, she could look forward to that day. There was only one fly in the ointment - Ginny, she wouldn't share Jim with her, never. She didn't mind too much now and again while things were like they were, but if she married Jim and became Mrs Megan Moore then Ginny could go to hell, Jim would belong to her alone, she could find someone else to bed, she was brazen enough, some of the things she came out with when they were having a threesome, well really! Ginny also was wondering what would happen between herself and Jim, she was sick of sharing him with dumb Meg, 'thick as two short shits' thought Ginny, but she knew that she had to handle Jim carefully, he was a strange animal was Jim Moore, one wrong word and it would be, "fuck off Ginny and don't come back." She too wondered about his life with Sal Moore, he never had a good word to say for her and the way he took Ginny night after night and Meg too he mustn't have had any with Sal at home. Now he looked sad and haunted and his moods had got worse, he drank more now than before and he would stop suddenly in the middle of a right good session when Ginny thought she would die with the pleasure of it, she would cry, "fuck me Jim," and he would go all crazy-looking and bugger off trying to hold down the biggest erection she had ever seen so that he could pull on his pants. She had tried to coax him back to bed but no, he would be gone and that would be all thank you, Ginny would lay in the bed and finger herself until she climaxed and lie in a big shuddering heap and she would always be ready the next time Jim took her to bed. She was ready to meet Jim's family and she would wheedle her way into his house sometime soon. After having nothing for years she could do with a home of her own and money, a regular wage packet and Jim Moore in her bed every night, aye that would suit her very well, she would set the wheels in motion or by god her name wasn't Ginny Wilkinson.

CHAPTER TWO

On the Brink of War

The wireless was crackling and Harry was trying to listen in. Chamberlain had gone over to meet Hitler to discuss Poland and everyone was holding their breath. Peggy watched his face looking for reassurance, "what's 'appnin Harry?" she asked him, "nothin lass, can't 'ear it very well, I'll 'af t' take th'accumulator to Sid's for't t'be charged up." "Will there be a war Harry diya think?" went on Peggy, she was more anxious every day now that she knew she was going to have a baby, they hadn't told anyone yet, she would be due in October and Cameo would have been 19 years old on the 28th so it was a little bit touchy at the moment. If war was declared Harry would be called up to serve his country, Peggy couldn't think about that, she was too afraid, she put it to the back of her mind and thought about the baby she was carrying. She and Harry were overjoyed, they had longed for one for ages and now everything was going well apart from Hitler of course. She had been knitting and sowing for weeks and flew about hiding it when anyone came round, she was a little shy and didn't want to tell anyone about it for a while, it was their little secret, hers and Harry's. Peggy had watched him since the deaths of his Mam and dearest sister Camy, she knew it had hit him very hard, and with it his hatred for his father had grown. The lads would hear tales of Jim and his floozies Meg and Ginny and would curse him for tarnishing the memory of their mother by being seen in the company of such tarts. Bridgevale was a small village where everyone knew about everyone else and what they didn't know at No. 9 would be made up by the time the story had reached No. 20 and unmarried draws could be heard dropping three streets away. "Mind you," Ada would say, "there's now't like a bit of 'armless gossip," it cheered everybody up and you could have a damned good belly laugh.

Ada was busy with the tea getting ready for the family, young Jim and his were coming round and Harry and Peggy too. Ada wondered if Peggy would tell them she was expecting, Ada knew the signs and was never wrong, she wished Sal was here, she wanted to tell someone, she had always told Sal, by 'eck they had some laughs, Ada missed nothing and no-one was safe from her knowing gaze. By-gum her wind was bad tonight, her guts was rattlin' she wafted the tea towel around to get rid of the stink she had just made - it wouldn't do to have the house stinkin'. The family arrived, first Harry and Peggy and then Jim, Tilly and Sally-Vicky (as they now referred to her). They sat down at the large kitchen table, the gleaming white cloth was starched to perfection. They were having salad and beef, left over from the roast from dinner time, Ada's new baked bread and butter which had to be tasted to be believed. There was plenty for everyone and later on, after several cups of tea came home-made cake and jam tarts, when they had all eaten far too much and couldn't manage a single crumb more, they departed to the parlour. Sally-Vicky fell asleep and Ada tucked her up on a chair. The others sat round talking about the everyday things that happened in the village. Ada sent Lizzie off home with Joe and Alex, she would see they washed and got ready for bed. "That lass is a treasure!" she told the others once more, "it's like havin' Camy all over again, she's a little angel," she stopped short thinking of the other one who was an angel now, she wished she hadn't said it now, anyway, they knew what she meant. Ted offered the menfolk cigars but no-one smoked now, Harry used to, until Peggy was "inth' family way," he didn't bother anymore, it made her cough and bark so it couldn't be good for her. "Is Jim coming round for his tea?" asked Tilly, "eh no lass," answered Ada. "Ave left 'im some inth' larder, he can get 'is own for a change, bet e'll be off owt wi' his tarts," said Harry and the womenfolk looked at each other and sniggered, "he must be as fit as a butcher's dog to cope wi' two," said young Jim. Ada scolded him, "now Jim none o' that talk please, not in my 'ouse." "Sorry Aunty," said Jim sheepishly, she gave him a hug to show there was no harm done, "lets talk about summat else," she said, "anybody got any good news, owt to tell?" her eyes swept the room and landed on Peggy, she went bright red and looked down at her feet. Harry started to laugh, "by 'eck Aunty, you don't miss a bloody trick d'ya?" The others all looked up at him and Peggy, Tilly jumped up and flung her arms round Peggy and the pair of them burst into tears. The men shook hands and laughed. Ada stood back waiting for her answer when they had all calmed down Harry told Ada and the others that Peggy was due in October, Ada's thoughts immediately flew to Camy and she started to sob as if her heart would break. "Sorry Aunty," said Peggy holding Ada gently in her arms, "that's why we didn't say anything before." Ada wept quietly for a while then blew her nose and hugged them all, "dunna ya worry about an old fossil like me," she said, "I'm that pleased, really I am, it's best bit o' news we've had for a long while," they all agreed, Ted brought out the sherry and they all drank "good health" to Harry and Peggy for the new arrival. When they had all gone home Ada went round to Sal's to make sure that everything was okay. She still called the house "Sal's" she couldn't bring herself to say "Jim's" it would stick in her throat. The kids were in bed and Lizzie had made sure that everything was neat and tidy, it wasn't as shabby and it used to be, Ada and Ted had made various improvements, things Sal would not have bothered with, it was a warm, comfortable home now only lacking what it had never had, the warmth and love of a wife and mother, " eh, our Sal," said Ada to herself, "you were a strange one and no mistake," fancy having a lover and being left with child, then thinking the child dead and never loving Jim Moore or her nine children, after all those years of grieving to find the child not only alive but wanting the hand of your daughter - his sister. Ada thanked God that Sal had been spared the deaths of Camy and Finton, those two so in love her old heart ached thinking of the sheer hell they must have gone through before they had hurled themselves into the deep fast flowing Goyt. Anyway, a new baby was on the way so things were getting better at last, Ted was sure there would be a war, Ada prayed there would not be. She sat for some time thinking of the past and reminiscing, wondering what Sal would have said about the new baby, she wouldn't have shown much interest, she never did, and all those years and never a word to her only sister. They could have shared so much together, Ada was sure she could have helped her sister come to terms with it, instead of bottling it up, trusting no-one with her secret. The back door opened and in came Jim Moore, Ada jumped up startled, he was surprised to see her this late, he nodded, " 'evenin' Ada," " 'evenin' Jim, I'll be off, I must have dozed off or summat," she made for the door, "Oh, by th' way, Harry's wife's expectin' a baby in October," she watched his face, his expression didn't change, "Oh reet," he said, that was all. She left and walked to her own door. What a bloody cold fish he was, Sal was better owt the bloody way. She slammed the door too, waking up Ted who'd fallen asleep in the chair, "hell fire Ada, what's up wi' thee?" he snorted. "Sorry Ted," she answered, "that bloody cow'd fish up th' road. Lets go t'bed, I'm tired out." Ted knew when to leave her alone so he locked up and made sure the fire was safe and followed Ada up the stairs. In bed she hugged Ted tightly and thanked God again for him, "why couldn't our Sal find someone like her Ted?" she cried, "eh, by 'eck Ada your Sal wouldn't 'ave settled for a boring old fart like me," they both laughed, "thank God for boring old farts," said Ada, “that’s all”.

Over at Mary and Brian's house they had just retired to bed, Mary's body was racked with sobs, Brian held her close, Harry had called to tell them about the baby and they had hugged him and pumped his hand, all the back slapping and congratulations and when he had left Mary had crumpled like a soft rag doll. She had been trying for a baby for a couple of years now, nothing was happening, Brian tried to comfort her as best he could.

"Dunna fret lass, it'll be alreet." Now with this latest news she was inconsolable, Brian didn't know what to do, he would have a word with Ada next day, see if she could help in any way, she always seemed to be so wise - like an old owl. He was upset for Mary but more so worried at the thoughts of a war in Europe, what would happen if he were called up? He tried not to think about it, there would be no more trying for babies, he enjoyed that part of it. Mary had urged him to make love to her at every opportunity hoping to get caught and he had obliged every time he felt like it, "now...let's try now Mary," he coaxed her stroking her firm round breasts, when he felt the nipples hardening he knew she wanted him too and he turned her over pulling off her nightie. He kissed her urgently, she responded hungrily, his hand slid down her legs and she opened them willingly, he stroked her inside thigh and ran his fingers along her clitoris, she gasped and begged him to enter her but he wanted to play with her a while. He slid down the bed and started to lick her first on her thighs then her vulva, she started to push him away, "don't do that Brian, you know I don't like it - it's dirty," she cried, but he laughed at her and just carried on. She wanted more now and almost screamed out loud. The smell and taste of her female parts drove him mad with desire, it wasn't very often she allowed him down there so he wanted to make the most of it, she was always more receptive after a bout of weeping. She tugged at his hair 'til it almost came out by the roots but it didn't put him off and he didn't finish until she was fully satisfied. Shuddering and panting clasping each other so tight not wanting the moment to end. Mary moaned wanting more, "Brian do it again - please," she begged, he felt himself getting hard almost immediately and rocked back and forth until they were both satisfied and utterly exhausted, "there'll be a baby there now Mary," he whispered softly, "there has to be after the shaggin' I've just given thee." "Brian, don't talk dirty," she chided, "you know I don't like it." "Not much," he laughed, "you forget what you ask me to do and say when you want it bad." "Oh Brian," she felt herself blushing to her roots, "I dunna know what comes over me," he turned her over and groped her breast, "I know exactly what comes over you," he quipped, "I do!" They laughed together the tears forgotten; it was good to be so in love and loved. Mary loved him very much and would never spurn his lovemaking and every time they did it she hoped she would get caught with the baby she longed for.

Ada couldn't sleep, "Ted?" she asked, "what did tha do with the buttercups our Lizzie took up th' churchyard?" she asked, "by 'eck Ada, what's wittlin' about now," groaned Ted, he was almost asleep, "what did tha do wi'em, ya didn't throw 'em away dids't?" "ey na lass, what d'ya tak me fer? I left 'em there, I'd taken up another vase just in case."

"Did th'flowers look reet nice?" asked Ada, "by the' did that lass, it's best kept grave in th'cemetry," "thanks t'thee Ted," added Ada tearful, "when art tha goin' up lass?" enquired Ted, "dunna know, not yet Ted, I canna go just yet. I'll try, I really will just thee bare wi' me wilt tha?" "Ada lass, dunna fret yoursen," he patted her back and lay still while she wept quietly giving her a little pat now and then so she knew he was with her in her sorrow. She couldn't bring herself to go to the graveyard after the funeral, she knew it wasn't right but her legs turned to jelly if she attempted to go. "I'll be alreet soon," she assured herself, "then I'll go up every week." Till then she would have to depend on Ted, he would do all the running about and everyone said it was a credit to him. Marble polished 'til it shone, grass trimmed, always flowers whenever possible, never a weed to be seen. Ada wondered what would happen to it when Ted and herself were gone, she imagined the kids one by one tending to the plot, but the one who stood out from all the rest was Lizzie, 'Aye that lass was turning out to be a goodun and no mistake,' she surrendered herself to the sandman and Ted was relieved, no more tears tonight, tomorrow would probably bring some more. Ted was the one who helped everyone else and was always glad to do so, but the happenings of the past year were taking their toll, everyone was too busy to see that Ted was looking poorly, he was often pale and a little breathless. 'I must cut down on food,' thought Ted, 'I'm eating far too much,' his weight had shot up over a stone in the past few months and also he was smoking cigars in his allotment shed, he went there often to get away from the tears and heartache that was all around him. He darn't let on to Ada, she would be livid, all the time tellin' everyone he only had one on special occasions now. Mind you they were safe in his storage box in his shed, Ada never walked up there, she only walked to the shops that was enough, being fat she struggled to walk very far. Ted remembered when they first met - Ada was about seven stone wet through, he could lift her off her feet and put her over a style, 'by 'eck them were the days,' she was a bundle of fun and energy and they always enjoyed themselves. They used to picnic a lot in the summertime, always strolling along the canal banks, they'd walk miles but never got to the end of it. They'd spread a cloth and get all the goodies out that Ada had baked or made, her favourite passion was food even then so it was no wonder all these years later they would look like two balloons. Ada was old fashioned and didn't believe in sex before marriage so Ted had to wait a year or two, by the time they got wed Ted was too afraid to try and she too shy, what a performance. They tried quite often but it was never very good, Ada only tried for babies and when they didn't arrive they stopped bothering altogether yet they were happy together and loved each other dearly, "sex isn't the be-all and end-all," said Ada more than once, "there are other things far more important." 'I bet Jim Moore wouldn't agree wi' that,' thought Ted, 'it seems to be all he wants in life, fancy havin three women at one time, shame on the man, would he always behave like a bloody animal?' Ted asked himself if he envied Jim but no, he'd never been good at sex so it didn't bother him none, let Jim get on with it, Ted was happy with his plump cuddly Ada, a good woman - salt of the earth was Ada.

Lying in her bed at No. 8 Mill Cottages, Lizzie was thinking about the future. She wanted to work in the Weaving Shed like her sister, she would work hard and earn good money and save some then she could travel to different parts of the country at holiday time like lots of people did, some even travelled across the world, God that would be amazing..... she hoped one day she would be able too. Teddy would be starting work next year and Joe was working for Mr Lamb the butcher - she always laughed at that, a very good name for a butcher. Joe delivered the orders on a huge black bicycle, he loved it, speeding round the village, everyone knew him and in spite of his father's reputation everyone liked Joe Moore. Teddy wanted to study drawing, he wanted to become an artist but Jim said he would have none of that talk and had got a job lined up at The Foundry for him. Teddy would cry about this, he hated The Foundry and longed to get away. To go to Paris and draw was his idea of heaven but he knew Jim wouldn't let him. Maybe one day when he was a bit older he would be able to run off and never come back, this thought kept him happy. He was a nice young lad was Teddy, always clean, never getting into mischief like his other brothers. His hair was a mass of lovely blonde curls and he had his mother's large dewy eyes, every one of the family loved his sensitivity and they chided him playfully about him really being born a girl, he didn't mind this, he knew they meant no harm, they all envied him his thick long lashes and curls wishing they had them. One day when he had done well for himself he would buy them all the things they had never had. Not his father though, 'there'd be nowt fer that bastard,' his pals' fathers would hug and kiss them, play games with them or take them fishing, not Jim Moore, he'd never had anything to do with any of his kids from the day that they were born. Anyway, by the time Teddy made good, the old get would be dead, but then he wouldn't be able to see his success, whichever way would be okay as long as he didn't fail, he couldn't fail, that would only mean a life working in The Foundry and the thought of that filled him with dread, he hated the smell of the place and the dirt and dust, the men with their red eyes and black faces, always spitting out great globs of phlegm, it was disgusting and Teddy thought he would rather die like Camy than ever have to work there. He would cry himself to sleep many nights just visualising himself working there, his face black his eyes stinging, his curls under layers of dust and dirt, no he could never follow his father and brothers into The Foundry, he would just have to work on Aunty Ada and Uncle Ted, they would help him to find something else - he was sure, young lads were always wanted at the Co-op for delivery and unloading foodstuffs, he would find out about it and get Uncle Ted to put his name down, yes that's what he would do, also there was the Calico Printing works in the next village, he might get on there, he could walk there along the canal every day, it wouldn't bother him, anything but the dreaded Foundry. With these thoughts he found it easier to get on with his life, yes it would be alright, he just knew it, everything would "work-out" like Ada would say, "every cloud had a silver lining."

Chapter Three

Call Up

The 3rd of September and their worst fears were realised, the Prime Minister had made a solemn announcement, his voice faltering with emotion, he told them after repeatedly trying to stop the invasion of Poland, he had no alternative but to declare war on Germany. So there it was, what everyone had dreaded all these months, the men gathered on street corners, the women cried and wiped their eyes on the corner of their pinafores, they would wring their hands in despair, who would go off to war and who would stay behind? All anyone could do was wait and see and hope for the best. Ada remembered the 1914-18 war and steadfast as always knew that they would all pull together no matter what life threw at them.

The small buff coloured envelopes started to arrive through the letter boxes, faces drained of colour and panic seized every male who received one. Tilly almost screamed when she picked up the post, young Jim ran towards her, "it's alright Tilly, don't worry," he said as he looked with fear and yet great anticipation at the letter in her hand. He was one of the few who wanted to fight for his country, he opened the letter carefully, it told him his King and Country needed him and to report for duty to RAF Biggin Hill. He didn't know where it was but he would soon find out. The date was one week away, so he had a lot to do in that time. Tilly cried for hours, Mr and Mrs Bennett were sent for, in they came, white as sheets, not only was Jim called up, so was Arthur, and Jean was also beside herself. "It has to be faced," said young Jim calmly and sensibly, "we have a job to do and hopefully we shall all return safely." Mrs Bennett was the next to speak, "I have been told," she said, "that Foundry workers and the like don't have to go, they will be needed here to make war planes and ammunition," she said. Tilly sprang up overjoyed at this news, "Oh Jim" she cried, "you won't have to go." Jim told her to calm down, "Tilly I have to go, I couldn't live with mis'en if I didn't." Tilly couldn't understand this and flew upstairs amid a fit of weeping, Mr Bennett understood, he'd done his bit in the last war and was glad that he had, it hadn't been easy, far from it, but he felt more of a man for fighting his corner. He looked his wife in the eye and bade her stop this talk, "men have to fight wars and women should back them to the hilt," he stated. She agreed on that but still hoped that Jim and Arthur would try to stay put, she didn't want either of them to be killed and the thought of the latter made her weep too. "Best put kettle on," said Mr Bennett, a strong cup of tea was called for.

Meanwhile, at big Jim Moore's, the post had arrived too, one for Jim to say his services would be required at the Foundry for the time being. He was glad of this, but all the same he would go if he was called up, although thoughts of nights without Meg and Ginny he could well do without. He wondered if his sons would be called up, they were of age so probably would be. Times like this he was glad Sal wasn't here, hard as she was on her kids she wouldn't have wanted to see them going off to war. It might be a good thing for Jim and Harry, knock the bloody softness out of 'em, but still, how would he feel if they lost their lives. Jim didn't want to dwell on this so he shut it out of his mind, "by 'ell" he said to himself, "the buggers'd send me of to bloody Hitler first chance they got. I wonder if fatty gets called up, now that would be worth watching" he could picture Ted in uniform "burstin' at'seems," with Ada in full ships regalia at the front door. Poor old Ted, fancy bein' married to that old Fartarse all those years, it made him chuckle to himself.

Harry had his call-up papers too, Peggy urged him to stay at the Foundry, for a while anyway, so he said he would until it was clear what was happening. So everyone was caught up in the trapping of war, it was on everyone's lips from morning 'til night, the womenfolk stood on every corner of every street, wringing their hands and trying hard not to cry, few of them wanted their men to go off to war, mind you one or two couldn't wait to get rid of their men and fantasised about what they would get up to the minute the train pulled out of the station. There were also a few males who couldn't wait either for the women's husbands to bugger off, then they would be round like a shot, to give them a good seeing to, "can't have them going short!" Tom Scully said to himself, he was safe at the Foundry so he didn't have to go, "by 'eck, all them women left alone, it would be paradise," The thought of it gave him a bloody great hard-on, "get up here woman," he shouted downstairs to his down-trodden wife, "and bloody well hurry up!" He couldn't wait for her to get her clothes off so he pushed her up against the closed door and shoved his dick up her knicker leg, 'by 'ell, what a time he was goin' to 'ave, all them women queuing' up for it.' He didn't bother to look at his wife's face, didn't see her dead fish eyes, wrinkled skin, old bruises, a face 35 years old looking 76. She would have loved him to go off to war and never come back, to get away from this bloody grim life, seven kids, little money and his demands for sex whenever he wanted it, she hated it every time. He never washed himself between each coupling and he stank like a bloody Pole Cat, what with his "stale beer and fags" breath too it was sheer hell every time, and him thinking he was God's gift to women.

Ada and Ted were having a cuppa and talking about Jim and Harry's call-up. Ada had been weeping on and off all day, Ted tried to console her as best he could but it was hard work, "na then Ada, tha canna go on like this, your goin' t'kill thee sen." "I know Ted, but I canna lose any more o'family, I just canna." He knew she hadn't got over the loss of Sally and Camy yet, it was too early. They'd all laughed at him sat listening to th'wireless, goin' on about Chamberlain and stories of war, now they could see he had been right all along, he never said "I told yer so," he didn't need to. Ada was glad that Ted wouldn't have to go, but knew he would probably volunteer for A.R.P. work. "Has drunken bugger bin sent fer?" she asked Ted. "No lass, he wunna haft' go bein' int' Foundry, he'll be needed there." "No bugger'd miss 'im anyway," she said. "Our Jean 'n Mary'll be beside the' sens wi' worry, where will it all end Ted? I wish I were dead an' owt on it all, I really do." Ted put his arm around his portly wife and hugged her to him, "now come on lass, We've a lot to be thankful fer, we'll do all we can to get along. Maybe it wunna last long, yer nere' know eh owd girl? Cheer up Ada." Ada blew her nose loudly and let off at the same time, "sorry Ted," she tittered, "me wind's playin' me up summat awful." Ted was glad something could make her laugh anyway. He walked away quickly, the stink was terrible, "bloody 'ell Ada, has't shit?" he asked. "Now Ted, no need fer that," said Ada going red in the face but they both started to laugh 'til they almost cried, "what wi' state o'th' country an' thy wind," said Ted, "it's God 'elp us all, I dunna know which is worst!" They went up to bed a little happier than they had been, a laugh was good for you, they knew that. Tomorrow was another day, there would be something else to worry about soon enough.

Lizzie had just gone up to bed after finishing all her jobs for the day, she was afraid of the things everyone was talking about. There wasn't anyone to talk to about things like this now that Camy was gone, she missed her big sister very much and the tears weren't very far away. Joe was always tired out after work and Teddy was in a world of his own. Little Alex needed her though and she was glad of that, she was the mother here now for him and she fussed about him which made Jim mad as hell, he would shout and ball at Lizzie, not that she took much notice of him. He wasn't in the house very often, after tea he would be off 'til late at night, sometimes she would hear him crying out for Sal. She was petrified that Sal's ghost was walking about the house, she would get under the covers and not dare look out 'til morning. Jim was late home that night, Ginny had been pestering him to bring her home to meet the family, he didn't want her here but when booze was in him and sex was on a plate he would forget that he didn't want her and then he would have to think up excuses why he couldn't take her there. Time was fast running out and he knew one day she would have her way, she was a very determined woman was Ginny, different than Meg, she was a little gem was Meg, he thought about her in his house, but no, no-one could take Sal's place never, unless he got so pissed up and did something really bloody stupid.

Lizzie wondered what would happen to her brothers when they went away to war, would they come back or, like Camy, never be seen again. She wished she was older and could go to work and not have to spend her days cleaning, everyone helped but it was damned hard and she got sick of it, she wanted to play out with her friends from school but she couldn't, there was always jobs to be done, shopping, cleaning, ironing..... Aunty Ada did the cooking and tried to do as much of the cleaning as she could but she had her own house to see to so couldn't do everything. Even so, it was a lot for young girl and many felt sorry for the poor soul. Her fingers were sore from the peg rug she was making, it was cutting up the old clothes that was the worst part, coats were hard to cut into strips and she wished them all in Hell every time she had to start a new one. They were as heavy as lead too and her back was nearly broken each time she put the damned thing down. 'Why can't we have nice carpets like Eveline's mother had,' she moaned, their house was wonderful, the furniture shone like silver and they had patterned carpets in every room and up the stairs too. She loved to sit on the stairs and just feel at it. At home they had bare wood that had to be scrubbed every week, the peg rugs did manage to cover up a little bit here and there at the top and bottom of the staircase. She decided to walk over to Uncle Ted's allotment, he usually cheered her up, the sounds of digging and clipping could be heard long before she got there. Ted was sat in his shed having a quiet smoke, he was startled when Lizzie walked in, "how-do Uncle Ted," she called. Ted jumped up as if a wasp had stung him. "By 'eck lass tha gave me a turn I can tell thee. I thout it were our Ada." Lizzie giggled, "Uncle Ted tha't smokin'?" "Ay, an' dunna let on to Ada or my life won't be worth livin' " he exclaimed. "I wunna say owt," she laughed back at him. "What do'st want lass?" he asked her. "Nowt really," she answered and stood fidgeting in the doorway. "Oh sit thee down girl an' shut th' door," said Ted, afeared Ada might be his next visitor. Lizzie sat down on the up-turned bucket he patted, "now what's up wi' thee? Come on, Tell Uncle Ted," he smiled and his face lit up, he was a kind man was Ted. "Well Uncle Ted, I was wonderin' what would 'appen to our Jim and Harry when they go away." Ted could see that the youngster was worried and he had to think for a while before he could answer her. "well lass," he said "you munna go worryin' your pretty little 'ed abart things like that, they'll be alreet, I went to war tha knows an' I came back alreet." He told her a little about the fighting and the life in the trenches nothing gory, he made light about much of it. "Will the' get killed? Eveline ses the' will," she asked, her large eyes getting larger by the second. "Ee nay, the' wunna be kill't," answered Ted, "dunna thee go lisnin' to silly tittle tattle na then. By 'eck tha dust cum up wi' daftest things," said Ted shaking his head, he puffed deeply on his cigar and Lizzie started to cough and splutter, "tha's better be off lass," said Ted, "an' dunna let our Ada smell thee or a'm dun fo'." Lizzie got up to go and Ted followed her out of the shed, "canna 'ave sum o' them flowers?" she asked Ted. "Aye tha' can that lass," and he went to get his cutters. The smell of blossoms filled the air and Lizzie closed her eyes and had a good long sniff. This was how she always thought of Uncle Ted at the allotment - a hint of cigar and the scent of flowers. Ted collected a large bunch of Dahlias and gave them to Lizzie, "yer dad'l like 'em," he laughed, "put 'em in a nice flower vase on th' sideboard. These meet bi th'last ones, it'll be a veg patch from now on I reckon." "What dust mean?" asked Lizzie. "Well lass, in war time we've to grow all't vegetables we can, there'll be a shortage like as not." Lizzie didn't understand but she didn't like to say so. She waved "ta-ra" to Ted and set off home with her flowers, looking down at them she was aware that crawling out of her beautiful Dahlias were spiders. She shrieked with horror and dropped the lot, "bloody 'ell," she cried, she hated spiders, what was she to do. Well, plucking up courage she picked them up one by one, gave them a good shake and held them at arms length, she scuttled home as fast as she could, looking out for the creepy crawlies all the way. Enlisting Alex's help she let him put them in the vase of water and onto the sideboard, they did look lovely but she darn't say anything about the spiders, she was mesmerised with them and couldn't stop looking. Aunty Ada made her jump, she hadn't heard her come into the house, "what ar't up to lass?" asked Ada when Lizzie jumped up with fright. "Oh Aunty thart feared me t'death!" shouted Lizzie, anyway, they were soon laughing it off. "I see tha's bin to Uncle Ted for 'em," said Ada, "what were 'e up ter?" Lizzie went scarlet as she muttered, "nuthin' Aunty." Ada chuckled to herself, "dunna s'pose 'e were 'avin a crafty smoke?" "Oh no Aunty, 'e werna doin' that, he were 'ard at work in th'allottment," she spluttered. Ada had to laugh again, "he shuddna be smokin' it's bad fer 'im tha knows Lizzie, tha must tell me if tha sees 'im. Think on lass." "Oh aye Aunty, a will," she made an excuse and trotted off out the road. Ada sighed, she hoped that Ted didn't smoke too much, he wasn't very well, he never complained but he wasn't looking his usual self. There was nothing she could put her finger on but Ted wasn't well, he thought she hadn't noticed but there wasn't much escaped Ada. All this war mongerin' was doin' him no good, he'd never really got over the first one. He'd only bin a lad himself and now Jim and Harry would have to go too. Ada dried her tears for the umpteenth time, mustn't dwell on it, there was work to be done.

Lizzie busied herself out of the way of Aunty Ada, she didn't want to let Uncle Ted down, "there was nowt worse than a blabber-mouth" she'd heard said many times and she didn't want to tell lies to Ada so keep out o'th' way she did 'til tea was ready. Big Jim came in from work, had his tea and settled back in his chair for fortywinks. The others ate in near silence, Alex and Lizzie whispered to each other and Joe and Teddy were trying sign language, they were getting better at it, it was better than a hefty whack across the Brain Box from Jim if they disturbed him. Joe wanted to listen to the wireless so he crept out to meet his pal Johnny Lomas, they would go into Johnny's shed and try out the cat's whisker. Teddy went upstairs to read his book, so that left Alex and Lizzie to be as quiet as they could. After clearing the table and washing the dishes, creeping about like a thief, Lizzie was glad when she heard Jim go out of the back door, he never said "I'm off" or anything, but she knew he wouldn't be back 'til late. Alex charged round the house and they made enough noise to wake the dead, it was grand. Ada was round after a while and she got Alex ready for bed, Lizzie had some ironing to do so she got on with it, "can tha do a bit with 'peg rug our Lizzie?" asked Ada. "Aye, alreet Aunty, just a bit, ironing meks me tired," she answered thinking, 'bloody 'ell fire, the soddin' rug agen,' she hated the bloody thing. There was a knock at the back door, it was Eveline, "can Lizzie come out to play?" she asked. "Not t'neet," answered Ada, "the lass 'as things to do." Eveline looked across the room at Lizzie ironing, she felt sorry for her friend. "Oh reet then," she answered, "ta-ra" and she was gone. Lizzie would have liked to run about in the warm September evening but no, it wasn't for her now that Mam and Camy had gone. Hot salty tears welled up in her eyes, "na then lass," remarked Ada, "dunna get upset 'cos there's a few jobs to be dun, tha munna get cryin' 'cos thee friend's owt playin'." "It's not that Aunty," answered Lizzie, "I were just thinkin' of Mam an' our Camy," and her little shoulders shook with emotion. Ada felt the tears in her eyes too and she swallowed a lump in her throat, "Aye Lizzie, it still 'urts, I miss 'em too lass tha knows. Dunna thee cry anymore, come on lets 'ave a nice cuppa eh?" Lizzie tried to smile through her tears and nodded her head. "Lets put 'kettle on eh Polly," said Ada and they both smiled at that, a cuppa was always Ada's answer to every problem. They sat and talked for a long time with several cups of tea. Ada had a fag and it was like old times with Sal, Lizzie was a good listener and sensible too. Ada told her stories about Sal and herself and Uncle Ted, about their Dad Sam and about Camy and Finton, they cried again and had another cuppa but after a while they both felt better for it. It had done them good and Ada thanked God for young Lizzie Moore, what they would do without her she couldn't imagine. "One day lass when thart a bit older, tha'll look back on days like this'n and you'll wonder 'ow tha put up wi' it all but things'll get better, mark my words." Joe came in and wondered what the matter was, "we've bin pipin' our eyes," said Ada, "we're women, we're entitled." Joe looked puzzled, scratched his head, said "goodnight" and was off to bed picking up Alex on the way. He was fast asleep on the chair by the fire, they had forgotten about him. "By gum, it's gettin' late," said Ada, "tha'd better get thesen off to bed. Leave ironing 'til tomorra." "It's alreet Aunty, I'll just do a bit more first while th'iron's still hot." So Ada went home and Lizzie got on with the ironing. When that was finished she thought she would do a bit of the peg rug, it was hard work and she was just getting into her stride when the back door opened and she jumped with fright, it was Jim Moore in a really bad mood. He took one look at her and bellowed, "what the bloody 'ell are you doin' up?" "I didna know it were late dad," she stammered. She got up and started forward but she stood on the heavy rug and she fell over in a big heap. "Jesus Christ all bloody mighty!" shouted Jim, "another bloody idiot in the bleedin' 'ouse." He sighed, walked over to the chair by the fire and his gaze came to rest on the vase of flowers on the sideboard. He looked long and hard at the procession of spiders and earwigs running about, in and out, "what the fuckin' 'ell," he snarled. His fist came down and swept the vase, flowers, water, spiders and earwigs to the floor with a crash.

"Clean that bastard lot up now an' get to bed," he bellowed, "what the fuckin' 'ell is goin' on in this bastardin' 'ouse?" He marched off up the stairs to his bedroom and the house shook with the slam of the door. Lizzie looked at the mess and wondered how she was going to tackle this, the glass, water and flowers she could manage but the spiders and earwigs.....never! She stood rooted to the spot when she heard someone coming quietly down the stairs, it was Joe. His gaze took in the flowers etc and he looked from them to Lizzie. "Come on Liz, let's get it cleaned up then." He knew she was afraid of creepy crawlies so he just gathered everything up and put them in the bin outside, he even mopped up the water and squashed anything left alive with the mop. Lizzie would have hugged him but she knew he wouldn't want her to but she thanked him over and over again. "Get off to bed our Lizzie," he told her, "it's school inth' mornin'and they'll be too tired to do owt." She went up to bed and was glad to go, Joe would see to the fire and lock the doors, he was a good lad Joe, 'don't sen' 'im off to war Jesus' she asked in her prayers 'not Joe or Alex or Jim or Harry just Dad, yes he could go. Jim could go, Big Bully Jim, we won't miss that bugger.

Chapter Four

Tom Scully

It was official, Harry, Jim and Arthur had their papers through giving them instructions on where to get to their units. Jim was to go to Biggin Hill to train as a fighter Pilot, Harry to the Infantry Head Quarters in Hastings and Arthur wanted to go into the Navy so he was off to Portsmouth. There was nothing they could say or do, they had to go. The women wept and wrung their hands in anguish, Tilly thought her heart would break in two. Peggy set her shoulders and tried to remain as calm as she could, not wanting Harry to think she couldn't cope. Jean was trying to be strong for Arthur and young Elizabeth Jean. They were to leave in five days' time and everyone was trying their level best to help, it wasn't going to be easy parting, they were all so very much in love. Lizzie lay in her small bed at night and wondered if there was a God in Heaven, he'd already taken Mam and Camy, now he was after her Jim and Harry, what a little bugger he was thought Lizzie, "well yer canna 'ave 'em!" she shouted to herself, "so there, tha can 'ave me dad instead," she offered, "take big Jim Moore God, an' leave th'rest at 'ome." The day dawned, it was cold and looked like it might snow, Jim and Tilly made love over and over again, each time like it might be there last. They clung together and vowed to be faithful to each other whatever might happen. When Sally Vicky awoke and jumped into their bed they hugged and kissed each other and Jim's eyes filled with tears as he looked down on the face of his beautiful little girl. Golden curls, big blue eyes and long dark lashes like spiders swept over her eyes as she blinked away the tears, she could feel the heartache in the house and didn't understand. Daddy was saying "goodbye" but she didn't know why. Over at Harry's, Peggy was trying very hard not to break down, the baby kicked inside her and she wished it would stop. She didn't want to have the baby on her own, she wanted Harry with her to hold her hand and kiss her pains away. She had witnessed enough births to know what was in store for her.

Harry watched her out of the corner of his eye, he groaned inside with pain, how could he leave her now when she needed him so badly? He had let her down, he knew, they had planned this baby together and now it was due he was off leaving her to cope alone. The thoughts of war and fighting for his country did pick him up a bit, he wished he could have stayed home until the baby arrived, he would have felt better about Peggy, what if she died? Some women did die in childbirth, panic seized him and he leapt to his feet almost squealing with anguish. He ran to Peggy and gathered her in his arms and his tears began to fall, they stood like this sobbing together for what seemed like an age, their tears were spent, they couldn't manage another and with this Harry said his goodbyes and off he went down the street cold and frosty, his breath causing great clouds of steam around him. He prayed to God to take care of all of his loved ones and asked to be spared and to return home as soon as was possible. He heard the sound of boots on the cobbles behind him, turning he caught sight of Jim, they strode down to the station together neither speaking a word, too gutted to talk. They were joined a few minutes later by Arthur, he was in sombre mood also, going back over and over in his mind the most marvellous love-making, he had enjoyed hours of it and he felt a stirring in his loins, 'good God' he thought to himself, 'it's no use having a hard on now, don't know when I'll ever get another one;' only thoughts of Jean filled his mind. The train pulled into the little station and they were soon aboard. Lots of familiar faces smiled at them and wished them "God's speed". As the train left the station they looked out towards their respective homes and feasted on them until they were specks in the distance. Bridgevale was out of sight, they wondered when they would return. Harry began to talk about the laugh they'd had at the "Goyt Inn" the night before, they'd had a damned good send off. Big Jim had been in but left without wishing his sons farewell, "what a bastard" they all echoed, "shan't be missin' him eh," they laughed. Jim thought of writing to Adolf Hitler to tell him about his double; Jim Moore, they'd really get on well together the pair of bloody lunatics. They laughed for a while and sat back to watch the landscape change around them. When they reached Piccadilly Station in Manchester they all had their own ways to make to different parts of the country. Jim and Harry shook hands with Arthur and wished him well and he walked away to find his connection. The two brothers faced each other and tears sprang up into their eyes, they both tried to speak but words came out as a strangled cry, they held each other hard and rocked back and forth on the cold, hard platform. This was the first time in their young lives that they would ever be apart, they looked into each other's eyes and both knew that the love was felt deep down for one from the other, they had slept together all their young lives. Their first days at school, toboggan races down the three hollers, swimmin' in th'cut, starting work, their first fag and a pint at the "Goyt" hidin' from their dad who would have skinned 'em alive. Then had come their girlfriends, marriage and the pregnancies, their loss of Mam and sister Camy and now they were going off to war, they may never see each other again, they wrung each others hands and turned away blinded by a thousand tears. 'God bless you brother' they sounded in their minds, 'God keep you safe from harm'. They were lost in the steam and mist, a whistle sounded far away, a swirl of smoke, a footfall and they were gone.

Tom Scully staggered out of the pub, it was early on but he hadn't got any money left so he was going home, he'd give his wife Maggie a bloody good hidin' when he got there, it were her fault spending' th' bloody money on food and bleedin' rent. He didn't give a bloody damn about the necessities of life. He worked his balls off in the bastard Foundry every day and he was entitled to a drink and that was that. So what if the missis couldn't make ends meet on what he gave her? She would have to get on wi' it, fuckin' ugly miserable bastard she was, never a bleedin' smile, and fuck, she was bloody useless, she couldn't fuck a duck. He was unaware of someone behind him and he staggered backward colliding with Mary. She lurched sideways and fell in a heap, a pain shot through her ankle, "Bloody 'ell!" she cried out. Tom Scully sobered up almost immediately, "sorry lass, I didna see thee there, I fell on that cobblestone," he helped her up and dusted her down as best he could in the lamplight. The ankle wouldn't take her weight and she winced with pain, quick as a flash his arm was round her waist and he pulled her to him to support her. She tried to pull away but the pain was unbearable and she leaned on him even more. Tom was in seventh heaven, his arm round the Moore girl, by 'eck she was beautiful and the smell of her perfume; well he'd never known anything like it. "I'll soon 'ave thee 'ome lassy, dunna thee fret". Mary wasn't bothered who she was with at this very moment, she was in agony and just wanted to get home. They made a right sketch; hobbling up the street. At last they were at Mary's door, "I'll be all reet now Mr Scully," she told him, "thanks ever so much." "Nay lass," said Tom, he wouldn't hear of it, "gimme them there keys and just thee owd onta th'wall," she did as she was told and he half carried her into the parlour. It was warm and sweet smelling, there was a glow from the fire and Tom Scully caught his breath; by God, she looked absolutely beautiful.

"M...Mary," he stammered, but could say no more. She looked up at him, in the soft glow he didn't look too bad, 'he must have been a good looking' man at one time' she thought. "You've been very kind Mr Scully, and thanks ever so, I'll be all reet now," but she wasn't and the pain was terrific, she cried out and tears started to fall. Tom put his arms around her to comfort her but she pushed him away, "Wilt'tha light gas for me?" she asked him. "Right oh," he answered her, he was reluctant but he got out his matches and lit the gas mantle and turned it down to a gentle hiss, "I'll get tha a bowl of water and towel," he said and strode into the kitchen, she shouted after him to be careful int the dark and told him where everything was kept. He poured hot water from the kettle that was nestling by the fire and in no time her foot was soaking in the warm water and Comfry leaves that she had added. "Sit down Mr Scully," she bade him. "Please Mary, call me Tom, I canna do wi' th "Mr" all the time." He looked around him and took in the neat clean room, everything gleaming, smelling of polish and God knows what else. He thought about his own shit-hole stinkin' of piss, worse than a bloody doss 'ouse. God she was a lucky girl to 'ave all this, and 'er born a Moore - the piss poorest in the bloody village. "By gum lass tha's got a place like a palace," he stammered, he also realised he must look like a bloody dog and smell like one as well. She thanked him for his kindness, "wilt tha 'ave a cuppa tea Tom?" she asked him. "Nay lass, I'll be off now," he couldn't wait to get out the door, "ta-ra," he said and was gone. She was just getting her breath back when the door opened again, she almost screamed in fright. "I'm sorry lass," he shouted to her, "sorry, dunna ferget to lock the door," and he was gone again leaving a cold blast of air behind him. 'How kind and thoughtful of him' she said to herself, she had always hated him from afar, but he had gone out of his way to be kind to her so she had to judge him accordingly. Mind you, he reeked of booze, still it wasn't any of her business, she saw the best in everyone, a sweet nature just like the other girls in her family. Down the street Tom Scully was brooding, wishing he were better off, that his clothes were a little cleaner and that he didn't smell like a bloody pole-cat, what a lass, Jesus Christ, why couldn't he have had someone like her? He wanted to kiss her and hug her tightly to him and boy did he want to fuck her, his mind raced ahead of himself thinking about what a marvellous coupling that would be. By the time he reached his own doorstep his hard-on was so hard you could have knocked a nail in with it. He rushed upstairs to find Maggie but she wasn't there, he ran round the house like a headless chicken waking up all the kids, they were frightened to death of what would happen and they began to wail and screech. "Shut you're fuckin' mouths now or I'll shut the bastards for thee," he yelled, they shut up but the look of terror in their eyes was bad enough. "Where's thee Mam," he demanded of Ruby the eldest. "She went round

Lily's, Dad," said Ruby, "to borra some bread." "Reet," said Tom, "get back t'thee bed, I'll settle the bugger when she gets back." 'Right ye little bastard' said Tom to himself, 'as soon as me back's turned she's off.' He sat in the darkness, it was cold and dank and the smell of pissed up mattresses filled the house. The more he thought about Mary the darker his mood became. Suddenly the back door opened and in came Maggie; she was out of breath from running. She put her shawl over the chair and was just putting the bread on the table when she saw the cigarette glowing the dark, before she could utter a sound Tom was up and snarling, "you fucking whore, where the fuck have you bin 'til now?" She tried to explain about the bread but you couldn't reason with a bloody madman. He thrashed the living daylights out of her and didn't stop 'til he was too weak to hit her again. Maggie lay on the flag floor like a broken toy not daring to moan or utter a word. Just when she thought he was going up to bed he turned and crossed over to her, she steeled herself for another barrage of blows, instead he rolled her on her back, hoisted up her clothes and gave her a right good seeing to all the while thinking it should be Mary he was giving it to. 'I'll have her' he told himself, 'by God I will, I'll 'ave 'er beggin' fer it if it's the last bloody thing I ever do.'

Mary was quite unaware of the thoughts going through Tom Scully's head, she hobbled over to the front door and locked it like he had told her. She tidied up as best she could and made her way painfully up the stairs to her lonely bed, her thoughts turned to Brian and the tears flowed easily. Brian was the next to get his papers, Mary had thought he would be alright for a while but no, he had to go and the parting was as painful as the others, if not more so, Mary hadn't conceived so her heartbreak was worse wondering if they would ever be together again to try. Where was her darling now, was he safe, was he missing her? He would have kissed her ankle better and would probably have kissed her everywhere else too, the thoughts ran through her mind and she lay in her bed and rocked back and forth thinking about her loved one, she sobbed as if her heart would break, finally falling into a fitful sleep in the early hours of the morning.

Over at Harry's house Peggy awoke with a niggling pain that just wouldn't go away. She felt dreadful and got out of bed, she lit the gas light and had a glass of water, the niggle seemed to go away after a while and she got back into bed, why wasn't Harry here with her, she felt sorry for herself, he should be here to hold her close and tell her not to worry. Suddenly she felt a gush and the next second she was sat in a pool of water.

"Oh my God!" she cried, she knew that the waters broke when you were in labour but she was early, the baby wasn't due for a week....well, it was now. Out of bed she got again and banged on the wall with a mallet that her dad had given her. It was 2.15 am and everywhere was quiet and still. A banging on the wall from next door told her that her message had got through, her next-door neighbours would then knock for her parents two doors down. They had wanted her to stay with them when Harry was called up but she wouldn't hear of it preferring to stay in the bed where she could recall her love life with her darling Harry. Hearing a knock at the front door she slowly made her way down the stairs after she had lit a candle, she ushered in her Mum and Dad who looked white with worry. "It's all reet Mam, me waters broke so I guess it's time eh?" "You'll be all reet Peggy," cooed her mum Jen, "I'll get the water boiling," she said and flew around getting things ready. "What about Midwife Mam, hadn't Dad better get 'er?" she asked. "Eh lass, not yet, tha'll be a fair few hours before tha'll need 'er." Peg's face suddenly crumpled up in agony as a contraction gripped her like a vice, she squealed like a pig, as it eased off she began to cry, "bloody 'ell Mam, that 'urt, how many of them will a get?" "Peggy," said Jen, "no need to blaspheme," she didn't hold with cursing and swearing. "I'm sorry Peg but you'll have quite a lot more before baby arrives." "God almighty," said Peggy to herself, "more of that, I'll die," she said out loud. "Dunna be daft lass," her mother assured her, "tha'll be fine, just do as you're told an' everythin' will be as reet as rain." Pain after pain shot through her young body and she squealed and cried with every one. It went on for hours; at half past seven Peggy's dad Bert went round to get the Midwife, she was out with another expectant mother and her old man didn't know when she would be back but he would leave a message. With that Bert reluctantly trudged back to Peggy's, he'd be better off at work but knew Jen wuddna hear of it. "Blast it all," was the nearest he got to swearing, "what a life, listening to his lass squealing like a pig hour after hour, a young woman ran past him, her clogs ringing out on the cobble stones; she was late and her face was etched with worry. 'I hope she has a good excuse' thought Bert, 'she'll be for th' highjump fer sure.' Back at Peggy's the same cries came from up stairs, "is she 'ere Bert," shouted Jen running down the stairs, "na lass," answered Bert "she's owt at another birth but as soon as she's back her hubby said he'd send her round." Jen was mad as could be, "what shall I tell our Peg, she's in agony," she wrung her hands and tears sprang into her weary eyes, it was hard to watch your little girl go through so much pain even when you knew it would all be worth it in the end. She remembered her own confinement with Peggy and a tremor ran through her, she'd never had anymore after her; one was quite enough. "I wish Harry were 'ere," she whispered, "he could do the things I'm doin' much better." "Mam!" shouted Peggy, "Mam, where are ya!" Jen bounded back up the stairs and reassured Peg that all was well and the midwife was on her way. By 12.30 Jen had had enough, she flew out of the front door and was hammering at the midwife's door in no time at all, the nurse answered it quickly, "I'm on me way Mrs Barlow, I've just called 'ome to get some supplies," she said in her matter of fact tone. Jen was beside herself with worry, "she must have summat fer th' pain nurse," she ranted "it's bin ten hours now and she canna go on any longer." They scurried along the streets and the curtains twitched at each house they passed. Ada quickly heard the news and set off to Peggy's, she couldn't walk very well but she had to do her bit, for Harry at least. The Midwife gave Peggy something to drink, it didn't do much for the pain but she calmed her down and Peggy was relieved to see her after looking at her mother for the past ten hours. Jen's face said; don't die my little girl and Peggy was scarred to death she would indeed die. She had never in her wildest dreams thought that childbirth would be this painful, it was sheer agony and she wondered how much more she could take. "Harry, where are you" she cried out loud, "Harry!" but he wasn't there, he couldn't hear her. Another hour passed and the nurse decided to help her along, she reached for her long sharp scissors and snip snip, she had cut the flesh to make more room for the baby's head to get through. The sheet was awash with bright red blood and Jen almost passed out. "Come on now Peggy, push as 'ard as tha can," urged the nurse. Peggy did just that and in no time at all the baby was out and spluttering and gasping. Peggy laid back, too exhausted to look at the baby, she hadn't the strength to ask if it were a boy or girl. Jen glanced down eagerly to see and cried out, "it's a boy Peggy, it's a beautiful baby boy," they both burst into tears of joy and hugged each other tightly. The Midwife washed the baby and wrapped him in a white linen cloth, she then handed him over to his mother as she gazed at him in wonder, he looked up at her, it was just like looking into Harry's eyes, "Mam, he's just like Harry," she whispered. She began to whimper softly, "Oh Harry darlin' I wish you could be 'ere with us." "Hast tha got a name fer 'im then?" asked the Midwife smiling broadly, happy at the outcome. "It's Harry," she answered, "young Harry." "Very nice," said the Midwife. Downstairs Ada was waiting for the cry of the new born baby but he didn't cry at all, he just gazed around contented. "Come up Ada," shouted Jen, "come and see young Harry." Ada pulled herself up the steep staircase puffing and panting. She was handed the baby boy and she cried long and loud, "by gum he's just like our Harry was when he was born. I can see 'im now, my he's a grand little chap, he's lookin' all round like he knows what's goin' on, by 'eck 'e's goin' t'be a clever lad, mark my words," chuckled Ada, "I'm allis reet, you'll see."

Harry Moore stood in the NAAFI, everyone seemed to be enjoying themselves, the band played, many were dancing; some cheek to cheek, 'by 'eck' thought Harry, 'only been 'ere a few weeks and they've forgotten their wives and sweethearts already.' His heart was heavy, he missed Peggy really bad and he worried about how she would cope when she went into labour. 'I should have been with her' he told himself over and over again. He was jolted out of his daydream by a tug on his sleeve, he looked down to see a tiny blonde about five foot nothing, she was a beauty too, "havin' a dance?" she asked him. "Er, no," he answered, "I dunna....canna," he stammered, "can't dance," he blushed beetroot red. "I'm not very good myself," offered the girl, "but we can try can't we?" He couldn't refuse her, she was so appealing, "aye, we can 'ave a do at it." He guided her to the dance floor and took her rather clumsily in his arms, the band was playing it was a really nice sound and it tugged at his heartstrings. He held the girl really close and suddenly realised what he was doing, he pushed her slightly away, "sorry," he said looking down at her. "Oh, it's alright, really," she answered, she smiled broadly and showed the most perfect white teeth, her lips were painted bright red and she looked absolutely divine. He shouldn't be thinking like this but he couldn't help himself and he surrendered to the moment, it was nice and it felt right, after all he wasn't doing anything wrong. The dance ended and he escorted her off the dance floor. "My name's Harry," he told her, "Harry Moore." "Right, I'm Pamela, nice to meet you," she laughed. "Can I get you a drink Pamela," asked Harry. "Oh thanks very much," she answered, "Gin and Tonic would be nice." 'Bloody 'ell' thought Harry, he'd never met a woman who drank before apart from a sherry at Christmas or a shandy at the Goyt Inn, that's the most Peggy and the other womenfolk ever had. He hadn't got very much money and he didn't know how much a Gin and Tonic would cost him so he looked around for a familiar face; he spotted Scouser, "hey Scouser," he hollered, the young Liverpudlian came over all swagger and cockiness, "what's up whack?" he asked. "What's price of a Gin and Tonic?" he asked. "Bloody 'ell whack, what ya want a G and T for, not fer me, fer 'er eh? asked the Scouser. Harry pointed to the girl Pamela who stood waiting, "Oh right man, it's about one shilling and sixpence." "God almighty, I canna afford that." "Leave it t'me whack," said Scouser, he headed off with Harry in tow, he had a quick word with one of the lads on the bar, slipped him a coin....."Hey Presto," he shouted and handed a glass to Harry then turned a left. Harry made his way back to Pamela, he handed her the drink, she thanked him and had a good swig, her smile told him that all was well. They began to talk about themselves in turn. Pamela was an only child from a wealthy family in Hampshire, her parents hadn't wanted her to join up but she wanted to go and they couldn't stop her, she chose the Army and wanted to be an officer quite quickly. Harry told her about himself and Peggy and the imminent birth. He's truly in love with his wife observed Pamela, how nice, he must be a really nice man, he was tall and handsome too, that she couldn't help but notice. He told her about his brothers Jim and Joe, Teddy and Alex and also about Mary, Jean and Lizzie. He couldn't mention his father or Sal and Camy. After all she was a stranger, wouldn't be right to tell all his family history. Before they knew it the dance was over and everyone was off to their billets, "I'll walk you to your quarters," he volunteered and off they went, it wasn't very far and he bade her goodnight. It had been a very pleasant evening and he was happy for the first time since he'd left Peggy behind in Bridgevale. He couldn't get Pamela out of his mind, he was very surprised at himself because her beautiful smile came into his mind over and over again. He went to sleep thinking about her, the smile wouldn't go away.

Meanwhile, Harry wasn't the only one to have enjoyed themselves tonight; Pamela was deep in thought too - God he was handsome for sure and such a caring sensitive person, that had come across without a doubt, he really was something though Harry Moore, she said his name over and over again, 'he's married, his wife's expecting their first baby. Come on Pamela, for goodness sake don't go falling for a married man, no...no I won't, I'll keep right away from him,' she thought to herself, but something stirred deep down in her that she couldn't understand, she thumped the pillows and settled into an uneasy sleep.

The next morning Harry was told to report to his Warrant Officer, he wondered what was wrong, what had he done, he was trembling inside. The officer shook his hand heartily, "congratulations Moore," he bellowed, "you're the proud father of a baby son born yesterday, 24th October 1939," he read from a telegram that Jen had sent. "To be named Harry after yourself I believe." Harry was delighted, 'oh well done Peggy, well done' sang Harry to himself, "thank you Sir," he beamed, "thank you." "Don't you want to go home to see your son?" asked the officer as Harry made for the door (having forgotten to salute too). "Oh yes Sir, thank you Sir," he answered going back to the desk. "Right you can have a couple of days because of the length of the journey, if you set off now you could be back home before dark, Okay old man?" and he shook Harry's hand again. Harry scuttled off to sort out his pass and pack a few belongings. His mates were dead envious of him, "bloody jammy sod," said Rob, the best of Harry's pals, "well done anyway, have a great time daddy." They all laughed, "you won't get yer leg over!" shouted Scouser, "not 'til it heals up." "Bloody hell Scouser, must you be so bloody course?" hollered someone from the shower room. Harry was on his way out of the Barracks and a blonde head bobbed in the distance, he tried to see if it was Pamela. Anyway, the most important thing was going home to Peggy and his new baby son, but somehow he didn't feel quite as happy about it as he should have been. The train journey home was long and boring, he tried to sleep but a bubbly blonde with a smile to light up the sky crept into his mind; what the hell was he thinking about, it wasn't like Harry, strong dependable loving Harry, who loved his Peggy with all his heart, he was just going through a rough patch what with the war being on it would all turn out okay in the end. Yes, it would be all right once he got home to Bridgevale. There was no-one to meet him at the station, it was the last train and most people would have been in bed hours ago because of their early start in the morning. The ticket collector shook his hand and bade him welcome home, "tha'll be 'ere to see th'new baby then." "Aye, that's reet," said Harry wondering how he had come to that conclusion, 'na, I'm 'ere to see the bloody May Queen' he said to himself. It wasn't like Harry at all and he couldn't understand himself. In no time at all he was home, back to his snug warm cottage and rushing up the stairs to embrace his darling Peggy. She looked radiant and handed him Baby Harry with a look so proud he had a lump in his throat. "He's just like thee Harry," said Peggy. Harry couldn't see the resemblance but his son was indeed a most handsome baby. "He hardly cries," said Peggy, "he's so good Harry," they clasped each other tightly and Harry felt himself becoming aroused, it had been a fair few weeks since they had made love, he stroked Peggy's breasts and bent to kiss her mouth. He was startled to find she was pushing him away, "No Harry, not yet I've got to get reet first." Harry felt like a dirty old man, "sorry Peg," he said, "I'll go and put the kettle on," and he went downstairs. Peggy could tell he was upset and she felt sorry for what she had said, still it wouldn't be for long although she didn't really want to make love yet, she had been told that she could get caught quickly with another baby if she did. After what she had been through she couldn't stand that again, she'd been sure she was going to die whilst in labour, it was the most horrendous pain that she had ever felt in her life and if she had to go through it again she would for Harry but not yet; no, not yet. Harry was back upstairs with a cup of tea for her, he wore a sheepish grin, "sorry Peg," he told her, "I shuddna have been like that wi' thee, I've missed thee that bad." "I know," answered Peggy, "I know darlin' one, just be patient wi' me, please Harry, it will be all reet soon." They hugged each other for a long time until they were interrupted by Jen, it was time for the baby feed and Harry had to go back downstairs. He would have preferred to wait and watch his young son suckling on those luscious breasts, he could taste them himself, 'bloody 'ell, I'd better have a walk in the cold' he told himself, "I'm goin' round t'see Aunty Ada and 'kids," he shouted upstairs and off he went. Bert was on his way to see Harry and they almost collided, Bert shook his hand and thumped him on his back 'til he felt sore. "Reet lad," said Bert, "we're off for a pint t'wet baby's 'ed." Harry told him he wanted to see the kids and Ada first so they arranged to meet in the Goyt Inn in an hour. Ada burst into tears when he walked through the door, he hugged her tight and almost wept himself, Ted did the usual hand shake and back slapping, 'God' thought Harry, 'if everybody slaps me back today I'm gonna be in bloody agony.' "Where art stationed lad?" asked Uncle Ted. "Little place outside London called Hastings," answered Harry, "it's a smite different to this place too, very different," suddenly his mind went back to the dance and Pamela, the beautiful blonde and her even white teeth, that smile that lit up her whole face and those blue eyes and long dark lashes......he jolted himself out of his reverie, what the hell was happening to him? Aunty Ada was staring at him, "art alreet lad?" she enquired, "tha looks a bit lost in thought." "Sorry Aunty, it's a bit strange bein' away from Peggy an' all." "Dunna go upsettin' lad," scolded Uncle Ted, "na then, let's 'ave a cuppa and gossip." "I canna stay long, am meetin' Bert in th' Goyt fer t'wet baby's 'ed." Ada tutted, "drinkin' in th' day time, ey, whatever next!" Ted invited himself along too so Harry didn't see his young brother or sister, he would meet up with them before his return. Bert was waiting in the Goyt Inn where Mr Jenkins was ready to shake his hand but Harry managed to keep his back well out of reach. They enjoyed a few games of Dominoes and caught up with the local gossip. "Has anyone heard from our Jim?" he asked. "Well," answered Ted, "Tilly 'ad a letter las'week an' 'e reckoned 'e were 'avin' flyin' lessons, a bloody pilot in th'makin', I never thowt we'd 'ave one o'them in th'family." Harry felt very proud of Jim, "great news that Uncle, just great." "Aye, as long as he dusnna get shot down," added old Joe in the corner of the snug. Everyone knew he'd been badly wounded while in the last war. "Ee, dunna fret Joe, nowt'l 'appen to our Jim, we're too bloody good fer Jerry." They all had a good laugh and Harry relaxed in the cosy warm atmosphere of the Goyt snug, he couldn't tell them anything about the war effort because he didn't really know anything, he was still square bashing and that was about all he could talk about, that and the shine on his boots; you could see the hairs up your nose in them. On their return to Chapel Street they bade one another goodbye, Harry would be going back in the morning and Bert would be at work. "Look after thee sen, na think on," said Bert, he thought the world of Harry, "an' thee," answered Harry, "look after the wife and baby, alreet?" Jen was looking down her nose, "by 'eck, drinkin; in th'day time, whatever next, tha'll be joinin' th' crows on th'railin's," she moaned, everyone knew crows were the men who spent their days waiting for the pub to open leaning on the railings outside. Harry laughed, "dunna tha call me a crow y'owd rat-bag." Jen let him get off with that because he'd had a drink. "Your tea's in th'oven," she said, "best get it now afore it's dried up." He was feeling quite hungry and was glad to sit and eat. Jen went home after much cooing and clucking, Harry tucked into his tea of Hot-Pot and it was bloody lovely. Suddenly into his mind flashed a picture of a pretty blonde lass in uniform, he felt a strange sensation in the pit of his stomach, Jesus, what on earth did he keep harking back to her for? He lost his appetite and couldn't eat the rest of his tea so he went out to the dustbin and threw it away. Best not let the womenfolk see it, they would call him ungrateful, after all, there was a war on, "waste not, want not" was their motto. He felt tired out, what with the journey home and the bar, so he went up to the bedroom, Peggy was lying there resting, he undressed and climbed in naked beside her and took her in his arms, "no Harry, not yet," she moaned at him, "I've only just 'ad the baby, I canna do that yet." It was very unlike Harry, he had always been kindness itself but he was greatly aroused and he wanted to make love to his darling wife, he kissed her everywhere he could reach and she struggled out of his grasp, "Harry!" she shouted out loud and awoke baby Harry who started to cry, "now look what you've done," she scolded him, "an' you look what you've done," answered Harry and pulled back the covers to show her his erection, once they would have laughed and clung to each other but not now, she gathered the baby up and began to pace the floor patting his back to soothe him back to sleep. Harry laid back and covered himself up, he began to wonder what Pamela would have done if she had seen his erection, he fell asleep imagining how wonderful it would have been and Peggy was glad to see him asleep, what could she do, she loved him so much she didn't want to turn him away from her, he would be going back in the morning and she might never see him again, she was full of self loathing and cursed her insensitivity. She got back into bed later on and cuddled up to Harry but he was fast asleep and she couldn't wake him. She laid awake most of the night partly because she wanted to watch Harry in bed with her again knowing that he would soon be gone again and also watchful for baby Harry, she didn't want him to cry and wake up his father. At dawn she lay looking around her at the bedroom that they had lovingly decorated together, they couldn't afford wall covering so they had distempered the walls pale pink and using a small sponge, they had stippled all over, also they had put up a border that Jen had managed to get hold of for them, anyway, it looked very good and she was proud of it, a couple of pictures and old photographs and it was done. There was a washstand complete with cream basin and matching jug - wedding presents from Bert and Jen and the bed, one Uncle Ted had bought from a friend of his and Ada's, it was big and comfy and they had loved every moment they had spent in it together, until tonight that was, it was also the first time they hadn't slept in each others arms. Peggy began to weep softly and couldn't stop, this woke up Harry from his troubled sleep, he held out his arms for her and she nestled in them, "what's up Peg?" he asked her, she tried to whisper about what she had been feeling, "dunna ye fret, we're alreet, ya know that," he held her tight, he could feel her breast large and swollen with milk pressing up to his chest, he was immediately aroused again, this time he knew she would have to do something about it. He pressed it to her body whilst at the same time he pulled her breast free from restrictions of her nightie and began to kiss it and then he started to suck the nipple, milk began to pour out and he gagged on it, "Hell fire Peg, it's awful," he spluttered and quickly covered it up with the nightie again, he took her hand as she laughed at him and guided it to his erection, she slowly began to caress him and then the strokes became more urgent, she gritted her teeth; God her arm was hurting, faster and faster she pulled and deeper and deeper he groaned, "oh Peg, Peg," he pleaded, "let me love you." 'No way in this world,' she thought and kept up the pressure until he came to a shuddering climax and lay panting for breath, Peggy was exhausted and her arm would never be the same again. They both lay for ages unable to move, the baby began to stir so Peg had to get up, her breasts were hurting with milk so she was glad that he would soon feed and she would be a bit more comfortable. Harry got up for a wee in the chamber pot or "guzzunda" and then decided to get up and dressed, he had to see the family before he caught the 9.30 train so there was plenty to be done it was only 5.55 am but people were scurrying off to work every way he looked out of the window, all the lamps were lit and it looked like it might be a nice day, dry and a little cold. Round at the Moore house the kids were overjoyed to see him, he had waited for Jim to go to work and then gone inside, Lizzie jumped up into his arms, "Harry I've missed you," she shrieked and he twirled her round and round 'til she was dizzy. Teddy shook his hand and Joe too, little Alex threw his arms around him and hugged him close, "I've sinth' baby," he said, "he's like a little kitten." "Well I 'ope not," said Harry, "I dunna want 'im growin' up lookin' like a cat!" They all laughed and then the back door opened and in sailed Ada, she came round every morning early to see that they were ready for school and work. Harry gave her a big hug, he looked around the house where he had lived and where his mother had existed; that's all you could call it really, she hadn't had much of a life with Big Jim - the bastard. Ada saw the fears spring to his eyes as he looked around the room and she knew what he was thinking, "hast got kettle on Lizzie?" she scolded, "come on, let's 'ave a cuppa." They did just that and in no time at all Harry was off, he met a few of the neighbours and exchanged a few pleasantries with them and upon reaching his home he was filled with a deep sense of loss, he didn't understand it but it persisted throughout the morning. He had to prize himself away from Peggy, she was in floods of tears again, she whispered in his ear so that her parents couldn't hear, "I'll make it up to you Harry, I promise we'll have the best lovemaking in the whole world when you come home again." Harry was ashamed of himself, what had he done to her; he'd been home 48 hours and all he had wanted was sex. He held her close and kissed her cheek, "Peggy darlin' dunna go sayin' that, I just want to be with thee, it dusna matta about the other, dunna ye go frettin' about it you know I love thee with all me 'art," she clung to him even more and wept again, "Oh Harry, I do love thee so much," she wailed. He drew away and headed for the door, he hated to leave her so upset but he had to go for the train and he flew down the cobbled streets. Someone shouted to him but he couldn't stop and by the time he reached the station the train was ready for leaving, "by gum, that were a close shave lad," said the ticket seller. "Aye it were," he answered and leapt into a carriage. He felt an elation he couldn't quite understand at first then the blonde hair and wonderful smile came into his mind, he was going back and he would be seeing Pamela. He cursed himself but he just couldn't help himself, he watched through the window as the train pulled out of Bridgevale station, the houses, the Foundry, the tall chimney perched high above the Goyt Mill weaving shed, the house where he had been born he could make out the rooftop, then they were gone only the cemetery was visible and his thoughts flew to Mam and Camy and that Irish lad Finton, his half brother, what a revelation that was, it had filled their minds for months, he wished Camy had been spared he would have loved for her to be alive and happy, she was a beauty and so loveable everyone liked her, he would never understand why she did what she did, never as long as he lived, he sat back and looked around him. The carriage wanted a clean and it stank of smoke like a tarry bonfire smoke, he closed his eyes and settled down to sleep for a while until he reached Manchester station then he would be running around like a headless chicken looking for his connecting trains.

Chapter Five

Enchanting Coral

Jim Moore had heard that his second son Harry had been home on leave to see his new baby boy, they hadn't clapped eyes on each other which was probably for the best, there was no love lost between them. Ginny goaded him about it and he rounded on her and told her to shut her fucking big mouth, "you know now't about it so shut it slut!" he bellowed at her, she hadn't meant for it to be like this, what she intended was quite the opposite to turn him away from his family and more towards herself. Anyway, it had backfired on her so she sat sulking. Jim took one look at her petulant face and marched out slamming the door behind him with a salvo of four letter words left hanging on the night air. Ginny was pissed off about this, she was no nearer getting round Jim to move her into his house, what the bloody 'ell do I 'ave to do, she pondered, all she had to fight with were her figure, her face and her easy way to please a man in any sexual position. Next time he came round she would use all her womanly wiles to snare him.

Jim banged on Meg's door and she jumped up in alarm, "where's fire?" she asked as she let him in. "Dunna you fucking well start," bellowed Jim. "I'm not startin' owt Jim, whatever's up wi' thee?" "Now't that a good shaggin' wi' thee wunna put reet," he nodded towards the bed and Meg dutifully obliged, whatever was up with Jim Meg wished it would happen every week, she had never had it so good as on that day, Jim was insatiable and they were at it for hours. 'He must love me' thought Meg 'after what we've done together, he must'. He lay snoring in her bed exhausted at last and she gazed at him feeling so much love for him she felt like weeping. She wished he would ask her to move in with him but he never did. She wondered about Ginny if he had seen her today, she knew that Ginny was sharpening her claws and vowed to keep out of her way. They both wanted Jim, which one would get him only time would tell. Meg thought that she would die if he didn't choose her, she loved him so much, she may be a tart but she wasn't a bad one.

Mary was feeling a bit let down too, Harry hadn't called round to see her, she knew he hadn't got very long and he would have wanted to be with his wife and baby but he could have said "hello" it wasn't like Harry at all, he was such a caring person. She was having a moan to Jean who hadn't seen him either, "I canna understand it," she said to Mary, "it's not like our Harry, he must have been overjoyed at th' birth an' we disappeared from 'is mind." Mary was still hobbling around, her ankle still a bit swollen, it didn't help having to work at the Mill weaving every day, the floors were hard cold stone and they seemed to draw the very strength from your legs. She had told Jean about Tom Scully and Jean's hackles were raised, "he was probably drunk when he knocked you over our Mary," she scolded, "fancy lettin' the likes of 'im in yer 'ouse, he could 'ave done anythin' to ya," she did a mock shudder. Mary laughed out loud, "dunna be sa daft, 'e were reet gentlemanly." "Oh my God," she rolled her eyes in the sockets, "dirty, smelly drunken swine, 'ed be more like it," she chided. "Mary, dunna 'ave 'im inth' 'ouse agin wilt tha promise me?" Mary promised and they started on about baby Harry, glad that he hadn't been born on Camy's birthday which would have been tomorrow the 28th, she would have been 19 years old, their eyes met and they began to weep for their darling Camy, she was so badly missed by them all. Elizabeth Jean wondered what the matter was and joined in so they stopped crying, dried their eyes and decided to go up to the graveyard they next day and take some nice flowers, they would take Lizzie with them too and little Alex. Mary walked home up the cobbled streets, it was a cold clear evening and she dawdled along thinking about Brian, wondering how he was, hoping he was missing her like she missed him, just the thought of him reduced her to tears, what with Camy and him she felt almost like she was drowning in tears, she became aware of someone beside her and turning she was Tom Scully. "How do, Miss Moore," he called. "Oh hello, how art?" "Ee reet champion thanks, how's th' ankle?" "Gettin' better." He could see that she was still hobbling, he was looking quite clean and tidy and he smelt of shaving lotion, "'ast tha bin cryin' Miss Moore?" he asked her observing her tear filled eyes. "Just a bit, it would've bin me sister Camy's 19th Birthday tomorra an' I was missin' 'er tha knows an' then wi Brian bein' away an' all," the tears were coming back again, Tom didn't like to see her upset, "come on lass, let's get thee 'ome, a drop o brandy'll do thee the world o good," he told her. In no time at all they were at her door, she unlocked it and was about to bid him goodnight but he quickly followed her inside, "I canna leave thee upset like this," he told her, he was being very kind and she was lonely, Jean's words came to her but he hadn't harmed her so it was all right. The fire was laid ready to be lit but she said she wouldn't bother, she'd have an early night. She sat in the fireside chair and in the gas light he thought how beautiful and sad she looked, she pointed to the sideboard, "tha'll find some brandy in they're," he did and he boiled some water in the kettle an poured them both a reet good measure she spluttered and gasped, "it was awful," she said to Tom, "just hold yer nose an' down it ," was his reply, so she did and her eyes ran like waterfalls. "The next one will be even better," he told her and he added sugar to it stirring it well, "no ta," said Mary, "I canna drink any more, am non used to it." "Taste it," he coaxed her, "you'll feel grand when it goes down," so she did with the sugar it wasn't quite as bad. "Let's 'ave a look at this ankle," he said and before she could answer her shoe was off and he was stroking her leg, "by 'eck that's much better Miss Moore," he said. "It's Mary, me name's Mary Bailey not Moore, I'm Mrs Bailey," her speech was slurred and she felt hot all over. Tom Scully looked up into her eyes, he didn't want to frighten her so he began to flatter her, told her what a lovely girl she was and how everyone liked her, he continued to stroke her ankle and he looked deep into her eyes. She felt a bit squiffy and in the gas light he looked quite nice, he had been a nice lookin' bloke and he hadn't quite lost it all. His hand travelled slowly up her leg and she shuddered, he stopped he got up and mixed her another brandy and hot water with sugar, "tha'll feel better after this Mary, ye'll sleep like a top," to himself he was thinking, 'with me on top,' he was greatly aroused but in the gas light she couldn't see it. By the time she had finished the drink she was absolutely pissed, she started to giggle and then burst into tears, Tom took the opportunity to comfort her, his arms wrapped 'round her shoulders and he hugged her to him, turning her face 'round to his he kissed her on her nose, then her neck, she flinched away from him but he held her tight and then found her moist lips, he kissed them gently at first and then when she didn't respond he drew back, "come on lass," he coaxed her, "let me help thee upth' stairs," he pulled her to her feet but she couldn't walk unaided and he half carried her up the steep staircase, she was trying to tell him something but the words came out all wrong, "by 'eck you are in a way lass," he told her, "it's a good job I'm 'ere fer thee, how art goin' ta thank me?" he asked. Her eyes were rolling about in her head and the room was whizzing 'round, "Oh please," she squealed, "I feel sick," he could make that out all right, he bundled her into the bedroom and held out the basin from off the washstand, he could just about make things out in the dim light from the street lamp. She was as sick as a dog, when she had finished retching her guts up he undressed her gently 'til she was naked on the bed, she couldn't stop him she was too ill, she knew it wasn't right but all she could whisper was, "please no...don't.....stop," feebly. In seconds Tom had stripped off too, he felt at his hardness and was proud of it, he straddled Mary and opened her legs wide, "you're goin' ta get summat tha's never 'ad afore," he told her and he eased himself into her, she was dry and it was hard going but it didn't put him off she was mortified but powerless to resist, she felt herself aroused and couldn't believe it , she didn't want this man inside her but at the same time it felt so good, if her head would stop swimming about she would be all right she could stop him and send him off home, he rode her deeply and with great joy he adored her, he worshipped her and at last he was inside her, she was his goddess. He gripped her buttocks and pulled her even closer to him, he wished to be as one with her he began to kiss her again but she turned her head away, "stop it," she mumbled, "stop it," but she was also matching him thrust for thrust, "stop, please," she pleaded, "we canna do this, we mustna do it, it's wrong." "Mary me darlin' girl, it's right, we were made fer each other we're meant to be doin this love me back lass he urged love me back come on." She tried as hard as her pelvis would let her, she pulled his face back to hers and kissed him deeply, her tongue flicking in and out of his mouth until he almost screamed with the passion of it, they climaxed together and laid in each other's arms for a very long time. Mary fell asleep but Tom Scully didn't, he wanted to savour every inch of her body, he stroked her naked breasts they weren't large but firm, nice breasts, he'd always said owt more than a handful were wasted. He ran his hands up and down her legs and buttocks, by 'eck she were a beauty, her skin felt like silk and the aroma of her body made him go weak at the knees. He began to caress her and upon waking Mary shouted out "bloody 'ell," what on earth was she doing, it was almost daybreak, "you'll 'ave to go," she pleaded "afore anybody sees thee leavin'," he knew it made sense so reluctantly he dressed and walked over to the bed, "we must do this a lot more Mary," she couldn't look at him, she lay shivering under the covers, "dust that 'ear me Mary?" he spoke louder this time. "Aye all reet," she muttered. "I'm lookin' forward to more," he drooled "lots more." He kissed her head and was gone down the stairs, she listened for the back door to close but heard nothing, she wrapped her dressing gown around her and crept down, he had gone without a sound, she locked the back door. "Oh my God," she started to cry "whatever 'ave I done?" she darn't think about it, it was too disgusting, "Oh my God, how could I 'ave , it was awful," she got a bowl of water still warm from the fire oven and started to wash herself down, she was very tender below, "no bloody wonder," she coloured up scarlet when she remembered. The size of it, she knew she had enjoyed it but didn't want to admit it even to herself. Never again, it must never happen again, what could she do to stop it he was a very determined man was Tom Scully, what he wanted he got, seemingly he'd had her very easily and she was supposed to be a good girl, 'I'm no better than a tart,' Mary thought to herself, 'I'm worse than Meg or Ginny.' She cried bitter tears, what would her Brian think of her, he must never find out, never or she would do what Camy had done she wouldn't be able to live with herself. It was Saturday morning, Camy's birthday and, thank God, no work today, no weaving at the Mill, after the night she'd had she wouldn't have had the strength. She still felt dirty and couldn't get the nights goings on out of her mind, she filled the copper with water and boiled it up, it took about an hour then she fetched in the tin bath from the back yard and put it in front of the kitchen fire, then she filled the bath with water from the copper into this she crumbled half of one of her precious bath cubes, having lowered herself in she lay back and let the warm scented water soak into her skin. There was a knock t the back door luckily she had locked it and drawn the kitchen curtains too, she began to shake, it must be Tom Scully, Oh God, what could she do, she did the only thing she could, she remained perfectly still and quiet. "Mary!" a voice shouted out to her, "Mary art thayer?" it was Jean with the flowers for Camy's grave. "I'm havin' a bath Jean, can tha wait a minute," answered Mary thanking God it wasn't Tom Scully. She stood up and wrapped a towel 'round her body and stepping out of the bath she padded over to the door and turned the key, Jean came bustling in with Elizabeth Jean in her bassinet. She looked at Mary and asked, "whatever's up wi' thee?" "Nowt," answered Mary "I'll just get me dressed." "It's non bath neet, what's up?" "Bloody 'ell Jean, I can 'ave a bath if I want one wi'owt permission canna ey?" "Oh dear, ya got out o'th' bed wrong side this mornin' then, tha'rt in a bad mood and no mistake." She noticed Marys back and shoulders were red and had long red marks running down them and the tops of her arms had what looked like finger prints on them. "Whatever 'ast tha bin up to?" she whispered to Mary, who burst into tears and fled up the stairs. Jean knew instinctively that something was very wrong and she felt panic seizing her, "Mary!" she almost screamed, "whats 'appened, tell me fer Gods sake." She could hear Mary weeping loudly, great sobs racked her body, "I'll go bloody mad in a minute if tha dussna tell me," she almost screamed. Elizabeth Jean started to wail, "Oh God, now look what I've dun," she lifted the little one out of her bassinet and climbed up the steep staircase and followed the sound of sobbing, Mary was laid like a rag doll on her bed raked with sobs, uncontrollable, the towel all askew.

Jean observed her buttocks, they were bruised and scratched, there were bites on her neck like the ones you give your lover. "Oh Christ almighty, Mary," she squawked, "ast tha taken a lover?" Mary looked her in the eye and then burst into another fit of tears. Someone was knocking at the door, Mary let out a strangled cry and the panic in her eyes was plain to see. "Hold the baby," Jean ordered and thrust Elizabeth Jean into her arms, she was ready for whoever stood there, she snatched open the back door half expecting a mad man, it was Lizzie, "art thee ready?" asked Lizzie, Jean just stood looking gormless, "what?" she asked. "Art tha ready fer th' bone-yard?" Lizzie couldn't understand why Jean looked so upset. "Well now Lizzie tha can do me a great big favour, wilt tha take th' baby fer a walk inth' bassinet, our Mary's feelin' a bit poorly." Lizzie was only to pleased and Jean went up the stairs to bring down the child. Having got them out of the way with instructions to be away for the next hour or two Jean reluctantly went back upstairs to Mary. She had dressed by this time but she just sat looking vulnerable like a china doll, "dust tha want to tell me Mary?" With faltering voice Mary went over the nights happenings, Jean was aghast, "Christ all bloody mighty Mary, whatever came over thee, I told thee not to 'ave owt to do wi' that dirty bugger," she gave an involuntary shudder, "I'd rather 'ave died than let that filthy bastard near me." Mary collapsed into another sobbing bout. Jean knew it was doing no good keep harpin' on about the dirty old man, she had to help Mary over this before she collapsed, "right then our Mary, lets get out inth' fresh air, take them flowers up th' grave, say 'ow do to our Camy." Mary let herself be led like a little puppy, "pull thee sen together before somebody notices," said Jean rather sharply. Mary tried her best, by the time they had found Lizzie and the baby and walked to the boneyard it was getting quite late in the afternoon, clouds were whipping past and it looked like it might rain at any minute. They sat beside the grave and talked about Camy and Finton, how probably by now if things hadn't turned out the way they had, that the two would have been married and so very happy. Lizzie added that she thought they were happy together in another world. "I might be joinin' them soon," said Mary still in the depths of despair. "What dust tha mean our Mary?" asked Lizzie. "Oh take na notice of 'er," snapped Jean, "she's talkin' daft as usual." "Mary never talks daft," said Lizzie. Mary began to cry again, Lizzie couldn't understand it at first and looked puzzled then it dawned on her, "you're missin' Brian," she babbled on, "he'll be all reet dunna worry we'll look after thee wunna we Jean." "Aye that we will Lizzie, that we will. Come on lets get back afore it rains or we'll be like drowned rats." They took one last look at the headstone and realised they hadn't mentioned Mam, they looked at each other feeling a little ashamed, 'couldn't be helped' thought Jean and pushed it to the back of her mind. Off they trundled down the steep hill, what a walk it was, they were all glad to reach the cobbled streets again. "Tha'd best be off 'ome Lizzie," said Jean and they bade each other goodbye. "Tha'd better come 'ome wi' me Mary, I canna 'ave thee stayin' by thee sen, come on," it was starting to rain; they had only just made it in time as they reached Jean's door the heavens opened. Arthur stood there, Jean squealed and rushed into his arms, "what tha doin' 'ome?" she asked him, "me eyesight's too bad, they wunna 'ave me," he answered, "they sent me back 'ome," he was beaming all over his face. "Thank God," said Jean. He was a bit put out, he liked to have his family to himself, he didn't like visitors much, Mary noted the look he passed to Jean, "Mary's not too well Arthur so she's stoppin' 'ere for a bit." "No I'm not Arthur I'm all reet an' I'm goin' 'ome in a little while," said Mary. Arthur looked relieved, "Oh reet lass," he said. "Lets get tea on shall we," muttered Jean staring with vexation at both Arthur and Mary in turn. Soon they were sat around the parlour table eating boiled ham and pork pie with a nice crisp salad and crusty home baked bread, the cloth was hand embroidered and even the napkins were hand made, everything looked clean and wholesome and they ate heartily except for Mary who pretended to. Jean persuaded Mary to stay for just the one night so Arthur went round to her place to make sure the fire was out and he emptied the bath, what the 'ell had she left that for?...he knew Mary was very house-proud and he couldn't understand what had made her leave it like that. He hoped it wasn't anything that would keep her away for too long, the sooner she was back here the better, he wanted to be alone with his wife to kiss and caress her when he felt like it, to stroke her cheek and laugh with her about the day's events. He was a private man was Arthur, Mary would say dull but Jean loved him with all her heart and only saw the best in him. He was a good man and he adored their little girl. There was a knock at the door, " 'ang on!" he shouted, he put the dirty towels into the laundry basket and strode to the door....there was no-one there, he looked down the back yards, no, not a soul, well that were very strange he definitely heard a knock, well let 'em beggar off if they couldna wait. Later on he related the tale to Mary and Jean who looked frightened and ill at ease, "by 'eck, you're a daft pair an' no mistake," he laughed

"it were only a knock not a visit from th'devil," worse thought Jean, much bloody worse, she looked across at Mary, she still couldn't believe what had gone on between them two, he had obviously got her drunk before he had violated her, he should be bloody well hung but why had she let the bloody snake into her house in the first place? They had agreed to keep it their secret, no-one was ever to know, if this got out in Bridgevale she would be shunned by all who knew her, Jean could imagine the tongues wagging, "there's no smoke without fire......tied her up did he......knocked the bloody door down," eh by 'eck they would have a friggin' field day. Jean scolded herself, I've got to stop this swearin' even if it's only in my thoughts, she sounded like her dad and she didn't want to be tarred with the same brush.

Lizzie was doing a few chores before going to bed, she kept thinking about Mary and how sad she was, she wished Brian would come home to her then she would be all right, she'd never seen Mary this way and she had told Auntie Ada about it, Ada was puzzled too, Mary was a strong girl, she wasn't the sort to go to pieces without her man, she was logical, level headed, brought up with Jim Moore as a father you were anything but soft. Ada would go round when she had a minute; Sunday morning after Mary came back from Sunday School. The back door opened and Jim Moore stood glowering, "what's tha doin' up 'til this bastard time?" he growled at Lizzie, "I'm just," "ne'er mind," he cut her short, "just get up the bleedin' stairs now," he shrieked at her, his eyes blazing. 'He's gone stark ravin' mad' thought Lizzie and she ran up the stairs as fast as she could, she was undressed and in bed in a jiffy and started to cry, 'bloody 'ell, I didna do owt, bloody old sod, I hope he dies an' I won't visit his bloody grave' she cried herself to sleep. Downstairs Jim was pacing the floor, he was pissed off with the lot of them, Meg and Ginny were both mythering about moving in with him here, he didn't want either of them in Sals place but they were wearing him down and he was fast running out of excuses. He threw his boots down by the fire grate and climbed the stairs to his lonely room, he hadn't bothered with a candle tonight so it was pitch black. He undressed and walked towards the bed remembering when Sal would be laid there her body warm and soft, he would take her night after night and never once did she respond to his sexual activities. It would have been so good if she had done, Meg and Ginny would welcome him with open arms, they would never be cold like Sal, cold and unfeeling, well if she was why did he still love her, why did he weep for her, she never loved him she hated him so why did he feel this way, he couldn't understand it, he wanted her so badly it hurt. He clutched at his guts and moaned. "Oh Sal, Sal tha bloody well bewitched me, tha's cast a bloody spell on me, what canna do, I'll go bleedin' mad if I dunna get that woman out a my bloody 'ead." He eventually fell into a fitfull sleep and he dreamt about Sal trying to drown him, he was gasping for air and screaming. Someone was shaking him, he leapt up in bed, what the...it was Lizzie, "what's matter dad, you were shoutin'," she was shivering with fear, "nowt, piss off back to bed and dunna bloody wake me agen," she scuttled off clutching the candle, he lit his and looked at the cheap clock at the side of the bed, it was 4.30 am best get some sleep, fancy bein' wakened up at this bloody time of night, he'd have something to say to that daft cow in the mornin'. He was sick of being on his own, he'd decided to ask Meg to move in with him, no more nights alone he couldn't stand anymore, Meg would be the best, she was more placid, not as good in bed as Ginny but she would make a better wife, he stopped, what the bloody 'ell, "WIFE" he didna want a wife, a mistress that's what he wanted a bloody mistress aye that would be best, he'd ask Meg the next night after work.

At R.A.F. Biggin Hill young Jim Moore was into his fourth week of training, he loved every moment of it and couldn't wait to get up and away, he had learned eagerly the technological side of things and atmospherics, his written work was neat and articulate and his instructor was very pleased with him, he was popular with the other men and got on well with everyone. He hoped to win his wings pretty soon and then he could write and tell Tilly all about it. Tilly the love of his young life, he missed her terribly but the job had to be done, couldn't let Jerry have his own way or Uncle Ted would have his guts for garters. There was only one flaw in Jim's make-up and that was the broad Derbyshire accent, he was ribbed about it constantly and he was trying to speak a little better, more like the other chaps with their plummy voices. He wondered how Sally Victoria was, was she missing her daddy like he was missing her, she was a little beauty and one day she would be all grown up and married with children of her own. He didn't want to think about that but hoped the world would be a safer place for them to live in than it was right now. Getting back to his hut he saw a letter from Tilly waiting on his bed, he felt a great excitement and couldn't wait to read it. Tilly's writing wasn't up to much and he felt a strange embarrassment wishing she could write and spell better, he didn't want anyone to see it but he was still overjoyed to hear from her. So Harry was a father, that was good news, old Harry, he knew he would be cock-a-hoop, he would have to find out where he was and send his best. Tilly hadn't seen him when he came home on leave but had reports from the others, everyone was well, Sally Vicky sent her daddy a huge kiss and Tilly missed him so much. They had all taken flowers to the grave on the 28th, he had forgotten, he had been so busy, yes Camy, his lovely sister, what a bloody shit life she had. His eyes were brimming with tears, "a Dear John old man?" asked Charles Feathergill passing by, "Oh no, just news of a birth in th'family," he winced, why couldn't he have said "in THE family," "Oh jolly good show old man, top hole," added Charles. He was a nice chap but very posh, what Auntie Ada would call "upper crust". "Shall we go and try a couple old man?" shouted Charles. Jim nodded in answer and got on with his letter. He wrote back full of tales about his new life here at the base and about his wish to fly, he didn't mention anything about the lads and how posh they were. Charles and Jack Benson were waiting for him to finish off, "bloody hell old man, my bloody throats parched like a rasp, hurry up do!" shouted the latter, Jim shoved the letter under his pillow and ran out after the pair. "Can't a man write to 'is wife wi'out you buggers purgin'?" he moaned at them in mock dismay, "no-one of your age should have a bloody wife and kid Jim," scolded Charles, "women were meant to fuck and leave then go on to the next one, a much better arrangement he added bitterly, 'Oh dear, he'd been crossed badly' thought Jim. They headed for the local pub which was a few yards up the road, the "White Horse Inn" it was a lively place full of service men and women and a few locals who liked to tell a tale or two for a pint. Jim ordered two pints for himself and Jack and a whisky for Charles and they strode over to watch a game of darts, it was a good game and they put their names down to play the winners. Charles was deep in conversation with a dark haired lass, she was quite a beauty, Jim had to attract his attention, "we're on," he mouthed, Charles indicated that he had understood. They started off without him and he dashed over at the very last minute, "first things first old bean," he smiled like the cat that's got the cream, "got to get my bloody leg over soon or I'll go stark raving mad," he broke out in raucous laughter, "what, what." He was a bugger and no mistake thought Jim, he looked over at the dark haired girl in uniform, she had a stunning figure but she looked cold and haughty, with her was another cracker, she had deep auburn hair and her skin looked tanned and smooth, she laughed out loud and she had a mouth to die for, perfect teeth and luscious lips, a few freckles here and there, she was about 5'6" to 7" nice legs too. Jim pulled himself up sharp, what was he thinking about, she's not a patch on my Tilly. The girl looked across at him aware that he was starring at her, he turned away quickly and turned bright red. The only girl he had ever known intimately was Tilly, they met at school and were never apart 'til now, he would die without her and he loved her more than life itself. She wouldn't be very pleased to see him ogling this young servicewoman, he got on with the game but he was aware that the girl was watching him, he began to show off a bit and play the clown. He looked up to see her giggling at him, he smiled at her, Charles was aware of this, "I say old man, it's about time you were introduced to Coral," he pushed them together, "this is Jim Moore, I'll leave the rest to you." "Hello

Jim," said Coral, he stammered something stupid, "nice to meet thee," he said, she was a bit taken back with the thick accent, he noticed right away and he felt uneasy. "I'll get back to th'game," he told her and excused himself. Stuck up buggers he said to himself, he got himself another pint and got rid of it pretty quickly. He was playing better than ever, the years of practice at the Goyt Inn had paid off. Sod Coral and all the others like her, anyway, what sort of a bloody name was Coral, no-one could beat his Tilly, she was an angel and Sally Victoria, they were the only women he wanted in his life. Charles and Jack were talking to the girls so Jim headed off back to the hut. He headed for the showers and had a good soak and by the time he got back it was time for lights out. Jack sailed over to him from his bunk, "you buggered off rapid tonight Jim, you should have stayed." "Why?" asked Jim. Charles joined in the conversation, "our Red Head really fancies you, what." "Oh yes," added Jack, "Coral has the hots for you Jim." "Dunna be so bloody daft," answered Jim, " I'm married and that's way I'll stay, I dunna want any stuck up bitch." Charles and Jack roared with laughter, "you havn't got it stuck up yet old man," said Charles, "but play you cards right and you could well do just that." Jim didn't want to hear anymore of their banter and he put his head under the pillow where he found the letter he had written to Tilly earlier on. God bless you Tilly and my little girl, he wouldn't swap them for anyone never, never. Coral lay in her small bed in the hut, she went over and over the nights happenings, Jim Moore, now he was handsome, God she couldn't stop thinking about him, this had never happened to her before. She liked men but didn't really care for anyone in particular she had seen enough misery with her own family. She was the youngest of three sisters, her father was living in New Zealand with his sheep farmer girlfriend, mother Gloria had a new boyfriend every other week. She was always pissed and would scream at anyone and anything who got in her way when she was lurching around the house, the times her mother's beau's had tried to paw her or grab her breasts she had lost count of, the one good thing about living in a large house was you could hide very easily. She had spent hours sitting in un-used rooms, going through cupboards and drawers, trying clothes on from overfull wardrobes. Her sisters were a lot older than she at 18 years. Fran was 26 and Deborah was 28, they had both been married and both marriages had failed miserably, now they too cavorted about with every available male they could find. That was why Coral couldn't understand why she felt this way about Jim Moore, she was always so anti-men. She had joined up immediately to escape the family but was sure that she was doing the right thing marking out a career for herself in the air force. She missed her mother and sisters a little bit but on the whole life was better without too much of them. She fell asleep thinking about Jim Moore, she didn't know yet that he was married with a child. Morning came too soon, it always did, Coral had only just closed her eyes, "dammit," she said out loud to her best friend Daphne, "the bags under my eyes will be large enough to pack my uniform in soon." "I know what you mean my dear, it's dreadful isn't it. Must get some egg white, I'll have a word with Johnny in the cookhouse, see what he can do." Coral was scrambling about looking for a decent pair of stockings, "bloody hell, they're all laddered, what do I do with them?" Daphne came to her rescue, "here you are," she laughed, "have these, I've got plenty." "Yes and we know how," she laughed back. "Shh Coral, we don't want the others to know." The other girls were running about, too busy with their own lives to worry about silly vain Daphne. "Come on you lot!" shouted the Corporal, "lets be 'avin you." They all marched off to the mess for breakfast, Coral searched with her eyes for anyone who looked like Jim Moore but no, he wasn't here, she sat down rather glum, she didn't want any breakfast. "Come on old girl, whatever's the matter with you, you normally eat for two." "Oh, my stomach's a bit off, it's nothing really." "The drink," said Daffers, "you had far too many." Coral agreed with her, just go away and shut up she wanted to shout at her but she couldn't do that, she was too well mannered. "Oh I say," said Daffers "look who's over there, the dishy guy with the terrible accent, broad Yorkshire or something." Coral was incensed, "Daphne don't be so cruel, I think it's a lovely warm accent." Daffers studied her closely, "Oh I see, got the hots for him have we?" "No but he does look very nice, you can't judge a book by it's cover," she spouted. "Anything you say dear," added Daphne, "anything you say," raising her eyebrows to show she wasn't a fool. Jim felt her eyes upon him and looked round to see her, their eyes met and both felt an electric shock run through them, they both looked away embarrassed but not before both Charles and Daphne had witnessed the look, they then grinned at each other and pretended to fan themselves meaning the two had the hots. Jim felt really mad at himself, what was wrong with him, he'd only been away from his family a short while and here he was gazing at a bit of skirt. He was glad that Tilly couldn't read his thoughts and hoped that she wasn't giving the eye to anyone back home. "Come on old chap!" shouted Charles in his ear, he jumped up like a startled fawn. "Bloody 'ell, bugger off you damned fool," he hollered back. "Lets go, work to be done," he ambled off to the aircraft hanger without a backward glance. 'He doesn't want to know me' thought Coral, 'well I'll have to try harder, never give up, that's our family motto and if it isn't it should be.' After training had ended that day Charles,

Jack and Jim headed for the pub again, Jim knew he shouldn't but was secretly hoping to see Coral again. Daphne was there with some of the others but not Coral, Jim was really disappointed but he couldn't bring himself to ask about her, he was glad when he could get away from the others who were all pairing up. He felt like a fish out of water. "It's a pity Coral couldn't make it tonight," said Daphne looking straight into Jim's eyes, he pretended he couldn't remember her, "she had other fish to fry." He felt a pang of jealousy, it hit him right to the pit of his stomach. He wanted to demand where she was but couldn't, "I'm off then, see thee in't mornin'," he called over to the other men. Daphne was trying not to sneer at his broad accent but she failed miserably. Stupid stuck up bitch thought Jim and he was glad to get away from them all, they had nothing in common and he suddenly wished he was home in Bridgevale. 'I'll sleep on it, maybe it will all look better in the light of day', Uncle Ted always said that, he thought about them all and wondered if they missed him. He wondered when he would get leave, not yet he knew he hadn't been there very long so no use askin' to go home. He decided to write to Harry, ask how he was, 'I bet he misses Peggy and the new baby boy, I hope we get leave together' he thought 'and be able to see each other again.' He missed his family very much. Coral had washed her hair, it was very thick and long, she wore it up but when she let it lose it was really wonderful, it took an awful lot of drying so she stayed in the block and wrote a few letters to friends. She was in bed almost asleep when Daphne came in, "your dreamboat was in all by himself," she whispered to Coral, "he looked all sad and alone and guess what, he's married with a child." Coral wanted to scream, she stifled a sob. She turned away so that Daphne couldn't see her eyes, "go to sleep," she managed to say without breaking down, "I'm tired." Daphne was a trifle put out, no reaction, perhaps she had been wrong, it wasn't like her at all, "Oh well, good night old girl," it would soon be morning, she was very happy though, she had just enjoyed the most wonderful love making session with Charles, he really knew how to please a woman, he knew all the right buttons to press, she wanted to savour it, go over and over it again and again in her mind so she left Coral alone. Coral was thankful, she shed a few tears, there was absolutely nothing she could do about Jim, he belonged to someone else and whatever else she may have been she wasn't a home wrecker. When she spotted Jim a few days latter she just ignored him, he felt a bit put out, 'what's up wi' 'er' he said to himself trying not to care but he did care, he felt really strange, he tried to put it out of his mind, "bloody women," he muttered. "Did I hear the fairer sex mentioned?" asked Jack beaming over his shoulder, "my favourite subject old sport."

"Oh bugger off," answered Jim, "you're girl bloody mad." They had a good laugh and went on their way. Tomorrow would be the day they had been waiting for, it would be chocks away and head for the skies, Jim couldn't wait for his first flight it was what he longed for all these weeks. Charles wanted them to go to the pub that night but Jim thought he would be best keeping a clear head and said no, Jack felt the same way so Charles went alone. Daphne was there with Coral and the conversation soon came round to Jim Moore, Daffers sniggered and poked fun at Coral, "she's got the hots for Jim has our friend Coral," she said rather too loudly, everyone looked round, coral thought she would die of shame, "really Daphne, there's no need for that, I certainly do not have the....em....whatever you said for anyone." "Oh no?" replied Daffers, the word is the hots and you have them believe me. I know what I'm talking about." "Well shove your opinions up you know where!" responded Coral and started to march off out of the bar. Charles caught hold of her arm and pulled her back, "now come on girls, stop this silly argy bargy, don't ruin your friendship for the sake of a few silly words." He was right, they smiled at each other, "sorry," said Daffers and held out her hand, Coral took it and they hugged each other warmly.

Wednesday dawned cold and drizzly, the men marched out from their blocks after breakfast, Jim was too nervous to eat, he felt sick with excitement. The Gloster Gauntlets, single engine biplanes peeped out from the morning mist like giant praying mantis. They had spent a lot of time in those on the ground getting to know the rudiments of flying. The Hurricane was the one they would be using today, they held six crew and the men were given their orders as to which part of the aircraft they should make their way to. Jim was lucky to be with Charles and Jack and also Billy Downs and Roger Evesham. After what seemed like hours of rehearsing they were strapped in and bumping along down the airfield, before they knew it they were airborne. They went up and down, banking almost upside down, a couple of the men lost their breakfasts, Jim was glad that he hadn't eaten that morning. It was terrific stuff and he loved every moment, soon they were back on terra ferma and all agreed it was the best feeling in the world just being up there gave them such a buzz. They asked their Chief Petty Officer when they would be having another go, "it's not a bloody game you bleedin' shower," he barked at them, " this is for bloody real, you will be learning to fly all this week and the best will go solo by this weekend, the rest can piss off," he snarled. Solo by weekend, bloody hell that was a bit nerve wracking, nevertheless they knew deep down that they would be able to do it, they were all so keen. "Right lads lets get some dinner and then we can give the girls a treat," said Charles, "show them our cock-pits, eh what?" they all hooted with laughter. Later on at the pub Jim got a chance to talk with Coral for the first time, she was easy to talk to and as the evening wore on Jim was glad he was with her, she asked about his wife and daughter and she saw the love in his eyes for his family, he was a really good sort was Jim Moore and she felt a sadness deep inside she had never known before, why did he have to be married, the nicest man on the whole camp and he had to be spoken for.

Saturday was upon them and they gathered in the hanger, waiting for the Flight Sergeant to tell them whom amongst them was going on to fly solo. Jim had so many butterflies in his stomach he feared he would pass out literally, at last the list was pinned up on the board and they eagerly jostled there to see if and where their names came on the list. Jim whooped with delight himself, Charles, Jack, Billy and Roger had all passed with distinction and would all be flying solo very soon. Jim thanked God for his help he knew he couldn't have done it alone; the five of them danced a jig much to the amusement of the other lads and the Flight Sergeant.

"Right you horrible shower let's get on with it then you can all go and get pissed," he roared.

"If there were a grade for getting pissed you lot would come tops every time." He chuckled.

The gang of five headed for the airfield and in turn took over the small single engine Gloster Gauntlets and with cries of tallyho soared into the skies.

When it was his turn Jim sat in the tiny cockpit and almost died from sheer terror.

"Come on Moore pull yourself together man." Shouted a loud voice in his earpiece making him almost jump out of his skin.

"Shall we send for Mammy to hold your bloody hand eh."

Jim was enraged who the hell was that bugger shouting at he'd show him. He got his brain engaged and automatically his hands and feet responded and in no time at all he was bumping down the airstrip, faster and faster he sped, the little plane shaking fit to fall to pieces. Going at full throttle he pulled back the joystick and in seconds soared up into the heavens he was so shocked to be up there alone that he momentarily panicked, and the little plane swung back and forth erratically. With sheer concentration he steadied the plane he was a Moore after all and his wife and family needed him, he didn't want to go down before he'd had a go at the enemy.

The training he'd received came into its own and soon he was soaring over fields and hedges, as he winged his way over the camp site he shouted "Yeehaa" as loud as he could. No one could hear him but he wasn't to know that, he became aware of a buzzing in his ears it was ground control he had been oblivious to their command. Sorry he stammered must have lost contact somehow, he was ordered back to the airfield and told to land in one piece if that was possible. Jim made a perfect landing and couldn't help but laugh when he spotted a couple of the Gloster's with the propellers tipped forward churned into the turf, arse's in the air he wondered who's.

Showering quickly he wanted to be out, to find Coral and tell her all about it. He reckoned without the rest of the lads they wanted to tell their day too, so it was later than normal when they finally got to the pub. Charles was cock-a-hoop he had done exceptionally well so he would reward himself he remarked.

"Did you hear about Johnny Balham?" Asked Roger turning from ordering the first round at the bar, they all looked up expectantly. "He bottled out, never left the field." Everyone was shocked, he had been one of the most likely to succeed following in the family tradition and all that.

"Well well they all echoed, you can never tell." "Wonder what will happen to him now." they all shock their heads not knowing the answer.

"Shit his pants, they led him away crying like a baby." Added Roger.

No-one could believe it, his father, grandfather and two uncles had all been decorated for valour; they would be terribly upset to say the least.

"They might team him up with the crew in the Hercules bombers," replied Jim feeling sorry for Johnny. "it doesn't mean he can't fly." He added. Charles chipped in that he could still be part of a team he was a jolly could chap the Air Force wouldn't want to lose him, everyone agreed it was a tough life and could have happened to any one of them. A huge smile lit up Charles face as Daphne sashayed into the pub, "Here's my reward chaps if I don't get my leg over tonight there is no justice." He chuckled.

Ordering a G & T he sauntered over to Daffers and proceeded to chat her up, relating the goings on of the day with Daphne suitably impressed. Jim tried to hide his disappointment from the others that Coral hadn't walked in with her friend, but they gave him some stick anyway, poor Jim a married man they said couldn't go out on the batter poor bugger. It was all light hearted fun and Jim took it in his stride, however he couldn't tell them that he had lost his heart to Coral and his feelings for her were deeper that any ocean. He wanted her more than he had ever wanted anything in his whole life and his body cried out for hers, where was she? Why didn't she appear? His eyes repeatedly scanned the pub searching for that wonderful head of auburn curls, the pub was busier than ever, new recruits coming in daily, hundreds of them. They couldn't get a game of cards or dominoes and time was laying heavy on Jim, then suddenly he looked up and his eyes met hers. They smiled and nodded to each other, Jim wanted to shout out loud thank god you're here but couldn't of course. Jim offered her a drink and she mouthed that she would have a beer, her stomach was in knots how could she get to be alone with him. This exchange didn't go unnoticed by Daphne and she immediately jumped up to make room for Coral at the table she shared with Charles, so by the time Jim returned with the drink his face visibly fell seeing Coral sitting with Daphne. Charles searched for a chair for Jim but there was none to be had, which pleased Daffers no end. So he returned to the bar reluctantly and tried not to keep glancing her way, however when he did and their eyes met a feeling so strong came over him it almost ripped him in half. Daphne pretended to visibly shudder with horror regaling about what a bumpkin that Jim Moore was, and how when he opened his mouth she wanted to stick a turnip in it. Charles had heard enough from Daphne she was such a crashing snob, but his wanted his end away so he didn't want upset her not tonight anyway he would leave that for another time. So whispering urgently in her ear about a certain something wanting to be in a certain place as soon as possible, they quickly got up to go but not before giving Jim the nod to get to the table fast. An overjoyed Jim was so eager to join her that he caught the corner of the table and upset all the glasses, almost sending them crashing to the floor. Jim blushed scarlet with embarrassment but Coral quickly put him at his ease, and when he apologised for the tenth time about his accent and how he wished he could speak like Charles or Roger she admonished him and let him know in no uncertain times that he was as good if not better than all of them. Coral slipped her hand across the table and he very quickly took hold of it and almost put it to his lips, he wanted to kiss it, he wanted to kiss her all over and his eyes must have betrayed his feelings for her. Then suddenly Daphne appeared looking in a total rage, her intimate moment with Charles hadn't lasted very long he had satisfied himself and couldn't be bothered to satisfy her. Now as soon as her back was turned the stupid country bumpkin was pawing her best friend, she wasn't having it and told him more or less where to go. Daphne having taken his seat turned her back on him and excluded him from the conversation, he had no choice but to head off back to the bar and rejoin his pals who slapped him on the back and handed him a couple of pints to drown his sorrows in.

Coral was seething with rage, how dare Daphne do this to her, wasn't she capable of looking after herself and she had been enjoying Jims company so much. Damn her thought Coral but she couldn't say anything, after all Jim was a married man with a child. Daphne was twittering on "I could see you were bored and that oaf was pawing you." She went on and on. Coral wasn't listening she was holding hands with Jim Moore gazing into his eyes wanting him as she had never wanted anyone before, she looked over at him longingly and he saw the look. Red hot pain shot through his whole body and he had to turn away before he did something he might regret, that Daphne needed a swift kick in the pants and he would love to give her one, maybe one day he would get the chance. Charles took note of this and slapped Jim on the back and roared to the others that Jim is having trouble getting into Coral's knickers, old Daffers put the boot in again, "Any suggestions you lot?" They all sniggered and almost fell about while Jim squirmed in embarrassment, him a married man whatever would his Tilly think about him. The feeling of guilt consumed him and he wished himself away from this lots and back home with his family, but he knew they meant well and tried to act as cheerful as he could under the circumstances.

A little while later when the banter became rather coarse Jim decided that he'd really had enough so he bade them all goodnight and strode off into the night with their laughter ringing in his ears. He became away of running footsteps and Coral's voice calling to him to wait, suddenly she was in his arms and their mouths were locked together. The passion left him weak at the knees, they walked a short distance to the cover of an old oak tree and there they swayed together holding, kissing, loving each other. Coral felt the hardness of his erection as he pressed his body urgently to hers, and she wanted him more than ever. His hand sought her breasts and he groped them softly at first and then harder and harder until she gasped with pain, "Let me help you Jim." she called to him huskily. Then pushing away gently she proceeded to unbutton her uniform and before he knew it her bra straps were pulled down, Jim released her breasts from her bra cups his hot tongue licking each one in turn, sucking on the hard protruding nipples. Coral moaned deeply with every move urging him on loving every moment wanting more and more, Jim tried not to think about Tilly he pushed her to the back of his mind while he explored the delights of Coral. He thrust his hand between her legs and stroked her hard and urgently, Coral squealed with pleasure and they both glanced up to see if anyone was around. Jim held her tightly against him, "I've got to make love to thee Coral."

"Not here Jim, please not here." She whispered, "But yes I want it too with all my heart." She was shaking so much with emotion she could hardly speak, both of them felt things that they had never felt before and they clung together.

"Where?" asked a trembling Jim, "Where my darling sweetest girl?", "Coral where shall we go I've got to have thee in me bed I want thee that bad it hurts," he groaned pressing his crotch harder and harder into her warm sensual body. Coral couldn't answer him, she didn't know where to go, she had never been in this sort of situation before. Thoughts of Jims wife and family suddenly came into her mind, and with a cry of great anguish she pulled herself from his arms and ran off down the dark unlit path to her billit. Jim was in a sort of trance and stood back looking after her, "Come back Coral," he shouted into the black and empty void. A voice from afar answered, "I say old boy, you have done something rather naughty to our Coral, she ran like the bloody devil was after her." It was Charles with the bloody Daphne in tow, Jim sighed trust her to witness the two of them. Jim couldn't care less about them he was totally shattered, and just wanted to find Coral and tell her how sorry he was for putting pressure on her, it was wrong of him and he hated himself for what he had done.

Without uttering a word to either of them he turned on his heel and was gone, Charles was a bit put out but Daphne ranted on about the man having the manners of a wart hog and it was no surprise to her.

"I say old girl steady on now," spluttered Charles, Daphne snapped at him "Don't call me old girl I am not an old girl." Charles looked down in the gloom and could just make out her scowling features, "Oh bugger off." He snapped at her and he immediately turned tail and went off leaving her alone in the dark. Well really thought Daphne what an utter shit to go off and leave her like that, she would find Coral and get to the bottom of whatever was going on. Fancy running after the Derbyshire Ox, had she no morals at all, no principles.

When she did find Coral later on, Coral didn't wish to discuss the matter with her so she undressed and climbed into her lumpy bunk, wishing she hadn't upset Charles. She had been ready for a good session with him that night, as the first had ended too soon, he was wanting it that bad that it hadn't lasted very long, never mind there was always tomorrow.

Coral wept quietly to herself wishing that she hadn't behaved like a little school girl, there was a war on, no one knew what was going to happen to them you had to make the most of every moment. Right now she should be in Jims arms in his bed anywhere but just be with him, her body began to twitch in places she had never felt before and she began to get hotter and hotter by the minute. Coral prayed for sleep to forget her longings, and hoped that her body would stop its incessant throbbing. Having no knowledge of lovemaking she didn't know what to expect or what to do, she only knew that whatever it entailed she wanted it as soon as possible with the wonderful Jim Moore. There and then she decided to out any thoughts of his wife out of her mind, she wasn't a vindictive person and would never knowingly hurt anyone but she had to have this time with Jim somewhere, somehow.

Meanwhile Jim lay in his bed thinking up ways to make love to Coral, he just had to have her by his side under him, on top, any way he could. The thoughts of it made him almost cry out with desire, Tilly would never know about it anyway he might get killed and then it wouldn't matter at all. He would die a very happy man if he could just have this time with Coral, to lie with her to hold her in his arms to love her, yes that was all that he would ask. Drifting off into a fitful sleep he called out her name many times, the shrill blaring tannoy awoke him early in the morning and he was convinced that he had never gone to sleep at all. Turning over in his bunk he decided not to get up, 'sod em all' he said to himself and pulled the blanket over his head. However Charles had news for him, "get up or it's the water bucket." Muttered his pal, thoughts of the water bucket changed his mind very quickly and he sprang out of bed uttering a string of abuse at Charles. "You're a bloody evil sod Chas why don't you bugger off and give me a rest." At this outburst Charles waded in about wartime and commitment and they were soon at each others throats.

"Now now girls," mocked a grinning Billy with his hands on his hips pretending to be really camp. He sashayed around, and watching his antics the two of them stopped their silly argument and burst out laughing.

Daphne took one look at Coral that morning and uttered "Dear god you look dreadful, what am I going to do with you?" Coral was feeling wretched enough without Daffers throwing in her two-penny worth. Her eyes were red and swollen from weeping, they say weeping doesn't do a girl favours the their right quoted a girl in the background. Daphne gave her a withering look and flounced out,

"Well Coral what you see in that country bumpkin I shall never understand." She twittered until Coral made a dash for the ablutions to get out of earshot,

"Well really," Daphne called out to anyone listening." Not to be put off she quickly followed Coral into the showers, "I only have your best interests at heart darling you know that." She drawled "You must get it out of your mind whatever it is you feel for the yokel."

"Must you always refer to Jim as the yokel or country bumpkin, Daphne it really is in bad taste," admonished Coral "if you can't speak of him without distaste then don't speak about him at all, it smacks of damned bad manners." Added Coral in a cold icy tone, Daphne stood bristling with indignation. The very idea that anyone would call her bad mannered was quite unthinkable, she was fuming but knew that Coral was not thinking clearly at that moment and she would give her the benefit of the doubt. The poor girl would come to her senses soon enough then she would need her shoulder to cry on, after she had been cast aside by the ghastly bumpkin. Now she would have to wait before asking what had made Coral run away from him last night, had she witnessed an attempted rape? If so why was she still sticking up for him? Wait long enough and all would be revealed she told herself, so she pretended to be all sweetness and light for the rest of the day.

Breakfast time was difficult for them both as neither Coral or Jim knew how to greet each other, should they speak like normal or ignore one another. They both tried hard not to meet each others eyes, but it became impossible and although there were literally hundreds of servicemen and women they almost collided on the way back from picking up their breakfast trays. Noticeably both trays held just a cup of coffee, neither one in the need of food. As their eyes met and held, the two of them felt an almighty force pulling them together, it was like a magnet and they were powerless. He wanted to kiss her delicate succulent mouth, she wished with all her heart that they could be alone. The mess was a vast place but suddenly it felt small and intimate, they became unaware of the throng around them and continued to gaze adoringly at each other. However as usual there was always a fly in the ointment and sure enough up sidled Daffers, "Let me help you with the tray darling." Proceeding to take the tray containing one lonely cup of coffee out of her hand. The spell was broken and the magic all gone it was back to reality with a bump. Jim managed to breath a sorry to her then she was led away to a table with Daphne, why couldn't the interfering cow leave her alone, it wasn't as if they had known each other for very long. Daphne had latched onto her the very first day on the camp and had become her so called best friend, interfering busybody more like it thought Coral but much too ladylike to tell her so.

Charles was busy talking to Jim but became aware that his pal wasn't listening to a word he was saying, he felt sorry for Jim and tapping his arm to get his attention whispered to him so that the others couldn't hear him, "Isay old chap you have got it bad haven't you? Didn't realise it had got to that stage sorry old boy." Jim tried with conviction to try and laugh it off, but the laugh hung awkwardly in the morning air. "I do know how you are feeling you know old stick," and a faraway look came into his eyes. Jim became aware of something profound and deep-rooted there, instinctively he knew that Charles had suffered a great deal too, perhaps one day he would tell him about it.

In no time breakfast was over and they were heading for the hangers, another flying lesson, another day in the sky, whereas before he couldn't wait for it, today he couldn't be bothered he just wanted to be with Coral and he felt really pissed off with everything.

The day went reasonably well and soon enough they were back from their training, Jim dashed off to be first in the showers, this was followed by a barrage of lewd comments from his comrades which was cut short by a tirade from the usually placid Charles. The men looked at each other and pulled their faces wondering what was up with the pair of them, it had to be woman trouble it always was.

Jim had decided to speak to Coral that very night and he wasn't going to be put off, even if he had to drag her away from the dragon Daphne. No, he would have to handle things delicately he didn't want Coral to get a bad name that wouldn't do at all, he knew that all the men on the camp regarded all the women as ground sheets for the officers thinking that was all they were fit for. So he would have to tread very carefully and not give food for thought, feeling very nervous he headed for the 'White Horse' assured by Charles that he would be along directly. Jim decided to have a bit of Dutch courage and quickly sank a couple of pints of beer, it didn't taste very good and he grimaced as he forced it down him. It wasn't as good as the beer he was used to at the 'Goyt Inn' and he wished that he was supping there instead, it set him off thinking about the folks back home and he began to feel all nostalgic and maudlin. In no time at all the pub was heaving and he scanned it for signs of Coral, wondering when she would show up if at all.

Coral however was off on a mission of her own, the pain she was feeling about Jim and knowing that she could never be with him. Had got to her so badly that she had requested to see her commanding officer and ask for a transfer away from there, away from Jim away from Daphne. Away from everyone before her heart was broken, the C.O was very pleased to see her he was a good man and cared deeply about his troops. He also liked a pretty face and none came prettier than Coral, he couldn't help but notice a well turned ankle and wonderful and wonderful legs too my what a stunner by gad. He ushered her to the huge leather chair opposite his own, behind the large polished desk covered with photographs of his family.

"Fire away medear," he boomed "what can I do for you?"

“Please sir,” whispered Coral, “may I ask for a transfer sir?”

“Speak up me dear can’t hear a bally word what,” he boomed out.

Coral began again a little louder, this time he could hear.

“Transfer, whatever for my dear?” he spluttered, "Not happy here what someone being beastly to you," his large moustache clearly bristled and twitched making him look really silly. Coral jumped out of her skin as he thumped the desk asking her, "not happy here then eh."

"It's rather personal sir," she stammered hanging her head as if in shame.

He cottoned on pretty quickly, "affairs of the heart what in the family way eh." Coral very quickly assured him that this was not the case and he was rather pleased about that, he didn't want to deal with anything messy. "Well what the blazes is it woman," he demanded. The tears began to flow and the C.O. was out of his depth, a large white handkerchief was produced and he pored her a glass of water and as she sipped it he looked at her and waited for her to compose herself. Coral looked into his eyes they were kind eyes honest eyes she knew that she could talk to him trust him, and at length Coral was able to explain to him about her problem.

"So you see sir I have to get away before it's to late," she finished. Then she sobbed quietly and the Commander was at a loss to know what to do for the best.

"Well it is a dilemma and no mistake my dear." "I will grant your request for a transfer right away and put the necessary wheels in motion so to speak," "however it will take a little time but not to long, and as you say this young man has acted with great restraint thankfully so you shouldn't have to deal with the situation again hopefully." "Try not to be too despondent my dear and may I say that I shall be very sorry indeed to loose you, you are highly skilled in radar tracking systems and will be invaluable to another team." With that he shook her hand and wished her all the best, she left his H.Q. feeling both happy and miserable and decided to call at the pub for a drink lord knows she needed one. Maybe Jim would be there she hoped so she would tell him about her decision to leave it was only right, suddenly it hit her like a thunderbolt what had she done, she would never see him again how could she live without seeing him. But she knew that she would have to face up to it one day soon. The pub came into view but she couldn't face it he might be there so she cut of back to her little hut to face the inquisition from Daphne, the latter wasn't there she was out looking for Coral wondering what she was up too. So Coral had a long soak in the tub washed her hair and did a little mending, and was just tucking herself in for the, night when a very irate Daffers appeared demanding to know where she had been all night. Coral laughed it of making up a tale about going for a walk and the bath and hair do clinched it for her, "well" said Daffers "the country" she was just going to say bumpkin when she noted the look that Coral shot at her. "Well he was in the `White Horse' looking the worse for drink," she went prattling on about drunks but Coral didn't hear her she was thinking about Jim, he must be suffering just like me and she put her head under the covers to hide her tears. Yes she had done the right thing, it was time to go things would only get worse if she stayed and she didn't know how much more she could take without giving in.

It only took a few days and the C.0. was as good as his word her orders came through to report to R.A.F Wharton in Cheshire on the 15th Dec, Coral was both excited and unbelievably sad at the news. Jim would have to be told she had kept out of his way so far, what with the training she had been under jumping from a blimp with a parachute strapped to her back had been absolute hell. Being terrified of heights the whole time didn't help, although she had fared better than Daffers who had fainted clean away the very first time and had never managed one jump through the course.

Her cries of what do we need a parachute for we're Radar for Gods sake went unheard, and the whole squadron felt that she had let them down not that she gave a fig what they thought of her.

The news of Corals posting filtered through eventually and Jim got to know, he sought her out and the devastation looked out from his eyes, "why" he wanted to know. Coral couldn't look him in the face her heart raced in her body until it shook her very being, "I have to go Jim you know that I can't go on it's best for both of us." "It canna be best if it hurts so much," he searched to try to find some eloquent words to say but none came. All he could do was wave his arms around like a bloody windmill flapping about feeling totally useless, "don't go Coral please don't go not if you care for me just a little bit." He pleaded, Coral began to weep and he steeped forward and pulled her into his eager arms, She was in his arms sobbing uncontrollably. Jim held her tight wishing she would stay there forever, then as her sobs subsided his lips sought hers and the kisses became more and more intense until they almost collapsed with the passion of it. Coral's legs almost gave way beneath her and she had to break away from him, "I love you Coral," he told her. "I love you too Jim that's why I have to go you know that there's no happy ending for us my darling," they clung to each and wept like their hearts would break. After much soul searching Jim plucked up the courage to ask Coral to spend one night with him before she left, she wanted that too but would never have suggested it herself. It was the only thing left to them to be together just one time. To make love, do all the things that young lovers do. Yes they would do it as soon as they possibly could; Jim would make all the necessary arrangements. He hugged her close, then watched her walk away until she was out of sight. Later on he enlisted the help of Charles and Billy swearing them to secrecy, and between them they arranged for the unhappy lovers to spend the night together in the guards hut out on the perimeter of the airfield. It was very isolated and no one but the duty guard would use it at night, he was slipped a few quid and a couple of packets of fags and he was happy to oblige a mate. They were told to expect the guard periodically marching past the hut, it was his duty just in case Jerry was lurking about out there. There didn't seem much chance but every thing had to be done by the book, and anyway he wouldn't be shoving his way in to have a butchers at them added Billy. It could only be arranged for Coral's last night so they would have to sit tight and wait, they decided not to tell Daffers because of her big mouth and her obvious distaste for Jim. How they would stop her searching for her friend when she didn't return that night they didn't know, they would have to leave that to Charles.

The final night was soon upon them and they scurried to the little van that would take them along the airstrip, outmanoeuvring Daffers at great cost. Charles had set them up with a small bottle of whisky and Jim poured two small glasses at once, they needed it to help them relax they were both very uptight. After about half a hour and several tots he led Coral to the bed in the corner of the hut, it was a bit shabby but the sheets were clean. They lay kissing each other passionately for some time, and then Jim who was worked up to near exploding gently began to undress her fumbling nervously with the many buttons. When he got down to the bra with its hooks and eyes he almost ripped it from her in his haste, as he wrestled with it her generous breasts tumbled from the white lacy cups and he uttered a low moan as he bent and kissed them all over. Jim cried out her name as he sucked the delicately perfumed flesh and Coral writhed in sheer ecstasy, in no time at all there clothing was slung all over the hut floor and Jim was gently easing his hand between her long silky legs. As his fingers found her vulva she let out a moan of pleasure, and when his hot breath reached the top of her legs followed by his tongue eagerly licking her clitoris she thought she would die out of sheer delight. When he finally entered her when he could wait no longer she cried out with pain, it felt like she was being ripped open with a knife. Jim remembered how Tilly had been their first time so he knew that to expect, but she didn't make him withdraw she pulled him even closer she wanted everything the pleasure and the pain. It was worth it because as he got a rhythm going she relaxed and the pain turned to intense wanting, wanting more until her body suffered the most incredible spasm. Coral cried out with sheer joy and Jim just kept on going until he had the most unbelievable ejaculation, they lay touching and kissing each other for a long time afterwards marvelling in the joy that they had brought to each other. Jim explored her body and fondled every curve, until he was hard and ready for her again. Guiding her hand to his manhood he let her put it in to her vagina, which she did with great delight. He then pulled her on top and urged her to take the lead, showing her to lean back for maximum effect at the critical moment. Jim marvelled at how quickly she adapted and couldn't' believe it when she began to massage him and ask for more, and taking his fingers held them to her swollen clitoris asked him to finger her which he did with delight and as she was about to climax he was in her riding her furiously, this time they were both squealing with the utter pleasure of it all. "I bet we've woken up the entire Camp," laughed Jim. Although neither of them cared a jot, "did you hear the bed springs creaking Jim." Asked Coral, "hear them I think everybody did and they'll be hearing some more soon." He promised. However all to soon the footsteps that had passed by all night long stopped outside, and the guard knocked on the door. "Time to go old mate he shouted to them," then added "sorry". Where had the time gone, it had gone to soon and the lovers dressed quickly fearing that they would be discovered. Coral trembled in the early morning light and clung to Jim as they left the hut, looking back it wasn't just a hut it was a lover's nest she would never forget it as long as she lived. It had been their place, her's and Jim's it would hold a special place in her heart. Suddenly her calmness had deserted her and she almost slumped to the ground in sheer agony and pain of parting from her man, they hugged once more then she pulled herself from his arms with all her strength and sped off into the morning mist. Jim could hear her sobbing loudly as she ran, her footsteps ringing out on the cold wet tarmac then in the swirling mist she was gone. Jim knew that he would never see her again and he wept like a child, how would he ever forget her and get on with his life, it was going to take a superhuman effort, and he didn't know if he could do it. Only time would tell. But at that moment he was distraught.

Chapter Six

Mary Faces the Music

Mary lay in her bed feeling very queasy she must have eaten something that didn't agree with her, better get up and ready for work she thought. As soon as her feet touched the ground she began to retch and only just managed to grab the washbasin, it wasn't proper sick just yellow bile, but she retched until she had nothing left in her stomach. After what seemed like hours she managed to get down the stairs, if she didn't get a move on she would be late for work. After a cup of tea she felt much better apart from a funny feeling in her head it felt like it was sitting about two feet off her shoulders, she almost ducked under the doorway. By eck i'm going loopy ready for the funny farm she chuckled to herself.

She didn't know how she managed to work that day she felt so peculiar, and when the hooter blew she thanked God for it. Mary should have called round to see Lizzie and the boys but she couldn't face them not today, she must get home and lay down for a while.

Just rounding market street she spotted Tom Scully a feeling of panic seized her and she scurried faster than ever praying he wouldn't see her. At last she reached her door and her shaky hand dropped the latchkey she bent down to retrieve it, "let me elp thee lass" it was him he had caught up with her.

"No thanks" she almost shouted at him, "I can manage ta very much." But he would hear non of it and before she knew it he was inside beckoning her in, the whole bloody street was watching what should she do. Best not to let on that anything was amiss so she smiled and followed him inside, Tom closed the door and locked it behind her and in a flash his arms where round her and his mouth was seeking hers, his hold tightened on her until she could hardly breath. "Stop it get off me," she told him not daring to shout in case anyone could hear them outside.

Tom wouldn't be put off and pulled her mouth round to his and began to kiss her with a passion, Mary tried to squirm out of his grasp. However he was far stronger and she was powerless plus the fact that she was feeling decidedly nauseous, and what with his breath reeking of booze she almost gagged. I'm going to faint she thought as the nausea swept over her in waves, "Please let me go" she begged. Tom felt her go limp in his arms and relaxed his hold on her, "sorry lass but if tha didna struggle so much." "It's bin weeks an I want thee that bad just kiss me Mary me darlin girl," "why woudna let me in tha knew I were knockin at'th door neet after neet."

"I've wanted thee that much just feel how much," he slurred, he reached for her hand and pulled it towards his bulging crotch. Mary almost screamed out loud snatching her hand away she tried to push him back towards the door with all the strength she could muster, "dunna thee bloody well dare just thee bugger off outa my ome." She almost spat at him as she reached for the key to unlock the door, Tom was to quick for her. "Oh none bloody good enough now e'h what's up some bugger else shaggin thee," "didn'a do a good enough job las time well I will this bugger." and with that he dragged her up the stairs and threw her on the bed.

Mary tried to fight him off with all the strength she had left in her, but it was no use she begged and implored him to stop but he was like a bloody maniac. He wanted sex with her and fuelled with the drink nothing was going to stop him, he stripped her off and gazed at her perfect figure saliva ran down the side of his mouth God she was a beauty. Franticly he pulled off his shirt and dropped his trousers he didn't wear underpants which Mary thought was disgusting, and the filthy boots and his feet as black as coal she shuddered over and over.

Tom leapt quickly onto the bed "look what I've got fer thee lass" Mary closed her eyes tight and refused to open them, "tha'll feel it in a minute Mary an tha'll beg fer it" he mumbled as he began to caress her breasts and suck the nipples. Mary caught a whiff of his body odour and began to retch and vomited all over the counterpane, "by ell that a dirty bugger Mary allis spewin up" he sneered at her. However it didn't put him off he wiped her mouth with the corner of the counterpane and threw it onto the floor, he then proceeded to kiss her body all over again.

Tom slid his hand down between her legs and forced them apart, "relax Mary tha'l enjoy it more" murmured Tom. He stroked her hairs and told her how lovely it was down there, then he fingered her clitoris slowly at first then faster and faster. Mary tried hard not to get aroused but it was no use she began to squirm and moan it felt so good, this was the sign he was waiting for and he was astride her and entered her easily and rode her deeply. Mary tried not to want it but it was no use, she was only human and she was without her beloved to see to her needs. Tom interrupted her thoughts "dust tha like it Mary," she couldn't answer she felt to ashamed and began to weep.

Afterwards Mary wanted to get dressed but Tom had other things planned for her, "lie still lass relax a bit till I can get it up agin." Not again thought Mary oh no she didn't want it again she just wanted him to go; she began to cry softly. "Na then lass tha's no need fer cryin tha knows tha wants it just as much as I do," he snuggled up to her body smelling her delicate perfume my she was a beauty. Tom got out of the bed and for a moment Mary thought the tears had worked, but he had only gone to get a towel which he handed to Mary "here lass wipe theesen down we dunna want it slippin out na do we." He gave her a dirty leer showing his filthy teeth, he was a course vulgar bugger what was she doing here in this situation.

Tom watched as Mary wiped the seaman from her vagina it gave him an instant hard on and he was on top of her and in her once more, in spite of everything her loathing for the man she couldn't help herself she wanted it again as much if not more than he did. Later he wanted her to suck his dick but this she could not do he was far to dirty and smelly and she retched at the very thought of it, after much pleading he gave up and sulked for a while then got dressed and went home Mary was ecstatic and after locking up the house she put out the tin bath and even though the water in the copper wasn't very hot she sat in it and scrubbed herself until her flesh was almost raw.

That was it never again would she let that dirty bugger into her home and she meant it too, so she had let him do all those filthy things to her and she felt shamed beyond belief that she had enjoyed it so much.

But it really was the end. Never never again would she let herself get in that situation she would rather die. Waves of nausea swept over her once again and she was sick right there in the bath and retched until she could retch no-more, I'm dying she thought and its my own fault its my sinful ways and me a regular churchgoer. I'm not fit to walk through the church doors or teach the little ones about Jesus, and I don't think I should.

After a few hours fitful sleep she decided to get up, the bedroom stank of vomit it was putrid. As soon as her feet touched the floor she began to retch once more the same yellow bile as before, a while latter when she felt up to it she stripped the bed and took the soiled linen downstairs to the kitchen and placed them in the dolly tub. which was filled up with warm water from the fireside boiler which meant many journeys back and forth from parlour to kitchen with a bowl, she added a measure of washing flakes and began to poss them down until she could poss no more.

It was rinsed many times and wrung through the mangle and on the washing line before 5.30am, the lamp lighter was doing his rounds also the sounds of the knocker up ratt-a-tat tatting on the windows tapping his way throughout the village. His presence unwelcome by every sleepyhead, snug and warm in there beds, he never needed to knock at Mary's window she had been brought up the Jim Moore way that was as good a grounding as anyone would ever need. Yet it had been good to be amongst her family and she missed them more than words could say, her eyes swam with tears as she remembered her beloved Camy and she thought her heart would break.

A little later she made herself some porridge and a slice of toast she hadn't eaten for quite a while, but it wasn't long before it was back again and the retching seemed to be never ending. Feeling like shit she set out for the mill it loomed large in the dawn light and she wished she didn't have to go there this morning; all she wanted to do was go to sleep and sleep all day long and forget the nightmare of the night before. Had anyone heard her shout how could she face her neighbours God she was a slut what would her dearest Brian think of his whore of a wife.

Having set off her looms she began to busy herself and the next moment she fainted and lay prone on the cold mill floor, everyone rushed to her side and soon she was back on her feet. shaking her head she muttered that she couldn't understand what had happened, "I must ave caught a bug or something I were sick this mornin " she stammered feeling very foolish. Glances were exchanged all around "Aye mornin sickness tha knows what that means thas caught summat all reet" laughed Fanny Johnson looking Mary straight in the eye. Mary stood there looking gormless then the truth hit her like a sledge hammer, a baby' was she expecting a baby.

The thought knocked her sideways and she passed out again, she came to in the warp room with the First Aider looking down on her. "Tha'd better get thee sen ome tha canna work in that state," Mary tried feebly to protest she felt stupid lying on a table in the warp room it reeked of oil and cotton and she felt sick again as they assailed her nostrils. No she couldn't be expecting she'd had her monthly after Brian's return to his unit, and had wept for hours knowing that she wouldn't be having the baby they both longed for.

So what was the matter with her, Tom Scully that was the matter Oh no God not with him the realization hit her like a ton of bricks. Not a baby with him she wept uncontrollably, someone wake me up from this bloody nightmare she cried out. The woman sent for her sister Jean not knowing what to do with the weeping girl, Her sister was soon by her side and helping her to her feet she led her to her house. "Whatever's up our Mary ast hurt thee sen" Jean wanted to know, all she had heard was innuendo about a baby being on the way that would be wonderful it was what she had been trying for since she got married. Now it looked like she had got her dearest wish.

Jean prattled on about how happy Brian would be and that she must write and tell him at once, she put the kettle on and glanced at Mary lying on the settle covered over with a knitted shawl looking as white as a sheet. "I can't tell him" she whispered "he wont be thrilled he'll hate me for the rest of his life." Jean looked at her sister and wondered why she was talking such rubbish she was puzzled, "It's the most wonderful thing to appen our Mary just give it a bit off time tha'1 see." "I've got to get rid of it" said Mary, Jean looked on in horror, "What dith say our Mary" she asked. "You heard me" answered her sister, "I've got to get rid of it now an tha's gotta elp me our Jean."

With this she burst into heartrending sobs and Jean held her in her arms fearing for her sanity, "Mary she yelled at her stop this stop it saying such terrible things." Their eyes meet and Jean saw the terror in her sisters, "it's non Brian's" she whispered "I wish to God it were." Sobs raked her body again and Jean didn't know what to do for the best, before she could stop herself Jean had blurted out "Tom Scully" she felt near to collapse herself now with this bombshell. "Oh no Mary not him tha must be wrong it canna be that bugger," Jean only had to look at her sisters face to know that she was speaking the truth. Jean tried her best to comfort her, "right Mary no one but us two knows about it so if we keep it to our'sens then no-one will ever find out about it not even Brian.

"Get that idea into thee ead an tha'l feel better our Mary", "dunna let on ta another soul an everythin will be allreet." Oh God what a bloody mess thought Jean trying not to imagine her sister with the disgusting Tom Scully, she had always been such a decent girl whatever had gotten into her to make her do such a thing. Jean had a sudden terrible loathing for the man and would have gladly throttled him had he been anywhere in sight, had she been a man by ell what she wouldn't have done to the bastard. "I'll have't leave thee Mary must get back ferth little un wilt tha be allreet", she inquired "I shanna be long."

Mary nodded her head in answer, "lock'th back door after me." said her sister and dunna unlock it until I shout thee dust err," Mary answered with another nod. "I shall av'e to bring Elizabeth with me will that be allreet,"

Mary didn't care if she brought the bloody light brigade with her but she didn't say so. Her sister was doing her best to help and Mary was to full of self pity to care what anyone did or didn't do, Catching sight of herself in the mirror she shuddered," I'm a prostitute, a whore, I've done everything they did without the payment." This made her laugh " yes I did get paid he left a deposit did Tom and I'll pay for'th rest of me life, and she laughed and laughed until she thought she was going mad.

Jean was beside herself with worry, "stop it Mary I canna stand it." Mary's eyes were wild "you canna stand it well I've got news fer thee I've got to bloody well stand it," "I've got a bastard inside of me an I dunna want it," " find someone fer me Jean get Polly Simmons she knows how to get rid." she begged her sister, "Mary stop it dunna say such things for God's sake the baby will be part of thee." "Just keep tellin thee'sen thine and Brian's," but Mary was not to be put off and after much begging and pleading Jean gave in and said that she would help although it went against everything she stood for.

After repeatedly swearing that she wouldn't tell the family Jean headed home under a very dark cloud, Mary quickly locking the door behind her terrified that Scully was around and trying to get back in. Bed would be the best place she decided she could escape the world up there pretend it hadn't happened, she crept between the clean sheets and wept for her Brian and for herself until she had no more tears left to shed and fell into a fitful sleep. In her sleep she pursued Tom Scully wanting him begging him to get into her bed, pawing him feeling his private parts she was without shame she wanted him so bad it hurt.

On awakening she felt shame and revulsion what would become of her she was beyond redemption, thoughts of Camy filled her mind perhaps she should do what her darling sister had done and end it all. At least she would be free of the pain and suffering she thought anything would be better than going through with the pregnancy, she couldn't have this child, this bastard no never it couldn't happen she would find a way out it was simple she would sort it out everything would be back to normal yes it would be all right. Feeling much better she made herself a cup of tea and a cheese sandwich and sat before the fire smiling to herself, but the smile didn't stay long as the vomiting began again and with it the fears the nagging doubts.

Meanwhile Jean was beside herself with worry whatever was she going to do, she couldn't approach Polly Simmons everyone would know about it in seconds. Perhaps Aunty Ada would help but she had promised Mary so that was out of the question, something had to be done but what. There was nothing for it she would enlist the help of her best friend Joyce Hibbert, she was beyond reproach loyal and trustworthy. With Elizabeth Jean in her bassinet she set of to visit Joyce at her home, rounding the corner of market street she almost collided with Maggie Scully.

Jean looked at the woman with distaste she was filthy dirty her clothes almost rags, good lord there was no need to be like that there was soap and water for heavens sake. However it was her eyes that Jean noticed most of all they were dead like a fish on the mongers slab, she bade Jean good day showing a mouthful of brown and yellow teeth. Jean felt a rush of sympathy for the downtrodden woman, small wonder she looked as she did married to that no good spineless bugger. "How do Maggie," she greeted her and passed by quickly before she could be dragged into any kind of conversation, one slip and God knows what could follow.

Joyce listened to her story and was clearly shocked, not Mary it just wasn't like her. "Oh Jean what can we do," Joyce was close to tears. "I dunna know but we've got to do summat and quick she's suicidal I tell thee Joyce," answered Jean. "Nay nay she would'na do owt silly like that," scolded Joyce "she knows Gods against anything like that."Jean gave her a withering look," I hope that reet Joyce but God has nowt to do wi this I'm sorry to say." They exchanged glances and pondered over the problem, "let me think a bit," said Joyce and she sat back in the armchair and closed her eyes.

Jean took Elizabeth into the back yard to play a while until Joyce called her back indoors, "There's only one way as far as I can see," she explained. "We canna trust anyone we know or telfth family so we shall ave'ta go an see them Scully's," Jean almost screamed out in protest at this outrageous suggestion. "Just a tick Jean," Snapped a miffed Joyce. "Just hear me out for goodness sake just let me tell thee." "We must go an talk to Maggie Scully an tell er, she wunna want it to go any further like the rest on us." "An if I'm any judge of character she will have sought the services of Polly Simmons a time or two, an er's to feared on im to blab to all an sundry."

Jean tried to take it all in, Joyce carried on "an once Maggie gets over'th shock of im an Mary well we can try canna we." Her voice trailed of waiting for her friend to reply, Jean knew it made sense but it wasn't without it's drawbacks but yes she could see that it was probably the only way. The two of them arranged for the men folk to mind the children that night, and set off after dark pretending they were going to visit an old school friend. Arthur hadn't been very pleased but with Elizabeth in bed he couldn't argue, Joyce's husband didn't mind he loved to read to his children at night so he was quite happy.

They knew that Tom Scully was usually out at the pub most nights either at the Goyt or Railway Hotel, they hoped that tonight was one of them. Never the less they were both as nervous as a bride on her wedding night and they visibly shook with fright, number eleven Bridge St. soon came into view, Jean knocked and stood back a pace or two. The door was opened by a youth of about ten he was badly dressed and his hair stood up on end with muck, he just looked at the two of them and waited for someone to say something. "Can we av'e a word wi thee Mam," asked Joyce since Jean been turned to stone all of a sudden. The lad bellowed as loud as he could "Mam tha't wanted" "who is it" she shouted back "I dunna know two biddies" he answered. This jolted Jean back to life cheeky bugger she thought to herself, "that'll do me lad" she told him and before she could admonish him any further Maggie Scully was there at the door, where she proceeded to give him a backhander over the head. "Who is it "she inquired peering out into the night, "ar'th bloody kids in trouble agin I'm bloody sick on it if I've tow'd em once I've tow'd em a dozen bloody times." "Maggie" Joyce snapped "can we av'e a word in private," by this time Maggie had recognized the two women.

"What dust tha want we me" she demanded, they looked like they were bringing bad news, well all the kids were in the house and if owt had happened to Tom then it could only be a blessing from God. "We av'ta talk to thee urgently Maggie can we come in," asked Jean. Maggie didn't want these two snotty cows in her house, but she had little choice so reluctantly she asked them inside. Holding the door just wide enough for them to squeeze through, the stench was the first thing to hit there nostrils they visibly reeled from the shock of it, both woman though they would be sick and had to steel themselves against it. It was piss and dirt mixed together, there eyes began to smart from the ammonia' and it took all their strength to stay on their feet. The place was filthy; a few shabby pieces of broken furniture littered the room a dirty rug in front of an empty fire grate. It was bitterly cold and damp and in spite of everything Jean felt a surge of pity for the downtrodden woman and her filthy children who lined the room, there were about seven of them their faces pinched and etched with grime dark circles under their eyes a pitiful bunch to behold.

Jean remembered the poverty they had suffered but they never had to live like this thank God, their home was always clean shabby maybe but always clean and polished. Her thoughts flew to her mother how hard she must have worked to keep the home like that with her brood it couldn't have been easy. She was jolted out of her reverie by Maggie "Piss off to bed now" she shouted at the kids and they flew up the stairs dressed only in their vests nothing else there arses blue with cold. "Sit thee'sens down " gestured Maggie to the two women they didn't dare sit in case they sat in piss so Jean said that they would prefer to stand thank you very much, "please the'sen" answered Maggie to tired to care what they did. As best they could they explained the situation to Tom's wife, who sat and listened open-mouthed her mouth opening wider as the story unfurled.

Maggie was angry at Mary how could she let another man into her bed, her supposed to be a respectable married woman an her man only just gone of to fight for King and country. Tom well nothing he ever did amazed her she was used to his philandering, but the Moore girl was above him and she was surprised at her for stooping so low. Jean was going on again about the brandy that Tom had plied her with, "oh I that'd be it the lass wuddna be used ter strong drink wi err igh moral principles" scoffed Maggie "non on it would be her fault blame it all on Tom" she spat out. Jean was quick to defend her sister but blamed her for her part in the fiasco too, "the thing is Maggie she dusna want this baby and the top an bottom of it is she want's rid." Jean could hardly believe she was saying these things but saying them she was and she cringed inwardly it was a nightmare.

Maggie began to weep calling Tom every filthy name under the sun telling them about the rotten life she had with him and about his womanizing throughout their marriage, she could understand how he would get Mary the worse for drink and then have his way with her he had done the same to her when they had first met many years ago. She left out the parts about how he was eyeing up their own girls saying how they would be ready for a good shagging off him soon, the thoughts of him drooling over them while playing with himself made her feel sick inside and him always walking about stark naked in front of them all the time with a great big erection telling them to look at what they could look forward too, and she decided that she wouldn't take his side he could go to hell. Jean would have liked to hug her and say a few kind words but she was so dirty she couldn't bring herself to touch her, Maggie was still going on "he makes me ave it every bloody day at least twice him's bloody sex mad him wants puttin down like a dog" she wailed.

Jean then broached the subject of Polly and Maggie readily agreed to help them all she could, she would approach Polly and get things started as soon as possible. They were both glad to leave Maggie's dirty house that night and breath good clean air, how could anyone live like that. Jean reported back to Mary and the lass wept with relief, "thanks for everything" wailed Mary "I'm non worth it tha should chuck me inth cut an leave me there." Jean clucked around her like a mother hen and assured her that everything would be hunky dory, however it didn't stop Mary moaning about Joyce knowing "she'll tel'th bloody village" she ranted and raved "every bugger will know what'll I do our Jean." off she went weeping again, Jean was getting a bit fed up with it. "I canna do it on me own I'm tryin me best our Mary," she scolded her sister trying her hardest not to loose her temper.

She wanted to shout out at her why did you drop your bloody knickers for the dirty bugger then its your own fault, but she couldn't do that her sister was hurting enough so she bit her tongue and putting on her coat headed for the door. "Right oh see thee in'th mornin then good night our Mar," and she was gone. Leaving Mary to weep and wail and feel sorry for herself, Jean scurried for home she was tired and wanted to get back to Arthur. He was wondering what was going on, he would be putting his foot down soon thought Jean he was getting fed up with all the arsin and fartin around he would put his size eleven's in and that would be that.

Next evening there was a knock at Arthur's door he opened it to find Maggie Scully standing there, looking like a frightened rabbit. "Is missis in" she asked timidly wondering if she should have scarpered when he answered the door, "nay she's at her sister Mary's" again he wanted to add but didn't. Before he could say another word she was gone clattering off down the cobbles hell for leather, he scratched his head and wondered what the likes of Maggie Scully wanted with his Jean. Strong words would have to be said, very strong words indeed and answers he wanted answers too. Maggie legged it to Mary's house she knew which one it was, the one with the whitest net curtains, cleanest doorstep, sparkling windows, and the dirtiest slut living in it. No she knew deep down that wasn't true, she remembered how Tom had forced her into having sex on their first date, his strength and determination to get what he wanted when he wanted it and wouldn't take no for an answer.

Tom had been young and quite handsome and she would have had him at any price, however had she known what her life would turn out like she would have run a mile from the monster. The years of abuse had taken there toll and she looked much older than she actually was, lined wrinkled face etched with muck a few brown rotting teeth, dead fish eyes that looked fed up with life and clothes like rags from the many jumble sales she attended which was all she could afford for herself and her brood. She was week and malnourished and had to stop and get her breath, she had enough on her plate without pissin around fer them stuck up buggers. Reaching Mary's door she knocked rather loudly felling a little pissed off with them all, the door was opened quickly by Jean with her hand clutching at her heart.

"God Maggie you scarred the wits out of me," she gasped "sorry I didn't mean too me hand slipped." said Maggie meekly, Jean pulled her quickly inside the house feared that someone might see her and wonder what they were doing with the likes of her. Mary had been sent packing up the stairs by Joyce as soon as they realized who there caller was, she didn't want the two of them to meet not yet anyway not while she was there. Maggie reported back that Polly had been approached and had agreed to see Mary that very night at ten thirty; they would need to take with them towels, cotton wool, salt, a white linen sheet, and five pounds in money. "Jesus Christ" shouted Jean "did she forget to ask fer me diamond tiara," Joyce was eyeing her with disgust for using the Lords name in vain, but she couldn't care less at the moment that was the least of her worries.

"Where can we get five pounds from she asked no-one in particular, Maggie headed for the door it wasn't her problem she had done her bit and now she was off. Jean remembered her manners and let her out thanking her for her help, Mary crept down the stairs wondering why Jean had shouted out like that what could have happened now. However the first thing she noticed was the putrid stench that Maggie had left behind, she covered her nose with her hand and muttered about it making her feel sick. Jean filled her in about the five pounds and Mary didn't bat an eye, "I've got a bit put by for a rainy day" she told her sister. "Well it's bloody poorin now" answered a fed up Jean, Joyce felt like laughing but didn't dare.

"Right lets get started then I'll get everything we need, but first of all I must go home and see to Elizabeth Jean and then we can get over to Polly's." she tried not to look at her sister who by this time was looking decidedly white with fear, Joyce assured her that she would be back within the hour. Jean knew that Arthur would have to be told so she set herself to

that task and set off for home, he wasn't very pleased that she would be going out again but once she had given him all the sordid details he became very concerned for Mary. Jean was a little surprised but put it down to her husbands kind nature, also he urged her not to let Mary go through with a termination. "She could die tha knows if owt goes wrong, that owt of thee depth lass."

Jean hadn't considered this and was filled with a terrible panic, "Oh Arthur dunna say that for Gods sake I've gotta elp err I canna let err down now." "Oh reet theres no one else to elp er to'th grave yard eh she can join tha Camy that'1 be all reet then," he retorted with venom. Jean burst into a torrent of tears "what'll we do oh

Arthur," she wailed they both became aware that Elizabeth Jean was standing watching them her little face crumpled huge tears filled her eyes. Jean gathered her precious little girl in her arms and hugged her close, "we shudna talk in front of little un Arthur it's non reet." and Jean proceeded to take the child to bed and hushed her cry's, it took a long time to reassure the child that Mummy and Daddy were not angry with each other, it took two stories and a song before Elizabeth fell asleep.

Wearily she came down the stairs and Arthur gathered her in his arms and held her close, he loved her very much and couldn't bear to see her in such torment. Gently he told her that she would have to be very careful about what she did that night, "Its against law Jean and tha can get inta trouble lass." and added "The lass could die," " which is worst avin a baby or endin up on'th mortuary slab wi Gertie Lowe washin thee down." Jean was convinced, it wasn't worth the risk, Mary couldn't go through with it she would have to talk her out of it. She kissed Arthur and set of shoulders set ready for the battle she knew was ahead, the door at her sisters was tightly locked and bolted and wasn't unlocked until Mary was sure who was outside.

Jean quickly explained the situation as Arthur had put it, Mary stood and listened white faced dark circles under her eyes, puffy with weeping. Jean was thankful that Brian wasn't around to see the state she was in, he would never forgive her if he ever found out. she prayed he never would, Mary was adamant she would go through it with or without Jean's help. "I'm non bothered about death I'd rather bloody die than ave is kid, I wunna ave it Jean never never so if tha want's to go ome thee go." Mary looked at her sister and tried a week watery smile, "I wunna fall out we thee our Jean dunna thee feel guilty tha's done more than tha need do fer me."

Jean could see that Mary's mind was made up and that there was no shifting her, she had tried her best and failed. well she couldn't desert her now in her darkest hour so she told her so and despite her protests she went to fetch the towels etc. that they would need for Polly Simmons, also there was Arthur to deal with he would be so angry but she had tried her best she could do no more and she was tired and weary with all of it. Where would it all end her heart was heavy as she trudged back home, having let herself into the house she collected the necessary odds and ends without even looking up at Arthur. He could tell by her expression not to ask what had gone on, so he just shrugged his shoulders and gave a deep sigh.

Joyce was waiting for her on her return to Mary's house, the atmosphere was tense the two women having little in common. Mary wondered why Jean bothered with her she was a right misery guts, and if she wafted that bloody bible in her face once more she would be wearing it. Thank goodness for the return of her sister another few minutes and she would have been done for murder, surely that's what she was planning anyway she was going to murder her baby. No it wasn't alive she tried to tell herself it hadn't moved it wasn't a living thing, she couldn't have it there was no chance of that it had to go and the sooner the better.

Jean nodded her head and they started out into the night, they met a few neighbours but weren't aware of them and didn't let on. Their footsteps echoed on the cobbled streets probably because they were almost deserted at that time of night, Jean thought it sounded like a drum beat sending out a message. Don't go, don't go don't go. It was an omen telling Mary not to go thought Jean, she wished she was a man then she could sock Mary on the jaw and drag her back while she was still alive. Polly Simmons door suddenly came into view and they all shrank back, would Mary cut and run. The two other women stood and waited wondering what her reaction would be, she strode purposely towards the door and knocked loudly.

The door was opened immediately by Polly she chuckled and ushered them in, the three of them couldn't take their eyes of the huge hairy warts on her chin. Their faces were a picture and made Polly chuckle even louder, "Bye eck tha looks a reet shady bunch" she cackled. Having ushered them into the back kitchen she immediately asked "which of thee is it then" and waited for a response. "It's me" answered Mary looking her straight in the eye, "I'm the one". "Reet lets get started sooner we do sooner it's over,"said Polly, gesturing towards the other two "tha two can wait in there" pointing towards another door. Jean wanted to stay but didn't like to argue so they tiptoed into the parlour "shut the door," shouted Polly after them. "Reet tha can pay me now I allis likes me money first" holding out her hand to Mary.

Polly urged Mary to take off all her clothes, she stood there in her bra and drawers feeling very vulnerable. Trembling from head to foot she didn't know which way to look, "get em off lass come on shape theesen tha dussna need them buggers on." "Ow far ast gone," she demanded her hairy warts dancing up and down as she spoke. Mary couldn't take her eyes of them. Polly asked her again louder this time at the same time drawing back a curtain across a large alcove. Mary didn't understand her and stood there looking foolish, "when didst fall." Still she stood there not knowing what Polly was saying, "Good God all bloody mighty when did'th dirty bugger shag thee." At last the penny dropped, "Oh reet aye" she began to sob. Never in all her life had she felt so dirty and so alone, "well shouted Polly once more."

Mary managed to whisper three weeks, Polly stormed up and down the room. "Three bloody weeks tha's wastin me time," "tha canna tell at three bleedin weeks." Tha might as well piss off ome now an save thee sen the bother o commin back," she was pushing Mary's clothes back at her wanting to be rid. However Mary was having none of it and raising her voice she let rip with a string of obscenities that would have put a navvie to shame, grabbing Polly by the shoulders she looked straight in the eye. "I'm avin a baby an I dunna need thee to tell me that, an I want rid now not next week or the bloody week after but now tonite." "Dus tha get that I canna ave it, I wunna ave it," her voice was rising to a scream. Polly knew that she had to do as the girl asked before she had some kind of breakdown. "Reet lass let's get on wi-it then," answered Polly quickly. "There's no guarantee that it] work tha know's," Polly added, "everybody's made different does see."

Mary shuddered. "It'1 work its gotta do I canna go on like this another day," "I can only do me best lass." Muttered Polly, "Get inth bath" she gestured at the hip bath behind the curtain. Mary duly obliged, it was very hot and she made as if to jump out but Polly pushed her back "thee otter the better fer thee lass just thee sit there for a while and drink this." Handing her a tin cup, "What is it?" Mary wanted to know. "Ner thee mind just drink the bugger up that's a good girl," mumbled Polly. Mary tried to drink the foul tasting brew but gagged on every sip, Polly was getting vexed, "get it down thee hold thee bloody nose or summat but just drink the bugger." Demanded Polly, "I canna drink it its vile" sobbed Mary handing the cup back to Polly.

Polly was seething by this time "Well tha might as well piss off ome now cos if tha dos'na drink it it canna do it's job savvy." She hissed at Mary, Mary set herself and holding her nose as tightly as she could she gulped down the evil brew. Hanging on to it was the hard part how she stopped herself from gagging she would never know, time after time she almost threw it back up. Never in her life had she felt so sick, even what she had been going through recently wasn't as bad as this. Polly added another kettle full of hot water to the bath, then handed her a refill of the vile brew. Mary began to sob again vowing she couldn't drink another mouthful, but Polly gave her the look that said drink up or bugger off so she drank.

Bringing the lot back up in the bath, Polly looked at her with contempt and passed her another drink.

So it went on a drink followed by vomit followed by a drink etc, pretty soon Mary didn't know whether she was sitting or flying. One minute laughing the next weeping hysterically, Polly bundled her out of the bath.

"Reet lie thee down on err,"she guided her towards the kitchen table and pushed her roughly onto it. "Dunna shove me about Polly Simmons," shouted an irate Mary. "I'll smack thee a bugger," "Oh very sorry thee majesty did I ferget me place." said Polly making a mock curtsy, "Get thee arse on'th bloody table and quick about it." she bellowed, she was getting heartily sick of Mary she didn't like the girl. What with her hairs and bloody graces and her lettin Tom Scully shag her well it didn't cut any ice with Polly, she had seen the end results too many times here in her kitchen.

Mary started to giggle and couldn't stop she knew it wasn't funny but the more she tried to stop the more she shook with laughter, in the end Polly whacked her one on the arse and it felt good. All the pent up feelings she harboured for Mary went into it, but being as how Mary was to pissed to notice she got away with it. Open yer legs hollered Polly trying to prize them apart God the bugger was hard work, "ger off you dirty bugger."

Mary spat at her and made to get off the table, although Polly was at her wits end she wanted to get the job done to her satisfaction. So she wheedled and cajoled and convinced Mary that it was in her best interests to let her do the deed, so Mary laid back and let the old woman do her job. It wasn't easy she looked around the room, if only it would stop spinning it wouldn't be so bad. The small kitchen was clean and tidy everything was in its proper place, a warm fire burned in the grate.

Polly's cat slept on the comfy fireside chair uninterested in the goings on around her, the pathetic squeals of young pregnant females had long since failed to send her scurrying out of the warmth of her bed into the cold night air.

The pain ripped through her like a knife Mary squealed like a pig ready for slaughter, Polly withdrew the implement from between her legs and tried to cover Mary's mouth to shut her up. "Tha'l ave bloody Bobby at'th door if tha dusna shurup," snarled a rather scarred Polly her face just inches away from Mary's. The sight of Polly's warts and facial hair wagging in her face was enough to send Mary into a fit of hysteria, and Polly almost smothered her trying to shut her up. Jean came running in from the parlour fearing the worst, Polly was forced to let Mary go but shouted at Jean to shut her sister up before the law came knocking at the door. Jean drew her sister close to her and soothed her as best she could, the sight of her straddled on the table showing everything she'd got wasn't a pretty sight. And all that squealing and screaming it was a nightmare, "what's the matter with her eyes." Jean wanted to know, "and her speech is slurred."

Polly tried to explain that quite a lot of alcohol had to be consumed to enable her to do the difficult part of her job, get em plastered first an then they dunna know quite what's goin on she told Jean. "Can't tha do summat a bit more humane tha that," demanded Jean who was feeling very vexed about the whole thing. "What does tha want me to do give err a bloody injection or summat would that suit thee," snapped back Polly. "I'm none qualified to do owt like that, tha knew that afore tha came ere I do best I can wi what I've got." Jean continued to tut and fuss over Mary and assure her all was well, while giving Polly looks that could kill. "Reet that's it take err ome I canna do owt wi the lass," snarled Polly "I've just about ad me gut's full o you bloody lot err's mard bloody soft." "Go on piss off an leave me in peace an dunna come back," she added. It took and age to get Mary dressed and Jean could gladly have rung her neck for her, Polly sat in a chair glowering at them the whole time, not saying a word. At last they set off up the street with Polly's last words ringing in there ear's, "tha wunna get a bloody penny back so dunna try." Jean was wishing she had clouted the old bag before they left, she wasn't a fighting sort of person but to see Polly going down like a sack of spuds would have given her a lot of pleasure. The woman was an animal she shouldn't be operating on young girls poor defenceless little buggers, many without family to support them. Thank God she had been there for Mary, thinking back to the sight of Polly with the long metal needle in her hand trying to insert it into her sisters private place gave her the shivers.

Mary was a dead weight and Jean and Joyce struggled to drag her along the dark cobbled streets, praying that they wouldn't meet anyone they knew. She threw up on every corner and the racket she made was enough to waken the dead, at times Jean would have liked to see her go down like the proverbial sack of spuds and stay there but who would deliver the blow.

Jean herself couldn't and Joyce was to much of a lady so unless a stranger with a grudge came by it wouldn't happen, her thoughts went back to Polly's place and the fight for the return of the five pounds. Polly had refused on the grounds that she had played her part providing the gin and Epsom salts, hot water and so forth. Jean had demanded to know where the towels, cotton wool and sheets were that she had taken round. No sign of them could be seen, and she demanded those back also. Polly however wouldn't budge so they had to leave empty handed, with Jean yelling tha dusna get paid fer tryin to murder folks. Polly brandishing the copper posser at them, and Joyce literally pushing them out of the door. "Tha'l none get away wi this tha'l pay mark my words," were Polly's last words.

The words rang again and again in Jean's head, what would that woman do how could she hurt their Mary. Please God let me get home and out of this nightmare situation, she prayed what a right carry on to be sure. Mary was acting up and the other two women were fed up with her antics, so Jean stopped and gave her a damned good shaking until her teeth rattled in her head. They then gathered speed and almost dragged the poor girl home her feet hardly touching the ground, Joyce spied one of Jean's nosy neighbours and quick as a flash they ducked into a very handy gennal and stayed there until they were sure that she had gone not forgetting to keep a hand over the drunken Mary's mouth.

Having reached Mary's front door they almost threw her inside the house, "get bath out." Jean asked Joyce, "whilst I undress err." In no time at all she had her clothes off, and coaxed her into the bath which Joyce had crept into the yard for like a thief in the night. They had to keep reassuring her that everything was alright, she moaned and whined non stop. Then threw up in the bath, so they had to drag her out and empty the tub. Which wasn't easy in the dead of night trying not to awaken the folks next door, who would wonder what was going on. Mary moaned constantly that she was going to die, and Jean mouthed to Joyce that she was going to murder her if she didn't shut up. They almost managed a smile but not quite, after what seemed an eternity they had her in a clean nightie and put her to bed, they didn't like to leave her but she was sleeping peacefully so they decided to get off home.

It was late and they were both tired and weary, Jean gave her friend a big hug and thanked her warmly for all her help and kindness. "I cuddna have done it wi'out thee," she told her. Joyce gave her a tired smile and replied, "I canna say it's bin a pleasant experience but tha can rest assured I wunna breath a word to a livin soul." Jean knew that her friend meant every word, and she nodded to her. No more words were necessary they bade one another goodnight. Jean locked her sisters door and ran for home as fast as she could along the dark cobbled street, there was a man standing on the corner and Jean almost screamed out in fright. "Sorry missis," he whispered to her. It was Tom Scully she recognised him at once, by the lamp light she gave him a look of intense hatred.

"Go home" she hissed "hasn't tha done enough mischief." Tom didn't like the look she gave him something was wrong and he didn't know what, he wasn't going to stop and find out either so he legged it up the street as fast as he could without a goodnight. Jean trembled from head to toe after encounter with him and was glad when she let herself into her house and its warmth and comfort, Arthur was waiting up for her and although she was very tired she had to relate the nights happenings to him. He was aghast and could hardly believe what Jean told him, he wanted to go to Mary and hold her close and kiss her better. However Jean held out her arms to him and wanted to be hugged to so he duly obliged, "Oh Arthur I never want to see another day like today never as long as I live." she told him and held him even tighter, Arthur reassured her that she had done her best and that she had nothing to reproach herself for. All the while his heart was aching for the girl lying in bed all alone with no-one to comfort her what he wouldn't give to be with her right now.

So the outcome of it all Jean told Arthur was that Mary was still with child, everything they had been through had been for nothing. They had lost the five pounds, sheets, towels, cotton wool, they would never get them back. You couldn't go to a woman like Polly Simmons and demand the return of your goods without attracting the attention of the neighbourhood, and that was something they did not want to do. Jean broke down when she related the time that Mary filled with gin and salts begged to die and go to Mam and Camy, Arthur thought it couldn't get any worse and he held his sobbing wife and longed for Mary. "I think that we should go and make sure that Mary's allreet," said Arthur. "Tha canna leave err on err own all neet," he added. Jean quickly agreed so they brought little Elizabeth down from her bed and wrapped her in a thick warm blanket, they then set off for Mary's down the dark street trying not to make a sound.

Tom Scully banged the front door as hard as he could, and taking the stairs two at a time he yanked open the bedroom door and bore down on his sleeping wife. Throwing back the filthy covers he dragged a startled Maggie out of the bed by her hair and dumped her on the floor, "right what the friggin ell is goin on." He demanded. Maggie was shocked and bewildered and was trying to get her head together, she had been in a deep sleep and felt groggy. "Well he demanded," Maggie hung her head not wanting to make eye contact with her irate husband. If she did it would be a bloody good hiding for her she knew that, "what dos't mean Tom." she stammered, "I've asked thee twice I'm non goin to ask thee agen." he told her menacingly, "dunna thee fuck abart wi me spill the fuckin beans now." with that his fist came down and crashed into the side of her face, Maggie let out a cry of pain and shrank back onto the floor.

This only fired Tom up even more and he gave her a pummelling with his fists, he laughed as he hit her.

There was something about hitting Maggie that he loved, the sound of his fist smacking into flesh and seeing her poor face twisted in agony it gave him an instant hard on. Although he would have preferred to beat her senseless he pulled up her nightie and yanked her legs apart, and pulling off his pants quickly he hissed at her "tha ought to be thankful fer this dick ere it wants to shag summat an that only bugger about so tha gets the pleasure on it. With that he was in her, she could put up with him shagging her it was better than a beating. It didn't take him very long and he was puffing and panting when he had finished, "reet lets be avin it then." He demanded,"

Dust tha mean about Mary Bailey" croaked Maggie, she could hardly breath after her ordeal. "Ah so that's it then" answered Tom not at all bothered that his wife knew about it. He gestured for her to continue, Maggie did in spasms and told him all about the baby and planned abortion. When Polly Simmons name was mentioned she heard a sharp intake of breath, but nothing else. "Then tha name were mentioned she almost screamed but I didna believe em an I teld em so," "well I telt Polly an she said to tell Mary Bailey to go round theere tonite an that she'd do'th job an that's all." Finished a very frightened Maggie wondering if he was going to go berserk, she mentally prepared herself for the onslaught. However it never came, Tom was good and scarred the thoughts of the Moore lads after him made him turn to jelly. He was all right thrashing women but when it came to facing up to his fellow man, well he was a cringing coward.

"Maggie I'd better lie low for a bit lass," he told her. Maggie was aghast he was talking to her not shouting at her, "tha knows as well as I do Jim Moore an is lot are bloody madmen tha dussna want me ta get beaten up by'Th mad Moores dust tha." The thoughts of Tom being beaten up by the Moore family were music to her poor boxed ears, and a sight she wouldn't have missed for the world. However she couldn't tell him that so she went along with what he had in mind, whatever that would be. "I'd best clear off fer a bit til'th coast is clear an theve fergotten abart me," he decided. "Ast'th get any brass" he wanted to know, "na non a penny." Answered a very happy Maggie, she would gladly have given him every cent she had just so long as he went. He had always kept her without so it wasn't any surprise to him, he didn't have anything to take with him so he just said ta ra and he was off into the night. Maggie was speechless for a while then she crept down the stairs and when she had searched the house and there was no sign of him, she locked the front and back doors and fell on her knees and prayed to God that he wouldn't return. Her girls would be safe from his evil lust and with no one to fuck and blind at them the boys would be better behaved, yes it would be good she would never live in fear again sobs of joy and relief racked her frail little body.

Arthur and Jean let themselves into Mary's house; all was quiet and still. Jean asked Arthur to go upstairs to have a look at Mary, whilst she settled Elizabeth down on the fireside chair and put the kettle on. Arthur was reluctant to go but Jean insisted, so he gingerly crept up the steep stairs, what a sight was to greet him. Mary was propped up in the bed; there was vomit all down her face and the counterpane was awash with it. The stench in the room made him want to throw up with her, her face was ashen and her eyes bulging out of there sockets were bright red rimmed. For a moment he studied her, the beautiful golden curls looked like coconut matting. He had seen better corpses, and for one awful moment, he thought she was.

"Mary art tha all reet," he whispered quietly. She just opened her eyes looked at him smiled weakly then shut them again, and then she began to sob softly as if her heart would break. Arthur crossed over to the blanket chest and rooted out some clean bedding, and then he went off downstairs and bounded back with a bowl of warm water and clean towels. Without a qualm he stripped off the soiled bedding and threw it down on the bedroom floor, then he removed her dirty night-dress which wasn't easy, it got stuck on her head. With a lot of tugging and pulling, it was off, revealing Mary in all her naked glory. Arthur sucked in his breath God if there was ever a more glorious sight in the world he had yet to see it, well Jean had made it crystal clear she wouldn't be coming up to help anymore tonight she'd had her guts full. Therefore, it was up to him and he got on with it, gentle as a lamb he did not give Mary any cause for alarm.

Mary just lay there and let him do whatever he had to do; while he dried her he could not help but get turned on by the sight of her delicious breasts and silky mound. What he would not give to take her in his arms, to kiss and caress her. To suck those pink tipped breasts, he became aware that she was looking at him intently and felt that she was able to read his mind. God he felt so ashamed what would she think of him, his face turned purple with embarrassment. "Can you put your nightie on," he asked her not able to meet her gaze. As he helped her up in the bed the tip of her left breast brushed the corner of his mouth, and sent a shiver throughout his body. It took all his strength to break away from her and walk to the other side of the bedroom, he was only human after all and he yearned for her longed for her with his very being.

Arthur pondered over the sorry situation with Tom Scully; he could understand why Tom wanted Mary any man would want to bed her. However, why had she let him do it to her, she must have wanted it, wanted it bad enough to let it happen more than once. He would have to put it out of his mind before it drove him crazy, he gathered up all the dirty bed linen and called over to the sickly lass to ask if she needed anything more before they set off home. Mary suddenly became all panic stricken and pleaded with him not to go, "dunna go yet please stay just a little bit longer Arthur."

Well he did not know what to do so he told her he would have a word with Jean, and off he went carrying the washing.

He put the question to Jean but she refused to stay, she wanted to get home and put her little one to bed and she was dog-tired herself. So he decided that he would stay and see to the washing put it in soak and get the worst out of it, and by the time that was done it would be getting light and Mary would feel less nervous and probably get off to sleep. He walked Jean and Elizabeth home fist of all, and then got the washing sorted out into the dolly tub. Then he made a pot of tea and took one up to Mary, she had slithered down in the bed so he put his arms around her and pulled her up. It took all the strength in his body to pull away from her, when all he wanted to do was to pull her to him and hold her in his arms like a lover would do. However he resisted the urge and handed her the cup of tea, "Thanks Arthur I dunna know what I'd ave done wi'out thee."

"I've reet shamed meesen I canna think what tha makes on me," she told him and tried a weak smile. The tears began to fall again and her body shook, Arthur tried to soothe her and told her not to worry. But she was inconsolable and before he knew what he was doing he had gathered her in his arms, what he had longed to do all night long and he held her close so close you wouldn't have got a spoon between them. They had never been close hadn't really ever got to know one another, but there was a bond between them now that would be there always. They stayed locked together for a very long time, one grateful for the other the other lost in a haze of longing.

Arthur knew that he must never let Mary know about his feelings for her he would keep them locked in his heart and treasure them, he would never abuse her in any way he was her brother in law and he wanted to keep her trust and friendship no matter what happened. However what he dreamt about her at night or his private thoughts in the daytime were his alone, and nothing to do with anyone else, and so long as he didn't let anyone know his feelings well that was fine he could live with that. When he had finished the washing and put away the dolly tub and posser and cleaned up, he checked on Mary she was fast asleep looking more like her old self. She had her colour back and he knew that she would be all right now the worst was over. Overcoming the urge to kiss her cheek he left the house and set of for home, it was getting light and folks were afoot and heading for their places of work and he would be joining them shortly there would be no sleep for him.

Jean called round the next morning to find Mary up and dressed, she had thought that her sister would have taken to her bed for a couple of days.

There was no need to tell anyone that she wouldn't be in to work today she was dressed and ready for it, Jean was assured that she was up to it so she gave in. "It didn't work did it our Jean," she asked. Jean didn't need to answer her face said it all. "I canna go through it any more it were," she couldn't go on. "I'll ave the baby an make best on it," Jean rushed to her and hugged her warmly and they wept softy together for a while. "Reet lets get on we it" said Mary "we'll ave eyes like rubber tyres if we dunna stop pipin em." Laughed the sisters, Jean was thankful that another visit to the dreaded Polly Simmons wouldn't be necessary. It didn't stop her thinking about the way they had been conned out of their money etc, they would put it down to experience and hope none of it ever came to light.

Chapter Seven

Ginny Moves In

Jim is was on his way to Meg's he had decided now was the time to ask her to move in with him, Should she start yawpin he might change his mind. So it was up to her, yoo hoo called someone from down the street. He didn't normally turn round for any kind of call but he knew who it was, and sure enough Ginny came running up to him panting for breath. She was looking her very best and it didn't go unnoticed, she could look stunning when she wanted to.

"By eck has't got a sweetheart waitin for thee" chided Jim, Ginny coloured up "tha nows I avna". She told him looking up at him from under long dark eyelashes, her eyes giving out unmistakable signals. "Well appen we'd better do summat about it," with that he took her arm and guided her down the street towards her home.

He'd had a fair few pints and sex was on his mind very much to the exclusion of Meg, or anyone else for that matter. Ginny was beside herself it was working, so far so good get him into bed and maybe. Just maybe, be patient time would tell. He really was a handsome man was Jim Moore despite the lines etched deep in his face, the loss of a couple of teeth did nothing to harm his charming smile. Still had plenty of thick dark hair thinning a little on the crown, but all in all looking good.

He bundled her up the stairs to her room, and had her stripped within moments, she worked hard on him and gave her all it was good. Jim begged for more they had sex in every position possible, at the end of it Jim asked her to move in with him.

He wasn't thinking rationally but he had done it now and there was no turning back.

If he could have sex like this every night then he wouldn't grumble, bedtimes with Ginny would be something to look forward too. He wouldn't need to go to the pub as regularly, he'd have her there warm and willing in his bed. Just the thoughts of it got him aroused again, Ginny was knackered but she couldn't blow it now she gritted her teeth and gave another marvellous performance.

Later on that day Jim took Ginny to his home for the very first time, Joe, Teddy, Lizzie and Alex were getting ready for bed. Jim told them in no uncertain terms that Ginny would be moving in right away, that was it no other explanations given. The children exchanged looks of horror and panic, Jim looked round at them in turn. Lost yer bastard tongues he shouted at them, they all jumped up like they had been shot.

Lizzie started to cry, the boys reluctantly whispered "Hello."

Jim turned to Ginny who was sizing up the opposition, as opposition it certainly was going to be. "Bloody waterworks at every turn dunna let it get thee down," "they'd drown in the buggers" snarled Jim. "Piss off up'th stairs" he shouted at Lizzie, "I canna stand it and rest of thee go on bugger off to bed."

They shuffled out of the room and were gone quickly and quietly, Ginny took in the kitchen it would need lots of improving to get it to her liking. Still Rome wasn't built in a day, it would do for now it was reasonably warm and comfortable. Ada always made sure that it was spotless clean, which wasn't easy with her weight to carry around she was always done in when she had finished.

Ginny was deep in thought there was no way she would be eating with this lot, couldn't see herself sitting down to dinner with Jim's brood. No they would eat together in the parlour she scrutinised it like an eagle, yes a small table from her place would be just the thing. That way she could caress and fondle him at will keep him happy that was what she intended to do.

"Dust tha want owt afore bed," asked Jim Ginny pretended to be shy, and gave him her best show of coyness. "I think av'ad everythin I need afore bed Jim," she whispered he took hold of her ample breasts and giggled them about, "there's plenty more where that came from" he assured her. "Oh Jim you are a caution an no mistake" giggled Ginny, they swayed together in the gaslight then with him tickling her and her squawking with glee they made their way noisily up the staircase.

The kids listened in awe at their bedroom door how could the bastard bring home this tramp, and parade her in front of them.

Telling them to piss off in their own home. Aunty Ada and Uncle Ted would have something to say about this in the morning by God they would, they'd soon owst her and good riddance too.

Lizzie continued to sob, Joe tried to comfort her. "Dunna thee fret our

Lizzie er arse'l be through back door afore her can get her drawers off," "bet there off already" chirped up Teddy. The boys began to snigger even little Alex who didn't really understand what was going on. He never cried for his mother he didn't really miss her very much, but he missed Camy and said a prayer for her every night.

They fell asleep trying not to listen to the grunts and cries, and mattress springs twanging with great gusto. What a bloody carry on they were bloody shameless, Joe's face burned with shame and embarrassment at his father's antics he wished Jim or Harry were .there. They would sort the bastard out, he would write to them and see if they could get home and put the trollop out of Mam's bed.

Jim and Ginny couldn't have cared less they'd had a great night what stamina they had, each time was better than the one before. Ginny couldn't sleep she'd worked bloody hard to get here, at last she had been rewarded and she intended to stay those snot nosed kids wouldn't hold her back. She would soon sort them out by hell she would, she had fought much tougher battles than this in her time.

Before she knew it Jim was hollering "we've overslept" he ranted "I'll be late ferth shift" he was on for six and it was ten minutes past. It put him in a right foul temper what with the booze and sex the night before, he caught sight of Ginny through the dressing table mirror. What a state she was without the raddle and her hair looked like a birds nest,

"What hast done Jim" he said out loud, Ginny looked up at him and held out her arms pouted her lips and tried to make her eyes smoulder with passion. "Thas gone bog eyed" said Jim turned his back on her and got dressed, then with a slam of the door he was gone. No bleedin breakfast or cup of tea. God help his workmates today they would be wishing they were somewhere else for sure anywhere but there.

Ginny drifted off to sleep after Jim left for work, she was still sleeping when Ada marched into the bedroom at eight thirty. "why anna them kids up an doin" she demanded "You bone idle bugger" Ginny was taken aback by the intrusion "piss off outa err you cheeky bugger" she hollered back trying to hide her nakedness from Ada with the bed covers. Her hand slipped from the counterpane and thumped her under the chin, she yelped Ada scowled

God she felt so stupid, Ada continued to stare at her last time she had been in this room her dearest Sal had been lying in the bed. Now it was occupied by a slut, a dirty brazen slut. They continued to stare each other out Ginny was the first to drop her eyes, Ada words tumbled out amide tears "thas none fit to lick my Sal's boots", adding "but tha wunna rein long mark my words tha'l be back onth slag-ep where tha belongs". "tha thinks tha's got it made but tha's very wrong very wrong indeed", "an dunna thee ferget arm one air of them littl'ens eads an I'll kill thee wi'me own two ands na think on."

With one last contemptuous look she added, "tha looks like a bloody cart-horse tha probably pisses like one." Then she walked out slamming the door with all her might wishing Ginny's head were in it, the windows rattled and the floorboards creaked as Ada waddled down the stairs a formidable sight to behold.

Tears of rage ran down her face, that bloody bastard Jim Moore why couldn't he be called up and never come back, they'd been getting on a little better since Sal died. But this was an insult to them all, his dick had got in the way off all reason. It was all he thought about, sex mad bugger a dog would be castrated for less.

Joe, Teddy, Alex and Lizzie were all agog, "is she goin Aunty" they chorused. Ada shook her head "dunna ask me err's brazen an as ard faced as a pot dog," "we shall ave to see what thee father as to say cos i'm none commin back if that pie-cans eer." Lizzie begged her Aunt to let them move in with her and Uncle Ted, "we'll see what appens Lizzie dunna thee fret get thee of to school come on shape theselves."

"Mr Lamb will be givin thee yer cards if tha dossna get of sharp, "she added to Joe, when they were ready she ushered them out off the house and taking a last look round she closed the door of her sisters home. She would not be setting foot there again until things were back to normal, until the floozy had been dispatched. There would be no-more succulent meals for Jim, he could live on love see where it got him. He could nibble on her big tits when he was hungry that would suit him very well the bloody animal. Ada could not wait to tell Ted, but as she burst through the door she became aware of him bent double his face screwed up in agony. "Ted whatever's up wi thee", she shouted

"It's all reet Ada," he managed to wheeze and gestured for her to leave him alone. Ada was beside herself with worry, eventually Ted's colour returned and he was able to sit down and talk about it. "It's nowt to worry over Ada" he tried to pacify her, but she wouldn't be put off. "Tha's goin to see Dr Marshall this mornin if I ave to carry thee there me self," that was final and he hadn't the strength to argue.

The tale she was about to tell him would wait for another day, he wasn't up to it best find out what was ailing him and get him better then there would be time for other things. They plodded up the hill to Dr Marshall's surgery, both overweight and out of breath. Ted held on to the railings outside looking very pale, Ada was seized with a panic she hadn't felt since Sal was first taken ill. Ted became aware and tried his best to reassure her, "thall ave't cut down on me tater ash Ada" he joked.

Ada wasn't in any mood for banter, and she almost pushed him through the door. The receptionist was told in no uncertain terms that Ted needed to see the Doctor right away, "can tha sit down Ada whispered the young woman an'th Doctor will see thee as soon as he can ther's all this lot afore thee" she gestured at around eight or nine people already waiting.

There was nothing else to do so they sat and waited their turn, Ada huffing and puffing tutting and clucking with indignation, telling everyone who cared to listen about the unfairness of it all." We ner come err an no wonder when folks ave to wait fer ours on end," After about an hour and a half they finally saw Doctor Marshall, he greeted them warmly he always found time to talk to his patients put them at ease.

Ada was quick off the mark about Ted's symptoms with him protesting repeatedly that there was nowt wrong with him that a tonic wouldn't cure,"I'll be the judge of that Ted" said the Doctor. Ted was given a right good going over, at last he sat down and when he spoke to them his voice was very sombre. "Right Ted it looks like you might have a little problem with the old ticker."

"Not Ted" gasped Ada "no tha must be wrong it canna be that not after our Sal," the Doctor held up his hand "let me finish if you do exactly as I tell you all will be well." "It doesn't have to be all doom and gloom," "firstly you will have to loose a lot of weight Ted and you can do it with Ada's help." Ada added that he could count on her, "and the cigars Ted they will have to go too." "They are putting a strain on your heart and you will be better off without them, they help to clog up your arteries it isn't good Ted."

Ted could tell by the tone of his voice that it was serious, "right then I'm puttin mesen in thy ands Doc where do we go from err." The Doctor continued "I want you to go to the hospital for a few tests, nothing to worry about," "will you do that for me Ted." "Aye I will that" answered Ted. "I'll see to that Doctor dunna fret," added Ada she felt a little better knowing that Ted could be helped.

On the homeward journey Ada told him about the floozy moving into Sal's, Ted was aghast "the dirty bugger and under them kids noses by ell he's a lot to answer for Ada the bloody tom cat." "He deserves a dammed good iddin an its about time he got one by eck if I were a bit younger an fitter," Ada told him to calm down and think about his heart. "Weve got to get thee better Ted let bloody mad man get on wi'it you come first from now on."

they swept past Jim's house taking care not to look up in case the slut was around, whatever would the neighbours think to see them skulking about. "That bugger brings nowt but shame on'th family Ted," Ada moaned as they let themselves into their own house. "I'm ready fer me dinner" answered Ted not wanting to talk about Jim any more, Ada gave him one of her looks and pulled out the diet sheet that the Doctor had given her.

"Reet lets see what tha can ave" she started to titter and her ample frame shook from head to toe, "one thin slice of bread, no butter, one boiled egg,no salt,"it's non funny Ada" snapped Ted he was roaring hungry and could have eaten a horse and come back forth saddle. "Dunna gi me any kids grub Ada me guts is empty" he complained, "what do'st want me to do Ted ignore'th Doctor's advise."

Ted could see that she was worried about him and at a loss what to do for the best, "well allreet then but I dunna know ow I'll get on wi it." "Tha can ave two eggs just this once," beamed Ada happy that he wasn't going to be awkward. "Wilt tha cut me bread into little soldiers fer me," their eyes met and they collapsed into fits of laughter.

Ted wondered if life without Ada's lovely grub would be worth living, he couldn't exist on rabbit food even if it was in his best interest. He decided to go over to his allotment and have a crafty cigar he couldn't give up everything not all at once anyway. He would cut down but not out never, he would probably get bombed out of his house so why worry jerry might have other plans for them all.

Round at Jim's Ginny was having a good old root round, for letters etc. he might have other women she only knew about Meg. That bitch would be out of bounds from now on bye bye Meg, she could piss off Jim was hers and she would be Mrs Moore before too long. The house was a bit shabby and could do with livening up a bit she would soon see to that, she would bring her brightly covered cushions and throw overs and her gramophone and records get into party mood yes it would be good once she got stuck in.

Ginny lit another fag and draped herself across the settle she couldn't be bothered with food but Jim would want some, she would get his girl to make him some give the nosy little bugger something to do. Then she would go to her rooms to pick up her magazine before she died of boredom, straightening her stocking seams she set off grinning like a Cheshire cat at the neighbours who stood and stared at her.

Oh yes this was the life a mistress, what a laugh a scarlet woman that's me like Vivian Leigh as Scarlet O'Hara in 'Gone with the Wind' the film was just out and every one was talking about it, she must get to see it soon. Every curtain twitched along the row as she made her way up the street, her high heels clicking on the cobbles. Two old girls were nattering near the end of the ginnal they gave her the head to toe treatment, they folded their arms across their chests puffed out like pigeons and glared at her as she approached them.

Ginny wasn't bothered by the two old bags she looked them straight in the eye one by one, "why don't you piss off" she told them "clutterin up the bloody street tha makes it look untidy." Well they gasped what a bleedin cheek one was lost for words but the other one Betty Jones never was "at least we dunna drop our draws fer any bugger who passes by tha must be riddled wi decease tha dirty tramp." Ginny laughed out loud "no bugger ed look at thee twice so tha's no chance of the draws bein dropped, bloody Air Force might think they were windsocks"

The two women didn't know what windsocks where but didn't like to show their ignorance they only knew it was an insult, they turned their backs on Ginny to dismiss her. "Funny smell" said Betty "like a bloody dead skunk," they held their noses until she was well past them. Ginny laughed even louder it was going to be fun living down this street if today was anything to go by.

Feeling very bitchy she decided to call on Meg, who had been up all night her eyes red with weeping. Jim hadn't turned up and she had waited practically all night long for him, he was going to ask her to move in with him she just knew it and she couldn't wait to say yes. "What dust tha want" she asked not inviting Ginny into her room, "Oh nowt really just came to get me things," "If there's owt you want feel free." "What dust'tha mean get thee things" her heart skipping with delight, she's going thank God Meg was whooping with delight inside.

But her next words sent her reeling, "I've moved in with Jim" she said with great delight. Then waited for Meg's response, who tried bravely to compose herself but it proved impossible. Huge tears like diamonds tumbled from her large blue eyes, she almost choked with shock slamming the door in Ginny's face she ran to her bed and proceeded to break her heart.

Ginny listened to the heart rendering sobs and laughed until she felt dizzy, there was no sympathy from her for the silly little bitch. Let her get on with it "Go on cry you silly bugger you'll piss less" she shouted through the closed door, by eck it was turning out to be a very good day all round she was enjoying it immensely. And tonight she would be in Jim's bed, what a life all this and heaven too she crowed. Skipping to her room she set about removing everything that could be useful to her, after several journeys she was worn out and decided to have a bath and relax.

The tin bath was heavy and cumbersome, and carting the water back and forth was a bloody bind. But at last she was soaking in the tub and had almost fallen asleep when the door burst open and in came Joe, she jumped up, he got the shock of his life and ran out again. There was water all over the place and she was bloody pissed off with it, well the little bugger could mop up when he came back.

Then it hit her he had seen her naked, and it was probably the first time well that would give him something to think about for sure. Jim would have to be told about it she was entitled to her privacy, yet it gave her a buzz to think about the youngster running down the street with a face as red as a smacked arse. She began to laugh and stamped her foot it shot along the bottom of the soapy tub and she landed in a heap, legs in the air, head under the water spluttering and gasping for breath she emerged feeling very foolish and thankful that no-one was around to witness it.

Joe was legging it back to the butchers shop he wouldn't be finishing early after all, he would find something to do keep himself busy. He tried to erase the pictures of Ginny out of his head but it was impossible, all wet and soapy those huge breasts and her hairy bits. He felt a throbbing in his groin, fancy Dad sleeping with that every night lucky bugger. Floozy she might be but she had a stunning figure, by eck he was almost drooling he swallowed hard.

Mrs Lamb was surprised to see him back, "what's up Joe duss,na ve an ome to go to." Joe went bright red "I fo'got to clean'th bike" he lied and headed for the back yard, where his bicycle stood as clean as a new pin. He began to wash it again wishing the soapy sponge was washing Ginny instead, he cleaned all her little nook's and crannies with extra care and lovingly polished her shiny bits. Mrs Lamb observer all this from inside the shop, what's up wi lad she wondered the way he was washing that bike. Well she'd never seen anything like it, he must think it's human poor lad she shook her head. Best give him some steak and kidney to take home feed him up a bit her answer to everything was to have a good feed and all would be well.

Ginny was tired out she left the bath of water and got into bed for a nap, there was plenty of time till Jim came home from work. when the kids came home from school they couldn't believe it, no-one had ever left the bath like that before. It smelled really nice and Lizzie wished that she could use it, they all set to even Alex and in no time at all the bath was hung up in the yard, water moped up with the towels and everything shipshape, tea prepared just as Jim came in from work.

His eyes swept the room for Ginny she wasn't there perhaps she had gone back to her own place. He hoped she had it had been a mistake and he knew it was the sex he just couldn't resist her, she flashed her tits and he was a goner. He ate his tea not bothering to ask anyone of her whereabouts, Joe couldn't have looked him in the eye anyway and coloured up every time his father looked his way. What's up with that daft sod thought Jim he's probably had a bollocking off his boss old Lamy serves him right soft sod he'll learn.

Jim got washed and thumped up the stairs to change he must see Meg right away beg her forgiveness, what he would say to Ginny he didn't know he would give her a slap if she got stroppy. Suddenly there she was in front of him fast asleep in bed, in the daytime too it was unheard of unless you were poorly. Ginny awoke and saw his disapproving look, Jim darlin she cooed and throwing back the covers she displayed her ample charms. Once more Jim was hooked he got an immediate hard on and in seconds he was inside her he wouldn't be looking for Meg tonight that was certain

Poor Meg she had sobbed for hours after her visit from Ginny, how could Jim do this to her. He'd almost said the words as good as, now she'd moved in Poison she was and he would be sorry he'd rue the day that he would. Meg's heart was broken she loved Jim so much, she had stayed in the background when Sal was alive hadn't been proud of what she had done but her love for Jim was unshakeable.

Her love had kept her going waiting for the day when he would ask her to move in, now that wasn't to be. She would have to move on she couldn't stay there and watch the tart with her man, no anything but that to have it rubbed in day after day she couldn't take it. She would go back to Derby, visit old friends and perhaps find a job there and somewhere to live and try to forget the happenings in Bridgevale.

By eight o'clock that night she had everything packed, with one last lingering look around her little room she turned and left. The last train to Derby was ready to leave and she scuttled down the platform, and as the carriage door closed behind her the train pulled out and she was on her way her small plump body racked with sobs.

Lizzie was complaining to Aunty Ada and Uncle Ted, "we'ad to empty'th bath an clean up when we came ome from school, an she were i'bed." "Di'th ear that Ted" said Ada "what a bloody carry'on" Ted cleared his throat he didn't approve of swearing in front of the children. Ada hadn't time for fripperies "come on Ted what's to be done," she asked "can I come an live err" begged Lizzie. "Please Aunty an Joe, Teddy an Alex,"

"Good God little un we canna du that thee dad would go mad," answered Ada gathering Lizzie to her ample bosom. It was going to be very hard for all the kids now that Jim had moved his woman in, but what could they do. Ada didn't want the kids to witness the goings on between the pair of tomcats, it could turn a youngsters mind she was sure.

"I'll ave'ta ave words wi Jim," Ada told Ted "summats got'be said it'l ave be sorted one way orth other. She waited for Ted to argue with her but he didn't and she was quite surprised, that's that then it would be done tonight. "Na then Lizzie dunna thee worry wen sort it out tha'l see," Lizzie went home feeling a little happier now that Ada and Ted would be sorting it out.

A torrent of abuse met her as she let herself into the house, "shut the bleedin door fer Christ's" sake she squealed she had her dress patterns laid out on the floor and the draught had sent them all flying to every corner of the room. Sorry she stammered, Ginny gave her a withering look. "Are all you lot thick," she demanded. Cheeky bugger thought Lizzie she's the thick one wantin Jim Moore, only an idiot would want him.

"Pick em up" bellowed Ginny "an in'th proper order," Lizzie wanted to shout out to her you put them on the rotten floor you pick them up. However she dardn't so she duly obliged, then she got on with her chores while silly Ginny buggered about with cushions and rugs. They were all gaudy colours and looked hideous against the other furnishings.

When she had finished Ginny started on herself, nail polish on her hands and feet. Lizzie was aghast she had never seen anyone do it before, but had to admit they did look nice but wouldn't have told her so not for all the tea in china.

"What'le I do fer tea," she asked Ginny. Ginny was livid "ow the ell do I know," she ranted "I'm non err to cater to you bloody lot, do whatever you do normaly an make some fer me too." She walked off up the stairs ranting to herself, "what the hell am I doin err they need a bloody work horse an I'm not the bugger."

Lizzie was glad to see the back of her and got on with the tea, I'll give her poison an kill her that'd be best she thought to herself, but she didn't know of any so that was out. Never mind our Jim or Harry would soon sort her out once they knew, once the word got round from Jean and Mary who she would waste no time in telling straight after tea.

Joe and Teddy were playing silly buggers whispering together, they couldn't look Ginny in the face and their antics were getting on Lizzie's nerves. After tea was over and the pots were washed she set of with Alex, Jim and Ginny had gone to the pub so they wouldn't be missed. Jean was pleased to see them and gave them a kiss and a hug, she listened to their tale of woe the poor kids what a life they had.

Jim Moore was a bloody shit and no mistake, and the tart he had moved into there mothers home was an insult to her memory. All make-up and breasts reeking of cheap perfume, but she was probably very good in bed and that's what Jim Moore would want her for. Jean blushed beetroot red at the thought's of it, a mental picture of herself and Arthur in bed making her blush even redder.

Lizzie asked her to write to Jim and Harry, they would sort him out she was sure. Jean assured her she would and they felt a bit happier, she also put them off visiting Mary "she's non to well at'th moment" she told them "Arthur's just gone round to see if she's all reet". So they trooped back home feeling a little better now that something would be done.

Round at Mary's Arthur was having a cup of tea, he was feeling very mixed up he had feelings for Mary he shouldn't have and yet he couldn't keep away from her. always making excuses to go round just to see her sit a while have a talk to be near her anything, she didn't realise this and was completely unaware. Mary would have been shocked to the core had she the slightest idea, she was always telling Jean what a treasure he was and cried often at the kindness they showed to her.

The baby was here to stay and nothing was going to change that fact, so she had to accept it and make sure that Brian never found out. As long as Tom Scully stayed away and Maggie said nowt all would be well, she didn't like the underhanded way she would have to deal with it, but it was the only way she could save face and not hurt Brian he might be killed or wounded no-one knew so she had to keep up a front and that was that. He would never be hurt by anything else she would make sure no matter how she was hurting inside.

Her thoughts suddenly flew to her mother Sally, she had been through a similar sort of dilemma herself when very young. Many times she had thought how could she, and now look it had happened to her not with a man she adored like Sally had it seemed. But with a dirty scruffy cretin who was no good to man nor beast, her heart was heavy yet at the same time what she remembered through the boozy glow was of pure animal lust.

Her colour deepened at her memories, what on earth had gotten into her well Tom obviously to put it crudely. Had she tried hard enough could she have stopped him he was only human after all, but she had laid back and enjoyed it just like he had. If she hadn't been caught she might have gone on enjoying it even now, no, no, no, never, she wouldn't she bitterly regretted it all and she would never ever do it again as long as she lived. The sooner she put Tom out off her mind the better it would be and then she could get on with her life; her one prayer would be that her baby wouldn't look like him. He or She would be loved and cherished no matter what, by herself and all her family she knew that for certain. Mary cursed the wave of nausea that swept over her and ran for the sink just in time to retch her guts up, and after several minutes she sank down onto her knees like a rag doll absolutely lifeless unable even to stand.

Arthur stood in the kitchen doorway and watched all this, it took all his strength to stop himself from walking up to her and gathering her up into his arms. Mary was aware of him standing there, "I'm all reet now Arthur" she gasped and staggered over to the table and held on to it. "Na thas not" replied Arthur I dunna remember Jean like this get thee sen up to'th Doc's an tell im ow that feelin,"Mary giggled at this "by eck I dunna think so I'd be laughed out of'th place I'm only havin a baby it is'na an illness tha knows." "Aye I can see that burstin wi good elth Ive seen better lookin corpses," "Oh put'th kettle on an shut up" snapped Mary a little too sharply. She noted his hurt expression, "Sorry" she said quickly "I didd'na mean to snap at thee Arthur," "I dunna know what I'd do without thee." He looked away unable to meet her gaze couldn't look into those eyes and maybe give the game away there were enough complications.

Best leave things as they were keep his feelings to himself, he didn't want to hurt Jean or Mary he loved them both too much. He believed in fidelity and prayed for God to help him through this difficult time, they had another cuppa then he bade her ta ra. He was a lovely man was Arthur thought Mary their Jean was a lucky woman to have him, she wished she had got to know him better when he was courting Jean they'd never exchanged more than a dozen words in all those years, my what a strange family they were and no mistake. Well they had never been brought up to show any affection Jim and Sally had seen to that, never say sorry when a clout round the ear hole would do. Mary knew that she would have to see Lizzie and the boys now that Jim had moved his woman in, some made out she was a prostitute well that would be about right for him, he wouldn't want a decent woman in his life or maybe a decent woman wouldn't want him. What was he thinking about letting all this go on in front of the kids it just wasn't on, they had suffered enough in there short lives and could do without it.

Poor Lizzie she had taken over where Camy had left off, the new drudge slogging her guts out night and day, and no reward at the end of it. Something would have to be done about them, they would have to be taken in by the family one way or another Jim wouldn't want them getting in the way of his sexual antics and her mind boggled at the thoughts of those two at it. Ada and Ted would have to be sought out and asked to do something to help and soon, she could just picture Ada sailing forth into battle like Bodicea, her face beetroot red, hair standing on end in spite of her many curlers to tame it down. And poor old Ted at the rear to back her up what a sight they were, formidable came to mind. However she couldn't face them yet not while the sickness was so bad, she would have to wait until she was feeling better and then tackle the problem. Also try to put her own troubles behind her, it was still hard to come to terms with what she had done and how easily it had happened. Brian would never forgive her if he ever found out, she would never tell him she would rather die than have him find out how low she had stooped. To the gutter in fact that was how low, she shuddered involuntarily with disgust and self loathing. she would have to put it to the back of her mind, and keep it there for ever she would be like Scarlet O'Hara she wouldn't think about it because tomorrow was another day.

Chapter Eight

Goodbye My Love

Mary was back at her looms in the weaving mill, some days she thought she would go stark raving mad .The baby she had so lovingly planned with Brian had been put there by a filthy dirty beer swilling sex maniac a wart a festering boil. What was she going to do! Hold her head up high, that's what her sister Jean had told her make just one little slip and they would be on her like a pack of rabid dogs.

Her life wouldn't be worth living if the truth came out, they had seen it all before many times. She would have to grin and bear it, smile through gritted teeth pretend she was happy beyond her wildest dreams. However there were people who knew, Maggie Scully for one, Polly Simmons, Joyce Hibbert, and the filth of course Tom. She just had to hope and pray that they kept quiet , with a bit of luck she might miscarry , she'd thought about throwing herself down the stairs or taking poison anything to get rid of the thing inside her, but she didn't want to die not that she couldn't leave her darling Brian know matter what .

So she wore a frozen smile all day, every day. Making small talk about babies, knitting little booties and mittens, as far as anyone could see she was a happy young mother to be. until till such time as anyone opened their mouths that was, then whatever happened would have to be dealt with. Jean watched her like a hawk and would fight tooth and nail for her beloved sister if need be, she knew how Mary felt about the baby and her loathing and disgust for herself and Tom Scully. Try as she might she still couldn't understand how Mary had got herself involved with the scruffy oyk, but the dirty deed was done and couldn't be undone they had tried God help them now they would have to wait and see.

She would have words with the others involved and have them promise never to breath a word or they would have her to deal with, none of the other members of the family would be told unless it became absolutely necessary. Aunty Ada would faint away it might kill her, they would have to be very careful lots of people could be hurt in many way and they didn't want that. Mary spent most of her nights weeping for her beloved Brian she had written to tell him the marvellous news under Jeans instruction, and his response had knocked her for six.

If there was a happier man on the planet he had yet to be found, how could she ever tell him the truth crush him break him . No he must never be told never ever she would take her shame to the grave with her. Ada was a little worried about Mary she missed nothing few thing got past her she was a wise old bird` that lass is goin't ave a difficult time mark me words` she told Ted` she's non appy in er-sen,` eatin nowt ers stick thin canna be good ferth babbie`. `Eh Ada thas gotta ave summat to worry thesen about or that non reet`, he replied. "` Ast-tha ever known me be wrong Ted," dunna know much but by ell i know when summats wrong wi me own`. Ted decided it was time to visit the allotment he didn't want a slanging match with Ada he wasn't feeling to well and he was ready for a cigar I'll be off then he muttered.

`O reet thar bugger off dunna thee stay an talk to me I'm nowt `. He could hear her moaning as he sallied forth down the road glad to get away for a while to enjoy the peace and quiet of his allotment have a cigar, and relax let the cares of the world go by have a cat nap out of harms way women! they could be a bloody pain in the arse sometimes.

He was best out of their way his chest felt really tight and his breathing had become ragged, upon reaching his garden shed he busied himself doing a few odd jobs , tidying up the plant pots and stacking them into neat piles . Taking his big scissors he went of outside and cut the last of the chrysanthemums they were beauties Ada would love them, she always maintained they were her favourite flower .

Ted had won the cup with them for best at the show a couple of weeks earlier he had felt very proud , he was a good gardener keen as mustard some said his sweet-peas had won first prize earlier on in the year . Then he'd had a couple of seconds with his dahlias and first and second with cabbage and cauliflower's not to mention leeks , beetroot , and carrots yes he'd done very nicely thank you his hard work had paid off dividends .

He wrapped some newspaper around the flowers and placed them gently on to the floor at the side of his chair he felt tired and sank into his comfy chair , 'by eck' he gasped thankful to be there at last phew! 'thout i'd never make it' he said to no-one in particular. He reached for his favourite cigar and lite up by eck it was good this is the life for me he thought as he sank back on the cushions, suddenly he was seized by a terrific pain in his chest he let out a cry of agony `Ada ` `Ada` they were the last words he would ever utter he died with her name on his lips.

Jim Holmes heard Ted call out, he was passing by having just finished digging over his plot he looked inside the shed "did'st call me oud mate" he inquired. The sight of Ted was enough to tell him that the man was in a bad way by eck what should he do , first of all he picked up the smoking cigar that Ted had dropped onto his jacket he stubbed it out quickly. Next he felt his pulse there was nothing he listened for his breathing no he wasn't breathing either, he then pulled Ted gently to the floor and laid him in the recovery position and unbuttoned his shirt pulled up his vest and began to massage his chest.

He even tried mouth to mouth resuscitation but poor old Ted was beyond worldly help, there was nothing more he could do he had done his very best. Jim felt heart sorry to see his old mate like this it was a shock and he realize that he had lost a very good friend one of the best, whatever would Ada do without him and who would tell her!. There were the sound of footsteps outside Jim shouted out "give us a 'and" he turned to see young Lizzie standing in the doorway, he didn't want her to see her beloved uncle like this.

Very quietly he told her to go for help she may have been very young but Lizzie was wise beyond her years, she sped off not bothering with passers-by going right to the Doctors front door. After knocking loudly she waited breathless, the door was opened by the housekeeper who was not amused` what dust-tha think that doin` she demanded. Lizzie spoke quietly yet there was a great urgency in her tone she asked that the Doctor be told to go to the allotment where uncle Ted had been taken very poorly, `aye reet away `came the response she could tell that this was a genuine request the child was death pale.

`Tha'd best go an tell thee Aunty Ada` she advised, `that's a good lass,` `yes missis` answered Lizzie and sped off down the road to where Ada would be unaware that uncle Ted was poorly. She forgot to knock at the door Ada was a stickler for good manners and began to chastise her, there was something in her eyes that made Ada stop in her tracks. `what's up lass` she asked, Lizzie gulped her voice seemed to have gone. `Spit it out Lizzie it canna be that bad`, Ada tried to laugh but the laughter died in her throat.

`Its uncle Ted` she managed` where is e` Ada whispered, `allotment Aunty i've tel't Doctor`. `That a good lass Lizzie na go'an tell our Jean to come reet away an thee go an look after littlens`, oh dear god please let my Ted be alright she uttered over and over to herself. Something told her that it was going to be bad news she felt a great unease, now and then she felt a great foreboding panic seized her Ted "Ted dunna thee dare ta leave me."

She collapsed onto the settle in floods of tears she knew in her heart that her beloved Ted had left her , how could she carry on without him he was her right hand her rock it was Ted and Ada always was always had been. She hadn't got over the loss of Sal and Camy yet she was still in mourning how could Ted think of leaving her, no he'd be fine the old bugger would walk in through the back door any minute. She felt like screaming where was Jean where were they when she needed them, the door opened she wheeled round `Ted `she shouted! it was Jean she ran to her aunt and held her tightly in her arms.

Jean began to sob and in that moment Ada knew that her Ted had died she let out a pitiful scream sounding like a wounded animal and her legs buckled under her, it took all Jeans strength to lower her back onto the settle God help us whatever where they going to do. The back door opened suddenly and Dr Hallam strode in he knew there was no time for niceties, Jean was relieved to see him she didn't know what to do Ada was absolutely distraught what could she say or do comfort her dearest Aunt.

The kindly Dr held Ada's hands and spoke to her calmly and frankly, `you can be sure that Ted didn't suffer he wouldn't have been in very much pain Mrs Harris`. `he's at rest now `,`he has been poorly for a long time now more ill than you ever knew`. `Ted didn't want you worry about him he knew you had more than enough on your plate as it was`. Ada's big red face crumpled into a thousand tears and her body shook from head to foot, unfortunately her wind was playing up too and she let out a very loud trump quickly followed by another.

Jean felt embarrassed and didn't know what to say` er wilt tha ave a cup'a tea Dr` she asked?` thank you Jean` he answered` that would be very nice I think your Aunty might have need of a good strong cup too.` Jean busied herself in the kitchen making the tea thankful for something to do , every now and then Ada would break into a fresh bout of weeping accompanied by a burst of wind. She couldn't hold her cup of tea in her shaking hands and it fell to the floor luckily it didn't break and the tea was soon mopped up, there was another knock at the door the Dr quickly dashed to open it he spoke to however it was then turned to Ada .

`Are you ready to have Ted home Mrs Harris`, he asked solemnly. Her Ted home! of course this was his home and she wanted to see him , to hold him in her arms and tell him she hadn't meant it when she had told him to bugger of that morning. Not knowing that he would never return, never walk through the door again she steeled herself . Aye she said to the Dr I'm ready, he beckoned to someone outside and the door was propped wide open while the undertakers men bore in the recently deceased Ted Harris .

Ada ushered them into the parlour and Ted was laid on the large settle `shall i send for Mrs Lowe` asked Dr Hallam Ada's head jerked up at this request , `that wunna be necessary thank thee all the same I'll see to it me'sen my Ted would want me ta see to everythin`. She went and knelt down at Ted's side and collapsed into floods of tears once more. After that there was a stream of neighbours and friends also the large family, the small cottage was bursting at the seams everyone was shocked and saddened at the loss of Ted .

Even Jim Moore was shocked and that wasn't easy he had been convinced that Ted would live forever, although he'd always said that he ate to much. He looked upon the grief stricken Ada and however much he disliked her he wouldn't have wished this on her, even the sight of her large red face didn't bring him down into fits of laughter like it normally did .

Jim didn't stay very long he couldn't do with weeping and wailing he was of to the pub as soon as was decent he would be glad of a bit of fresh air too he could tell that Ada was having trouble with her wind it was about time some one opened the window. At last everyone but the family had gone home and Ada began her task of undressing Ted, she was helped by Jean and Mary who for the first time in weeks forgot about her own problems.

Lizzie was there to a good little help in every way when they got down to the underwear Ada thought it was time that Lizzie went home to see to Alex and put him to bed, she hugged her little niece to her large bosom and they had another weep together Ada knew that Lizzie had loved Ted very much and she was grieving too. I'll need thee in't mornin lass bright an early said Ada ther's lots to do , aye Aunty i wunna let thee down she bade goodnight to Jean and Mary and let herself out it was pitch dark and she suddenly felt afraid and she ran like hell to her own doorstep slamming the door behind her.

Ginny jumped up in fright what the bloody ell! she ran at Lizzie and smacked her up the side of her head, `don't you dare do that ever again` she raged `you scared me out of me wits` . This was just too much for Lizzie and she burst into floods of tears and ran upstairs,` you'll piss less` Ginny shouted at her. What a bloody family this was she would have to get rid of the buggers and soon, she didn't know how but it had to be done Jim would have to see to it

What with the little fat man dropping dead in his cabbage patch and his even fatter than a pig wife wailing up and down , life here was getting pretty grim. Ginny didn't care for this housewife image she didn't mind the drinking and having a good time and loved the good seeing- to's Jim gave her in bed almost every night.

But he still expected his shirts to be washed and dinner on the table not only for himself but for all his brood too, it was getting to much for her and she didn't know how much more she could put up with. Christmas would be upon them soon and she wasn't going to be lumbered with the trappings of that lot, she would have to invent some long lost relative and rush to there side in there hour of need anything to get away from this bloody lot.

Ada looked down upon the face of her dearest Ted he was sleeping he couldn't be dead not her man, speak to me she whispered to herself blink once if you can here me Ted. He didn't blink nor did he speak, Ada continued to sponge him down gently the way you would a child her tears falling onto his chest. Jean and Mary tried to help but they felt useless and very uncomfortable, it was very personal this laying out and they both wished that Ada had used the services of Maggie Lowe who enjoyed every minute.

Like Ada always used to say she wouldn't swap it for a gold clock, but Ada didn't want Maggie any where near her Ted hard as it was she would do what had to be done. At long last the job was done and Ted was dressed up in his best Sunday suit and they were left panting and sweating like three rag dolls, but that wasn't the end of it Ada wanted the house cleaning from top to bottom. They knew that if they didn't help her she would struggle on by herself so after a cup of tea they set too, they didn't have time to worry about the rest of the family it was a good thing that they all had someone to rely on.

Arthur would see to Elizabeth Jean and young Lizzie would take care of Teddy, Joe, and Alex. Mary was secretly hoping that she would miscarry all this tugging and pulling it might just do the trick, anything to rid her of this thing she was carrying she hated it more with every day that dawned. Maybe God would punish her she hoped not she felt afraid because of her terrible thoughts and wishes, if she hadn't kept on wishing for a baby this might not have happened if she had just been patient a little longer.

"Are you going to stay tonight" Jean was asking her "oh yes o course i will "she replied, they both brushed aside Ada's protest's of being alright on her own" No Aunty we shanna do that were here as long as tha wants us." She was duly put to bed absolutely exhausted they hoped that she would sleep, Jean went home it was two o'clock in the morning the darkness enveloped her and she felt a little frightened.

Her pace quickened and soon she was running as she rounded the corner her feet left the ground it was icy, she landed on her back and bumped her head she was in agony. The rest of the way home was at snails pace why had she run like that now she would be in pain for days and there was so much to be done. How could she have been so stupid there was nothing to be afraid of at all, her mind had been playing tricks with her it often did in the dark.

Suddenly it hit her that Uncle Ted had died, there had been so much to do she hadn't had time to think about it . She was suddenly racked with pain in her chest and the tears came raining down, she lent against a wall for support " oh Uncle Ted whatever shall we do we-out thee." Life would never be the same again,

Ada was unable to sleep she tossed and turned and wept, life without Ted was unthinkable there was a war on what would happen to them all . Just when she needed him the most he had left her, she alone would have to cope with all that life threw at her. Sal would be there to great him and Camy too! yes he would be safe with them, how could he be safe he's dead what on earth was she thinking oh God help me please.

She drifted into a fitful sleep all night was spent searching for Ted he was always just around the next corner, but she never found him all she wanted was for him to know she hadn't meant to say bugger off. She had loved him with all her heart and would do so till the day she died, at last morning came and she was able to go downstairs and sit with her dearest man.

She held his hand and wept quietly she knew this would be the last time, very soon the undertakers would be arriving and he would be gone. Ted looked splendid in his very best suit, white shirt and tie, his shoes polished like glass. His hair slicked back from his face it stuck up on the top always had it would never lay down no matter what they did to it, well it didn't matter any more Ada stroked his brow and wiped away the tears that had fallen from her eyes down onto his.

Mary was on her way down the stairs so Ada bent to kiss Ted good bye one last time then scuttled into the kitchen to make a pot of tea, it wouldn't do to be seen mauling the dead. Although know-one would have thought any the less of her she had her funny ways did Ada, "ast tha slept Aunty "? asked Mary "aye a little bit lass" Mary gathered her Aunty into her arms and hugged her close they wept together softly. “Oh Aunty am that sorry i dunna know what ta sa," " i know lass i know “they were startled by a knock at the door. They wiped there eyes and Mary went to answer it , Joe Robinson and his son Joe where there with Ted's coffin .

They doffed there caps and bade her "good mornin" "come in" said Mary , they would have been up all night making the coffin a perfect fit for Ted they looked tired . “Wilt tha ave a cuppa" she asked, they nodded in response "aye that'd be reet welcome thanks missis". Ada and Mary bustled about in the kitchen out of the way of the undertakers they had there job to do, eventually they took the tea out to the two men who were mopping their brow. Their's wasn't an easy job by no means, Ted was now ensconced in his bed where he would sleep for all eternity.

Seeing him like this started Ada off again into a fit of weeping, the others stood about with head bowed the men were used to it after many years but it never got any easier especially when the deceased was liked and respected by them. Joe and his son finished of their tea and thanked the two women ," we'll be putting the lid on now Mrs Harris is there anything you'll be wanting to put in with him" gesturing towards the coffin Ada looked bewildered.

She was almost blinded with tears, and her face looked fatter and redder than ever. "Sometimes folk like ter put in favourite pictures an trinkets an such", added Joe Jnr Ada thought for a moment then she ambled noisily up the stairs they could all hear her trumping loudly. They all started to move about embarrassed by her wind, Mary stifled a giggle she didn't want to laugh but it kept on bubbling to the surface.

At last Ada was back and in her hand she held a cigar she gently folded Ted's hand around it ," he can ave one wi- im foth journey "she cried" there were nowt he loved better than is cigar". The two men nodded their agreement , they then proceeded to screw down the coffin lid and in know time at all they were out of the door and gone . Not before they had arranged the funeral for Tuesday 19th December at 10 o'clock, by half past eight the house was full to bursting again every one wanting to do there bit. Teddy and Joe were doing all the errands, the girls were busy ordering food for the funeral tea.

Sorting out all available cups and saucers, plates, napkins, teapots and the like. The house was far too small to hold everyone so they would book the co-op rooms, and do the catering themselves Ada would be kept busy baking it would keep her mind off Ted a little. Hopefully she wouldn't have much time to think about his death, no-one was talking a bout Christmas either they couldn't face it without their beloved Uncle, who would carve the turkey! it was unthinkable for anyone else to do it but have to they would. Mary was telling Jean about the previous night and how she hadn't slept a wink, the thoughts of Uncle Ted's corpse on the settle below gave her the heebie-jeebies.

Ada's wind through-out the night was unbearable "she never stopped our Jean" giggled Mary, Ada turned round at that moment and the two women felt ashamed as she told everyone what a great help they had been to her and how she wouldn't know what to do without them. They both loved her very much but everyone needed a little laughter now and again, it kept them sane . Perhaps she would laugh about it herself one day when the deep sense of mourning had been taken over by memories, when they would be able to say remember when Uncle Ted said so and so.

Jim was in for a surprise on his return from work that Saturday afternoon Ginny was waiting on the doorstep suitcase in hand ," what's up" he asked. "It's me cousin Gwen she's bin taken very ill I've got to go to her right away," "I did'na know tha ad a cousin Gwen" answered Jim. "Well I have "replied Ginny" she lives in Llanelli and I must catch the next train Jim "," Llanelli where the bleedin ells that when it's at ome". " Oh come on Jim it's not my fault don't be like this I'll be back as quick as I can," Jim Moore was a very shrewd man he wasn't easily fooled , he had noticed Ginny's displeasure looking after his brood he had seen her moody sulky expression many times when she wasn't aware that he was watching her .

" Right lady" said Jim" you go off to Llan bloody ethlee and dunna thee come back" ," take all thee stuff what tha leaves beind will go in't bin ". "Jim what's up with thee I'll be back after Christmas I promise", "no tha wunna tha goo's now an tha can fuck off for good." He went inside and slammed the door with all his might, she wouldn't make a bloody fool out of him by God. Jim expected her to come running back inside but she didn't , when he went to look later on she was gone . Good bloody riddance he thought to himself he would go and look for Meg someone had said she had buggered off she wouldn't be far away he was sure.

Ginny was pissed of with Jim showing her up in front of the neighbours there he was shouting and effing at her, well she wouldn't put up with it she would come back when she was good and ready she caught her train. Jim was furious, that bitch could piss off for good what a cow she was. Well she had met her bloody match, he ran around gathering up her belongings bellowing like a bull. The kids ran out of the house down to Ada's , she couldn't really be bothered with anyone and duly ambled off upstairs to leave Mary to deal with them.

"What's goin on now" she asked,"it's that Ginny" answered Joe. "errs gon-nth train ", Mary didn't understand . "What do'st mean gone weer ", "she's packed err case an gon onth train our Mary." said Alex, an i ope she's non commin back," his little face was a picture. "Well what a todo where has't her gone too," Mary wanted to know. Joe answered quickly, "errs gon ta lanbloodyethlee" he was felling very important being the only one who knew.

"Joe! scolded Mary "ther's no need fer swearin", "'I'm only tellin thee what wer said."answered Joe quite crestfallen,"I'd best get our Lizzie"said Mary and she shouted up the stairs for her to come down and look after the others. Lizzie duly obliged and took them home, fearing the worst from Jim Moore. However there was no sign of him, "he must'a gonth pub" beamed Lizzie. They danced round in a circle cheering loudly, so loudly they didn't hear the back door open.

Jim Moore surveyed his family, "What art cheerin fer is it cause thee Uncle Ted's dropped dead or summat else." The kids turned in horror they all started to squeal in unison, however Jim could see the funny side off it all though he didn't want them to know. He stood with arms folded waiting for an answer, they hung there heads not knowing what to say. "Right well if tha dunna know what that laugh'in at tha must all be bloody barmy an we all know barmy buggers live inth nutouse," "so tha'd best piss off there an be quick about it."

They didn't know what to do and wandered aimlessly round the house, this was to much for little Alex and he began to cry. Jim couldn't stand crying kids and made for the door, I'll deal with thee later an tha can answer me question is that understood." he bellowed they nodded their heads in answer. With a slam of the door he was gone and they breathed a sigh of relief, they all ran to the back door to see what he had been up to. The dustbin was full and overflowing filled with Ginny's belongings" bye eke" said Lizzie ""e's throw'd lot out ", they rushed to get their hands on the spoils.

There were shoes, frocks, jewellery, etc, hanging out of the bin. Alex sorted out some things for himself and Teddy and Joe scrambled to get there share too," come on Lizzie get thesen some stuff" urged the boys. Lizzie would have liked too but she was afraid of the consequences should Jim decided to retrieve them when he came home after having a skin full," I'm avin nowt of ern " she told them" an you'll be best leavin em too". Teddy was in his element with all the gee gaws he loved glittery things and lots of colour, Ada always said he would wear a frock if they let him.

It was the last straw when he held up a bustier, Lizzie snatched it from him and told him she would have words with Aunty Ada, several neighbours had gathered outside to tut tut about the goings on at no 8 and Lizzie felt ashamed that they were watching them like hawks riffling the bin. She pulled Alex inside despite his protests and gestured for the other two to follow, back inside they went with heads bowed.

Lizzie shot back outside with a pair of knickers she had wrestled from Teddy's grasp and threw them in the bin, he howled loudly they were bright red with black trimming and he wanted them. He was older than Lizzie and wasn't going to put up with her bullying; he made for the back door to retrieve the knickers when there was a knock at the front door. They all went very quiet Lizzie looked round at them all it was always her who had to do every thing, she opened it to see Mrs Hibbert standing there she waved her walking stick at Lizzie and told her that her father would be informed about the terrible racket that had been going on.

Lizzie started to say how sorry she was but she was cut short by the irate woman, she didn't want to hear lame excuses and if there was anymore of it the police would be called. The Moore children were petrified God almighty Jim would kill them all," come on we'd best get over to Aunty Ada's" said Lizzie. the boys rushed upstairs to find hidey holes for their spoils somewhere away from the beady eyes of Jim Moore, Mary was busy helping Ada with the preparation for all the baking that had to be done, there was much to do before the funeral on Tuesday.

There was fresh bread to be baked, veal and ham pies, cheese and onion, game, chicken and mushroom. Apple and cinnamon, plum, bilberry, jam tarts, butterfly cakes, tea loaves, a large fruit cake. Also two big hams to boil, half a dozen chickens to roast and a whole salmon to steam. Plus the salad, lettuce, tomatoes, cucumber, cress, spring onions, beetroot and a nice big cheese board. That would be about right they couldn't think of anything else.

Luckily all the family had taken on a certain amount each so hopefully all would be ready on time, Jean called round to let them know she had dispatched telegrams to Jim and Harry so all being well they would be home in time, Ada was pleased about this, the arrival of all her large family was very important at this time it was expected it was showing respect for a loved one. Everyone knew that the larger the congregation the higher the esteem for that person, Ada began to weep once again "them lad's el be besdide em sens." she wailed "the'll be that upset fer their Uncle Ted," Jean and Mary had to ignore her they couldn't break down every time with her or nothing would get done. "I've put tablecloths anth napkins in'th parlor Aunty" fussed Jean trying to distract Ada from her sorrow, but it only served to set her off again. "Thas bin that good to me tha two God knows what i'd do wi'out thee "and off she went again her wind started to play her up and loud trumps echoed round the kitchen, it took all their strength not to break down into fits of laughter.

They were saved by the return of Lizzie and the lads, they were all cowed down and anyone could see that something was afoot. "Whatevers up wi thee" echoed Jean and Mary, "it werner our fault chirped up Joe "it were all that owd misery guts". Everyone looked towards Ada but she wasn't ready to resume her role as matriarch just yet, she shook her head and walked back to the kitchen they would have to sort it out for themselves. "Come on Lizzie lets be avin it" demanded Jean," what'ast bin up too this time." "well "began Lizzie "we thout Dad were out at pub an we were just dancin round a bit," an'th next news theere es standin lookin at us it feert us death." "An then we went out-toth bin an all her stuffs throwd out," "so them lot" gesturing towards Joe Teddy and Alex "were rootin al'th things an keepin em." She paused for breath, Jean and Mary were all agog at this news and exchanged knowing glances.

Lizzie continued "Teddy wer takin er knickers an I took em off im an put em back inth bin," " I did'na know what they were" whispered Teddy going scarlet with embarrassment. Lizzie wouldn't be put off , "then he started shoutin anth next thing old ibbert were knockin an sayin as ow she were sendin ferth police." "I'll be kilt an i've done nowt," moaned Lizzie. The lads looked shamefaced and didn't know what to do" we did'na mean to cause bother", said Teddy "it were just a bit o fun." Jean and Mary knew that the four of them were sorry for their actions and didn't deserve to have a thrashing from Jim, between them they managed to convince them that Mrs Hibbert would see reason once she had been pacified.

They would take her a fresh baked loaf as soon as it came out of the oven ," fancy'th slut clearin off then our Mary wonder what err's bin up too" whispered Jean . Mary thought about it then answered, "nowt any worse than I've done." She was wearing her martyr look the one that Jean loathed, "oh come on dunna start that agen, lets change subject." Lizzie was puzzled "what ast'tha done Mary," Jean gave her a look fit to kill. " Tha'd best be off an get these three sin-too make sure they wash their ans an faces," "an dunna fe'get the'se meat'n taater pie in'th oven." Joe looked a bit miffed he was a working lad now he didn't need to be told to wash his hands and face, not by Lizzie or anyone else.

But he didn't say anything not yet, but he would when he had the opportunity. Jean hustled them out pretty quickly, which didn't go unnoticed by Ada who had been stood in the doorway for a little while observing. "Has'st owt to say," she asked directly to Mary. "Mary blushed deep red, Jean tried her best to distract Ada but she was having none ove it. Then Mary started to sob and sobbed as if her heart would break, she was inconsolable. Ada felt alarmed, "good God whatever's matter." She rushed over to the sobbing girl and held her in her arms, "e'h lass it canna be that bad tell thee Aunty Ada." "Get it off thee cheast," "I telt thee Uncle Ted on Friday mornin just afore e went down to'th allotment." "I said summats wrong wi our Mary er's none reet," Jean begged Mary not to tell.

Aunty's got enough ferth worry about she dunna need it, but it was too late if they didn't tell it would look like she wasn't trusted. That was bad enough but if she knew what then, there was no way out they looked at each other. " Tha'll ave to tell er our Jean I canna, "shouted Mary and with that she bolted up the stairs like a bat out off hell. Ada turned to Jean her eyes wide with alarm, "is it that bad lass." "Worse" replied Jean, and went on to tell the sordid sorry tale about Tom Scully.

She didn't spare her Aunt any details but tried not to paint her sister as black as Tom, emphasizing the drink he had plied her with. Ada was shocked beyond belief she demanded to know how many people knew, then she went to ponder the whole sad issue. "By ell Ted"she said aloud, "I did'na know how reet I were." Where was he! where was her Ted, he would know what to do he would help. H'ed picked a bugger of a time to die and leave her too it , now what was to be done about Mary.

Ted would have been wise and philosophical, nothing could be done she knew that without question. They had visited Polly Simmons and she had failed, so what could Ada do. There was only one thing to do hold that girl in her arms and reassure her that all would be well, she would have her baby to care for and love it would be part of herself the best part. and she must never dwell on the past it was the future now that mattered, and they would make the best of it for the sake of Uncle Ted and all he held dear.

Ada went of in search of Mary who was laid on the bed in the back room," them stairs'll be death o me" she panted. She sat on the bed and urged Mary to look up at her, "come on lass dunna thee fret no moor." "Thee Uncle Ted would'na want thee to," "oh Aunty" cried Mary and threw herself into Ada's arms. Where she sobbed till she had no-more tears to shed, till she was a wrung out rag. There would be no recriminations they would get on with the tasks ahead, there was still much to be done before the funeral on Tuesday.

Jim Moore was sent for at the foundry on Monday morning and told to hurry up, what the bloody hell was up now he thought as he hurried to the bosses office. "Phone call for thee Jim" shouted Ben Lowe above the noise of the foundry, Jim didn't like to answer the phone it was alien to him and he picked it up with some misgivings. "Hello " he bellowed, "Dad it's Harry," Jim was to stunned to answer . "At thee there," "aye " answered Jim at last. "wil't tha tell Aunty Ada I'm reet sorry about Uncle Ted," " an that I canna get ome for'th funeral". There was a long silence, again Harry asked "art there Dad" "aye said Jim reet I'll let err know." He was uncomfortable, not knowing what to say to his son. "Right'o I'll see thee then", he said and he was gone.

Jim stood looking gormless at the phone, Ben was watching him. “He’s gone” Jim told him, "put'th phone down then" said Ben. Jim duly obliged, turned and stomped off back to his work muttering about having to tell Ada about it. By hell he's a cold fish thought Ben he'd never even asked his son how he was keeping, but that was Jim Moore for you no one would ever get to know the man. If his own family couldn't then who could, still he was a damned good worker and that's what he was there for he could do the work of two men and never complain.

A cablegram arrived for Ada; Jean opened It. "Oh Aunty It's from our Jim," "he canna get leave he says he'll write an he sends is love." Ada was very upset about this she had hoped that all her family would be with her on Tuesday morning, but you couldn't argue with the Air ministry. "It canna be elped lad would've tried is best, an our Harry will be ere I'm sure." Ada dabbed at her eyes once more, "Ted'll understand es watchin ore us all'th time" moaned Ada the tears followed quickly, there was a knock at the back door and in came Tilly with Sally Victoria. "Can I elp wi owt” she asked, Jean didn't know where to start there was so much to do.

"Ther's co-op room'th get ready," " an all'th pots take up." replied Jean, "reet thats the job fer me where dust I start" answered Tilly, Jean began to sort out the pots and cutlery etc, Ada came in from the kitchen and Sally Vicky ran to her for a hug. Ada swept her up to her ample bosom and kissed her fondly, "I'm reet sorry our Jim canna come ome Tilly lass." said Ada , Tilly looked puzzled. "What dust mean Aunty," "well lass we'ne add a telegram this mornin sayin as owe he could'na get leave."Ada told her, Tilly tried not to show her feelings. She didn't get much news from Jim these days still it wasn't like him not to let her know, but things were different there was a war on now.

She pushed the hurt to the back of her mind she would think about it later on when she was alone, they dispatched Sally Vicky off to no 8 to be looked after by Lizzie with instructions not to let her out of the door, it got dark early and she would soon be lost and with the canal being just down the road. They went on and on till Lizzie felt like screaming, bloody hell did they think she was a child! They were playing together when Jim came home from work, ignoring his grandchild he shouted for Lizzie to be off and tell Ada that Harry had telephoned to say he wasn't able to get leave for the funeral.

Lizzie rushed around getting Sally's hat and coat on, then they hurried to Ada's where she told them what Jim had said. This was to much for Ada she collapsed in tears, her Jim and Harry not coming. It was unthinkable she needed them now more than ever, dam the bloody war, damn Hitler.

She lumbered up the stairs and flung herself on the bed calling for her beloved Ted, why was everyone she loved leaving her where were they! Who would escort her to the funeral, it was always the sons or nephews.

It would have to be Teddy and Joe, they would need new suits. "Jean," "Mary" she hollered from the stairs "it'll ave'th be Teddy an Joe the'll av'ta ave new suits," "can't tha sort it out fer me!" "If my Ted were in'th grave he'd be spinnin now," added Ada. "Can anythin else go wrong," she muttered to anyone and everyone. "That bloody ittler'l bomb us in'th church that'll be next thing," "you mark my words." The two girls looked over at each other and shrugged their shoulders, yet another task to do would it never end.

It was always the womenfolk who where left with the lions share every time, the men sat back on there arses or went to the pub. Jean was hoping that Arthur wouldn't mind being left to look after Elizabeth Jean again, she had hardly seen her little girl since Ted had died. There was nothing she could do about it, the family needed her help and she would always do her very best come what may. Mary was about as much use as a wet paper bag she was traumatised by her own misfortunes and couldn't really cope.

However she tried her best, and Jean loved her for it. Although at times looking at the pair of them piping their eyes, and their pained expressions almost made her give up. Harry's wife Peggy had called with an offer of help but she had baby Harry and he needed breast feeding every couple of hours, so she would just be another dead leg as far as Jean was concerned. Various neighbours had offered help so maybe she could find them something to do, the windows wanted cleaning she wondered how many of them would volunteer to clean them not bloody many.

The pies , "Aunty how long ast pies bin inth oven," she hollered up the stairs . Ada could be heard thundering about overhead, then eventually thumping down the staircase. "they'll be black as chimney back, " she was moaning . " Jean open'th oven door lass see if owt can be rescued," the door was duly opened revealing two perfect pies. “He anna quite gidden up on us" she uttered looking skywards, not as you'd notice thought Jean. Mary was dispatched to search through the best of Teddy and Joe's suit's for the funeral, they would escort their Aunty following the hearse. They would be wearing the suit's they'd had last year for their Mam and Camy's burial, with Lizzie's help the trouser bottoms were taken down a bit.

They had both grown quite a lot in the twelve months, the sleeves were all right they had been a little long so fitted well now. The pressing was only just finished off when Jim came home, he wasn't very pleased to see Mary there. She felt very strange in his presence it had been a long time since she had lived at home, nearly done she told him wanting to be off as quick as possible. He gave her a withering look more at her slightly swollen stomach than anything else, he'd heard she was expecting her first. Well he wasn't interested let her get on with it always bloody crying and moaning, she could have done with a few lessons from Sal.

Now there was a woman you never heard her wailing and carrying one, she just got on with it . pity none of them took after there mother, mind you she was a one off was Sal what a woman. His throat constricted and he felt the tears welling up in his eyes, by God he missed her he would have given anything to find her waiting up for him. Mary watched him wondering what he was staring at, she jerked her head at Lizzie telling her to get off to bed before he started.

He was a strange animal was Jim Moore, with the habits off them to sometimes. The door clicked quietly and Jim came out of his reverie, he was alone they had both gone good riddance he thought to himself. The funeral was tomorrow he didn't want to go but old Ted hadn't been a bad old stick, he would pay his respects it was the least he could do. He often thought about how he would have managed without them when Sal had died, yes they hadn't deserted him when the chips were down.

Ada would have shed her fare share of tears, whatever he thought about her she loved her man he had been happy with her. Yes he would give her that she had given her man a warm comfortable home, good vitals, too good maybe. True he had to escape to his allotment but she never chastised him about it, all in all he'd been a happy man had Ted Harris. His lifestyle wouldn't have suited Jim but each to his own, he would go to the funeral stay a few minutes and then bugger off to the pub and make some inquiries about Meg.

That had been a big mistake taking in Ginny he knew he preferred Meg, but when the drink was in him and Ginny was rubbing her tits in his face and his dick was throbbing. There was nothing to be done until he'd used it on whichever was handy, he would look for Meg and they would have a good old time she would look after the kids. She liked kids so that wouldn't be a problem, she would cook and wash too yes he would find her. Everyone was up at the crack of dawn on the Tuesday morning there were still jobs to be done, the kids had a day off school and Joe was having half a day.

He didn't want to be hanging around all day long, funerals were sad occasions and the sooner it was over the better for every body. The flowers were the first things to arrive, they came in all colours and sizes little posies, sprays, small wreaths, large wreaths. The scent of them filled the air, it was a cold crisp morning and they probably wouldn't survive for many hours.

Which was a shame because they were very expensive this time of year, next was the hearse to bring Ted home for his final journey.

A trestle was erected and the coffin placed upon it , then surrounded by the family flowers. There was a huge cross that completely covered the coffin lid, it was from Ada every flower that Ted had loved was in it. The family were speechless when they saw it they had never seen the like before, Ada was to upset to write on the card so she dictated what she wanted to say to Jean and the tender loving message was then completed. The coffin was then opened up and everyone was urged to say their farewells to Ted Harris the youngsters were a little afraid and didn't know what to do.

However Ada gently coaxed them into touching his hand and saying good-bye, she didn't force them to kiss his face as she herself did. Well he was her beloved and he would never hurt her, they would understand themselves one day understand the pain and anguish. She didn't envy them what was to be but one day it would be upon them as sure as eggs were eggs, well that was in the future so it was best not to dwell on it.

Various members of the family were dispatched to the co-op tea rooms with the food, it was an awesome task there was enough food to feed the entire village. The family didn't want to stint they had been to weddings and funerals where the food had run out leaving guests without a crumb, it wasn't going to happen to them. Ted Harris would have the best send off they could afford, and folks would remember it for many a year to come. Ada wouldn't be short of a bob or two, they had always saved for a rainy day and not having children had meant that it was easier to save money when you hadn't got little mouths to feed.

Although they had always seemed to be feeding Sal's brood and clothing one or the other, but they had never begrudged the help they had given. The family had meant the world to herself and Ted and it would have been a poorer place without them, yes they had loved everyone of Sal and Jim's children like they were their own and wouldn't have had it any other way. Joe, Teddy Lizzie and Alex arrived at their Aunt's to be inspected it wasn't necessary they were a credit to the family, their Aunt beamed at them through her tears they would do her proud she knew.

People began to arrive and soon the little house was bursting at the seams, they had to stand outside. The street was filled with folks bending reading the condolence cards, they couldn't remember ever seeing so many flowers. It was the mark of the man Ted had been liked and respected by many people and he would be very much missed, not only by his own kith and kin. Numerous men and women filed into the house to pay there respects and remarked how good Ted was looking, Mary couldn't understand this she thought he looked awful white/grey face and the eyes not quite closed he looked ghastly to her she could hardly bear to look at him it wasn't the uncle she had known and loved.

At last the coffin lid was screwed down and Ted was born out onto the street and placed in the hearse, the top was filled to capacity with flowers from the family. Ada's cross on top of the coffin, she was escorted out of the house by Joe and Teddy dressed from head to toe in black. Her small plump body racked with sobs, one look at Ada and the whole of the female population of Bridgevale burst into tears. The large black Daimler backed up to the door and the uniformed driver leapt out, he swept open the passenger door and steered Ada and the two young men inside. The rest of the family and friends and neighbours followed behind having picked up their wreaths and sprays, they walked in sombre mood as the cortege wound it's way up to the churchyard.

The rest of the village gawked behind lace curtains or from front doorsteps, they'd never seen anything like it in all their years not even when Alderman Bentley had died and he was a bigwig. Polly Simmons looked out at the scene from her parlour window by hell what a fuss and to-do, she caught sight of Jean and Mary and hissed under her breath. Them buggers who did they think they were the telling off that Jean had given her warning her never to mention the night that her sister had tried to get rid of the baby. Well they could just go and piss in their hat she wasn't bothered about them or their threats, and what had Maggie Scully got to do with it that she would like to know too.

She would find out one way or another that was for sure, and then they could look out they would find Polly Simmons a very bad enemy. Big Jim Moore surveyed the whole show, well you live and learn the man was thought better of in death than he was in life. The sight of his family did nothing to move him, there was Jean her husband Arthur, Mary with Lizzie and Alex, Ada with Joe and Teddy, Ted's brother Albert and his snotty wife Minnie. Their son Alfred, and his wife Mildred. Their daughter Cicily her husband John, children Benjamin and Alice, they all knew about Jim and they looked on him with disdain, he couldn't give a damn he'd never set eyes on such a boring lot of bastards in his life.

Also he knew that Ted himself hadn't cared very much for them either, so he wasn't such a bad judge of character after all. The coffin was taken from the hearse and born towards the Church where it was placed onto a plinth, the mourners filed in behind it and it took quite a long time for the large congregation to be seated. The Very Reverend Booth welcomed them all to the celebration of the life of Edward Harris whose virtues he extolled for many a long time, they sang the hymn Jerusalem Ted's favourite which reduced Ada to floods of tears.

Joe and Teddy held her hands tightly as her little plump body buckled under her grief, the family held their breath and prayed her wind wasn't playing her up. However the Doctor had given her a potion to calm it down and all was well, the singing could be heard from one side of the village to the other from the foundry to the dark satanic mill. One of Ted's pals stood up in the pulpit to give a eulogy, he spoke of Ted the man loyal and trusted by one and all.

Ted the Soldier his bravery in the trenches who had saved many of his troop from certain death at the risk of his own, This was news to Ada and she wept anew her Ted the hero well she wasn't surprised not in the least she had married one in a million and thanked God for him. Her biggest regret was that the Lord had taken him away so suddenly; it would have been nice to have had him a little longer. The next hymn was Ada's favourite chosen with great care "THE OLD RUGGED CROSS" she would sing it when she was happy baking in the kitchen or cleaning the bedroom, Ted would listen and know all was well with the world well his and Ada's anyway.

This time all was not well but she had to put on a brave face for Ted's sake, she knew he was looking down on her so everything had to be right.. Everyone sang with great gusto and although Ada tried the words would not come out, they just seemed to stick in her throat. After yet another sermon by the Vicar which seamed to go on for ever the final hymn was played, it was The Lord's My Shepherd and it was the one hymn that both Ted and Ada liked very much.

They could harmonize together on this one very well, what with Ted's deep baritone and Ada's soft contralto. Ada felt a panic inside her she wanted to scream out loud wanted to run outside and look for Ted, to be reassured that he was there and her little world hadn't fallen apart. To be told that yes they would sing the hymn together again, and yes Ted was still here. Then why was she here dressed from head to toe in widows weeds, "get me outta er please" she begged of Joe and Teddy. They were dumbstruck not knowing what to do," old on Aunty we'st be out in a minute". They held on to her hand a little tighter and pulled her closer, and sure enough they were soon filing out of the church behind the coffin.

Joe had a quick word in his father's ear much to everyone's surprise and Jim Moore took his place at the graveside, Ada was unaware that Jim was holding her hand she was unaware of everything. As Ted's coffin was lowered into the ground Ada's grief was to much to bare and she sank to the ground in a dead faint, Jims strong arms were there to lift her up like she was a doll he loosened the buttons at the top of her dress and untied the ribbons on her bonnet.

Everyone rushed forward but there was no need he had done all that was required as soon as she came round Jim melted into the background so that she wouldn't know the last thing he wanted was gratitude. Everyone was muttering about the side of Jim Moore that he never showed there certainly was more to the man than met the eye, soon people were wending there way back down the hill towards the co-op tea rooms where everyone was invited.

They were in for a feast fit for a king it was the best spread folks had seen for a long time and they all tucked in, the only one who didn't turn up was Jim he couldn't be doin with it all he had shown his respects and that was that. After a glass or two of sherry Ada was less fraught and even managed a smile now and then, but it was a day that she would never forget. The saddest day of her life come to that, Ted and herself had often spoken about who might die first he was always adamant that he wanted to be the first to go. "I cuddna live wi-out thee Ada," he would almost whisper.

They didn't like to go on about it to much, well Ted had got his wish and Ada was left to get on with her life as best she could. One or two of Ted's old cronies started a sing song in the corner they had supped a pint or two, and were ready for a bit of a warble. They seamed to sing everyone of his favourites and Ada got more and more tearful and wished they would stop, however Bert Barlow Peggy's dad came over to Ada and asked her to join them in a chorus or two.

Although she protested strongly they won her over and soon she was singing along with the rest, and despite everything she enjoyed it and could have gone on all night and was sorry when everyone started to leave. She then decided to help the family to clear up the tearooms, they wanted her to go home and rest but she would have none of it and set too with great gusto.

When everything was cleared and packed away they sent the lads off with leftover food there were plenty of families who would be glad of it, da could imagine the look on Franny Withals face when they turned up at her door with half a ham on the bone and a basket of bread and cakes. That would keep her twelve kids fed for a day or two she could see them like vultures swooping down on the basket and it brought a smile to her sad old face.

Chapter Nine

Matthew Stakes His Claim

Harry was feeling miserable he should have been there at the funeral, he had tried his level best but with the visit home to see baby Harry so recent it had been impossible to get away again. How would his dear Aunty Ada be holding up, he knew she would be devastated at the loss of Uncle Ted. What a shock it had been when he had received the sad news, he couldn't imagine Bridgevale without him he was a one off was Ted. He could never be replaced, his eyes brimmed with unshed tears dear Uncle Ted who would have thought the last time he saw him would really be the last. Bye eck what a way to go having a crafty cigar in his allotment shed, and the bloody Grim Reaper waiting for him. Poor bugger all he wanted was a quiet life with his Ada, alas they would never see the like of him again. He was snapped out of his reverie by his mate Rob, "are we goin to the pub then or what" "oh reet let's go then " answered Harry. They dully set off "sorry mate I'm just thinkin o'th family back om what wi funeral an all," said Harry to his friend. "Don't worry about it pal it happens to us all sometime or other," they walked the rest of the way in silence neither of them knowing what to say to the other. The Griffin was warm and cosy and with the Christmas decorations looked very festive and inviting, the two ordered pints and searched for seats there were none so they leaned against the wall for support. Harry soon became aware of Pamela who was seated with a couple of her friends across the room, she hadn't seen him and she was totally relaxed she laughed out-loud and filled the room with her happiness. She was beautiful thought Harry that smile those perfect teeth, he shook himself mentally come on think about Peggy she had a beautiful smile too. Try as he might he couldn't get her out of his mind, she became aware of him and turned slowly. Their eyes met Harry felt a strange sensation run through his body the like of which he had never known, bloody hell what's up with me he wondered. He nodded hello towards her and quickly turned away not knowing what to do, Rob was quick to spot this and started to rib his mate about it. Harry changed the subject and noticing that a place was vacant at the domino game he hurried over to join in, it shut Rob up for a while and he was thankful for that he wanted a little time to compose himself. Although he was normally a very good player he couldn't concentrate and he was soon out off the game, he lost a couple of pence but it didn't matter he would win it back another night. Uncle Ted would have tutted about it had he been at the Goyt Inn back home, some of them were so good they could have played for England and their boast was they never lost a penny. When he left the table and looked around for Pamela she was gone, he felt quite put out at this and scanned the pub room by room but she had left without a word. What had he expected from her anyway she could do whatever she liked it was nothing to do with him, he didn't own her he only knew the magic had gone out of the place the minute she left it. "Let's go Rob" he said to his pal "I've had enough ferth neet," "I'm just having a game of darts Harry will you wait for me." Harry didn't want to hang around so he bade his pal goodnight and left the Griffin, he hadn't walked very far when he came across Pamela she was having words with some guy Harry didn't know. They seemed to be having a bit of a bull and cow but not shouting, I don't want to here anymore about it Pamela was saying to the soldier now leave me alone. With that she walked away and almost collided with Harry, "sorry" she almost snapped then noticed who it was. "I do apologize" "It's all reet no arm done"said Harry who couldn't believe his luck, he couldn't have timed it better if he'd tried. "dustha want any elp" he gave the soldier the gaze that back in Bridgvale would have sent Jack the Ripper scuttlin off home, however he couldn't see Harry too well in the gloom and didn't feel threatened by him. "She's not worth having pal " answered the man "good luck" and he turned on his heel and was lost in the autumn mist, "I must look like a tart lurking around in the dark accosting men." Pamela told him, he wanted to tell her that was the last thing he was thinking but he suddenly became tongue tied. He just stood staring at her for what seemed ages, she began to feel uncomfortable "I'll be off then " she said and turned to go." Hang on dunna go let me walk thee back" Harry fell into step beside her happy for the first time in days, this was where he wanted to be more than anything else in the world and he intended to make the most of every moment.

He couldn't contain himself he had to know who the man was so he made a feeble attempt at being diplomatic and failed miserably, " he was just asking me the time," Pamela told him. But he knew she wasn't being honest with him and after all it was none of his damn business, so he decided to let the matter drop for the time being. They both started to talk at the same time which made them laugh, then both of them said "after you" which set them off again. "thanks Harry this is my billet," she was saying goodnight before he had time to draw breath. As he stood with his mouth wide open she was gone, "bloody ell"he exclaimed out-loud. “What’s up mate didn't you get any" shouted a squaddie passing by, "never mind next time e'h "and he roared with laughter. Harry couldn't for the life of him see the funny side of it, all he knew was that he'd blown it and all the things he had wanted to ask her well all he could do was hope there would be a next time and soon. By the time he had reached his own quarters he was feeling full of remorse, reality had returned and thoughts of Peggy and young Harry filled his mind. What a bastard he was he didn't deserve them "Sorry Peg " he said aloud I wunna do it agin, he hoped he could keep his promise he had to the situation was hopeless he threw himself onto his bunk and lay there for what seemed an eternity trying to blot out the memory of Pamela What would the family think of him if they knew what a dirty rat he was, lusting after another woman when he had his Peggy she was the finest woman in the whole world and he didn't deserve her. He was turning into another Jim Moore and the thoughts of it made him shudder, anyone but him he didn't want to end up Jim the second not ever. He would keep himself to himself from now on stay faithful to his Peggy and be a good husband and father, with those thoughts he undressed and climbed into his lonely bed and tried to sleep

Pamela too was unable to sleep, every time she saw Harry Moore it became harder to turn away and pretend nothing was happening to her. She knew it was and there wasn't very much she could do about it, he filled her every waking moment and it was wrong she couldn't have him he was spoken for and she would have to get on with her life without him. The very next time they meet she would ignore him that would be best try to act nonchalant if she didn't encourage him then he would turn to someone else, that didn't make her feel better about the situation either she thumped her pillow and almost cried out in anguish "please let me be strong lord" she whispered.

Neither of them managed to get a lot of sleep that night, and by morning they were exhausted and snapped at everyone they came into contact with. None of their friends could understand what was wrong with them and put it down to the pressures of war, every day was filled with square bashing and map reading also tank driving and vehicle maintenance. Always lots to do until the evening time then they either pressed there uniforms or polished there shoes till they shone like glass, went to the pub or the NAAFI played cards, dominoes, or darts.

Harry decided to keep away from the Griffin that night he would write to Peggy and tell her how much he loved her and baby Harry, and urge her to hurry with a photograph of his son before he forgot what he looked like. He did love her very dearly the only trouble was that he wanted Pamela so much more, yes wanted her that was the difference he loved Peggy but lusted after Pamela. The upshot was he wanted to make love to his wife but wanted sex with the other, wanted it so bad he could think of little else it was becoming harder and harder to disguise his permanent hard on. Having spent considerable time on his letter to Peggy he decided to get it posted right away and made for the post box, which was situated just outside the NAAFI as he approached he could see that some kind of party was going on. He stood and gazed in through the window and there was Pamela with her arms around some officer hugging each other, he felt sick inside and turned away quickly and almost ran he was glad of his Peggy she wouldn't be gadding about with any man she could get her hands on thank God. He was almost back at his billet when he realised that he hadn't posted his letter, he scurried back and almost collided with Pamela he was going to say sorry but the words stuck in his throat. Instead he just ignored her and walked away she stood open mouthed not knowing what to say "Harry", she managed at last but he just kept going and went on his way. Pamela couldn't believe it the few times that she had meet Harry he had behaved impeccably, she knew she hadn't done anything to upset him so it must be it must be bad news from home or maybe he had been having trouble with someone in his platoon. It didn't make her feel any better and she made her way slowly back to her quarters, perhaps tomorrow he would be his usual self. She couldn't bear to think that he would never speak to her again, even though she had decided not to see too much of him not for his sake but for her own peace of mind and her sanity. Neither of them got much sleep that night and what little they did get was filled with strange dark dreams, the tannoy cut through their troubled sleep and both felt that they hadn't slept at all.

Harry was in a foul mood and couldn't be bothered to talk to anyone at all, his mates tried to rally round him but it was no use and they gave up and decided to leave him to get on with whatever was wrong with him. Harry decided to ask if he could go home for Christmas surely they could tell him that much he wasn't asking for the world, he knocked at the door of his C.O. after waiting for what seemed like an age he was ushered in. His C.O. made him aware immediately that his time wasn't to be wasted and snapped with impatience "come on man spit it out get on with it", Harry stammered out his request and thought the officer was going to have a fit as his face turned purple. "Jesus Christ is that all you think about you horrible little man," screeched his C,O," how long have you been here five bleedin minutes and all you ever want is leave," "leave to go here leave to go bloody there where will it end." He threw his hands in the air in a gesture of despair , and with eyes filled with hatred and venom dripping from every pore he beckoned Harry to come closer. "Do not I repeat do not ever cross my path again," "get out of hear and do not return at any cost there will be no leave for Santa's visit, or should the King call or the bloody Archbishop of bleedin Canterbury savvy." he almost fell over in his temper. Harry saluted quickly and almost ran out of the office; "thank you sir thank you" was all he could say. Once outside he breathed a sigh of relief thank God that was over, wonder what was the matter with him he thought to himself the silly bugger almost had a fit. Well that was that he wouldn't be going home for Christmas so he would get on with it , he smiled perhaps Pamela would be staying there too for Christmas he hoped so he knew he shouldn't but he hoped so.

Jim wasn't having such a good time either since Coral had left, he was bereft to say the least. One day he was fine the next nothing could go right for him and he made everyone's lives a misery, however they all understood and sympathized and hoped that he would come out of it in due course. Charles, Jack, Billy, and Roger all tried their very best and rallied round him, but Daphne on the other hand had lost her dear friend and confidant and she blamed Jim totally for this. Nothing that was said to her made the slightest difference she had been thwarted, and what galled her most was the fact that Coral had fallen for a nothing a simpleton why the man couldn't even speak properly. He was a country bumpkin what on earth had she seen in him, and him married too with a young child. The old saying while the cats away sprang to mind she wondered who would be next on his list, it wouldn't be her that was for sure let him dare come sniffing round and he would get a lashing of her tongue the very thought made her cringe. Of course she didn't know Jim and she would never want too, if she had taken the time she would have found him to be a caring loving man a man in great torment pulling himself apart to try to come to terms with his lot. Daphne was a snob and only her own well being concerned her everything else paled into insignificance, that anyone else might have an opinion would never occur to her such was she. Jim wouldn't have cared what Daphne thought she was at the bottom of his list anyway, he didn't care for spineless people or what their thoughts were. All he could think about was Coral where was she, did she miss him, Had she met someone else. The very meaning of it filled him with such pain he thought he would die, and what about Tilly his darling his young wife and their little girl. He loved them too so much they were never far from his thoughts, he never set out to hurt them and he hoped he never would.

He would get on with the job he had to do in this war and if he lived through it then he would return home to Bridgevale and his beloved family, he had been given one night with Coral and if that was to be all, then he would cherish the memory of it forever in his heart. If however they were thrown together at some time in the future he couldn't promise not to want her in his bed again. The lads were waiting for him to go to the pub so he trudged of after them, they were doing their best to help him bless them all so he tried his hardest to meet them half way which wasn't easy when your heart was aching. He looked around the pub hoping he might catch sight of a beautiful girl with auburn hair but there were none and his heart sank again, whose for a game of doms he shouted too loud perhaps everyone looked up. Not many noticed the tears that were lying unshed in his large blue eyes, one or two of his mates did Charles thumped him on the back, " well done old man well done "he whispered "you'll come through it mark my word by jove." Jim played like a demon and won every game and he drowned his sorrows with pint after pint of beer, he was counting his winnings he'd done very well he punched the air" Uncle Ted will be proud o me "he shouted out. The realization of what he had said suddenly hit him and he stopped dead in his tracks, Uncle Ted had died it was his funeral today and he had been wallowing in his own self pity to the effect that he had forgotten. Jim was consumed with shame he'd never had a thought for Aunty Ada and what she was going through or the rest of his family, he couldn't believe his callousness and he collapsed in a flood of tears. The other customers paid little heed to him there was always someone pissed and feeling sorry for themselves there was a war on and feelings often ran high he would get over it he would have to. Charles and the gang carried Jim back to the billet and almost threw him onto the bed he had kicked and struggled all the way and their patience was wearing a little thin, "come on old boy" urged Charles" lets get your togs off," but Jim was still feeling belligerent and totally refused to Co-operate-operate so they left him to his own devises and got on with their own ablutions. They were all in the shower when young Timothy Osborne came in to tell them that Jim was throwing up all over the place, others were wanting him to be thrown into the glasshouse. With towels hastily draped around their waists they descended on the sickly Jim Moore he was in a mess, "right let's get him in the shower clothes and all" said Charles. So it was all hands on deck and the poor wretched man was bundled into the shower still dressed in his uniform, once the vomit had been removed they undressed him and in no time at all they had him dried off and into a clean bed. Tim hung his uniform on the pipes and hoped for the best he couldn't just leave it lying on the shower room floor, he wondered what had happened to make Jim go off like this he was always such an agreeable chap one of the nicest in the regiment. He had heard that Jim's Uncle had passed away but even so one didn't kick up such a stink, he wasn't aware of Coral and the repercussions that Jim had been trying to cope with. Lights out were called and they were plunged into darkness they had only just made it in the nick of time everyone hoped that Jim would sleep and that they could get some piece. Jim had however sobered up somewhat in the shower and was feeling pretty much ashamed of himself and knew that wild horses wouldn't drag another sound out off him, he cursed himself and decided that it was time he grew up and behaved like a man he would put the past behind him and get on with whatever life was left to him because in times of war nothing was certain.

It would soon be Christmas and it would be the first time he had been away from his family and also the first for his Aunty Ada without her beloved Ted , he wondered how she would cope he knew that she would be grief stricken. The rest of the family would rally round her and help her all they could he knew that much perhaps his little Sally Victoria would be a tower of strength for her, sometimes children could be a boon at times like those. He wondered how the funeral had progressed it would have been a very sad affair, and knowing his Aunty it would be followed by a lavish spread even if there was a war on.

Tomorrow he would buy two cards one for Tilly and Sally to wish them a merry Christmas and the other would be a bereavement card to let his dearest Aunty know that he was thinking about her, with these thoughts he drifted of to sleep much to the delight of every one in his billet.

Coral was having trouble getting off to sleep she was home on Christmas leave with her mother and sisters, she had tagged along to every party they had attended and even though she was bored rigid she had to get out to stop herself thinking about Jim Moore. The heartache was still there she missed him so very much and longed for him daily and more so nightly, when her body ached for his touch. In her mind she would retrace every step she took that last night with him from beginning to end over and over again, the sexual joy and pleasure that she had felt until she was a shuddering wreck. Often she would cry out for him at her height of passion and her family were left to wonder what had happened to her to cause her such heartache, she hadn't been able to disguise her heartache from them much as she had tried but they wouldn't dream of questioning her it wasn't there style she would tell them when she was good and ready. Deborah wasn't all that bothered really she was having man trouble herself and couldn't handle anyone else's problems; Frances was a little more sympathetic and did her best to help her sister through the bad patch. Knowing her sister wasn't an easy target for men it had to be something really special that had happened to her, whatever it was it had hit her very hard and she was suffering greatly because of it. The family didn't pry it was their motto never pry into other peoples lives and hope they reciprocate, anyway time was a great healer she knew that from personal experience she had lost count of the many times that she had been in love or rather thought she was. Gloria was fed up with her daughters miserable face but she wouldn't be home long just a few days over Christmas and then off again so she would try to put up with her until then, nothing was going to spoil her festive mood she had her sights set on a gorgeous creature who had just moved into the district. He was all teeth and eyes and she couldn't wait to get into his trousers she almost drooled at the thought of it, he was probably very large down below oh God she hoped he was it had been an age since she had felt a decent sized dick and the thoughts of it kept her going. Roll on Christmas then she had a good excuse to get him over to the house to one of her famous party's, then if everything worked according to plan she would have him for dinner, supper and breakfast. Yes he was going to be a very happy man and she would be an even happier woman, very sore hopefully but very very happy. The invitations must be sent off right away she didn't want anyone else getting in, have him first was her motto then everyone else could have a go just so long as she got first fuck. There would have to be plenty of booze and oodles of food to keep everyone happy, they would have to enlist the help of the local girls they were always willing to work for a fare price. Deborah and Frances would invite their friends but Coral would be too crestfallen to bother with anyone, still she might meet up with someone on the night stranger things had happened one could only hope.

Crestfallen was the understatement of the year as far as Coral was concerned, she was utterly devastated how could she go on every day was sheer torment. Jim where are you she wanted to shout out loud to scream, would this hurt inside her ever go away. Perhaps if she wrote to Daphne and asked for news of Jim, but she hated Jim so maybe that wasn't such a good idea and she had been particularly miffed that Coral had asked for a transfer without even consulting her. Whatever was she to do, she would ask her over to Mothers party yes that was a good idea once she arrived

Coral would be able to get the news out of her. On the other hand Daphne might well be going home for Christmas, there was only one way to find out get writing. So letters were duly sent off both from Coral and her mother and sisters, each eagerly awaiting a reply. Gloria had ascertained the name of the new man and a little about him, he was Matthew Spencer recently widowed, age forty two he was something big at the ministry by all accounts someone going places if all was to be believed . A few days later reply's began to arrive they were snatched up off the mat before they had time to fall, each new day brought another acceptance and at last the one from Daphne arrived. Coral could barely open it she was all fingers and thumbs, at first it was full of admonishments for clearing of so fast but then Daphne assured her that she would be delighted to stay for a few days over Christmas and looked forward to meeting Coral at the station on the twenty forth at two thirty in the afternoon. Coral was ecstatic soon she would know all about Jim Moore and what if anything he had been getting up to, the rest of the family couldn't fail to notice the change in her and thanked the lord for it. It had to be the man she was pinning for, they wouldn't have to worry anymore so that was good it let everyone get on with there tasks there was still so much to do. Matthew Spencer also replied to the effect that he would be happy to accept their kind invitation, not as happy as I will be thought Gloria not half as happy.

All was ready at last it was Christmas eve and after much preparation they could all sit back and relax, the tree stood resplendent in the lounge looking magnificent festooned from top to toe with every conceivable bauble imaginable. Every lamp and light fitting was covered with a deep pink scarf or cloth to tone the brightness down and cast a warm glow, complexions were shown to be infinitely softer and more appealing. It was getting dark already and it was only just after two o'clock Coral was preparing to meet Daffers at the railway station her tummy was doing somersaults she felt physically sick, what have I done she moaned to herself she just knew it was going to be a disaster she didn't want Daffers there at all why in hell's name had she asked her to come it was only to find out about Jim Moore that was all. But she had left him transferred to another unit for God's sake just to get away from him so why was she wanting to know, her mother was calling to her asking if she required the use of the car to go to the station so she ran downstairs to pick up the keys. There was the third degree to go into first of all about the petrol, then not driving too fast and thirdly not to smoke in the wretched thing. which was ludicrous as she had never smoked in her life, then the ceremonial keys were duly handed over and after shout's of do be careful with it she was of. It was the car her mother was going on about not Coral, the car was the most important thing it was her gateway to freedom.

The train was on time a few passengers filtered off and for one moment Coral's heart leapt perhaps she wasn't on it, but no there she was trilling away to some poor unsuspecting fool sashaying down the platform flashing a well turned ankle. Cooee darling she trilled to Coral and immediately flung her arms around her, the poor chap she was waffling to turned out to be the person she had elected to carry her suitcase for her they didn't stand a chance when Daffers turned on the charm. The journey back to the house was a nightmare Daphne didn't pause to draw breath, Coral couldn't get a word in edgeways and as soon as they stepped over the threshold she started again to Coral's mother and sisters. Coral managed to escape and fled up to her room thank god that they weren't sharing at least she would be able to get some peace up there away from her, anyway the party would be starting in a few hours so there would be plenty of people for her to chat too.

Coral busied herself getting ready she wasn't really bothered about her appearance there wouldn't be anyone there to look her best for, nevertheless one didn't attend mothers party's looking like something the cat dragged in. Lying in the bath day dreaming about Jim Moore her peace was shattered by the sound of banging and shouting, it was Daffers begging to be let in, she had only just arrived and already Coral was heartily sick of her. She wanted to shout out piss off but it wouldn't have been very nice of her after all she had invited her to stay for Christmas so she would just have to grin and bare it, so Daphne took over the bathroom and Coral went of to dry her hair berating herself for bringing the wretched girl down there. It was funny really when they were stationed together they were really good mates but now Coral couldn't stand the sight of her former friend and could only hope that the time would pass quickly and Daffers would be gone, she made a mental note never to invite her again. The party was in full swing when Matthew Spencer arrived Gloria swept to his side like a vulture ready to eat his prey, he felt a little alarmed at the boldness of the woman and made his mind up there and then that he wouldn't tarry long . However upon being introduced to the family he quickly changed his mind, he looked into the eyes of the beautiful Coral and he was a goner, to say it was love at first sight wasn't far wrong he almost groaned aloud. He couldn't believe it when she made a feeble excuse and almost ran off, his eyes scoured the room for sight of her and this thing was pulling at his arm gazing into his face and almost mauling him to death. Gloria paraded him around like a prize bull and he was heartily sick of it, he made an excuse to go to the bathroom and almost had to prize himself away from the dreadful woman. Gloria offered to go with him to hold anything that might need holding, nudge, nudge, wink, wink, followed by raucous laughter, he might have gone home under normal circumstances but he had to see Coral again he must find her he made his way up the stairs and unashamedly looked in every room. The bathroom on the top floor was locked and he called out to whoever was within to vacate the room as soon as possible, after several minutes Coral emerged and Matthew's heart leapt in his chest. Her eyes were red with weeping and it took all his strength not to gather her up in his arms and hold her close to him," can I talk to you "he asked her shyly. Coral replied that she wasn't really in the mood for talking and made to go down the stairs, "please" he implored her" I must speak with you I really must" Coral was puzzled by this and agreed to stay awhile. Matthew was having trouble with his voice one second it was gone, the next he sounded like a strangled duck. " Forgive me for being so forward " he managed to say, "it's just that I er um " he was drowning , his eyes were pleading with her to help him. " It's alright relax please," trying to suppress her laughter. "it can't be that bad can it," her eyes twinkled as the light held on to her tears. Matthew marvelled at her, here she was in tears yet still caring enough to show compassion for his distress, he looked deep into her beautiful blue eyes and wanted to die right there and then.

"We have been introduced haven't we" he stated, "so I hope you wont think me rude and arrogant". "Oh no certainly not", replied Coral "please continue," " Coral" he murmured he made the name sound sensual and something stirred deep down inside her. "Please don't think ill of me it's just that," he continued to struggle for words. "Something wonderful happened to me the moment I saw you," he noted the hostile look that she gave him. "Please don't look at me like that," he implored "I know it sounds pretty pathetic but it is true I assure you." He continued to gaze into her eyes and much as she tried she just couldn't lay into him and tell him to drop dead or slap his face, they stood face to face for what seemed an eternity, then suddenly she didn't know how , they were in each others arms and she was enjoying the most delicious kiss. It started slowly at first then got deeper and deeper until she though she would pass out, his tongue was licking her's it was thee most sensual feeling a hotness swept over her, the last time she had felt like this was when she was with Jim.. realization dawned and she pulled herself away he tried to pull her back , "no no no" she cried out" please let me go," he moaned deeply and unwillingly let her go. "I'm sorry" he muttered "I didn't mean to distress you in any way please forgive me Coral," "It was my fault as well as yours" answered Coral and walked away quickly. Matthew wanted to run after her and beg her to stay, but he knew that it was futile there was always tomorrow that was sure, the way that she had kissed him back told him that much, he knew it wasn't a lost cause. With that knowledge he could face another day yes tomorrow was another day and he would fight for her by hell he would and he would win.

Chapter Ten

Croeso y Cymru

Ginny was felling really fed up she was missing Jim, there was no-one to match him in-between the sheets and her loins were aching for a really good shagging. The family were kindness itself but she hadn't met anyone who came up to Jim's standards, and they expected her to go to Chapel all the time and her not being religious well it went against the grain. She had been staying with her cousin Gwen in Lwynhendy, Llanelli, it was a small town but with quite a bit of industry, plenty of work for those who wanted it. The colliery's were all around too and most of the men worked down the pit, it was backbreaking work and the men looked done in when they made their weary way up to the surface. After they had coughed their guts up and tried to wash of the worst of the coal dust, all they wanted was a warm bed to crawl into and to sleep till their next shift. The wives would try to keep the rest of the family quiet as best they could, but if the kids were noisy and they woke up their Dad well out came the thick leather belt and God help them. He would show no mercy, and they would lie on their beds hoping that the draught from the window would cool the welts on their backs.

It was a hard life but at the weekends the men folk would let their hair down and have a damned good time, and the singing it had to be heard to be believed. The men had voices like angels and you would have had to be made of stone not to be moved by them, everyone would join in the rousing chorus and even Ginny would shed a tear and try to join in although her voice could be likened to a corncrake. She had decided to move on from Gwen's and visit her second cousin Di Evans in Haverfordwest, but first of all she would have to say hello to her Aunt Selena who lived in Locher a couple of miles away and some distant relative in nearby Gorsinion . The families held great store from a visit by relatives and it wasn't the done thing to exclude them or woe betide you, duty had to be done at whatever cost Ginny didn't want the witches curse on her and many believed in them. So it was that on a cold wintry morning Ginny said her good-byes to Gwen and the family, and traipsed of to the bus stop lugging her large suitcase which almost dragged her down to the pavement. One or two people she had gotten aquatinted with shouted their good-bye's and wished her a merry Christmas, the bus arrived and it was almost full to bursting although room was made for her next to a huge woman carrying a whopping great turkey. The bird had been dressed and looked vulgar in it's nakedness, Ginny tried not to stare at it or the woman either but she couldn't help herself and every now and then their eyes meet. The woman began to shout rather loudly to someone sitting at the front of the bus, it was all in Welsh so Ginny couldn't understand a word of it but she had the distinct impression that it was directed at herself. Let em piss off she thought they were ignorant buggers, she would have mouthed off but for the fact that she was alone and there were many of them. However she made a mental note that if she saw the fat cow again she would slap her fat face for her or her name wasn't Ginny Wilkinson, her mind drifted on to thoughts of Jim Moore she would have to go back to Bridgevale soon or she would loose him and she couldn't bear the thought of that. He was one hell of a stud was Jim and once more her body ached for contact with him, she would have to find someone to give her a right good seeing too before she exploded from wanting it so bad. The old bus shuddered to a standstill and after much heaving Ginny was standing at the bus-stop looking fed up and lost, it had been many years since she had visited her old Aunt Selena and she had forgotten her way to the house. She closed her eyes and tried to remember way back when she had gotten of the bus with her mother which route she had taken, soon she had a picture in her mind and yes she could remember the way. The tiny cottage looked just as she remembered it gleaming windows, scrubbed front step , tidy garden , the womenfolk prided themselves on there cleanliness. Every house would be spotless clean even if the pit was next door to them, her knock at the door was answered by a young lad and on listening to her explanation of who she was he led her through the house to the back kitchen. Her Aunt sat before a roaring fire, if there was one thing they had in abundance in Wales it was coal. The old girl looked up" who is it" she asked "it's your niece Ginny from England," answered the lad, he made her sound like a foreigner silly bugger thought Ginny. " Hello Aunty how are you " she called to the old girl Selena looked her up and down and answered back in a lovely lilting Welsh accent "very nice to see you my dear " "you'll be one of Myfanwy daughters " she waited for a response. "That's right Aunty I promised Mam that I would call one day when I was visiting," "she died didn't she " asked

Selena . "Yes eight years ago next month the twenty sixth," "I'll be eighty nine next year " said her Aunt she loved to tell everyone "and it's not because of a blameless life either I've supped many a glass of ale, smoked all my life, had one or two lovers." She began to cackle and almost choked at the memory of it all, Ginny took stock of her Aunt she was still a very handsome woman she had been a beauty in her youth the family used to tell stories about her love life, her Aunt was saying "your mother was always a bit of a fast one if I remember rightly " "no Aunty not me Mam she were very quiet," "it were me Aunty Jess she were man mad me Mam always used to say." "That's right my dear I remember now Jess she was a wild one and no mistake, whatever happened to the girl." "Well we don't know Mam said she went of with the gypsies years ago we did try to find her when Mam died but it were useless," Selena was watching the young woman carefully weighing her up she'd heard that Ginny was a bit of a tart who drifted from one man to another in rapid succession. She liked a girl with guts but there was a difference between a tramp and a good sort, her brother Arfon Ginny's father had been a wild one too, much as she loved him she couldn't tame him nor could the rest of the family. They had given him too much rope when he was a young lad and he almost hanged himself many times, after one particularly bad incident he had run off to England to escape the law and while in search of work in Nottingham he was followed by Myfanwy who he had left behind pregnant in Llocher they had gotten married. And despite moving up and down the country and having three more children Arfon left her for some floozy he'd picked up in a bar, the penniless family had thumbed rides all the way back home and had stayed with Myfanwys family for a couple of years. That was until they had word that Arfon wanted his wife back again so the silly woman went back to him dragging the kids with her, he was ill by this time to much booze had rotted his guts and he was in constant pain. He berated his wife and children from dawn till dusk and they hated his guts for it, but his wife brought up to believe that marriage was for better or worse till death do us part refused to leave his side. In the end she followed him quickly to the graveyard and didn't have a penny to leave to the four kids, Ginny being the eldest at twelve ran away when she found out that they were to be put into care it wasn't for her the bloody workhouse or someone's punch bag she'd had enough of that thank you very much. You had to be cunning and devious, light fingered too and quick on your feet, and she was all these and more, much more. She'd gotten into a few scrapes and had finally ended up in Bridgevale and meet Jim Moore and he was the man she wanted more than anyone else she'd ever known, and she was determined to have him come what may but not his bloody family they would have to go where she didn't know but they would definitely have to go somewhere.

The more she talked the more Selena disliked her she didn't know why but there was something rotten about the girl and Selena would be glad to see the back of her, there was something about her eyes they were to close together they reminded her of a hyena she shuddered like someone had walked over her grave. "You'll be taking your leave of us then," she inquired to Ginny "we'll be having tea soon". It was her dismissal and she felt stupid, "yes right then I'll be off it was nice to see you Aunt Selena" she didn't mean it and vowed she wouldn't be back, her Aunt nodded but couldn't bring herself to return the compliment. The young lad saw her to the door and without a word shut it behind her, Ginny stood for a while bloody hell she thought what a way to treat visiting relatives she has come out of her way to visit the old cow and not even a cup of tea, well she could piss up her leg this would be the last time she would be visiting this part of the world. There was a long wait for the bus and Ginny was just about pissed off by the time it arrived

She decided to forgo Gorsinon and travel on to Haverfordwest she might get a better welcome there and if she didn't then they could all go and jump over a bloody cliff, she couldn't care less she was becoming very despondent with the South Wales contingent .the bus took the scenic coastal route and Ginny sat back and enjoyed the beautiful view, the wide sweep of Swansea Bay the Mumbles, Oxwitch Bay, Port Inon in the distance. By the side of the road at tables beautifully set out on snow white clothes sat the cockle women, resplendent in their welsh national costumes. They toiled from the crack of dawn to find the cockles in the sand, dangerous work at the best of times. Then they were washed and set out to be sold to make enough to feed there family's, even so there was never enough to go round after all their toil. Later on it was the beauty of Saundersfoot as yet unspoiled God she could live there no problem it was a dream, soon she was sleeping and didn't waken till they had reached Haverfordwest she was startled out of her sleep by the driver shouting and balling there was no need for it and she wanted to tell him so in no uncertain terms but bit her tongue for the second time in as many days. Having lumbered of the bus with her heavy suitcase she then had to ask the way to her cousin Di's place it was well past midnight and pitch black all the street lamps were out because the black out law was in-force, there didn't appear to be anyone around they had disappeared like bloody cockroaches. The bus driver was off too and try as she might he wouldn't stop and help her, "you bastard "she shouted after him "you bloody bastard" she set forth with a string of obscenities at the man he wouldn't be able to hear her but she had to vent her rage onto someone. A sound behind her made her jump out of her skin, someone cleared their throat. "Who's there" she asked, the figure revealed itself it was a Policeman. "And what have we here a fishwife" he inquired, "are you aware that it's after midnight" he asked her "and language like that is not tolerated around these parts not even from a man". Ginny was far from caring what the bloody daft copper thought about her, but she knew that she would have to be careful and pretend remorse. " I'm so sorry officer I was so frightened of the dark I panic't " she responded and tried to manage a few tears but couldn't quite squeeze any out. "You'll be best coming down to the station with me and we can sort you out" he told her in a manner not to be argued with, so she followed in the dark like a silly school child. She was fuming inside, the bastard could have helped with her luggage it was damned heavy and more than once she almost fell over it. At last they arrived at the small police station and she was glad to get into the warmth it was freezing outside. "Take a seat" the officer told her and she gladly did so, he asked her various questions and after being told the name of the person she had come to see he was a little putout. He had removed his helmet by this time and Ginny felt a ripple of excitement run through her whole body, he was gorgeous six foot something and my was he handsome. "Well well" he said and something in Welsh which she couldn't understand then he began to chuckle, Ginny was furious she didn't enjoy being laughed at "don't mind me "she told him sarcastically. He stopped laughing at once and simply stared at her until she blushed deep red, at last he put her out of her misery. "I'll be taking you to your cousins house then," and he opened the door before picking up her suitcase. "Oh and by the way my names Di Evans your second cousin," he emphasized the second. Ginny's mouth dropped open that wide you could have fitted your suitcase in it, well that was it she wasn't going to stay there, her cousin a bloody flatfoot no way in the world. "Mam will put you up for a while that is if you won't be staying very long "he told her "we haven't the room for anyone to stay long term if you get my meaning. Yes she got his bloody meaning the bloody piss-ant she wouldn't be staying long that was sure, she followed on behind him her mind in a turmoil she would have to get back to Jim as soon as possible the good time she had been expecting wasn't happening at all and she very much doubted it would. The tiny cottage he took her to was warm and spotless clean but she didn't feel any welcome in it his mother her great Aunt was in bed by this time but she was awake and shouted to Di asking why he was home and who was with him, he went up to tell her and there were lots of mutterings. At last her great Aunt came down the stairs to greet her if you could call it that," Why didn't you let us know that you where visiting my girl "she almost shouted at Ginny who shrank away into a corner. " I'm sorry Aunty I meant to really I did," "never mind we will have to make the best of it for now" she set about lugging blankets and pillows into the small parlour. Ginny took in the tiny wiry frame that was her great Aunt small she may be but she looked as strong as a horse," I'll have to be off now Mam" shouted Di and with a nod good-night he was gone. "God love you "shouted back his Mother "Bless him "he's a good lad the best a Mother could ever wish for." I bet he is thought Ginny to herself bloody well bound to be, salt of the bloody earth the sun rises at the sight of his arse Christ all bloody mighty what on earth had made her come here. She wanted a piss but she would have to ask the old bag where the cludgy was, she steeled herself " excuse me for asking Aunty but I need the lavatory" the old girl shrugged her shoulders in dismay "it's tryin to make you a bed up I am "she answered. Then she almost ran past Ginny into the kitchen muttering as she went then a lighted candle was thrust into her hands, "it's out there down the garden" she almost spat out. The back door was opened and she was herded outside and the door shut tightly behind her, the candle blew out immediately and she was enveloped in pitch blackness. She wanted to scream out loud but she couldn't give the old boot the pleasure of it, so she squared her shoulders and stuck out her chest I'll show the old cow thought Ginny that I will. In the darkness she could make-out the silhouette of a small building so she ventured forth slowly one step at a time, she had to grit her teeth her guts was full of pittle and if she didn't go soon she would piss her pants for sure. She didn't remember what happened next all she knew was that she was sitting on the ground in a pool of her own piss, with hens squawking and flapping all around her making enough noise to waken the dead. In no time at all it seemed the whole bloody neighbourhood was out with torches and lamps to survey her plight, Ginny hung her head in shame anyone else would have cried but not Ginny she was as hard and tough as steel she wouldn't cry never. If she were to turn on the waterworks it would be to her own advantage nothing more, the villagers where having a right old time at her expense and to add insult to injury they were speaking in Welsh and she couldn't understand one single word. As she lay in her uncomfortable bed in what was left of the night she was busy plotting, she would hurt the old cow by God she would some way that would cut her to the quick.

It hadn't helped that Di had turned up to see her sat in her own piss, he didn't laugh but she could see the look of distaste on his face. I'll have him she promised herself the bloody sanctimonious bastard, she had meant to leave the next day but she would hang on a day or too more until she had her revenge then and only then would she leave.

Ginny was sweetness and light sugar and spice, butter wouldn't melt, she tiptoed around like the good fairy anything that dear Aunty Blod wanted dear Aunty Blod would have. Blod wasn't taken in by Ginny but she let her think she was, the jungle drums had been very busy since she had descended on an unsuspecting Wales. However they were quick to learn and her appalling behaviour since her arrival was not going to be tolerated, she had tried to bed every male she had come into contact with but none would take her on not even the village idiot. Talk about a laughing stock, but the only one who didn't know was Ginny herself. Cousin Di however was trying to be fare he tried not to listen to village gossip and being the law enforcement officer tried to detach himself from such, he wasn't aware that every time he was around Ginny alone and she flashed a well turned ankle or a little bosom it was anything other than planned. She had gotten him to take her out to the pub one night and she had been on her very best behaviour showing a side to herself that was totally unnatural, he however was taken in by it and admonished his mother who flew into a terrible rage. " Why can't you live and let live Mam he begged her she'll be off home as soon as Christmas is over," his Mother let rip with a stream of Welsh unfit for the ears of children. Di knew there was no talking to her when she was in this mood so he sauntered off to the bar and ordered another pint, Ginny was talking to some men she had just met and was all giggly like a school girl pretending to be shy and innocent. But if she could have had her way her knickers would have been of and she would have been straddling one of them over the table, God she groaned to herself if I don't get some dick soon I'm bloody well going to explode she was desperate for it could think of little else what a bloody life without it. However she had a plan, when they returned to the cottage she put on the milk for the bedtime drink that they had every night and insisted that her Aunt relax she'd had a few and knowing that she had sung Mafanwy with excellence and been applauded all night long on the strength of it she was more than happy, Blod knew she had a fine voice one of the best in the valley but constantly needed reassurance. Ginny brought in the nightcap," I've put in a little brandy Aunty not much just enough". "Enough for what girl" asked Blod "well to help you sleep that's all" added Ginny. "Why do I need help to sleep?" said Blod Ginny couldn't be bothered to answer, get it down your stupid old throat she wanted to shout at her Aunt, Blod took a swig and almost choked it was well and truly laced. It was damned good too and she drank every drop, "I'll bid you goodnight then and a merry Christmas."

Ginny had almost forgotten it was Christmas Eve and bade her Aunt the seasons greetings, Di kissed his Mother and wished her a merry Christmas too. She told him not to be to long before he went to bed himself, Ginny winced at this him a grown man why didn't he tell her to piss off bloody mammies boy. Ginny handed Di his brandy laced milk and waited for him to down it, when he had done so she offered him another which he refused "well goodnight then Ginny merry Christmas "she wished him the same and he was gone. For the next hour she sat patiently and then she started to undress, for a while she admired her body in the looking glass yes she had a good figure and she would be using it for seduction very soon. Her most scanty see-through black nightie was all that was required then up the stairs she crept as quietly as she could, the bedroom door squeaked a little but she was inside in a flash and in Di's bed even quicker. The drink had slowed his reflexes down and he murmured sleepily something unintelligible, Ginny began to kiss his neck softly and stroke him gently he began to resist but she silenced his mouth with her own and all the time caressing his limp dick. However it didn't remain limp for very long and then she began to wonder if it would ever stop growing, in seconds his mouth had sought her breast and he sucked so hard on her nipple she almost screamed out with pain. Ginny straddled him quickly and the feeling of him entering her was a joy almost to much to bear, Di's hands gripped her buttocks and drew her down even harder onto his shaft. They quickly got a rhythm going and Ginny was ready to explode with pleasure God it was so good she had waited weeks for this it didn't matter that he was her second cousin, or that she didn't particularly care about the man it was sex and it was good and it was what her body craved. Suddenly she felt a blow on her head and then another followed by a scream and a cursing like she had never heard before it was Blod she was trying to pull Ginny off her son and Ginny was trying to hang on. However nature took its course and the dick was limp once more and slid out of her, and what with him trying to push her off and Blod pulling her there was only one way to go and she hit the bedroom floor with an almighty thud. Blod was going in for the kill and rained blow after blow upon her at last Di had hold of his Mother and led her away to her own room, Ginny was well and truly pissed off and gathering herself together she sloped of down the stairs to the parlour. Blod was still ranting and raving and the names she was calling Ginny were terrible to hear, after what seemed like an eternity Di walked into her room. "I think you had better keep out off Mam's way for the rest of your stay Ginny let her settle down," "I'm off first thing " muttered Ginny "so you needn't worry " "Its Christmas day tomorrow there wont be any public transport so you'll have to stay and probably Boxing day too." answered Di and with a shrug of his shoulders he made for the door then added "pity Mam couldn't have left us for just a few seconds longer" then he was gone, so he was as pissed off about it as she was he had wanted it probably as bad as she had it made her feel better. Perhaps they would get another chance to finish off what they had started, she wondered if there was a large carrot in the house she could use one right now. Her laughter filled the room the old bag would come in and take it off her if she thought she was enjoying herself.

Chapter Eleven

Fred Tries His Hand

Jean knocked loudly on Mary's front door, there was no answer but Jean knew for certain that her sister was at home. She shouted through the letterbox "I knows that in our Mary so stop playin silly buggers an open'th door," after a few moments the door opened an inch and Mary peered out. Her hair was lank and greasy and hung around her face like a tasselled cover, her once large clear eyes were dull and lifeless, appearance unkempt.

"What dos't want" she demanded rudely, Jean was taken aback. "Dunna you talk to me like that our Mary an bloody well let me in now", she demanded, her sister reluctantly opened the door and stood back to let her enter. "Right let's be avin it" asked Jean "ast'tha seen thee arse or summat",

Mary made her way to the kitchen and sat down at the table folding her arms and continued to look belligerent, Jean's gaze swept round the room it was untidy, dust was gathering in every corner and it didn't smell to sweet either. Mary had always been so house-proud her little home had always been kept spotless she had always loved to keep it immaculate.

"I dunna want to talk about owt just leave me alone our Jean", mumbled her sister. "But tha canna keep it all bottled inside thee thas got to let it out lass come on it's non like thee",

Well give me summat that'll get rid o this bastard I'm carryin an I'll be alreet agen". Snarled Mary" that's only thing that'll put things right."

Jean gave a huge sigh what was she going to do with this sister of hers, she had never seen such a change in anyone before. Everyone had put it down to her condition it took some woman that way they said, everyone was different no-one ever the same. Thank God that Brian wasn't there to witness any of it what would he have said or done,

"Mary please try, you've got to for Brian's sake if no-one else's." "let me help you to clean up" she urged. "Oh me ouse is dirty now is it" demanded Mary in a rage now. She jumped up and headed for the stairs, "clean the bugger then do what tha want's an then piss off."

Jean began to weep what a bloody carry on, she was only trying to help her sister. They had always been so close had always loved each other so dearly. Mary turned at the top of the stairs and her heart lurched inside her, what was she doing, how could she behave towards her dear sister like this when she was only trying to help.

She ran back down the stairs and threw her arms around the weeping Jean, "I'm that sorry our Jean please forgive me she begged." They held onto each other and wept together quietly, when they had dried there tears and gathered themselves they put the kettle on and made a pot of tea. Mary realized that come what may she would have to go through the pregnancy and make the best of the situation, for her baby and her husband. With Jean's help they cleaned up the house then went out to buy her shopping and call on Aunty Ada who still needed there help and support.

It had been three months since Ted's demise but the pain in Ada's heart was just as intense, and she missed him more every day that dawned. Getting up in the morning and existing was all that she could do, and it would have been her choice to join Ted as soon as possible if it were left to her. Besides there were Sal's kids to think about, and Mary who had made such a bloody mess of her life they needed her help and being Ada she couldn't let them down.

Jean knocked softly on the door and swept inside followed by Mary, they greeted their Aunty with a hug and kiss. Ada felt the thin bony frame belonging to the pregnant Mary and her heart thudded in her chest, dear God the girl was wasting away, she should be bonny now and as fit as a flea.

She held her at arms length and looked into her face, the sight of her reduced her Aunty to tears of despair. Jean put the kettle on and got her Aunty busy in the kitchen, and chastised Mary for upsetting there dear Aunty. "You've really got to try harder our Mary we can't upset Aunty Ada anymore can't you see the effect its having on her," Mary was all for dissolving into floods of tears but Jean stopped her in her tracks. "We'll ave none of that I've add enough bloody tears to last me a soddin life time, smile an keep smilin."

So Mary did as she was told for once and her smile was more of a grimace, she looked so strange that Jean collapsed in a fit of laughter. Ada rushed in from the kitchen to see what was so funny and just the sight of Jean convulsed in a heap on the floor reduced them all into peels of mirth, two of them didn't know what they were laughing at but it was hysterically funny anyway and it was better than crying all the time. They were worn out from all the laughter but all agreed it had done them the world of good.

After a cup of tea they all felt a little less tense, and able to talk about the things they had been putting off since the day Ted had died. The sisters listened to their Aunty talk about her beloved man of the kindness he had always shown to everyone, his knack of turning a raging storm into calm and soothing the most savage beast. His many brave deeds in the war, his help with money to many who had needed it without question. And always in the strictest confidence, of his worry about Hitler and the ensuing war always wanting to protect his loved ones.

He had been spared that now and Ada was glad about it, the tears began to flow steadily and she buried her face in her pinafore. The girls sat quiet and let her weep and weep she did, her fat little frame shook for what seemed an eternity and when she could cry no more she blew her nose loudly and made for the kitchen to make yet another pot of tea.

Ada then turned to Mary and told her how worried she was about her, "ow ast bin bearin up lass" she asked "thas non lookin to well." Remembering Jean's words, Mary assured her Aunty that all was well with her and the unborn baby. "I'll be allreet when'th sickness stops Aunty its gettin better alth time" she lied, her Aunty was relieved to hear this and said so in no uncertain terms.

Jean smiled warmly at her sister and silently thanked her, Ada had enough to cope with at the moment and more stress could not be heaped upon her. "He's opt-it" added Mary, "dun a bunk thank God". Know one wanted to talk about him and there was an eirie silence, "ast sin that floozy" asked Ada breaking the silence. The sisters knew that she was referring to Ginny, Jean answered that she had seen her but only in passing and that they hadn't acknowledged each other.

Mary didn't bother she knew that she was as big a floozy as Ginny and therefore couldn't cast the first stone, that's why she had given up taking the class at Sunday school she wasn't fit to teach young children about God and being without sin. That was rich her the most sinful woman in Bridgevale daring to tell others how to behave, well not any more, she wouldn't be going to church again or Sunday school not even to christen her baby when it was born she wasn't fit and she knew it.

"Come on Mary lets be off I've got to pick up Elizabeth Jean from Joyce's and I'm late as it is," Mary was jerked back to reality. "Sorry Jean" whispered Mary, she had her martyr look on and Jean couldn't stand it. She wanted to slap her face and tell her to snap out of it, but she knew that her sister was suffering badly. And she didn't want to hurt her anymore than necessary, but sometimes she wished that she could be a bit more grown up have a little backbone.

Good-byes were said to Ada and promises of a return visit soon, and they were off leaving Ada to wonder what was to become of Mary. She had changed so much over the last few months; Ada's heart was heavy what on earth had the lass been thinking of giving herself to that bloody awful Tom Scully. It would have been more believable if she had fallen pregnant to some good looking young chap with potential, something to offer the lass stability perhaps. But no a boozer a no good wife beater a man who kept his children without food and proper clothes, a man who would take his last farthing to the bookies rather than give it to his wife for food.

Ada was baffled what on earth could have possessed the lass to behave the way she had, true Jean had told her that Tom had plied her with drink and she wasn't used to it. Even so it was hard to swallow, could it have been the lovemaking some women actually liked it. Herself she never had, but look at Jim's floozy's Ginny and Meg, they must they were always at it to hear everyone talk. Ada began to wonder if she had missed out on anything maybe if she had married someone else, no never her Ted was all she had ever wanted.

Still there was a nagging doubt.

She wondered about Ginny there had been a remarkable change in her since she came back from Wales, she was quieter very subdued some said. Perhaps a dear one had passed away, perhaps she had a heart after all. That thought was soon put out of her head as the door opened and in trouped Lizzie, Alex & Teddy, they were in such a state they had forgotten to knock. Ada let them get away with it this time, but not again she was a stickler for good manners.

"Whatever's up" she demanded, "its that Ginny" they chorused. "One at a time if tha dunna mind" shouted Ada "it's bedlam in ere," "right Lizzie lets ere it." "Well Aunty" began Lizzie "we were just finishin tidyin up an er telt us all to piss er oh sorry Aunty" Lizzie didn't know where to look, Ada was beside herself with anger. “It’s all reet leave it wi me I'll sort it," having said that she gathered up her shawl and headed for the door.

Ada's knocking on Jim's door could be heard three streets away, the door was whipped open by a very irate Ginny who was ready to give the culprit a damned good tongue lashing. "Oh it's you” she said calmly, and stood with arms akimbo on the step. Ada spoke softly but her eyes betrayed her feelings, "I wont be left standin outside my own sisters house by you or any other trollop, so stand aside and quick about it" said Ada quietly but with venom dripping from every word. Ginny was feeling a bit uneasy the little fat woman was an unknown quantity, and she didn't want to get Jim's back up not now not after what she had been through.

The icy cold wind whipped up Ada's shawl and wrapped it around her head, just when she wanted to be at her most menacing. Damn it all she swore as she tried to disentangle herself from the stupid shawl, Ginny looked on trying not to laugh at Ada's plight the woman was spinning about trying to remove the shawl from her head. Her face was redder than ever when she eventually disentangled herself and she puffed and panted as if she had climbed Mt Everest, unable to speak she sank down on her sister Sal's settle and sat there for a good five minutes until she got her breath back.

"Right lady when best get right to-th. point " spouted Ada in her sternest voice "Im non, avin them kids used like door mats, their non used to it" "they've just lost their mother for Gods sake " hast tha no compassion at all." ! "ast tha any idea what theve suffered! she looked into cold icy eyes set in a granite face. No there was no feeling there no compassion just emptiness, hardness, bitterness. A shell in which a thing existed, "I can see I wont get any feeling out of thee that as hard a character as ever iv'e come across in all me years" added Ada. "But I'll tell thee this, if tha ill'treats anyone of our Sals kids if tha arms one air on their eads then by God tha'll ave me to deal wi and mark my word I make a very bad enemy."

Ada didn't wait for a reply she simply walked out of the door with as much dignity as she could muster, Ginny wanted to laugh but the laughter stuck in her throat. There was something in the threat from the little fat one that she didn't like, no she didn't like it at all.

Perhaps she knew, no she couldn't it wasn't possible. She broke out in a cold sweat and the memory of her last day in Haverfordwest came flooding back, her throat constricted she couldn't swallow. Panic seized her, suddenly a bout of coughing and spluttering griped her it was as if her breath had been cut off from her body. Ginny lurched to the kitchen and grabbed a glass trying desperately to fill it with water, but it slipped out of her hand and smashed to pieces on the floor.

I'm going to die she thought and I haven't done all the things that I always wanted to do, her heart was going to explode any second, Ginny sank to her knees on the kitchen floor and waited for the end to come. There was nothing she could do about it, her eyes swam with tears of self pity damn it all there was so much living left in her. The front door opened and in came Jim bringing an icy blast with him, his eyes met Ginny's "what the fuckin ell's goin òn "he shouted at the top of his voice, and ran to pick her up from the floor.

Memories of Sal on her deathbed came vividly back to him, Ginny let herself be gathered up and deposited on the settle. "whatever's up wi thee " demanded Jim "ast bin on'th piss " he couldn't smell any ale on her breath, still there were spirits that left no odour so she could have bean drinking all day long. However she was deathly pale perhaps she was genuinely poorly if she would say something it would help, "shall I call'th doctor out Ginny" he asked her. Her breathing was less laboured and she began to feel a little better, she managed to assure him that she would be alright. "Just let me rest up a minute Jim and I'll be fine", murmured the frightened woman. Her heart wasn't racing so fast now thank the lord she would live, yes she would be fine she would do all the things she thought she never would.

The tears began to flow and sobs racked her body, Jim couldn't stand weeping women so he left her there in the parlour and off he went to the kitchen to get himself some food he was starving. He shook his head what the bloody hell was wrong with the woman, perhaps it was her time of the month, he was feeling a bit pissed of with Ginny just when he thought he was rid of her and almost had Meg in his sights up she pops as large as life.

There was something different about her he couldn't put his finger on it but there was definitely a change about her, he had tried to piss her off with every obscenity in the book but she had clung to him and would not be budged. It didn't matter that he had thrown all her belongings in the dustbin, even her most treasured possessions nothing he could say or do would make her leave his house. So there she was and there she wanted to stay, how he would ever get her out and Meg in he didn't know but he would keep trying. All this weeping wasn't like her at all something had happened to her in Wales, but she wouldn't talk about it and if he asked her anything her face became a mask of fear.

The kids returned later on after having their tea with Ada so they were ready for bed, they didn't look at Ginny the old cow was lying on the settle looking like a wet dishrag. "I bet Dad's gin er a good iddin "chortled Joe, "she's bin showin er tit's off again" how well he remembered the eyeful he had of her core she had a lot to show off too. Lizzie scolded him for his dirty talk "I'll tell Aunty Ada she'll settle yer ash" Joe only giggled more and set of Teddy and Alex and the three of them couldn't stop. There was a roar from the bottom of the stairs, it was Jim and he let them know in no uncertain terms what would happen to them if they didn't shut their fucking mouths.

They all laid quietly for a while then Teddy piped up "are there two f's or one in fucking, there laughter could be heard down the street. As could their squeals as Jim gave them all a good walloping, even Lizzie who hadn't been laughing. She cried for Camy wishing she were there to comfort her, she wondered if Camy was ever as unhappy as she was perhaps that was why she had killed herself. Maybe I'll kill myself too, then he would be sorry the bastard.

Mary was deep in thought as usual, as always about the baby she was carrying. Wishing as usual that it would die before it was born, she hated herself for thinking like this but on the other hand to have Tom Scully's bastard. God she would give her life to turn back the clock, she was convinced it would look just like him and then everyone would know. Her looms had all stopped and women were noticing the fact, she bustled about trying to get them all in order.

Suppose she fell in between the looms it just might bring about a miscarriage, she closed her eyes and tried to will herself to fall into the machinery but she couldn't do it. She cursed her weakness she was useless, scorching hot tears ran down her face and she bent down and rummaged in her weft tin to hide herself from prying eyes. The baby kicked inside her and she wanted to hit out at it and shout at the top of her voice stop it, stop it.

She was aware of someone at her side and looked up to the leering gaze of Fred Wright he took in the tears of despair; his expression changed it softened quite considerably. "whatever's up lass tha's in a reet state err let's give thee a hand", Mary wanted to snap at him tell him to piss off and leave her alone but she couldn't the words stuck in her throat. Fred set off tidying up her looms, and in no time at all everything was as it should be.

A couple of the women asked him what was the matter and he gestured back that she was a bit tearful, the women gestured to each other that she was a bit of a mard arse and she would piss less. What would she do when her tenth was on the way wondered one or two of them, she would have something to cry about then by hell.

Later on when she had finished work and she was walking up the yard heading for home, Fred caught up with her. "art tha feelin better lass", he asked her. She answered that she was O.K "that's the ticket it wunna allis be dark at seven", he added. They chatted on not really knowing what to say to each other, when they reached Mary's door he bade her goodnight. "If tha feels lonely Mary tha can allis talk to me anytime tha knows", Mary thanked him she knew of his reputation and thought to herself not bloody likely.

The house was cold and felt empty she would be glad when the war was over and Brian was back home, she didn't bother to light the fire just heated herself some soup and when it was finished she went of to her lonely bed. There was no one to talk to, to hold in her arms to love. Her body ached for her man every muscle twitched inside her and the baby started to kick, leave me alone you bastard she shouted at it and she rocked back and forth in her despair.

Next day at the mill wasn't much better, and Mary began to think she was going mad her head swam and she couldn't focus properly her eyes were seeing double of everything. Nellie Brown worked near to Mary and she could see that the woman was far from well, leaving her looms in charge of another woman she ventured over to Mary. "whatever's up Mary" inquired Nellie, "I dunna rightly know Nellie I canna see proper" answered Mary.

Nellie stopped all Mary's looms and tidied up for her, getting her coat for her she told her she was taking her home. "I canna go ome Nellie Mr Entwistle'l skin me alive," moaned Mary, "well tha canna do thee work in that state, an leave the big footed old bugger to me." Monty the loom oiler was wanting to get his job done and was hovering about wondering what was going on, Nellie told him what was happening.

Monty and his mate Archie both liked Mary very much and were sympathetic about her distress, they tried to make her laugh with their daft antics but she just wasn't in the mood. All eyes were on them as they walked out of the mill, tongues were clacking ten to the dozen; Mary felt stupid and hung her head as if in shame. On the way they bumped into Fred Wright and he wanted to know the in's and out's, "nosy bugger " muttered Nellie "we'd better put a notice up on'th board wouldn't want the bugger's to miss out on anythin."

Mary was duly taken home and Nellie lite the fire for her and put on the kettle, "shall I ask Doc Sawbones to call round on thee lass" she asked "I'll be fine in a bit Nellie onist dunna worry," " tha'd best be gettin back afore tha gets in trouble" urged Mary. So Nellie scuttled off back to the mill promising to call on her way back from work, the fireguard was put round the fire and the door locked and Mary climbed up the stairs to bed.

A loud knocking awoke her some hours later, what was it, she didn't know where she was for a few moments. Then she remembered it would be Nellie, opening the bedroom window she shouted out. Sure enough it was Nellie she just wanted to know that Mary was alright, after much re-assurance she was gone disappearing into the darkness. The house was warm and Mary felt better she put a little more coal onto the fire and re-laxed with a cup of tea, things didn't seem as bad at that moment.

She started to doze in the warmth of the fire she hadn't felt this well in ages, someone knocked at the back door stirring her out of her reverie. "Who is it" she shouted, "It's me" came back the reply obviously a male. "Who's me" Mary asked again, she was at the door by this time. Thinking it was Arthur she unlocked the door and there stood Fred Wright, she was taken aback and wanted to slam the door shut again.

Her mind was in a turmoil what was she to do, she just stood there dumb struck. He took advantage of this and pushed his way into the kitchen, he was at his most oily. "Just thout I'd see if tha were feelin better" he told her "canna ave a lovely lass like thee poorly an left in er own na can we," she quickly assured him that she was feeling a lot better. "It's the baby she added colouring up she didn't know why, it sounded dirty as though she shouldn't be having one. Seeing him stood there reminded her of the time that Tom Scully had forced his way in and she felt a panic rise inside her, she wanted to scream out-loud.

Fred noticed that she was uncomfortable and quickly backed off," reet lass he told her look after theesen an dunna thee come back too'th mill till tha's properly better." Then with a "goodneet lass" he was gone, Mary locked the door and breathed a sigh of relief and wondered why she had felt so frightened he had behaved like a gentleman. Why did she think that every man she met wanted to get her into bed, all-right so he had a reputation but she hadn't actually ever seen him with anyone but his wife. The wife wasn't down at heel and didn't look neglected so he couldn't be that bad it was probably a case of give a dog a bad name.

Sleep came easier that night she felt a little more relaxed not as sickly, and awoke felling a little more refreshed and was ready for the day ahead. By the time she got to work she was feeling a bit off again but she put it to the back of her mind, the rent wouldn't pay it's self and food needed to be bought. Besides that there were baby clothes to knit and bedding for the pram and cot to buy, so she had to work and that was that, no two ways about it.

Five thirty couldn't come quick enough and Mary was half-way up the mill yard when Fred caught up with her, "how art feelin to'dy lass "he asked. Mary replied that she couldn't grumble, and hoped that no-one was watching them. Fred accompanied her as far as her house then he bade her goodnight, she breathed a sigh of relief as usual and let herself into her own home. There was a letter from Brian and a bill from the coal man waiting on the mat, and she eagerly opened the first.

It was full of his love for her and of how he missed her, a few details about what he was doing mostly drill and the like. She began to cry as if her heart would break, why wasn't he here with her when she needed him so badly. If he hadn't gone away the terrible deed wouldn't have been done, she wouldn't be in such torment. Mary went up to bed without anything to eat or drink she was to upset to bother all she wanted was her Brian back home safely.

Arthur had knocked and shouted for about ten minutes when the bedroom window opened and Mary appeared, he let her know who it was and she shouted that she was on her way down. "What's matter Arthur" she wanted to know she was nice and warm and comfy in her bed and now she would have to go back to it cold, "nowt lass Jean were worryin about thee and wanted to know tha were all reet." He could see that her eyes were swollen with weeping, "what's up then come on tell Uncle Arthur" he coaxed.

She pointed to the letter from Brian, "oh that answers me question" he exclaimed. "How's things at is end then" Mary told him as much as she wanted him to know and no more. There was no way she could tell him the juicy details contained in the letter, they were for her only to go over and over again in her lonely bed. They had a cup of tea together and then Arthur was off, he would have liked to have stayed and gathered her in his arms and reassured her that all would be well. To kiss her lovely warm mouth and stroke her beautiful glossy hair, but it was not to be, he had a wife of his own and she had a husband.

Arthur made his way home his mind in turmoil what was he going to do he loved Mary so much, he yearned for her night and day his body aching for her touch. Every moment was spent in imaginary lovemaking with her in every conceivable position; he wanted her so bad he could taste her. His mind went back to the night he had spent looking after her when the abortion had failed, he drooled at the memory of her luscious breasts he wanted to caress them with both his hands and his mouth.

Mary he murmured to himself oh Mary, how much longer could he go on like this wanting her so bad. He couldn't tell her never she loved Brian and she always would she would be appalled if she ever knew what he was wanting, no he would have to keep it to himself suffer in silence go bloody stark raving mad. On reaching his house he was glad that Jean was busy and didn't notice his distress or the bloody great hard-on straining at his trousers, it wouldn't go down so Jean was in for a nice surprise at bedtime and could hardly believe the shagging she got it was the best she had ever had. It was just as well that it was dark and she couldn't see Arthur's face as he desperately tried not to call out Mary's name wishing she was in his arms.

After their lovemaking was over Arthur wandered down the stairs and sat for a very long time feeling guilty about his passion for Mary, after all Jean was a marvellous wife and mother no-one could have better he knew that. Jean had a very good figure too smaller breasts but nicely rounded, she was spotlessly clean and kept their little girl Elizabeth Jean immaculate.

And most of all she loved him with all her heart and it would be broken if she ever knew how he felt about her sister.

Suddenly Jean was at his side making him jump out of his skin, "sorry Arthur I didn't mean to startle thee". she exclaimed "I wondered why tha were gone so long art tha allreet" Arthur quickly assured her that all was well and he was just making sure that the fireguard was in place. they went back to bed she puzzling about why he had lied to her it didn't take twenty minutes to check the fireguard, perhaps he was worrying about the war that must be it yes it was a worrying time for everyone poor Arthur bless him. She gave him a big hug and snuggled up to him in their comfy bed, he hugged her back sorry for his lust for her sister but the lust was still there and he turned Jean over again and thrilled her once more with his mighty erection Mary's name unutterable on his lips.

Mary however was completely unaware of Arthur's feelings for her she would have been aghast to say the least if she had known, she became aware of a tapping at the back door perhaps it was Arthur back again. Well she didn't want to be bothered again tonight so she just ignored whoever it was if they really wanted her they would shout her, she knew Lizzie and the boys would. Whoever it was soon went away so it couldn't have been very important, Mary made her way up to bed alone once more and when she had pulled the counterpane over her she dissolved into the usual fit of weeping sorry for herself and for her lot in life.

Fred Wright scurried away from Mary's back door he hadn't dared to knock loudly in case any of the neighbours were about, he cursed his bad luck how the hell was he going to get into her knickers at this bloody rate. Because by God he was going to get into them one way or another, he would have her and she would know that she had been had. Properly like she deserved he would have her screaming for more wanting him so bad, he stopped and rested for a moment the excitement was to much he was well and truly worked up he would have to give it to someone.

Fred made his way to Jessie's house and tapped gently on the back kitchen window, Jessie looked up from her book and could see that it was Fred. Hotness swept through her right down to her toes, oh Fred she gasped to herself whatever was he doing here this time of night. Her husband Jack had just gone up to bed he could come down at any moment, the excitement mounted in her she gestured to him to wait a moment. From the bottom of the stairs she called up to Jack "I shanna be long Jack I'm just goin'ta look fer'th cat it anna come in yet," "reet lass" came back the reply.

If he hadn't been so thick he would have remembered the cat curled up on the fireside chair next to Jessie, so she let herself out of the back door pretending to call in the cat trying not to burst into fits of laughter. Putting her fingers to her lips she pointed towards the cludgy and quickly glancing round to make sure that no-one was about they scurried in, as soon as the door was closed Fred was upon her his hands pushing up her nightie thankful she wasn't wearing any knickers. Equally she was undoing his buttons and had his dick out in seconds it was throbbing ready for action, between them they got it inserted in record time and proceeded to shag each other with great gusto.

They both enjoyed it standing up and when they had climaxed together they were totally spent and could hardly move, Jessie's legs had turned to jelly and she could hardly stand God he must love me a whole lot to want me so badly she thought. While he was giving it to Mary in his mind imagining it was she thrust up against him in the cludgy clinging whispering more, more, harder, harder trying her hardest not to scream out with wanting. Yes this is how it will be with Mary and soon very soon.

"Jessie at in there " shouted Jack from outside, they almost jumped out of their skins. "Aye Jack I wunna be a tick" answered back Jessie, "the cat's inth kitchen asleep tha must be goin ga ga" he added. Jessie pretended to have a bit of tummy trouble and told him to go in the house out of the cold night air, and assured him that she would be as quick as she could. They waited with baited breath for the sound of the back door closing, "God that were a close shave Fred " whispered Jessie "we nearly got cought out on'th job. "One of these days he'll catch thee shagin me then what'll thee do, "shag thee some more "added Fred.

This only added to the excitement and Fred was aroused once more, and despite Jessie's feeble no,no,no's he was up her again and it was every bit as good as the first. When Jessie finally got away from randy Fred she hardly had the strength to climb up the stairs, Jack was sat up in bed waiting for her. Which only ment one thing, Jessie pretended that her stomach was giving her gyp and tried her best to get out of it. But Jack wanted his fortnightly fumble and nothing she could say or do would dissuade him, so she pulled up her nightie and closed her eyes praying it would soon be over. "Bye eck that wet lass tha must be wantin it bad" mumbled a very happy Jack.

Chapter Twelve

The Confrontation

Jim sat alone on his bed his mind in turmoil, the stuck up toffee nosed Daphne had hardly been back from Christmas leave and couldn't wait to tell everyone the news about Coral. Knowing full well that it would reach the ears of the love struck Jim, of course it had been stretched beyond belief but Jim wasn't to know that. He moaned over and over again the name Matthew, what had happened between him and Coral was she really in love with him. How could she have forgotten Jim so soon, he would find the bastard and give him a bloody good hiding and the sooner the better.

Of course he knew that he was being stupid it was nothing to do with him what Coral did anymore, she was a free agent and could do whatever she wanted whenever she wanted with whoever she wanted. However it didn't stop him hurting inside he was in pain in agony if the truth were known, and he didn't know how to stop the hurt. Jim had thought about going AWOL but that wouldn't solve anything only make matters worse. Besides Daffers and her so-called friends were waiting to see how he would react and he couldn't let them see how much it had got to him, he would rather die than give them the satisfaction.

Going home to Tilly and his little girl should help him, a few days with them would give him a fresh outlook on life he would apply tomorrow for a spot of leave after all he hadn't see them at Christmas so he was due. This perked him up quite a bit and he felt he could get on with life once more, he strode of to the pub where his friends greeted him warmly whilst Daffers and CO were quite put out to see he was still of sound mind and not the snivelling wretch they would have him.

After a few pints thoughts of Coral swept back into his mind, he could picture her in every part of the pub and he wanted her so bad his heart ached. Jim wanted to shout out loud leave me alone for God's sake leave me alone, however he had to stifle the sounds before they came blurting out making him sound a right bloody idiot. Last orders were the finest words he had heard all day and he couldn't wait to get out into the still night air, to escape the searching gaze of the dreadful Daphne.

Charles and the rest of his mates could see what was going on and they swiftly dealt with the situation by heading back to their quarters as quickly as they could, each one pretending to be particularly tired and ready for a good night's sleep. Jim was thankful for their consideration, and undressing in double quick time he scrambled into his bed and covering his head with the blankets he wept as quietly as he could for some considerable time. The others tried not to let it get them down it was bad enough that they were training for War let alone thinking about loved ones and the like, if they let it get to them God knows what would happen.

Before Jim knew it He gave up and lurched out of bed and headed for the showers, a good cold one would wake him up for sure.

By the time he sat down to breakfast he was feeling human again and could face the world, his friends looked at him fondly and he was glad of them. He knew they were concerned for him and it made him feel good inside, they were truly friends he owed them a lot and one day he would repay them. Jim was flying solo across the channel to France today so he would have to have his wits about him, in no time at all he was up and away listening to the instructions from the base which wasn't always easy with all the crackle on the line.

His Spitfire soared above the clouds and he was all alone, he felt very vulnerable it was a very strange feeling and he wondered if he would ever get used to it. With a quick flip of the rudder the plane dipped down again and the ground was beneath him once more with a glimpse of rolling hills and tree's speeding past this was better, he headed for the coast his orders were to fly as low as he possible could over the channel and to turn back over water not land.

This he did to perfection and his base camp were more than pleased with him, he would have liked to see a little bit of France while he was so close he had never been anywhere really nor seen any other part of the world. The Spitfire spluttered and made a coughing sound Jim was filled with alarm, come on old girl he shouted to her just like he had heard the other men talk to their aircraft. He throttled back and headed home the little plane responded well and he was thankful, before long he was landing on the airstrip and although he had enjoyed it, he was happy to be on terra firma.

Charles was waiting for him in the hanger and they clasped hands warmly, they walked along together just pleased to be in each others company. "There's a new film on tonight "said Charles, "how about giving it a go old chap." Jim readily agreed "what is it" he inquired "Gone With The Wind" answered Charles. they had heard lots about it, the search for Scarlet O'hara ending with the finding of Vivian Leigh. "It's a weepy more for women wouldn't you say" asked Jim, Charles shrugged his shoulders "It might be worth watching we can always leave if we don't like it" was Charles's reply.

Their voices were inaudible as an Avro Anson ambled along the runway it was deafening so they waited for its engines to stop, Billy and Roger alighted and strode over pleased with themselves. They had enjoyed themselves enormously and couldn't resist showing off a bit, The other two asked them if they wanted to watch the film with them but they were in a drinking mood and quickly declined the offer. They made their way back to the hut for a shower and clean clothes shouting to each other about the days happenings, each one bragging a little about their flights and all were mightily impressed when they learned about Jim's solo flight over to France.

The film was captivating from start to finish and both Jim and Charles were lost in it's spell, they didn't weep at the end but were filled with a great sadness. Neither wanted to talk much their minds dwelling on personal thoughts, they both decided an early night was called for and bade one another goodnight. Sleep didn't come easily to either of them that night, but the morning brought a new day a day for getting on with the job in hand to fight the enemy and keep them from there shores make it safer for there beloved family's to walk about freely without fear. That was the task they had been given and they would do it to the best of their abilities, they would put their own problems on hold till the job was done.

Jim applied for a spot of leave and was granted one week starting from January 12th he was told to make the most of it as training was getting more intense now and there would be little leave given in the future, try as he might he couldn't help wishing he wasn't going home when he was actually on the train heading for Derbyshire. He had written to Tilly and she was over the moon as was Sally Vicky and the rest of the family, they were at the station to meet him and the sight of his wife and little girl reduced him to tears they were everything a man could ask for and he would try not to ask for more.

The first thing he had to do was to visit Aunty Ada he knew it would be stressful and he steeled himself, as soon as she opened the door to him Ada collapsed in a flood of tears and it was a long time before she was composed. Jim's heart went out to his beloved Aunty, Uncle Ted's death had devastated her and he wondered if she would ever recover from it. He held her close and gently stroked her hair telling her over and over again that everything would be all right, knowing full well that part of her had died with her husband

Tilly made a pot of tea and they sat together and talked about Ted, Ada wanted to tell Jim all about the events leading up to and following his death. In between Ada would break down with another bout of weeping, she went to the dresser and came up with a leather case on the inside were a couple of brushes with silver handles and a comb and a silver framed mirror, they were beautifully kept Ada handed them to Jim and told him they were now his. she didn't have to tell him to look after them she knew he would without question, "They went to'th last war an came back safe "said Ada "an the will agin."

Lizzie and the boy's burst through the back door and threw themselves at Jim he hugged them close in turn and remarked how they had grown, Ada let them off with their display of bad manners she knew how much they missed their brother. He listened to the tales about Ginny and their Father and was amazed that Jim was still up to his old tricks, "your uncle Ted was goin'th give the bugger a tongue lashin but " she shrugged her shoulders. There was a knock at the front door, it was Jean with little Elizabeth Jean and the siblings hugged each other tight.

"By eck everybody's growin up that fast hast thee all got cow muck in thee boots " shouted Jim "An where's our Mary" he noted the look the three women exchanged "what's up is er all reet" he asked Tilly didn't know very much only that Mary was expecting and that she wasn't very well. But Jim knew that something was wrong and he would find out in good time, Ada began to set the table for tea Jim could see that it was giving her something to occupy herself and although he wanted to get off home with Tilly and be alone with her he hadn't the heart to tell his dearest Aunty.

At long last the goodnights had been said the hugs and kisses exchanged and they were on their way home to their own little world Sally Vicky was tired out and was ready for bed she wasn't the only one, Jim and Tilly flung off their clothes hardly able to keep their hands off one another. Tilly reached for her nightie Jim shook his head "you wont be needin that my darlin" his voice husky with emotion, Tilly threw herself into his arms and he took her up against the bedroom wall. It had never been so good between them and they collapsed onto the bed exhausted, they continued to kiss and stroke each other telling each other how they missed one another and of the lovemaking they had longed for every night they were apart.

Jim tried his hardest not to think about Coral but she kept creeping into his mind and his longing for her did not diminish, "love me agen Jim" begged Tilly "I want more she urged. He was hard and ready again for his eager wife he couldn't believe she wanted so much, once was usually enough for Tilly. This went on thro-out the night she was insatiable and Jim was ecstatic their lovemaking took them to greater height's and they marvelled at each other, as daylight dawned Jim mumbled that they hadn't taken any precautions but Tilly didn't care," lets hope there's a baby there Jim or will be afore tha goes back we can practice agin if tha likes" Jim duly obliged.

When morning came they were both exhausted and wanted to stay in bed and sleep, but there was Sally Vicky to dress and get breakfast for. The child wanted to go for a walk with her Daddy, so that put an end to Jim's lie in. It was freezing cold outside so they put on their warmest clothes, "don't forget the duck bread Daddy" called little Sally. On their way towards the canal they passed a few of the neighbours, who pumped Jim's hand and wished him the best of health and strength in the difficult times ahead. They walked quite a way looking for the ducks but the canal was completely frozen over and there wasn't a duck to be seen, Sally began to cry and Jim had to make up a story fast about how the ducks had gone to another canal to buy food for their babies. His little girl wasn't very pleased about it but it stopped her weeping.

When will they come home she wanted to know, "in a day or two" he answered. They walked on passing a couple of barges stuck fast in the ice, and Jim reminisced about Aggie and Camy and wondered if Aggie was still working on her families barge. He remembered how heartbroken she had been after finding the bodies of Camy and Finton, huge tears flooded his eyes and a lump the size of a cricket ball stuck in his throat. Tilly hugged him to her breast and tried her best to comfort him, knowing how much he had loved his little sister.

Sally Vicky wanted to know why Daddy was crying, and was told by Mummy that Daddy was just so happy to be home with them. Sally Vicky reached out for Jim's hand and told him not to worry that she would take care of him, and Jim had to laugh at her serious little face and scooped her up and hugged her close thanking God for the gift of such a beautiful child. He couldn't ask for anything more than his Tilly and their precious child, forget Coral he told himself let her go get on with your life. If only he could do that, he knew he had to try. On the walk home Jim was taken aback by the number of boys and girls sliding up and down the ice on the canal, "It's dangerous to go right out on the ice it could give way at any time." He told Tilly, he knew from his own experience what it was like he had been on it many times in the past. "Ther'l be a tragedy one of these days mark my words, it's just waitin to appen."

Tilly had to drag him past the kids, he wanted to tell them to get off the ice. However she knew that they wouldn't take any notice of him, and she didn't want him to have a slanging match. Time was to precious to waste and she wanted to get home out of the cold, and sit before the warm fire with her beloved. In next to no time he would be on his way back to God knows what, and no knowing when she would see him again. The tears were welling in her eyes now, and she had to dab them away quickly with her handkerchief before Jim saw them. Thoughts of snuggling up together in front of the fire were quickly dismissed as Jim turned to tell her that he was popping round to see Mary, she tried to disguise her disappointment but Jim could see her face.

"Sweetheart I wunna be long," "I think summats wrong wi our Mary an I must go an see." Tilly hugged him tightly and told him it was ok, but duna thee be too long as we've things to do she added her face going scarlet with embarrassment. Jim laughed out loud as he headed up the road to Mary's house, by gum his missis was turning into a nymphomaniac and no mistake. He turned and waved to them before turning the corner, why couldn't he be content with what he had. Why was he always wanting more, Moore by name and more by nature. "Art'tha non spakin Jim lad " Jim was miles away deep in thought, he looked up to see Johnny Bignal . "Sorry mate I were bloody miles away, how art tha" he asked shaking his old pals hand as hard as he could.

They walked along side by side reminiscing about old times, Johnny was thinking about getting married to Jill his childhood sweetheart, but he didn't want to leave her a widow should he be called up. "I dunna rightly know what to do fer'th best," he told Jim. "Well I didn'a get a choice " added Jim. "Mind you my Tilly an little lass give me summat to look forword to when I'm away," then looking Johnny right in the eye he said "It's up to thee but given chance I'd say stay single till its all over" "There's a lot of temptation out there." Johnny was taken by surprise at this coming from Jim Moore, but he could see that there was a lot of pain in his pal's eyes and he felt a pity for him he didn't quite understand.

Jim bade his old mate farewell and knocked on Mary's door, it was a while before she answered it. Jim was shocked by the change in his sister and almost gasped out loud. She threw her arms into the air and squealed with delight her appearance changing dramatically from sadness to happiness in a split second. Jim picked her up and swung her around the parlour hugging her close, she felt like a bag of bones in his arms and he almost cried out in anguish. Whatever had happened to her, he would wait and see. They sat down in the kitchen and Mary poured them a cup of tea ,"there's something stronger if tha want's it." Mary asked him but he declined not before he spotted a glass of sherry or such-like by the kitchen sink.

"I believe congratulations are in order our kid," grinned Jim. Mary didn't look him in the face when she replied her voice almost inaudible, she steered the conversation away from her pregnancy very deftly, and in no time at all Jim was telling her all about his flying exploits. Each time he looked into his sister's eyes he was aware of her pain, and when he couldn't stand it any longer he blurted out "Mary whatevers up we thee." She coloured up and hung her head, "It canna be that bad our Mary" he urged. Mary began to weep the tears that were always close to the surface, and her pathetic little body shook with every sob.

Jim held her in his strong arms, "it canna be that bad sis it's only a baby tha knows." "tha'll be allreet ask our Tilly she were scarred tha knows." "I dunna want it Jim I wish it'd die" Jim was shocked to the core he couldn't believe what he was hearing, he shook his sister roughly "Mary what art sayin stop it." Mary pushed him away from her and rushed up the stairs and the bedroom door slammed behind her. Jim stood alone in the kitchen wondering whatever to do, he couldn't go barging up the stairs he was in torment. Mary had looked like some mad woman, he couldn't understand it, for years she had been trying for a baby and now she had her dearest wish she wanted it dead.

Jim decided to see Jean and ask her what was going on, she was very wise and would know what it was all about. Jean was pleased to see her handsome brother and they hugged each other warmly, and after a few pleasantries Jim asked her straight out,"Whatever's up wi our Mary." Jean tried to avert her gaze but Jim was having none of this," I'll wait until tha tells me." Jean could see that he was adamant, "I canna tell thee Jim our Mary has sworn me to secrecy an I canna break the promise I'm sorry." she added, "Well I'm sorry too Jean but when my level headed decent loving sister tells me she wishes the baby inside her would die, the baby she's longed for fer God knows how long then I want to know why."

"Has Brian done somethin bad to'th lass," he asked. Jean was quick to assure him that Brian had done nothing wrong, but repeated her previous answer that she wasn't at liberty to divulge the reason for Mary's outburst. Jim wasn't to be put off he would get to the bottom of it before his leave was up, "wilt tha go with me an see our Mary." he pleaded, he went on about it till Jean gave in. Leaving Arthur to look after Elizabeth Jean they set off together to see their sister neither one looking forward to the outcome, after knocking several times Jean was getting very angry knowing full well that her sister was in the house and was choosing to ignore them. "Right sod the neighbours," she ranted and proceeded to shout at the top of her lungs through the letterbox, telling her sister to get the door open pronto or else.

Jim was taken aback at his sisters outburst they had never acted like this before, what the bloody hell was going on. At last the door opened a fraction and Mary peered round the corner, "if thas told our Jim owt tha can bugger off" she hissed. Jean pushed her way into her sisters house followed by Jim, "I've said nowt" "yet" she added. "But I canna promise if tha talks to me like that " Mary wobbled over to the fireside chair and almost fell into it, Jean and Jim exchanged glances it was still morning and she was pissed. The water works followed and Jim bent down and gathered his little sister in his arms, he held her tenderly until she had no more tears to shed.

Jean made a cup of tea for the three of them, Mary told Jean she was sorry and asked her to leave them and she would tell Jim the truth. So Jean set of home thankful to be out of the way she didn't want to hear the sordid story over and over again, slowly the story came out between bouts of sobbing and at the end of it Jim was aghast. Anger wheeled inside him the like of which he hadn't felt since the last run in with his father big Jim Moore, he held Mary tightly assuring her that all would be well.. The story would go no further, no Tilly would not be told anything about it. Aunty Ada and Jean plus Arthur were the only others to know and that was enough, he didn't know about Joyce Hibbert. Mary then told him that Tom Scully had scarpered when his wife found out, not another one how many more know he thought bloody hell is there no end.

Jim's mind was in turmoil he vowed that he would have revenge on Tom Scully, the bastard would be made to pay for what he had done to the lovely Mary. He had more or less wrecked her life she would never be the same, before he left her he got her to promise that she would give up the drink it was doing her no good.

He reminded her of the drunken antics of their father Jim Moore, she didn't want to be like him so she promised that the drink would go down the sink. As she poured the sherry away Mary wondered if she would be able to keep her promise, or would the urge return.

Tilly was waiting by the window for Jim's return, as he rounded the corner her heart leapt in her chest. Her love for him was as great as it had always been, and she knew it would always be this way until the day that she died. Jim looked a little downcast and deep in thought she noticed, however as soon as he walked into the house he was his old self. Tilly asked if everything was all right with Mary, he assured her that all was well not daring to look her in the eye of course. "Where's little un" he asked. Tilly coloured up er "at me Mam's," she stammered her voice husky with emotion. Neither of them needed to say another word as they headed for the stairs.

Jean had called round to see Ada, she saw her most days, there were always tears for her Ted. She wasn't adjusting to being without him at all, and Jean wondered sometimes if her Aunty would keel over and follow her husband to the grave. Her suffering was so bad that she could hardly breath between sobs, Jean hated to se her poor Aunty suffer like this but what could she do. Ted couldn't be brought back and that was the only thing that would pacify her, so all the family could do was to be there for her. Jean had to laugh though, nothing put Ada off her food she was forever cooking and baking. Scoffing as soon as she brought food out of the oven hot pies, buns, puddings, pasties and cakes large and small. They would all be tasted to see if they came up to scratch, then when meal time came Ada would declare that she had gone past it and would be unable to eat a mouthful.

Then she would have to be coaxed into eating a morsel just to keep body and soul together, she really was a hoot. However they never wanted to be without her, and prayed for her well being. Life would be a lot duller without the little fat one, as the dreadful Ginny had christened her. " Ast'tha sin our Jim this mornin our Jean," Ada wanted to know. Jean knew what she meant; she nodded her head and went on to explain that she had left him with Mary. Ada shook her head and clucked like a hen, "whatever will'th lad think abart it all, there'll be murder done mark my words."

"If thee Uncle Ted were err," oh here we go thought Jean he wouldn't have been able to do anything about it either. Ada droned on and on about how Ted would have dealt with it in no time at all, and Jean tried to stifle a yawn. Ada was no fool and snapped at Jean, "am I keepin thee awake or summat." Here we go thought Jean dog house for me, "Sorry Aunty I did'na get much sleep las'neet tha knows." "well get theesen ome and ge'th bed" answered Ada "dun let me keep thee up." Bloody hell thought Jean she really is miffed, as skilfully as she could she went on to tell of her nights of worry over Mary. Also if it wasn't for Ada she wouldn't know what to do, well the whole family would be lost without her guidance. Ada sniffed and strutted about then agreed that she really was an asset to them all, phew out of the doghouse at last Jean was thankful and vowed to watch what she did or said in the future.

They had another cup of tea and Jean finally managed to get away without upsetting the applecart, she wished that her family would sort out their problems themselves without getting her involved she was sick of it. What with Mary, the kids and the dreaded Ginny, Ada without Ted, Tilly missing Jim, and Peggy without Harry it was getting to much. I'll join up an get away from the bloody lot of them she mused, then she would miss her darling little girl and Arthur. No that wasn't the answer, she would have to put up with it all and hope that things became less stressful. As she headed home to Arthur and her cosy cottage she realized she had a lot to be thankful for, she wouldn't change it for all the tea in china.

Jim was up and about early much to the disappointment of Tilly, who wanted to snuggle up to him for a little longer. However Jim wanted to have a word with Ginny and give her a piece of his mind, and perhaps sort out his bastard Father. His body trembled at the thoughts of it, but something had to be done for the sake of the little-ones. It was a Sunday so big Jim would be going to the pub so it wouldn't be hard to track him down, and that would leave Ginny alone hopefully unless she still went to the pub with him. He would take his little girl for a walk first of all, find the ducks for her to feed if there were any around.

Tilly was left behind to prepare the roast, she would rather have gone with them but someone had to do the cooking. Jim started up a conversation with one of the bargees who told him the best place to find a duck or two, before setting off he also asked him if he knew Aggie. The man looked at him a bit puzzled, "What dust'tha want wi likes on err." he wanted to know, "astna got a lass on thee own." Jim was quick to assure him that he didn't have an ulterior motive, "err went of with a tinker last back end." The man told him, "nowt's bin erd on err since, err were a rum little bugger an no mistake." Jim thanked him for his time and went of to search for the elusive ducks,

Tilly was a bit put out when Jim and Sally Vicky returned from their walk, no sooner had he handed over the child when he said he was just popping out and that he wouldn't be very long. Before Tilly could ask where too he was away, with her standing open-mouthed. Well bugger me she thought to herself, where on earth is he off to. It was a bit much going of like that when they only had a few days together, perhaps he was fed up with her she had noticed that he was preoccupied quiet a lot of the time. It would be the war she told herself, things were different now because of it. After all he was a pilot now trained to fly, her heart soared with pride for her man she told herself to be grateful for what she had and to thank the Lord.

Upon reaching his old home Jim had a strange feeling of nostalgia, mixed with a smattering of resentment and loathing. Hearing his knock Ginny answered the door and was somewhat taken aback at the sight of Jim's eldest standing there, "oh I" she stammered, she didn't know what to say to him. By hell he was a good looking man she was quick to observe, and she coloured up in his presence. Wondering is my hair O.K, and was thankful that she had made an effort with her makeup and clothing that morning. She began to simper and asked young Jim into the house, swaying her hips as she did so. Jim almost laughed out loud at the silly bitch's antics, what a bloody fright she looked like a bloody clown in the circus.

Ginny began to feel uncomfortable under Jim's hypnotic gaze, and she began to stutter and stammer and almost burst into tears. "What's goin on" he demanded, "why are the kids being treated like dirt. "havn'a they bin through enough wi'out all this crap, he bellowed at her. Ginny was reduced to tears, which was unusual for her being an ally cat. There was just something about the man that demanded respect, his bearing and manner and his eyes, they could see right through to your soul she was sure. Jim let rip with a stream of accusations, thumping his fist on the table as he did so. Ginny had no answers for him all she could do was promise that things would get better, she would do all she could to make life easier for the children. It wasn't like her to be so meek and humble, but she couldn't do anything about it all she could think about was getting into Jim's pant's.

Even after he had slammed the front door behind him, she still stood there transfixed. What a beautiful man God help me I've got to have him. It was all she could think about, there would be no dinner today she would go to the pub and hope he would be there. So of she trolled in her highest heels, and tightest skirt reeking of cheap perfume and caked with make-up. She would try the Railway Hotel first of all so in she swept.

Jim on the other hand headed for the Goyt Inn, where old man Jennings greeted him warmly. Everyone was pleased to see him apart from big Jim Moore who stood glowering at him from his place at the domino table, there was no greeting exchanged between father and son. They stood like a couple of lions eyeing each other up and down, fists clenched, jaws tightened , feet firmly planted on the beer stained carpet in the snug.

Big Jim was the first to speak, "so your home then? I'll bet Mr Hitler's glad about that Ee musta bin shackin in is boots know'in tha were after im." He roared with laughter at this, and expected his cronies to join in. However they sensed the tense atmosphere and no one dared, young Jim curled his lip and snarled at his Father "well I'm non feered to do me bit fer me country." "I'm non idin be'ind foundry wall, or a tarts skirt while me kids suffer a life of bloody purgatory." He didn't have time to say more as his Father launched himself at him like a torpedo, absolute pandemonium broke out and hatred stored for many a long year spilled out with a vengeance.

half a dozen of the men managed to separate them, but not before each of them had planted a couple of blows on one another. There was blood everywhere and one of the local women screamed like a pig, Mr Jennings live in barmaid Ethel took one look at the shimozell and fainted on the spot. Everyone was running around shouting and waving their arms about, but doing nothing. Before you could say kafuffle a whistle blew loud and shrill, and to everyone's surprise Constable Bradley was in the thick of it Quick as a flash he had the sussed out the situation and cuffed the two Moore's. The Black Maria was outside the pub in a flash and Father and Son were loaded inside it, one with a bloody nose and the other with an eye as black as a bog.

Bad news travels fast, and in no time at all the whole village knew all about it. Tilly was shocked to find the police at her door, but agreed to the police request to make sure that young Jim stayed out of the way of his Father for the duration of his leave. The poor girl was beside herself with worry whatever was he doing getting involved in a fight with the bloody awful Jim Moore, hadn't he said that he was going to see Mary she would want some answers when the bugger came home if they ever set him free. Tears of anger welled up in her eyes, all she had wanted was her Husband at her side for the precious time that he was home. However all he seemed to want was to be lying in a police cell having them the talk of the village, well it wasn't right and she would tell him so in no uncertain terms.

Ginny heard about the fight over in the Railway Hotel, trust her to be in the wrong place she always missed everything. She would have loved to see the young supple Jim give his arrogant Father a bloody good hiding, Just the thoughts of it sent waves of desire through her body so by the time Jim was set free with a caution to keep the peace or else, he was dragged up the stairs by a very demanding Ginny. The woman was insatiable; Jim laughed out loud at her antics and promised to get arrested more often if it meant he would be in for hot lust all afternoon. He had been amazed by young Jim's outburst in the pub, he was a real man now the RAF had seen to that, he felt a little bit of respect for his eldest good on him. It was about time his sons stood up to him instead of acting like big girls, one day they might thank him but he wouldn't hold his breath. Ginny's arm wrapped around him drawing him closer, she wanted more well that was his name and he made sure that she got much much more.

However things were a little strained at young Jim's house, Tilly was pulling her lip down to the floor and Jim had offered to sit on it. "I saw red as soon as I set eyes on'th bastard," snapped Jim "he were bloody well barracking an all sayin as ow old Hitler must be relieved knowin I were ome." They both burst out laughing at this in spite of the black eye it really was funny, If only he could have laughed about it with his father but no he never would. They were enemies, always were and would always be until death thought young Jim. What a family they were turning out to be, now there was Mary to worry about and dear old Aunty Ada how would she cope without her beloved Ted only time would tell

Sally Victoria wanted to know why they were falling about laughing, but they couldn't tell her the truth so Jim made up a tale and soon had her laughing with them. He didn't know how long it would be before he got to see them again after his leave so he intended to make the most of it, sod Jim Moore let him rot in hell it would be the best place for him. It was only six thirty but it didn't matter, "Let's go to bed Tilly." he asked, that was all she wanted to be in his arms. Tilly's knees almost buckled with the sheer longing for him and the tears sprang up in her beautiful eyes, quick as a flash she hurried up the stairs with Sally Vicky to get her into bed so that she and Jim could do all the things they wanted to do to each other. However she took care to ensure that their little one wouldn't feel neglected in any way, and Jim read her three stories before she felt the slightest bit tired. At last the little one was sleeping, Jim reached out for Tilly and she melted in his arms only for a fleeting moment did his thoughts turn to a certain red head.

Mary made her way up the steep stairs feeling even lonelier than before, she tossed and turned in her large empty bed thro-out the night and hardly closed her eyes. By the time she had fallen asleep it was getting up and going to work time, she felt half dead however would she be able to stand at her looms all day long. The nausea began as soon as she put her foot out of the bed, and she only had time to reach for the washbasin. After an age bent over the bowl, she was able to get washed and dressed and began to feel a little more human. With a cup of hot sweet tea inside her the only thing that she knew would stay down, she set off to work at the Weaving Mill stopping every few yards to wipe her mouth which was constantly filling up with saliva. Perhaps she had a toffee in her bag she had a good root round in it and at the bottom covered in fluff was half a glacier mint which had seen better days, however to Mary it was the finest mint in the world and after a quick wipe over on her coat sleeve it was being sucked to perfection and the nausea subsided.

Into the shed she rushed afraid of being late, the looms had started up but the Boss hadn't begun his rounds yet so all was well. Dinner time couldn't come fast enough and she almost collapsed with fatigue, "at all reet lass" it was Fred Wright. Oh no thought Mary not that bugger, she felt bad enough as it was without this bloody tripehound moochin about. Mary managed a week smile and told Fred she was fine thanks, "shall I fetch thee a cuppa," volunteered the creep. "No thanks" she almost snapped but managed to keep her voice calm, "I've lots to do." she told Fred and got on with her work. Fred stood feeling stupid for a few moments then turned on his heels and walked off muttering to himself, right thee stuck up bitch I'll have the bloody last laugh just you wait an see. I'll get thee in bed if it's the last bloody thing I do and tha wunna want anybody else when I've finished with thee.

Monty and Archie had been watching Fred's antics and beckoned to Mary, "tha want's ta watch out fer that randy bugger." said Monty "The dirty sod'le ave is and up thee kilt that fast tha wunna know what it thee," Archie added "he'd tup a moldy loaf the bloody ally cat." Mary laughed out loud, "tha dosna need worry I'm non daft, the bugger wunna get out wi me." Archie ginned a toothless grin and pulled a daft face, "dust tha know come ta think of it I wudna trust yon mon wi our cat an its a tom." he added, and off they sauntered like two book ends as daft as brushes they were, but the most lovable pair in the mill if not in the whole village.

Jessie was waiting for Fred so that they could have a little grope like they did most dinner times, however he was in such a state that he grabbed her and pushed her into the First Aid room which thankfully was empty. He gave her a right good seeing too and Jessie gazed up at him and with wonder, "eh by gum Fred tha must love me a reet lot to want me this bad." Fred glared at her but hadn't the heart to tell her it didn't matter who it was as long as it was female and would let him shag her, she was a silly bitch but she would do until Mary came round to his way of thinking then she could piss off back to the gormless bugger she had saddled herself with.

Mary was thankful when the day was over she couldn't have gone on a moment longer, she shouted goodnight to her work mates and set off home telling herself that she would go straight to bed her body needed sleep and lots of it. So without any food she went off to bed to tired to eat or drink, she slept like the dead and didn't even hear pervert Fred knocking on her door later on that night. Needles to say Fred was speechless with rage thinking she was ignoring him, by eck she would pay for this and to top it all when he called around at Jessie's for another round in the cludgy she had gone to bed. He would give her what for in the morning he would have her in floods of tears telling her that he wasn't going to see her ever again, she would beg him for it and eventually he would relent. It didn't matter to him that the poor woman hadn't done anything wrong, all that women were fit for was to lay on their backs with their legs wide open waiting for their men to service them and that was all.

It was time for young Jim to return to Biggin Hill, the time had flown so fast he couldn't believe it. The hiding he had promised his father would have to wait until next time, there were tearful farewell to be said and Aunty Ada clung to him almost as much as Tilly did. "Be safe young Jim dun thee let that bugger itler anywhere near thee an come ome soon dust'tha er," and she collapsed in a heap crying as if her heart would break. Jim had to drag himself away the tears blinding him, he was hoping no one would be around but he met just about everyone he knew. After prizing himself away from Tilly's arms and clinging to his little girl he felt like a rung out dish rag, and when he reached the station he was thankful to be on his own at last and he tried to compose himself. As the train pulled out of Bridgevale station Jim had mixed emotions he loved his darling Tilly, but a certain red head crept into his mind once more and it was hard to get her out of it. The last thing he saw was the tall mill chimney where his Mother has worked and most of his family, he hoped that his little Sally Victoria wouldn't have to work there he would search for something better for her when the time came.

Chapter Thirteen

Ginny's Last Stand

Tilly sat red eyed on her bed, still rumpled from her lovemaking with Jim. She wept until she felt her heart would break in two, little Sally Victoria looked on bewildered not knowing what to say to comfort her Mummy. "Daddy will be home soon," she piped up her voice wavering close to tears. Tilly gathered her up in her arms and did her best to be calm and reassuring knowing it wasn't good for her little girl to get too upset about things she didn't understand, forcing herself to laugh and plastering a false smile on her face she set about making the bed. However the image of herself and her beloved in the throws of passion was too much for her, and the tears began to flow again. The sight of her handsome pilot husband in full uniform dashing off to catch his train, turning to wave and smile at her was like a knife stabbing at her vitals. When would she see him again would he be shot down over Germany, Tilly almost screamed out with anguish anly managing to stop by biting hard on the counterpane pushing it into her mouth.

A coo'ee at the back door stopped her in her tracks, it was her mother. Composing herself quickly she called down the stairs "I'll be down in a tick." There wasn't time to wipe her eyes or comb her hair, and when she walked into the kitchen with Sally in her arms her mother took one look at her and rushed to pull her into her arms she didn't say anything just held her. After a while she took hold of little Sally and put her in the bassinet, and reaching out for Tilly she told her "that coming ome wi me we'll have a nice tea and tha can stay the'th night if tha want's too. Tilly readily agreed and of they tootled, she wasn't ready to be alone just yet she needed a little mollycoddling and she would get that from her parents. As they set of down the road she was hoping that she would be having another baby, they had certainly done everything in the book to make one her insides were on fire at the memory of it all. Their lovemaking got better each time and she marvelled at how good they were together, the sooner Jim came home again the sooner they could get back to where they left of . Her mother was going on and she hadn't heard a word, "sorry Mam", " I were just thinkin" and she coloured up hoping her mother couldn't tell what she had been thinking about.

Lizzie was dawdling down the road and almost fell over Sally Victoria's bassinet, "sorry Tilly I did'na see thee" she told them and without another word she bent down to hug and kiss her little niece. The two loved each other so much and it was plain to see, Tilly looked at her mother and without another word having to be said she asked Lizzie if she would like to have tea with little Sally Vicky. Lizzie was thrilled to be asked but she would have to get permission from Aunty Ada and she sped of up the road, and before they had reached Mrs Bennetts front door she was back and the broad smile on her face said it all.

It gave Tilly a breather having Lizzie play with her little girl, so they got on with the tea and by the time it was over and the crockery was washed and put away Tilly was feeling more her old self again. Feeling so much stronger Tilly decided to go home she assured her parents that she was fine, "My Jim canna go ome to his Mam and Dad he's gone off to war so I've gott'a be brave too fer him and fer Sally Victoria.

The little one wanted Lizzie to come home with her and had a little weep, so Lizzie ran off home to see if she could stay the night at Tilly's. Ginny couldn't have cared less but she didn't know what Jim would say. Lizzie pretended not to be bothered she knew that if Ginny thought she wanted to stay badly she would put a stop to it right away, so she sat down looking not a bit bothered. While in her heart she was praying she would be allowed to go she never stayed overnight anywhere only Aunty Ada's a couple of times when she was poorly. Ginny finely said yes she could go it would mean one less of Jim's brats to look after, Lizzie nodded her thanks and went quietly up the stairs to get her nightdress whispering goodnight to her brothers and hoping Alex wouldn't start moaning. He understood and kissed Lizzie goodnight and off she went, as soon as she got outside she whooped with joy.

Lizzie's feet flew down the cobbled streets and at last she was at Tilly's door, once she was inside she threw her arms around Tilly and hugged her close. "I didn'a think owd so and so would let me stay" Lizzie told her "so then I pretended it didn'a matta one way orth' tuther, if er thooght I wanted to stay reet bad then she wuddna ave let me." Tilly had to laugh at her even if she didn't feel like it, but she loved Lizzie and she was glad that the girl had got one over on her Dads Moll or whatever she was. Poor things they didn't have much of a life, she hugged Lizzie closer and told her how much they all loved her. "Lets have a feast," shouted Tilly and they ran around the house with their arms out playing aeroplane life was fun again.

When the two girls were tucked up in bed after repeated goodnights sleep tights don't let the bed bugs bite, Tilly was exhausted and after finishing of her mending and ironing she was ready for her own bed. It had started to snow and she was glad she was inside her warm cosy snug cottage, herself and young Jim had done all the decorating themselves and she loved it. The nearest thing to heaven that's what it was only one thing was missing, her heart lurched with the old familiar feeling and the tears sprang up in her eyes. As she crept into bed she could hear Sally Vicky still talking to a fast asleep Lizzie, she tiptoed into the room and shushed her little girl telling her that Lizzie had to be up early for school in the morning then climbed into her lonely bed to think about and weep for her man.

Up the road at big Jim's house he was throwing a tantrum because Lizzie was staying over at Tilly's, "dun thee give orders in my fuckin ouse, thar't a bleedin lodger an think on tha dusna tell any on my lot what they can an canna do. He staggered off up the stairs farting at every step, this made him laugh out loud he was a vulgar bugger at the best of times. Ginny pulled her face and thought of sleeping on the settle she didn't want to be smelling his rotten beery stench all night, however she knew if she did that he would be down the stairs ranting at her again . He would probably be wanting his oats and for once she didn't want to be bothered, but she was wrong Jim was thinking about Sal and he didn't want anyone else near him and if the tart came up the stairs and walked into his bedroom he would throw the cow down the bloody lot.

By the time Ginny ventured to bed Jim was in a drunken sleep, he was fully clothed but she didn't bother to undress him wakening him would be like waking the bloody devil. So she crept about as best she could and slept at the foot of the bed shivering in the cold with her coat wrapped around her, vowing that she would piss off at the first chance she got she wasn't going to atay here and be insulted night and day by that drunken bastard. She should have let Meg have him let him threaten her and knock her about, she would piss off as soon and let him go fuck himself she hated the bastard. However when Jim woke her in the early hours of the morning with a huge erection throbbing against her buttocks she leapt into his arms and forgot the previous events, in her mind she was in heaven and she wanted to stay there. all thought of leaving gone.

After seeing Lizzie of to school Tilly decided to look in on Peggy and her baby son Harry, they hugged each other warmly and Peggy remarked that Tilly had a twinkle in her eye. "Was it a good leave then," and both the young mothers burst out laughing both knowing what good meant. Tilly going bright red at the memory of it and hanging her head down so that Peggy couldn't see her face, little Harry started to cry and they took it in turns to comfort him. Tilly had forgotten the wonderful smell of a new baby and she began to feel really broody, Peggy looked on "if he's don'th job proper tha'l be avin another the'sen, Tilly laughed out loud again but she was thinking exactly the same thing. "Worse things appen at sea" she said, "I ope not" replied Peggy "there all men on ships." This set them of in peels of laughter again and made the baby cry, so Peggy reached out her large milk filled breast and put the baby on it. Sally Vicky was enthralled and couldn't take her eyes of them, "I's baba eatin Aunty Peggy." The little girl wanted to know, so Tilly had to explain as best she could at the same time hoping that before to long she would have another baby at her own breast.

It was a different story over at Mary's, she would gladly have given her baby to Tilly if it were possible to do so. The little flutterings she felt inside made her feel utterly retched, she would smack her enlarging stomach and tell the monster to stop it. It would have two heads be ghastly deformed and would live till it was a hundred years old, she would have to push it about in a wheelchair and everyone would gawp at it and fell sorry for her. Many times she had tried to throw herself down the steep staircase but her feet would turn to led weights and it was impossible so she had given up on that, poison was out she didn't really want to die and never see her loved ones again. Her only hope was that her baby would be stillborn, so she prayed nightly for this to happen.

The time dragged on while she worked at her looms and she wondered how could she go on like this, every day the same old drudgery. The thing would be born about June time so she would finish work around April or May depending on how things developed, she wished she could leave now. All this pretending that she was over the moon was getting her down, when all she wanted to do was shout from the rooftops that she didn't want the bastard and that she wished it would die. Mary tried to remember the good times when she was happy and carefree, with a ready smile and quick to laugh. Where had that young girl gone too, she wasn't here anymore in her place was this grumpy bitter complaining old hag and everyone must have noticed unless they were blind.

The whistle blew for home time and Mary was off like a shot, she didn't bother with anything to eat she just crept into her empty bed and wept for Brian and times gone bye. There was a knock at the back door but she ignored it, whoever it was could just bugger off she wasn't in the mood for company. It would be their Jean, she meant well but Mary just wanted to wallow in self pity and be left alone. However it wasn't Jean it was Fred, he stood shivering in the frosty night air mad as a hatter that she wouldn't answer the door. He muttered under his breath about the little tart and how she would pay for this, he would get his own back on her or his name wasn't Fred Wright.

Big Jim Moore was enjoying a last pint before he made his way home, he didn't feel much like going he was getting more fed up with Ginny and her moods as each day dawned. His thoughts kept on returning to little Meg, well not really little quite plump little Meg was more apt but she wouldn't stay out of his mind no matter what. Plump or otherwise she was what he wanted, so he had all the rampant sex he could ever wish for with Ginny and he had to admit it was mostly good. However the more she milked him dry with their marathon sessions the more his thoughts turned to Meg, perhaps she couldn't or more to the point wouldn't perform the sex acts that Ginny did but she was warm and she held him tight and made even him feel wanted. Even big Jim Moore needed to feel wanted and Meg was the only Woman to make him feel that way,

Sal had never wanted him if only she had held him just once like Meg did, things could have been so different. By God he had loved that woman but she was a bloody cold fish, she was happier going to her grave to return to William than staying alive with him and the children. Well it was no use bemoaning what could have been he had to get on with life and as far as he could see his life must include Meg, and he would find her as soon as he could. Ginny would have to go she was sick in the head had never been right since her return from Haverfordwest, and he was fed up with her constant carping and her weeping and wailing. The Woman was obviously not well but she wouldn't let him help her so she could just piss off out of his life and leave him to have a bit of peace and quiet, then he could concentrate on finding Meg. Thoughts of Meg's soft lips and ample breasts caused a stirring in his loins, better go home and use it on Ginny while she was still there she was always ready for it that was the problem.

Jim banged the front door behind him, he loved to see Ginny jump out of her skin. Ginny was looking sick and seedy and wasn't best pleased at his childish antics, one look at her petulant face was enough to send him off in one of his rages. Thoughts of a shag were forgotten in an instant as he snarled at her to get her bloody bags packed and to fuck of out of his house pronto, she began to weep not for the first time that night and pleaded and beseeched the angry Jim to forgive her she wasn't well she was going to see the Doctor in the morning. Doctor she was going to see him Jim couldn't take this in, Doctor meant illness and death first Sal then Ted. "I'm non avin thee dyin in my bleedin ouse tha can piss off and do it somewhere bloody else," shouted Jim at the top of his voice. Then added "I want thee out in'th mornin dust tha ear me O U T spells out get it." Ginny nodded her understanding and wept all the more, what a bastard he was she hated him when he was in this mood.

Jim banged his way up the stairs and slammed the bedroom door, after a while Ginny crept up after him and quietly undressed in the dark. Into the bed she crept and using all her cunning and carnal knowledge she soon had the reticent Jim where she wanted him, and before you could say boo he was astride her and giving her the ride of her life. forgotten were the threats of moments ago sheer lust had replaced them. Ginny smiled to herself she always won over her men they couldn't resist her, she was red hot and she knew it. The smile faded quickly though when she remembered where she had to go in the morning, there was something wrong she felt so peculiar. The Doctor would put her right she would be fine a few pills and back to her old self, she slept better after that and felt quite positive she has always faced her demons and she would continue to do so.

Morning came quickly and Jim was furious for letting his dick rule his head, he scowled at Ginny and as she tried to kiss him as he left for work he gave her a look which was pure hatred. Ginny shuddered involuntarily and she wished that she had smacked the bastard in the face, and the more she thought about it the more she wished she had slapped him into the middle of next week. Little Alex bore the brunt of her displeasure as she tore into him for tripping over Lizzie's shoes, she clouted him round the head and the torrent of abuse that followed wouldn't have been out of place in a fish market. Lizzie pulled him quickly aside out of her reach and took the next three blows to the face, they hurt like mad but Lizzie didn't utter a sound just stood and took it. Ginny was fuming by this time and ran up the stairs squealing like a stuck pig.

When she had calmed down she trotted back down the stairs to wash ready for her appointment, the brats had gone thank God she hated them with a vengeance and the sooner she got away from them all the better. Thoughts of pastures new filled her mind and she felt exited, yes she would be of let the fucking lot of them do their own dirty work she was sick of it. Deep down she knew that Jim would never marry her and if he did she would be nothing more than a bloody door mat, it wouldn't be easy to get someone as good in bed as Jim was but it would be great fun finding out. She would miss that part of the relationship but nothing else and certainly no one else, she hated all of Jim's kids apart from young Jim and she hadn't had chance to get to know him and he had looked at her like she was something the cat had dragged in. No she wouldn't miss any of the bastards not one, good riddance to bad rubbish let them all go piss in their clogs.

Down the street she trolled in her best stiletto heels reeking of cheap perfume, and caked with tacky makeup. The surgery was full to bursting and there wasn't a seat to be had, even the most genteel of gentlemen couldn't bring themselves to offer her their seat so she stood glowering at everyone who made eye contact with her. After what seemed like an eternity her turn came and she was sat facing Doctor Hallam, he tried not to show his dislike for her and coughed and spluttered until she began to tell him about her symptoms. "Pop onto the examination couch please," he asked her. Then adding "please remove your underwear," followed by another cough and splutter.

Ginny wasn't bothered about removing her underclothes she was used to men asking her to do just that all her life, she laughed inwardly at the antics of the poor Doctor what a drip he was she thought to herself he must have seen lots of motty minges in his time. It took all her strength not to snigger at him, she lay there and the poor man had to ask her to open her legs and relax. Well she thought she would burst into fits of laughter and closed her eyes in case she saw his face that would do it she wouldn't be able to control herself any longer, suddenly a pain the likes of which she had never known shot through her body. Ginny shot up trying hard not to scream, she was just about to accuse him of being to heavy handed but he apologized to her and quickly and told her to steel herself while he went deeper into her vagina.

Doctor Hallam's tone was very serious as he explained that something was amiss and he needed to take a swab of the neck of her womb, Ginny laid still and tried not to panic the pain was terrible and she bit her lip until it bled. When the Doctor finished he apologized once more and telling her to dress he began to mess around with the swab and a phial, "what's up wi me Doc." Ginny asked,"by eck it urt like mad." she complained. The Doctor told her that he would be sending the swab away to be looked at and that she would need to make an appointment for a couple of weeks time, he sounded very serious and Ginny felt afraid for the first time she shuddered as someone walked over her grave.

The short walk home seemed to go on for ever as the pain in her belly got worse, and if she could have kicked off her high heeled shoes she would have done. The pain she was feeling was exaggerated by the height of her shoes, however she would rather be killed with fashion than without it. On reaching the Goyt Inn she decided to be their first customer of the morning, and after greeting Mr Jennkins ordered a port and brandy to settle her guts. "Art'tha outa sorts lass" Jennings wanted to know, Ginny replied that she was suffering from a jippy belly and hoped that the drink would put her back on track.

Old Jennings was a very good judge of character and he knew that Ginny was no good, he couldn't pretend he liked the woman but it was none of his business what she got up to. He didn't agree with the way she had moved in with Jim Moore, and he heard tales about the way she treated the Moore children which rankled with him but it was nowt to do with him and he kept out of it. However he couldn't help but notice in broad daylight how yellowy her skin looked he didn't think it was the makeup she usually had caked on, even her eyes were yellow. There's summat badly wrong with the lass he thought, then to Ginny he asked "ast'tha bin to'th Doctors lass." Ginny looked up from the cigarette she was lighting, "why " she asked with a puzzled expression. "Oh nowt I were just wundrin," replied a sheepish Jennings. Ginny gave him a withering look and walked over to an empty table and sat down, nosy bastard she said to herself and downing the port and brandy in one she shouted to him for a refill.

Jennings was getting very angry with Ginny she was pissed and refused to leave the pub, he wanted his dinner and a lie down before opening again in the evening. What with his woman telling his meal was drying up, and wanting to tap the barrel of bitter for the evening he was getting quite fed up. In the end he enlisted the help of a few of his customers and they frog marched Ginny outside and dumped her protesting over a low wall, it wasn't a pretty sight seeing a drunken woman and the men folk were disgusted at her antics. One or two woman out doing their shopping gawped at the drunken slut and scuttled past as if she had the plague, dragging their small children past quickly.

Word got round to Jim Moore in the foundry about Ginny who was still hung over the wall, so he set of to beat the living daylights out of her. How dare the slut show him up she would have to go and the sooner the better, he would throw her out bodily if that was the only way she would go. There she was showing her arse, hanging over the wall. There was spew all down and around her and she stank like a polecat, Jim reeled from the state of her and didn't know what to do. He was just debating which plan of action to take when Doctor Hallam appeared at his side, the Doctor began to examine her as best he could taking her pulse and checking the pupils of her eyes. Jim started to apologise for the state of her but the good Doctor cut him short, "Miss Wilkinson's not in the best of health Jim she came to see me this morning." His tone of voice was enough to make Jim sit up and listen, "Be very gentle with her." He added.

How they got her back to Jim's house was a miracle and when she was put to bed he was vastly relieved, he vowed that was it she would never show him up again she would never get the chance. Doctor Hallam was looking at Jim in a puzzled way, "spit it out Doc if tha's owt to say lets be avin it." thundered Jim pulling himself up to his full height, the poor Doctor didn't know what to say or do as he looked up at the towering Jim. "I'm sorry its just that I was wondering how Miss Wilkinson came to get her problem," "what bleedin problem are we on with man I dunna know what tha means." Answered a very angry Jim Moore, the Doctor started for the door eager to escape Jim's wroth. "I'll know more when I get the results" he called as he almost ran out of the door. Jim was left to ponder over his remarks what was the daft bastard on about. He was as mad as the bloody daft cow up stairs, by Christ he hated the bitch with a vengeance.

Jim looked at the pills that the Doctor had left for Ginny, he almost threw them at Joe who had just come back from his delivery round. "Take thee's buggers up to yon bitch an push em down er bloody throat," poor Joe duly obliged and when he saw Ginny looking like death he felt very sorry for her. Forgetting how she had treated him that morning, he gently held her head up and gave her the pills with a little water. He was gazing at her when she opened her eyes fully and instead of thanking him for his kindness, she snapped at him and called him a pervert and told him to piss off. Joe was shocked at her reaction and scurried out of the room as fast as he could, right he said to himself she can piss off herself she's mad the bitch. Hot tears sprang up in his eyes and he wondered if life would ever get better, she wouldn't be there if Mam and Camy were still alive.

Ginny pulled the covers tighter around herself and muttered about young perverts and the like, the sooner she got out of this hell hole the quicker she would get better. If only Jim would keep his trousers on, the easier it would be for her to leave. Just the sight of him with an erection was enough for her to throw her draws in the air and spread her legs; well he could whistle from now on she'd had enough as soon as her test was back from the hospital she was off for good. The pain in her belly returned with a vengeance and she squealed like a pig and rolled about on the bed, no one bothered to come up and see if she was all right and she cursed the uncaring cold blooded bastards that they were.

"Rot in hell" she shouted at anyone who could hear her. Then she began to feel sorry for herself and the tears followed, still nobody bothered with her and she cried herself to sleep as the pills began to work.

Jim had gone back to work almost taking the door of its hinges as he left, Joe made himself scarce too back to his job at the butchers shop, glad to be out of earshot. What with Jim balling and shouting and Ginny squealing in pain he didn't know what to do, anyway he wasn't going back into that room again so she could get lost. As soon as his father left he followed, he passed Jean and she him where the fire was. He explained about Ginny and the way she had turned on him, "er call't me a pervert" mumbled a very bashful Joe. Jean ruffled his hair in an affectionate way and giggled to herself as he peddled off down the hill, poor lamb he didn't even know what a pervert was. That Ginny was sailing close to the wind and something had to be done about her and soon.

Jean wondered weather to call in on Ginny and have it out with her but as she had taken to her bed it would probably be best if she left it for a while, plus the fact that she was drunk too and in the middle of the day whatever next. Ada was aghast when Jean called in to tell her about the latest goings on but Jean knew that it would give Ada something to think about besides Ted, she needed some other diversion away from the dead so it was all grist to the mill as far as Jean was concerned. Ada was adamant that she would be calling round on the slut the very next morning, so Jean left her to work out her speech. It was time for the mill workers to finish for the night so she decided that she would wait for Mary and see how she was, as she hadn't seen her sister for a couple of weeks she was shocked at her appearance. Mary was even thinner than before and didn't look at all well, Mary wasn't best pleased to see her sister and thought here it comes.

And she was correct as Jean began to berate her about the weight loss and haggard appearance, "If tha's nowt to say other'n tha's lost weight our Jean then dunna bother." snapped an angry Mary and turned on her heel and headed of home leaving an angry Jean standing feeling foolish, hot tears welled in her eyes in her distress for her sister who looked so poorly. What was she going to do to help her, she decided that Brian would have to be informed, and told as little as possible but enough for him to be worried and let her know that he was worrying. Then maybe she would do something about it before it was to late and she had joined her Mother and Sister down the cemetery.

Arthur took the brunt of Jean's wrath, but he understood that it was all out of concern for her sister so he wasn't too put out. Anyway he was feeling just as concerned if not more'so but hiding his feelings well from his wife, he asked himself what on earth would the outcome of it all be. Mary might not survive the birth she wouldn't have the strength the way she was carrying on, starved half to death just existing to the point where folks were noticing.. The village loved a good story and the thoughts of Mary Moore dying in childbirth was a juicy bit of gossip to mull over and pass around, she was aware of this but didn't really care one way or the other. She was carrying a baby that she didn't want and all the love in the world couldn't change that, she was doomed she knew that for all eternity and the thoughts of it filled her with dread and self loathing.

The next day at work she was trying to avoid eye contact with Archie and Monty, they had exchanged looks and shaken their heads in dismay at the sight of the once lovely young girl glowing with heath and happiness. Her beautiful eyes were dead the sparkle had gone from them, they tried everything they could to make her laugh but it was no use she didn't want to know. Archie danced his silly jig which had never failed to leave her helpless with laughter, but it fell on stony ground. Monty told her one of his silly stories and she tried to manage a week half smile, no matter how they tried they couldn't help in any way to ease her suffering . One of her workmates had witnessed the carry on and called over to the men that Mary was a bloody mard'arse, and wondered what she would be like when she had a dozen brats to see to like herself. "Er needs a kick up'th bloody backside" she mouthed to them. Monty and Archie didn't answer they felt too miserable it was the first time there daft antics had failed to work and it hurt.

While Jean sat composing her letter to Mary's husband Brian her Aunty Ada was knocking on her late sisters door, ready for the tongue lashing she was going to give to Ginny. After repeated knockings the door was opened a fraction and a small voice bade her to go away, that was like a red rag to a bull and Ada pushed the door wide open and bowled in knocking Ginny to the floor as she did so. The words of wrath were silenced in her throat when her eyes met those of Ginny's, despite everything she heard herself ask "what on earth's up wi'thee." Ginny was too weak to get up from behind the door where she had fallen like a sack of spuds, and Ada reluctantly helped her up. She didn't answer Ada right away she was clearly in a lot of pain, Ada helped her over to the settle and sat her down.

Ada then proceeded to put the kettle on and made them both a cup of tea, she might hate the woman but she wasn't merciless. Ginny couldn't hold her cup so Ada helped her to drink the brew, which she galloped down as fast as she could. "Dos'th want another," asked Ada, Ginny nodded and enjoyed the second cup. Ada sat and waited for the woman to get herself together, Ginny for the first time in her life felt vulnerable she was too week to fight with the little fat woman she felt far to ill. At the time of Ada banging on the door she was trying to pack her belongings as best she could, she had to get away as soon as she possible.

At last she was able to carry on a conversation of sorts with Ada, she tried to explain that she was leaving and wouldn't be back again ever. This was good news to Ada and she almost shouted hooray out loud, "ast'tha bin to'th Doctors lass" inquired Ada. Ginny assured her that she had but didn't offer to tell her any other detail, "well I'l let thee get on then an I wunna say it's bin a pleasure" Ada told her after her offer of help was declined. At the door Ada turned and it was like looking back to when her Sal had lain on that very same settle dying, that lass is dying too the thought came into her head well well so that was the end of the troublesome Ginny she would run away to die like a wounded animal.

Ada trundled up the street to her cottage she hadn't had to have a slanging match with the dreadful Ginny and knowing she would soon be gone and never be back it was all anyone could ever ask for, she did feel a twinge of pity for the hapless woman but it didn't last for very long. The family would think that she had got rid of the thorn in their side well she wasn't going to enlighten them let them think what they liked it wouldn't hurt, as long as she cleared of the better it would be. Jim would no doubt start looking for another floozy to share his bed at the very first opportunity, by hell he was disgusting all he ever thought about was sex. He was an animal with no scruples, her poor Sal what she must have had to endure all those years no wonder she had wanted to die just to get away from him. There had been a time the night Sal had died that she had felt for him but his antics afterwards had swept all that away, now it was hatred once more for the bastard.

How she carried her suitcase and bags down the street Ginny would never know, her body was in excruciating pain and she almost collapsed, but the thoughts of her nosy neighbours craning there necks to see her leave kept her on her feet. No way in the world would they ever see her fall down arse over charlie peacock,

she would go as she arrived head held high shoulders back high heels clicking on the stony cobbles. The thick makeup hiding a sallow skin and anyone who had dared to look into her lacklustre eyes would have seen death staring back at them, she made it to the railway station and had to endure an hour long wait for the next train. It was bloody typical of this shitty one horse town she moaned, she was glad to be getting away from it and from Jim Moore and his bloody family. The whole lot of them were a pain in the arse except for the little fat one, they would never have become friends but they would have enjoyed some good battles. Wonder what she came knocking the door down for, thought Ginny she never did say what she wanted. The thoughts of Ada sat looking at her with her fat chins wobbling, little fat legs dangling of the floor and large fat tits heaving up and down was too much and in spite of her pain Ginny broke down into fits of laughter and almost choked

By the time the train arrived even later than it was expected Ginny was at her wits end, her pain was worse and she feared that she would die on the platform and never escape Bridgevale. As the train pulled away from the station she closed her eyes tight shut and kept them like that until she was sure that Bridgevale was well and truly out of sight, she never ever wanted to set eyes on it again as long as she lived. How long that would be she didn't know that bungling Doctor Hallam had gone on about septicaemia and something piercing the bowel, he had wanted her to go into hospital at once but she had refused point blank and marched out of the surgery. The tablets he gave her were dwindling but she would get some more somewhere they would help, all this because of the day she had left Haverfordwest and her cousin Dai had given her something to remember him by. Ginny tried desperately not to remember the tiny cell in the small police station, the overpowering smell of disinfectant the rough hard blanket on the rickety bunk bed and the truncheon..

Chapter Fourteen

Loss of an Angel

A cry of anguish broke the silence in the hut, men writing home to their loved ones looked up at each other. Jim Moore was doubled up in pain, Charles leaned over to him. "I say old chap having a spot of bother" he enquired; he noticed that Jim was clutching a newspaper. "Not bad news old boy," he asked. Jim was in obvious distress, Charles witnessed the pain in his eyes. Jim passed over the newspaper to his friend, there on the front page was the picture of a couple in wedding attire and Charles noted at once the beautiful smiling Coral.

The headlines ran MP Weds WRAF Beauty, then went on to describe the pair of them. Poor Jim the headline had been a severe shock to his system and he was fighting with all his strength to keep the tears at bay, he couldn't be seen to weep he was a man after all and it just wasn't done. Mathew Spencer had become an MP, now that was a catch for any young girl as Jim could plainly see.

Daffers had been right after all when she had told the tale about Coral and the man from the ministry. However she hadn't mentioned the forth-coming nuptials and Charles wondered why, it wasn't like her at all she enjoyed inflicting pain on young Jim. Charles decided to seek her out and find out as much as he could, young Jim Moore would have to be left to come to terms with the painful news as best he could.

The rest of the men got on with their tasks none of them wanted to interfere in any way. Jim crawled into his bed and tried to shut out the world, how could she do this to him had she never really loved him. Deep down inside he knew that it was nothing to do with him he was the married one, he was the one who had betrayed his wife. His darling Tilly at home unsuspecting worrying about his safety and well being never knowing or suspecting that her beloved husband who she adored, wanted and lusted after another woman every waking moment of his life.

Over at the White Horse Charles sought out Daphne, she wasn't hard to find braying like a donkey at some poor suspecting male. Charles liked her less and less each time he came into contact with her, she spotted him and quickly excused herself from the man doting on her every word and sped to his side. Wondering if a damned good shagging was on the agenda, her body craved a good seeing to and Charles was the man to do it he was the best she had ever known. Daphne whispered her desire quickly and urgently into his ear, and although he didn't really like her sex with her was too good to pass up.

Without even ordering a drink he turned and headed for the door with her quickly in tow, in moments they had reached their spot and without any pretence of foreplay were soon engaged in erotic sex, sheer animal attraction. When they were both spent and fully satisfied they returned to the White Horse, they were greeted with cheers and laughter but neither of them could care less.

Charles ordered the drinks and they sauntered over to a corner of the pub and sat themselves down, "Have you heard from Coral recently" he asked her. Daffers waffled on about not hearing from her so-called best friend, "haven't heard from the bitch for months she hasn't even had the good grace to answer my correspondence or telephone calls." Moaned Daffers, Charles then took great delight in telling about the newspaper article. Daphne flew of in a rage the likes of which he had never seen, he could hear her shouting married at the top of her voice followed by Judas and bloody bitch.

Charles laughed out loud and everyone wondered what he had said to her to make her so angry, he had got his end away before he had given her the bad news so that was fine he would have a good nights sleep now that he had emptied his little sack. However there was still the distressed Jim to deal with before lights out, he fortified himself with a double brandy and headed back to his hut. Thankfully Jim was asleep so he didn't have to put on his wise old owl head for which he was very grateful, he wondered how Jim would get over it, his love for Coral had been genuine.

Jim had lain doggo pretending to be asleep, he couldn't face any of his mates at the moment his mind was racing at a rate of knots. "Coral" he almost cried her name out loud, why oh why had she done this to him. How could she fall in love with someone else so soon, to have forgotten him like he had meant nothing at all to her. Hot tears sprang to his eyes once more, he cursed his female hormones he was fast turning into a big Jessie. Well he would have to come to terms with it she was a married woman now, she didn't want him that was plain to see. There was Tilly to think about, poor Tilly what on earth would she think if she ever knew ever found out.

Life had to go on he would try not to dwell on it, to wish Coral all the happiness in the world. However his heart still felt heavy in his chest when he finally drifted into a fitful sleep, dreaming endlessly of ghostly figures in wedding attire each one sure to be Coral until he turned them around then they were someone else.

Daphne was fuming to put it mildly, to think of that jumped up bitch she had once called her best friend. To get married without a word, to do so and not even invite her to the nuptials. Well it was unthinkable despicable and utterly rude in the extreme, she would never get over the slur. To be slighted in such a way made her blood boil, the contacts she could have made at the do, the men she could have met. There was bound to be wealthy husband material in abundance. Coral would have to be written to and scolded in the nicest possible way, she would have to run with the hare and the hounds otherwise she might never see her again. There was however one saving grace, Jim Moore this would wipe the smile of his smug face. He would probably be devastated crash his plane into the sea, or jump out over land and be likened to a pot of strawberry jam when they scooped up his remains. This thought would keep her going for a long time and she laughed until her eyes were streaming with tears, and everyone thought that she had gone completely mad.

The next morning as the men trudged towards the NAFFI Jim veered of in the direction of the hangers, the men were ready for this and in a couple of strides they had him by the arms and almost carried him inside. No one would listen to his protests about not being hungry or having a bad guts, he was dumped unceremoniously onto the chair and a large plate of buttered toast was placed in front of him. After much protesting he managed to eat four slices and felt better for it, he couldn't have managed the eggs and bacon but the toast was very good and after a couple of mugs of hot tea he began to feel human again. Blushing scarlet he managed to look into the eyes of Charles and the rest of his squadron, they took it in turns to playfully slap him across the head and a smile returned to his handsome face. He would be able to get on with his life now the shock had worn off a little, he would never forget Coral he would keep a special place for her in his heart and now and then take her out and think about her and hopefully not break down.

Sometime later skimming the treetops over the English countryside Jim thought about his brother Harry and wondered how he was coping with the war, he hadn't heard from him for some time now and he hoped that all was well with him. His son young Harry was a grand little chap and Jim wondered if himself and Tilly would ever have a son, he hoped so he was sure after his last leave that he had left one in the oven. However Tilly had written tearfully that it hadn't happened this time, so on his next leave they would have to work day and night to make sure that it did. Something that she was looking forward to immensely, Jim began to feel hot under the collar and thoughts of himself and Tilly in bed night and day baby making filled him with desire. As soon as his flight training was over he almost ran for the showers to cool his ardour, feeling bashful in case anyone noticed his hard on which just wouldn't go down he doubled up with laughter something he hadn't done for a long long time.

Billy shouted out to him that they were off to the "Horse" and would he be joining them, he felt ready for a pint or three and told Billy. "Try and stop me," he would be more positive, stop moaning about Coral and get on with his life. It wouldn't be easy he knew that, every now and then something would happen to bring him to his knees. The pain would be swift and excruciating but he would deal with it head on, he would drink to her good health that very night. And he did with a vengeance so much so that he had to be put to bed once again sobbing like a baby, all his good intentions out of the window. Next morning found him very ashamed of himself he wore his chin on his chest for much of the day, and any talk of food sent him rushing to the latrines. There would be no White Horse for him that night he had to pull himself together once and for all, there followed a visit from Charles who didn't beat about the bush and warned him that his mates were getting heartily feed up with his childish outbursts. This hit home and was probably the saving of him he knew that he couldn't go on like he was doing, Charles's parting words rang in his ears. "You can't aim a rifle at the hun with eyes full of tears old boy," "we have a bloody war to win."

Jim decided to write to Tilly but he couldn't even do that, he couldn't tell her about his drunken antics. Or the tears for another woman one he loved more than herself, no he couldn't do that. He would have to tell someone about it, get it off his chest. He would write to Harry he would understand and he wouldn't tell anyone about it, he could be trusted to the ends of the earth. So he wrote at length and poured out his heart and bared his very sole, afterwards he felt a lot better and was glad that he had someone to turn to in his hour of need. The post wouldn't have gone yet so he strolled over to the pillabox as he posted his mail a pretty young Air-woman sidled up to him, she was very provocative and he was quite taken aback. "Want a role in the hay," she asked him as brazen as you like. Jim brushed her aside quite rudely and snapped at her to clear of and behave herself she was obviously the worse for drink, anyway he was in this state because of his role in the hay with Coral. "Where's your hut," he demanded of her. “Block H" she answered, and before she could stop him he was frog-marching her down the path to Block H. All the shouting and swearing didn't stop him until he reached the hut door, and opening it up he almost threw her inside then marched swiftly away. He knew that what he had done was cruel and that he had humiliated her, however he had to show her the error of her ways before it was too late. Hopefully she wouldn't remember him the next day so he wouldn't have to hide from her and just maybe she would behave herself and save herself from someone who would take her up on her offer.

Jim arrived back at his hut just as Charles was escorting Daphne back to hers; she couldn't help herself making snide remarks about Jim. Calling him the country bumpkin, then saying he would be best employed back home on the farm growing spuds and turnips instead of trying to fly planes. “Can you imagine it a turnip piloting an aeroplane," she trilled and almost collapsed in a fit of laughter. Charles almost dragged her past Jim who didn't give a damn what she thought of him anyway, "sorry old boy." Mouthed his friend, then the were out of sight with her shrill tones ringing on the night air something about cow muck and bulls, Jim closed his ears to it she was a silly pathetic cow and he wouldn't waste his thoughts on her. Sod the silly bugger let her go to hell it would be the best place for her, it made Jim feel really angry but it stopped him dwelling on thoughts of Coral so it did some good and he got his first decent nights sleep for ages.

There was a tugging at his bed covers and Billy Downs was calling to him to get up, everyone else was up and about. Jim stretched and yawned he really had slept well and he felt the better for it, he burst into song on his way to the showers something he hadn't done for many a long time and all the lads burst into rapturous applause much to his embarrassment. "Piss Off", he shouted back over his shoulder and they all roared with laughter. Later on he teamed up with Charles Feathergill, Jack Benson, Billy Downs, and Roger Evesham. The Four Must've Beers plus One as they called themselves, today they were training in a Lancaster Bomber which looked huge on the outside but proved to be a different story on the inside. The space they had to occupy was small and cramped and some of them were almost bent double at the end of their stint. However the camaraderie helped to keep them all going and they really enjoyed themselves, although there was no sign of combat from over the water they had to be prepared at all costs.

Daphne decided to telephone the Bevan household and putting on her poshest accent she asked the telephonist to be put through to their number, the phone was answered quickly by a breathless female. Upon hearing Daphnes plumy tones she sounded rather upset, "sorry I was expecting someone else." Obviously a man thought Daphne, she quickly explained who she was and asked if it was possible to speak to Coral. It was Fran her sister, who remembered only to well the obnoxious snob, the crushing bore that was Daphne. "What do you want" she asked, Coral doesn't live here now she's married. Daphne was hardly able to contain her anger, how downright rude the girl was. Still she tried to wheedle some information out of the girl, gritting her teeth she tried again to worm her way in perhaps for an invitation to the house. "Not bloody likely" barked a furious Fran, "Go and bore somebody else you silly bugger" and with a hearty laugh she slammed down the phone. Daphne was livid, never in all her life had she been spoken to like that. It wasn't the end she would get in touch with Coral somehow, and find out what was happening.

Meanwhile back in Bridgevale Mary was in for a wonderful surprise, she had gone to bed early as usual to escape the bother of having to make herself any food. There came the usual knocking at the door, this time it was the front door, which was strange. Mary had long ago learned that Fred Wright came around to call a couple of times a week, she hadn't let on best to ignore the silly bugger and hope that he would get fed up and go away. No matter how he tried he would never get into her home, she had learned the hard way with Tom Scully ever to get caught like that again. In fact she would rather die than have anything to do with the pair of them, dirty filthy buggers they were sex mad that was all they ever thought of day and night. After a while the knocking was replaced by stone throwing at the window, and a mans voice was calling her name. Mary sat bolt upright in bed she would know that voice anywhere, it was Brian her Brian. It couldn't be he would have let her know, her mind was playing tricks with her. Steeling herself she crept out of bed and over to the window, sliding the curtain over just a fraction she peeped down to the street below, there looking up at her was her beloved Brian. Mary let out a huge squeal and dashed out of the bedroom and down the stairs in the pitch dark forgetting her safety and that of her baby, it seemed to take an age to unlock the door and then they were in each others arms both of them weeping uncontrollably.

After a while Brian extracted himself from Mary's arms and lit the gas light turning it up full, and what he saw reduced him almost to a gibbering wreck. When Jean had contacted him and told him about the state that his wife was in, not mentioning her infidelity of course. He had assumed she was just missing him, he wasn't prepared for this. A stranger stood before him a gaunt stick thin sickly woman, he had felt every bone in her body when he held her in his arms and the full luscious breasts that he used to marvel at were almost non-existent. His face said it all, and before he could say a word she had fled up to the sanctuary of her bedroom where she wept more bitter tears. Brian thought it better to leave her for a little while and he made his way to the kitchen and put on the kettle for a cup of tea, he would make her some soup and bread and butter. He had a weeks leave before he left England for a tour of duty in some part of Africa, the powers that be hadn't told him where exactly, in that week he would feed his wife and get her back to what she used to be. One or two of his mates had told him about sickness in pregnancy and the rapid weight loss, well he would be here to help and encourage her and in no time at all she would be the old Mary he knew and loved.

The kitchen cupboards were bare there wasn't a thing to eat, the same with the meat safe nothing at all. There was however a quarter of tea and some milk no sugar, so he made do with that and the bar of chocolate he had bought at the train station. He bounded up the stairs with his tray careful not to spill any and put it on the bedside table, he then gently gathered his frail young wife in his arms and dried her tears. After they had finished the tea and she had been almost bullied into eating the small bar of chocolate, they talked at length Mary assuring him that it was all to do with carrying the baby. Brian let her know about the week's leave before setting off abroad, she was very upset at this but he couldn't hide it from her and it would have been foolish to try. Jean's letter however would not be mentioned now or ever as far as he was concerned, but in his heart he thanked her for it.

As the two of them fondled and kissed each other Brian prepared to make love to his eager wife, the long months of separation had taken there toll and he was beside himself with joy and happiness. This is what he had wanted had longed for with all his heart, and just as he was about to enter her he felt her freeze suddenly beneath him and pull away so that he was left poised in mid air. He felt very foolish and didn't quite know what to do, Mary began to shake from head to foot as if in shock, and the tears were back with a vengeance. Brian soothed his troubled bride and told her not to fret, he cursed himself for being insensitive but at the same time wondered what to do about his erection that just would not go down. However this was solved later on when Mary decided to take matters into her own hands it was the least that she could do, she couldn't go through with the love-making much as she had wanted to something had happened to her at the most crucial moment, but she would be alright next time it was just that she had been used to doing without for such a long time.

For the first time in months she slept well and awoke felling on top of the world, as she opened her eyes Brian was gazing down at her tears streaming down his face. Mary pulled him to her and they hugged each other until she could hardly breath, the same thing happened as the night before and he was left high and dry. Trying not to show it he concentrated on listening to his baby in the womb and watched in amazement as it kicked with great gusto, "cricky" shouted Mary "I'm gonna be late fer'th shed and off she bounded to get ready. "Dunna go in today lass," begged Brian. "I canna just av'th time off tha knows," answered Mary "I'll ge'th sack. Making for the door she picked up her shawl as Brian asked her about her breakfast, "tha's made me late now I'l ave summat at work." Mary promised, "wait fer me I'll walk wi'thee said Brian and off they set arm in arm. It looked like the whole of Bridgevale were of to work that morning, clogs clattering on cobblestones some running others striding out with a purpose. Not Mary though she was dawdling didn't really want to go, she wished she could stay at home with her man she had missed him so much. And she must remember not to let him see how she really felt about the baby, she would have to make a pretence play the excited happy mother to be. Never letting him know how she really felt about the bastard inside her, after a long lingering kiss she was gone through the big swing doors and he was alone.

Right, "here goes" thought Brian as he headed for the door marked

'Works Manager' tapping lightly he waited, no reply so he knocked a little louder. A voice shouted "come in" he opened the door and peered around it. A young girl was sitting at a large desk filing her nails, she smiled at him showing a mouthful of pearly white teeth. "Can I help thee" she asked, "I was wundrin as ow I could see'th Boss." Answered Brian, "if that'ed be allreet." The young girl flashed him another beaming smile, "sit thee down a bit Mr Entwhistle's on his rounds of'Th mill he should'na be very long. Brian sat down and thanked the girl, she got on with her filing that was until the door flew open and Mr Entwhistle burst in. Then she turned into a whirlwind bustling about with papers and such, Brian was amazed. Mr Entwhistle nodded to him and he returned the nod, "can I elp thee" he enquired of Brian. Seeing the embarrassed look on the young mans face he ushered him into his own office and closed the door, "is it about Mary" he asked. "Well aye it is, I was wunderin if tha would let er ave a couple o days off". "She anna bin too good carryin'th baby, an bein'as ive got a few days leave." Turning red at this point he was relieved when Mr Entwhistle intervened, "it's all reet lad I can see fer mesen ow Mary's bin, a few days we thee will put the colour back in them cheeks on er's."

Brian was quite taken aback by this he had expected to put up some sort of a fight, however he had heard that Mr Entwhistle could be a very fair man. Things like bad workmanship etc were said to send him frantic with rage, Brian must have got him on a good day. Thanking him profusely he left the office and on his way out winked at the young girl, who unexpectedly winked back. By ek er's a forward madam an no mistake he thought to himself, thank heavens my Mary's non like that.

He headed up to the high street shops, he would buy some provisions fill the bare cupboards and cook something delicious for Mary's tea. His first stop was at Mr Lamb's butcher's shop where he received a warm welcome, young Joe came in from the back and he rushed up to Brian and wrung his hand. Huge tears welled in his eyes, "ast tha sin our Mary," he enquired of Brian. His brother-in-law nodded his head in reply, "dunna thee worry lad I'm goin't feed er'up an er'l be as right as ninepence tha'l see we'll ave ere better in no time at all".

Mr Lamb clucked sympathetically as he weighed out a quarter of steak and kidney, "non on ems same tha knows every woman's different, some on em tak to motherhood like a duck ta watta an others can ave a very difficult time."

"This ere will do err the world'a good put airs on her chest it will," he added with a chortle. Brian thanked him and before leaving called out to Joe asking him to call round and visit anytime that goes for the others too he added, meaning Lizzie, Teddy and Alex. By the time he arrived home there was fresh bread, vegetables, meat and a little fresh fruit some biscuits and cheese. At least the cupboards didn't look so bare, by the time Mary arrived home in a state of exhaustion a mouth-watering meal awaited her. "Did tha go an ask owd Entie if I could ave'th rest of'th week of," she shouted at him throwing her arms round him at the same time. " I did that lass so tha can put thee feet up an no arguments reet," said Brian. "Now just sniff at this tea Ive got thee ready an sit the down", however the aroma only set of Mary's nausea and instead of sitting down to her meal lovingly prepared for her, she spent most of the night throwing up.

Brian held his young wife in-between her bouts of sickness and cursed the powers that be who had kept him from her side, no wonder she was skin and bone the poor girl could keep nothing thing down. A visit to the Doctors was called for and the sooner the better, after putting Mary to bed and clearing away the uneaten food Brian made himself a cup of tea. A visit to Ada would be made too he would ask her advise, she knew Mary better than anyone. He wondered why she hadn't tried to fatten Mary up a bit, anyway he would ask. Thank the lord that Jean had taken the trouble to write and let him know the score, he would thank her in person tomorrow. There was also his Mother to see, why hadn't she been round to look after her Daughter-in -law he couldn't understand it at all. He would join his wife upstairs there was nothing else to do, so he cuddled up in their comfy bed and wondered how long it would be before she was able to let him make love to her his loins were aching with the want of it. His hands gently stroked her swollen belly, he felt afraid for his unborn child would it be alright could it survive in this tiny little maltreated body. He wouldn't be here to see his baby, he wondered if he ever would see it he hoped with all his heart that he would. One day to come home to Mary and a little son or daughter it was all any man could ever hope for. Brian didn't sleep very well that night, terrible nightmares filled his dreams and he was glad to wake up and be ride of them. Everywhere he turned had been filled with death scenes usually about Mary, dead in the bath, in the stream, at the foot of the stairs, in bed or draped over her looms at the mill. Try as he might he couldn't get the images out of his head, it scared him rigid and a terrible feeling of foreboding came over him. He let Mary stay in bed a lie in would do her good, and he dressed quickly and crept down the stairs so as not to wake her. It would have been nice to have lain there at her side waiting for her to awaken so that they could make love, he wondered if he would ever do it again and the thoughts of it were driving him mad. The two of them had always enjoyed such a good sex life especially when they had been baby making, they had been the best time's of all. Now the baby was made and it was almost killing his sweetheart, but what could he do about it other than pray to God that both of them would be all right.

What should he make his wife for her breakfast, bacon egg fried bread. Yes she used to love that, he would take it upstairs on a tray for her make a fuss make her feel wanted and loved. It would do her the world of good, and by the time he left she would be strong again. There was only one thing missing from the breakfast tray and that was a flower, but he hadn't got one so it would have to do without. standing it gingerly on the bed he gently stroked his wife's face until she opened her eyes, they were still beautiful but the dark circles under them spoilt the once exquisite setting.

"Breakfast'n bed melady," laughed Brian at his sleepy wife as she propped herself up with the large bolster. "Thar't ta good fer me tha knows I dunna deserve it," she mumbled shamefaced hanging her head. Brian almost snapped at her "Why what's tha dun wrong, nowt at all only carryin my kid an it makin thee badly al'th time. " "If tha want's to blame anyone fer'th state thart in then blame me lass I'm'th one as put the little un there."

Mary couldn't look him in the eye when he said that, so she didn't reply. The sight of the food he set in front of her made her feel sick to her stomach. It was all she could do not to upset the tray as she leapt out of bed and threw herself over the washbasin, where she retched and retched for what seemed like an age. Brian stood by bewildered once more at the sight of his young wife's plight, what could he do how could he help her. His nightmare was going to come true she would die and it was all his fault, she had been suffering all these months and no one had helped her. The words Jean had written to him sprang to mind, 'she won't let us help her ' she had said. Well perhaps it was correct maybe Mary had refused all help she could be very stubborn when she'd a mind. They set off to see Dr Hallam, Brian had insisted that she seek some kind of medical help. Mary looking deathly white Brian red faced with embarrassment, perhaps everyone would think that he was responsible for the deterioration in his young wife.

They didn't have to wait very long to see the Dr most of his patients had been in at the crack of dawn, and he was getting ready for his morning rounds. He took one look at the emaciated Mary and promptly laid her on the examination couch, "well Mary it takes the return of your husband to get you out to see me." He exclaimed, Brian asked him what he meant exactly, the Doctor then went on to tell him about his wife not attending any of her appointments to see him regarding the well being of her unborn baby. Brian was quite taken aback by this revelation and turned on Mary to hear her excuse; she didn't have one and only burst into tears. Well he couldn't scold her now so he shrugged his shoulders and looked helplessly at the Doctor, "what can you do" he asked to make her better. Dr Hallam scratched his head then proceeded to examine his patient, drawing the curtain across to allow a little privacy. When he was finished he called the nurse in to take a blood sample, and also asked Mary to see if she could provide him with a urine specimen. After the internal examination she had just gone through she was more than willing, they sat for a while waiting for the Doctor to give them the outcome. When he ushered them back into his surgery he came straight to the point and did not mince his words, after telling Mary off for neglecting her unborn baby he then went on about the care she would have to take now before it was to late. "The baby will probably be very small," unless you can get a lot more nourishment inside you," "maybe then things will get better." "You've got quite a bit of time before the birth so I urge you to try your very best if you want your baby to survive,"

Mary looked crestfallen, Brian a little angry. However they both nodded at the Doctor and Mary promised that from now on she would take better care of herself and her unborn child, it was just that she had felt so sick all the time. "I will give you something for that," added Doctor Hallam "however you must never take more than the stated dose and if it makes your symptoms more severe stop taking it right away." Mary assured him that she would and made for the door, "not so fast young lady" called the Doctor. "I want to see you here in this surgery in two weeks time weighing a little more than you do today," "so make an appointment on the way out good morning." At last they were outside and Mary breathed a sigh of relief, taking her husband's arm she smiled up at him. Brian didn't smile back he was puzzled as to why Mary hadn't been attending regular check up's at the surgery, after all she had longed for a baby, had wept bitter tears when she hadn't conceived over the years. Now that she was carrying their longed for child she was neglecting herself and putting the baby's life at risk, he didn't know what to make of it. Well he was home for a few days now so he would look after her and give her all the attention she wanted, pamper her and give her lots of love and hope it would do the trick. By the time he went back to his unit she would be on the better side, and he could leave her knowing that everything was going to be ok.

Ada was very pleased to see him and gave him a big hug, and sitting him down in the warm comfy kitchen she made a pot of tea and cut him a large wedge of her freshly baked cherry cake. Brian asked how she was coping without Ted and she answered truthfully that she wasn't really, that she never would and only death would release her from the pain of loosing him. "I'm non afeered o death tha'knows Brian cos'tha see Ted'll be waitin fer me," she went on and on about death and the dead and Brian was beginning to regret calling round. When she paused to draw breath he nipped in quick and asked her what she thought about the state of Mary, well she was caught off guard and coloured up bright red she didn't know what to say and spluttered and coughed. What was worse she couldn't look him in the eye which wasn't Ada she was the epitome of honesty and straight John Bull, "er wunna let us elp er an we'an tried lord knows we ave." Answered Ada she didn't know what to say she couldn't tell him the truth that was up to Mary herself, she wanted know part of it at all. What he would do if he found out the truth she couldn't imagine, all that she could hope for was that he never did find out.

Brian wasn't to be put off so easily, "why did'na she let thee elp er what's up wi'er." "I thoo'ht er were deein when I clapped eyes on er fust time," he added looking perplexed and angry. Ada couldn't answer him all she could say was that she and the rest of the family were here for Mary should she need them at any time day or night, she offered him another cup of tea which he declined saying that he needed to see Jean and then his mother in that order. Ada hugged him and prayed for his safekeeping God is wi'the lad she told him and waved goodbye from the doorstep, He didn't get any help from Jean who like Ada clamed up at the onset. "I sent fer thee cos our Mary wuddna let us elp er, and by eck we tried dunna thee think we did'na." "It's er ormones or summat like that," she added not knowing really what to say to the poor worried man. Then went on about how some woman suffered terribly with hormonal trouble, Brian had never heard about hormones so didn't quite understand and didn't know what to make of them he just wished that his wife didn't suffer from them whatever they were. Jean was glad when he made leave to go she had run out of excuses, and to say that her head was spinning was putting it mildly.

As Brian made his way to his Mother's house he felt that he was no better of for knowing what was ailing his young wife, and later at his Mothers he began to wish that he had never called on her. To say that she was miffed was an understatement; Mary had never been near to see her. When she had called round at Mary's house she was either always out or didn't answer the door, folks were gossiping about how ill she looked some saying that she would never survive the child's birth. Mrs Bailey had always loved Mary like a daughter and it had upset her no end to be treated like this, she had knitted and sown for the new baby until her fingers were raw. But his wife hadn't seen any of the layette that she was so lovingly preparing because she wasn't interested; Brian hugged his weeping Mum and tried to explain about the hormones and how ill his young wife was. Telling her how worried he was and that he wanted them all to try and help Mary as best they could, adding that he was being sent overseas when he returned from his leave, and didn't know when he would be back. This news sent his Mother into deeper despair and she cried as if her heart would break, as he held her Brian wondered if he would ever get back to his family and fear filled his mind.

When he had finally got away from his weeping Mother who he had got to promise to look after Mary for him he was exhausted, and getting back to Mary was the only thing left on his mind. His beloved had made an effort and dinner was almost ready, but just as she was dishing up the usual nausea swept over her and she had to dash off and left Brian to see to the rest. There he sat alone once more trying to eat the sausage and mash that Mary had so wanted to share with him, not really in the mood as he listened to her constant retching. "Did'tha take the jollop I picked up from'th chemist fer thee," he bellowed, getting no reply he looked in the cupboard and there was the medicine that Doctor Hallam had prescribed for the sickness sitting there unopened. He was furious why in Gods name hadn't she taken the bloody stuff, he would tear her off a strip when she had finished throwing up. However she wasn't looking too good later on when she returned to the table so he didn't go on at her, but he did get the medicine out of the cupboard and put it down in front of her. Sorry she told him I forgot, how could she forget to try out something that might ease her suffering he thought to himself. The months of sickness could have come to an end but she had forgotten to take it 'why' Brian wondered about Mary, what if she was loosing her marbles he had heard about women going mad when they were having babies. He would keep his eyes on her and help her to get better it was the least that he could do, so as soon as she looked a little better he spooned out a dose of the medication and made sure that it went down the hatch. Mary went up to bed for a rest and Brian tootled of to the shops for a few odds and ends, young Joe was just on his way home and Brian reminded him that he hadn't called round yet. This he promised to do the very next day so Brian promptly invited him for tea, and bring Teddy and Lizzie too he added. Then he set off for a stroll around the village to give Mary time to have a bit of kip he didn't want to wake her yet, on the way back passing the foundry he caught up with big Jim Moore who had just finished his shift. He was as black as a bog and looked fit to drop, Brian bade him good day and Jim nodded in return to his son-in-law. They chatted a little about this and that but Jim didn't enquire about his Daughter Mary once, then he was gone before anything else could be said. Brian scratched his head in bewilderment, what a family what a bloody sad bugger Jim Moore was; the more he met him the bigger stranger he became.

Arriving home he was surprised to see Mary was still in bed, she didn't want anything to eat so he made himself some sandwiches and a large mug of tea, and settled down to read a paper that he had found underneath the chair cushion it was a couple of months old but he hadn't read it before hadn't really had the time. It was all about the war apart from a wedding day picture of a Tory MP with his bride, a very pretty girl and they expected you to believe that she was in the WRAF never in a month of Sundays not her sort obviously born with a silver spoon in her mouth he would say. There was nothing to do so he decided to join Mary in bed; perhaps she was up to a little lovemaking he hoped so he was about at bursting point and couldn't go on without much longer. As he snuggled up to his warm sleepy wife she turned over to face him, thank God for that he thought to himself and immediately ran his trembling hand up her legs, when she pushed him away with all her strength and called out something that sounded like Tom as she beat her fists at his body. Brian caught her hands and held them tight as she wriggled and squirmed, then she was fully awake and realised what she was doing. "Sorry Brian I'musta bin dreamin," she panted quite out of breath. "Who wer't dreamin over tha shouted summat like Tom," answered Brian. It was a good thing that the darkness now hid her face as it turned to scarlet and the panic in her eyes, "It were a nightmare I dunna remember shoutin." Added a very anxious Mary wondering if she was going to get found out before her man's leave was up, with that she cuddled up to him and encouraged him to have his way with her although neither of there hearts were in it.

As she lay afterwards hating every moment of their lovemaking she knew that she would be glad when he was gone, she had always adored him but just at this time she wanted to be on her own. After all she was unclean she might pass on something she had caught off the dirty Tom Scully onto her Brian, and if she shouted out again Tom's name then he would know for sure that she had been unfaithful to him so the sooner she was left alone the better it would be. There would be no more lovemaking for the duration of his leave, it had left her feeling sick to her stomach she did not want anymore of it, never again. At break of dawn when she felt him throbbing pressing hard onto her buttocks wanting it once again, she was out of bed like a shot feigning sickness for the first time. He was rolling about moaning and panting and she knew that he was giving himself hand relief, well he would have to get used to that from now on because that was all he would be getting unless he found another woman. Mary hoped with all her heart that he never would she did love him but just at this time she couldn't stand the sexual side of their marriage. Perhaps she would feel different about it after the baby was born but she doubted it very much, even reminding herself about the birth set her nerves jangling. To think that in a few months time she would have a little person to look after, to suckle at her breast how on earth was she going to deal with that when she would hate and loath it. Mary shuddered at the mere thought of it anyway it would hopefully be stillborn God willing, but while her husband was home she would pretend that it was the finest thing that had ever happened to her and hope that he believed her.

"Sorry darlin the medcin dunna seem'th be workin as yet," she whispered on her return. Brian couldn't blame her it wasn't her fault and drawing her close he assured her that she needn't worry and that all would be well, her hand sought his still proud manhood and she gave him more hand relief until he begged her to stop. Thank heaven for that she muttered to herself her bloody hand was in agony all that pulling and tugging men she thought, nothing but animals deep down animals the lot off them. Brian was happy and whistled all the way down the stairs where he proceeded to cook a large fry up, and unbelievably Mary didn't feel sick and tucked in with great gusto. "I told thee the Doctors jollop would do'th trick," Brian couldn't resist telling her over and over again until she threatened to throttle him. It was then that he remembered he had invited the kids for tea, Mary wasn't very pleased which wasn't like her at all but Brian assured her that he would be doing the cooking so not to worry it was all in hand. By the time they arrived breathless and full of fun, Mary was dreading them asking about the baby but they did endlessly. Going on and on about how lovely it would be and how Lizzie would take it out in the bassinet for walks, and then to top it all she asked Mary how many matinee coats she had knitted. Considering that she hadn't finished the first one she decided that a plan of action was called for, so as soon as Brian dished up the shepherd's pie she again feigned sickness and made for her bed to escape them.

Brian couldn't understand it the medicine should be working by now, if his wife didn't eat something soon she would disappear without trace. Lizzie wanted to take some food upstairs for Mary but was assured that when she was hungry she would be back down, everything fell a bit flat after that without their sister to talk to the kids were at a loss as to what to talk about. In the end they didn't stay very long after the meal that Brian had prepared for them, he was ill at ease worrying about his sickly wife and wanting to be with her. So they all shouted upstairs to Mary wishing her good night and hoping she would feel better soon, then trooped off down the dark street playing games as they went wishing that someone was waiting for their return. Anything would be better than an empty house and the prospect of Jim Moore returning in a drunken stupor; well they would be in bed long before he returned that was for sure. The boys and their sister practically ran the last few yards home just in case the Devil was after them, but they beat him to the door and hurriedly shut themselves in gasping for breath. After making sure that all was tidy in the house and the fire was safe they went up to bed, Lizzie called to Joe"dust'tha think our Mary's goi'th die." "Dunna talk so daft Lizzie tha shudd'na say such things tha'l ave our Alex cryin all neet," snapped back Joe.

Lizzie didn't know what to think about it all she was bewildered, other women had babies all the time and they didn't get thin and poorly like Mary they got fatter and fatter by the day. Lizzie had often wondered why they didn't burst like a balloon, and there was also the fact that since she started having the baby Mary hadn't been the same with any of them, where before she had always scooped them up in her arms and hugged and kissed them especially Alex. That had become a thing of the past she couldn't be bothered with them at all, and she hadn't been round to visit them for a long time. Aunty Ada said she didn't go round to her house either and it made her weep, she always added that Uncle Ted would be spinning in his grave if he knew.

Lizzie was brought back to reality rather quickly as the front door slammed, heralding the return of Jim Moore. He wasn't long before he was clumping up the stairs, and could be heard whistling loudly. Non of the children could quite take it in, big Jim didn't whistle but he was and he didn't even slam the bedroom door. Well well whatever had come over him they would be finding out never fear, it was the first time since Ginny left that they hadn't heard the regulation slamming of the door. Lizzie was glad that Ginny had finally slung her hook and she knew that the boys felt the same, they were forever sniggering about her and her sexy clothes. Not forgetting of course the time that Joe had seen everything she had when she was having a bath that day, as he repeated time after time the sight of them big tits would stay in his mind forever.

It was at the breakfast table next morning that their father told them that he would be away for a couple of days, he didn't say why and they didn't dare ask. However he did look mightily pleased with himself and the ear to ear grin just wouldn't go away, he told them that they would be sleeping at Aunty Ada's until his return and by eck they had better be good or else. So after countless warnings about their behaviour and not to lose the latchkey, and not to light the fire or have anyone in the house he was gone. The children breathed a sigh of relief and began to run around the house shouting at the tops of their voices, up and down the stairs whooping like Indians when suddenly the front door flew open and in strolled their father looking as mad as the Devil. "I knew tha'rd be like bloody idiots as soon as me back were turned," he roared and proceeded to give them all a clip round the ears. He then picked up the small overnight bag that he had deliberately left behind the settle and with a last threat of I'll kill thee bastards when I get's back, he was gone once more leaving them trembling with fear.

Round to Aunty Ada's they trooped after breakfast looking very sheepish, Ada who missed nothing looked at the lot of them and asked "what ast bin up to then." They hung their heads and didn't answer, until Ada repeated her question then Joe answered her. "Well we were just larkin about an he came back an caught us," "oh an I bet tha were actin like bloody fools eh." Snapped Ada "I allis tells thee non to let the bugger see thee actin bloody goat," but tha never listen to me so that'll av'th put up wi'th consequences tha'll never learn never as long as tha lives." Ada shook her head and muttered about banging her head against a brick wall and letting them get on with it, they were then given their orders as to sleeping arraignments for the next couple of nights then Joe rushed out to work and the others got ready for school. "Where's Dad gone too Aunty Ada," asked Lizzie "Im as wise as thee." Answered Ada, "just bloody swaned in an said as ow somut had cropped up an could I see to thee all." "Let's just pray he's non gone after that bloody floozy Ginny, if he brings that bugger back then I wash me soddin ands on Im." Ada went on and on until poor Lizzie wished that she hadn't asked and was thankful when it was time to leave for school.

When the children had left and Ada was tidying up after them she got to thinking about Jim and her eyes filled with tears, she hoped with all her heart that he wouldn't be returning with the bloody awful Ginny. The woman was nothing short of a prostitute and she oughtn't to be allowed in the same house as young impressionable children, what Sal would think about it all she didn't know she wept for Sal and for Cammy and her Ted. God how she missed them all life just wasn't the same and never would be again at least not for her, and death couldn't come too soon for her just to be with her loved ones that's all she asked. Life had become a chore for her there was no one to please, like she used to please Ted with her mouth-watering dishes and home baked bread. He used to love the smell of it when he walked through the door, "by gum lass tha's got a reet good batch in'th oven." Then he would laugh at the double meaning in it as Ada turned red with embarrassment, she would pretend to be outraged at him then they would laugh about it together and he would hug her close content to be together.

The memories came flooding back and poor old Ada almost collapsed under the weight of emotion, her heart pounded in her well padded chest and she wondered if she would go like Sal and then Ted heart trouble the pair of them. It was selfish she knew because if she went there would be no one to look after the children, although Jean and Mary could do it if they had to. Thinking about Mary she wondered how the girl was, what a change there had been in her she did look very ill. However there was nothing they could do to help her she had got herself into the mess and she would have to get herself out of it, she wouldn't accept their help anyway and they had tried lord knows they had. Ada still couldn't believe that Mary could have let herself be seduced by the dreadful Tom Scully, she had always been such a clean good living girl and if she had to stray why couldn't she have gone for some clean cut lad someone more her age. They would all have to pray extra hard that Brian wouldn't ever find out about it, it wasn't nice but the out-come would be much worse should he do so.

Well there were spuds to peel and the meat to put in the oven for when the kids came home so she had best get on with it, she would bake a nice fruit pie for them and make a rice pudding to go with it. There was nowt to beat a good fruit pie with lashings of creamy rice pudding with a good thick skin on the top, as she bent down to reach for the pie plate she let out an almighty fart. It made her shake with laughter what would Ted have said to her, something like "By eck Ada tha very nigh got me wi that one." Poor Ted he would have been such a comfort to her now that the lads had gone off to war, she would have been able to talk to him about her everyday worries and he would have reassured her that all would be well and everyone knew a trouble shared was a trouble halved. There was Sal's house to see to they might have left a mess behind so she had better get round their and see, there was so much to do and she could have done with a cat nap never mind she would have one when she had finished the pie. It would be nice to have the children for a couple of nights she didn't like being in the house on her own very much, she had always been a little nervous of the dark and swore she never slept. However those who had stayed the night could tell a different story about noises in the house, mainly farting and horrendous snoring coming from Ada's bedroom.

The kids enjoyed their stay with Ada and she was more than pleased to have them, she always slept better knowing that she wasn't alone. So when Jim returned a couple of nights later she wasn't feeling very happy that they would be returning home just as she had gotten used to having them, he was beside himself with joy at what she didn't know. The kids were getting ready for bed so Ada assured him that one more night wouldn't hurt, he was quite keen on the idea much to her surprise and had soon disappeared into the night. Ada made the most of it and soon they had a singsong going and all took turns, they all had very good singing voices and Ada wept as she sat listening to them. Lizzie could never understand why her Aunty wept so often because when any of them wept she used to say that they would piss less, and she wondered if Ada would piss less but wouldn't dare ask her. This was the last night they would stay with Ada for a while at least, it was back to Father and his shouting and balling and the constant cleaning and tidying she got sick of it and wished that someone else would do it instead. Maybe one day she would escape and let them do there own dirty work, but she couldn't foresee that happening not yet anyway. When Ada tucked them up in bed she kissed them and hugged them tight the lads were a bit put out but tried not to show it, the old songs they had been singing had got her all nostalgic and she wept for days gone by. Lizzie felt guilty about her thoughts earlier and she hugged her Aunty back as hard as she could, she knew that they would be the poorer for not having her around.

Big Jim Moore raced back to his house as fast as he could his heart pounding in anticipation, flinging open the door and just standing there marvelling at the sight of Meg sitting in the fireside chair looking for all the world like she belonged there. He ran to her and scooped her up in his arms and kissed her hungrily, when he came up for air he told her the kids would be staying at Ada's for the night and suggested that they made the most of their time alone in the house. Which meant lets get to bed right away, which they did like two school kids dashing up the stairs shrieking with laughter. If anyone had seen Jim Moore they wouldn't have believed it, he was a dashing cavalier and Meg was his lady. He knew that she would never have the sexual expertise that Ginny possessed but he no longer wanted that sort of sex, he needed her soft womanly body and her shyness. The thrill he had when he witnessed her enjoyment of the lovemaking they shared with him the dominant partner hit him for six, Ginny had always enjoyed leading the way and while it was good sex it wasn't as enjoyable. With Meg it was a totally different story she was soft and yielding and a little afraid of letting herself go, which made it all the more interesting for Jim as he coaxed and wheedled her into different positions and the like leading to much more sexual fulfilment.

The next morning when the children returned home they were met by a very nervous Meg, so that was why their father had gone off for a couple of days. There he was actually smiling at them when he introduced them in turn to Meg, they each said hello and just stood and starred not really knowing what else to say. Jim asked them if they wanted any breakfast but Ada had fed them well so that idea was abandoned, so their father suggested that they help show Meg around the house as she would be living with them, and to help her all they could. The kids were amazed that Meg was moving in however she did look a lot nicer and kinder than Ginny so they each hoped that things would turn out for the better, Lizzie wondered if her prayer for someone else to do the cleaning had been answered and her heart leapt at the thoughts of it, what if her days as a skivvy were numbered yippee was all she wanted to say. "Do you go to church on Sundays," asked a nervous Meg. Lizzie answered that they always attended Sunday school, Meg then asked them if they would like her to go with them, the embarrassment they felt was taken over when Jim said that he had hoped that she would be going to the pub with him. Huge sighs of relief could be heard three streets away, and after the couple had left for the pub Lizzie couldn't wait to rush round and tell Ada.

Ada couldn't take it in another one of the buggers women what on earth was he thinking about, she would have to give him a piece of her mind and no mistake and the sooner the better. It was no use talking to him when he had ale inside him so she would have to wait for a suitable moment, perhaps it would be better to work on her first tell her to sling her bloody hook. The moll wasn't welcome not now not ever here in this house her Sal's house, it would always be Sal's house as far as Ada was concerned or as long as she lived. The kids went off to Sunday school and after a short time Meg returned to prepare their dinner, Jim hadn't wanted her to but she was determined so he had reluctantly let her go. As soon as she had left everything felt flat and all Jim wanted to do was follow her home and take her to bed, but he didn't get the chance as soon as her back was turned everyone clustered round wanting to know how he had found her again and was she here to stay. Jim told the tale about hearing that Meg was in Nottingham so he had a few contacts and he set off to find her, it hadn't been easy and he was almost exhausted when he sat down in a little café and who should come over to serve him but Meg. It had taken him a whole day to convince her that Ginny was no longer in the picture and that he only wanted her, then it was a case of getting her possessions together and leaving her room.

As soon as he possibly could Jim left the pub for home, he almost skipped down he road with joy. This was what he had always wanted this feeling of belonging to someone he never had that for Sal although he had adored her and Ginny, well she was a different story wanting her wasn't quite the same as belonging. He wondered if other men felt like this about their woman they were lucky buggers if they did, Ted would have done he was sure of that for all the years they were together. For the first time in his life Jim felt envious of Ted and sad for Ada, how she must miss him poor old girl he would try to be kinder to her. With this thought he burst into laughter him being kind to Ada the very idea, he would refrain from kicking the foundry dog next. No not that he always enjoyed giving the slobbering mutt the toe of his boot, and he was sure that the dog enjoyed it to it must do it ran at him every morning he went into work

Normally Jim would slam the front door off its hinges and scare the kids to death when he came home from the pub, but not today he didn't want to frighten Meg. A rather strange feeling swept over him and he recalled that he hadn't felt like that since the early days, the time when he had fallen so hopelessly in love with the beautiful Sally Smith. A lump the size of a cricket ball stuck in his throat and huge tears filled his eyes at the recollection, "oh Sal" by God he had loved her. He couldn't let Meg see him like this so as quickly as he went in he went back out again, and he walked blindly not knowing where he was going too the tears still filling his eyes. After a while he stopped walking and surveyed his surroundings, he was at the allotments so he made his way to where Ted used to garden and sat down on the bench where the old lad used to sit and contemplate. It wasn't as well kept as it used to be when Ted was in charge, but there were plenty of vegetables growing for the war effort. It was quite comfy and Jim relaxed thinking about the old days, he wished that Ted was still alive he would have liked to have chatted to him. He had always known that Ted hadn't much time for him and it had never bothered him before, but today he would have liked to chew the fat with him he didn't know why perhaps he was getting old. Sitting there comfy and relaxed with a belly full of beer he soon nodded off, and when he awoke a couple of hours later in darkness he panicked not knowing for a few moments where he was.

Glancing at his wristwatch he groaned deeply, bloody hell it was gone five o'clock Meg would be wondering where the hell he had got to. The dinner she had run home to cook would be ruined and probably in the dustbin, he scurried home as fast as he could not noticing the bog he slipped into. His best suit shoes and coat were covered in mud as he lay there ranting one second then laughing like a fool the next, staggering to his feet he made his way home unable to contain his mirth and burst out with uncontrollable laughter at regular intervals. When he finally reached the house and let himself in he was prepared for the verbal abuse he always warranted, however the children where all very quiet and Meg was nowhere in sight, he feared the worst but Joe assured him that she hadn't left she was in the bedroom weeping. Jim suddenly became aware that the children were staring at him open mouthed, he realised what a sight he must look caked all over in mud. "I slipped in'th mud up at'th allotments" he told them trying hard not to laugh out loud, making his way to the kitchen he discarded his muddy clothes on the floor and clad only in his long johns he dashed up the stairs before the youngsters caught sight of him. In next to no time he was lying on the bed next to a very tearful Meg begging her forgiveness, he told her about the walk to the allotments but not the reason why he went there in the first place. Thankfully she hadn't heard him come in from the pub, so he didn't have to try and explain that one thank the Lord. What could he have told her, that he was thinking about Sal.

Jim broke into fits of laughter and was uncontrollable, Meg was unable to quieten him and wondered why he was laughing was it at her expense.

After an age when he had calmed down she managed to get out of him the reason for his hysterical outburst, it was a combination of him running upstairs in his underwear afraid that the kids would see him. Then the thought of him making excuses and more or less begging for forgiveness, something that in Jim Moore's book was completely unheard of. Meg was sure that it was only for the better and he should be like that more often, she liked him like that and began to show her appreciation as best she knew how and Jim was eager to accept. When they were both spent lying In the darkness of the bedroom Jim felt the familiar lump in his throat, the one that always cried out Sally, why oh why couldn't they have been like this if only she had loved him. He knew that she never had not a little bit, if there had been just the tinniest bit of feeling for him but there never was and never would have been. Well he would be happy with Meg so sod every one else, and he cursed himself for his longing for his dead wife. Before he drifted off to sleep he confessed to her about the pile of muddy clothes that he had left on the kitchen floor, but Meg didn't mind she loved him desperately and reassured him that it didn't matter at all and not to worry and they drifted of to sleep happy in each others arms. Downstairs Joe, Teddy, Lizzie and Alex were all agog, their Father hadn't slammed the door. There hadn't been any shouting from above, what was going on. They could only hope that it remained this way for all of them, so making sure that the house was tidy and the fire was safe they trooped of to bed feeling a little happier.

The next morning Brian would be to returning to his camp and he was dreading the thought of leaving his sick wife, although she was looking a little better he was still worried about her. Trying not to show his concern too much he hugged her to him on their last night, perhaps she would respond to his advances and they would make love before he left for God knows where. However after trying everything he knew how he fell asleep exhausted hoping that perhaps morning would bring better rewards, Mary however was one step ahead and when he awoke she was already up and about. Brian was livid and tried desperately not to show it, and when his young wife appeared in the doorway with a cup of tea in her hand he threw back the covers to reveal an almighty hard on. Mary decided that she must make an effort and not let her man go back felling frustrated, after all she didn't know when she would see him again if ever and she did love him very much. The hand relief she gave him was better than nothing at all but it wasn't like being inside her feeling as one, holding her tight kissing her moist eager lips. Mary assured him of her love and argued her morning sickness cause, furious with herself for not wanting him like she had always done before but she was unclean and she mustn't forget that not ever.

Neither of them could eat they were filled with such mixed emotions, and now that the time had come Mary wished with all her heart things had been different. Brian didn't know what she had been up to behind his back, and there had been no need to lie and deceive. All that he had wanted was a little loving from the wife he adored before he left her to go off to war to fight for his country; it wasn't much to ask a bit of tenderness a hug a kiss. It might have led to other things so she had withheld her feelings just in case, and now when it was too late she wanted desperately to hold him in her arms and go to bed like they used to. To be like they were before would have been both agony and ecstasy, she tried but failed miserably to stem the flow of tears and they cascaded down relentlessly. Brian rushed to her side and scoped her up in his arms they clung together sobbing neither one ashamed of their tears, she promised him that next time would be different she would give him so much loving he would be exhausted. He reminded her that next time there would be a little one to see to so they may not get all the loving they wanted, Mary assured him that nothing would get in the way of their lovemaking it would be top priority. And she meant it too they would stay in bed for days on end, the baby hopefully would not exist it would have died at birth. They wouldn't have anything to stand in the way of making another one, a baby that would be both loved and wanted. It was something to look forward to something to aim for to get her out of this ghastly mess that she was in, it was time for Brian to go and he gently pulled away from her. "I've got to go sweetheart I dunna want to miss'th train" he told her, he did want to miss the train really but knew that he had to be on it he didn't want to classed a deserter. Mary just crumpled in a heap and he had to leave her there, his heart breaking at the sight of his young wife and he prayed to God that he would come back to her and their unborn child. Brian ran down the cobbled street knowing that the train would be pulling out of the station at any moment, his vision blinded by tears as he tried not to get waylaid by any well-wisher. Tearing along the platform he became aware of his Mother waiting there for him, her eyes awash with tears. "I knew tha wud'na ave time to say tarra to me," she wept. Brian gave her a big hug then ran for the train shouting back to her "sorry mam look after Mary fer me now think on", then he was gone as the train pulled out of the station leaving his mother distraught wondering if she would ever see him again. The woman cut a lonely figure as she trudged out of the station once she lost sight of the train, she wrung her hands together and wiped her eyes with the corner of her pinafore muttering to herself about how kids grow up and away from their Mothers when they find themselves a wife.

Mrs Bailey didn't think to call and see how Mary was coping without her husband all she could do was wallow in her own misery, and everyone she met along the street had a blow by blow account of how she had gone to the station to wave goodbye to her only son as he left for active service. Of how he couldn't leave his wife long enough to have a few words with his Mother before his departure, everyone tut tutted and said how true it was that sons broke there Mothers hearts. Each one echoing the timeworn phrase 'A Son's a Son till he finds a wife, but a Daughter's a Daughter all her life', and each one met with the same reply "tha never said a tru'er word by eck never a tru'er word. This was repeated to anyone who had the time to listen until she reached home, where she proceeded to throw herself down on the settle and weep for the son who she felt was lost to her in more ways than one.

Someone else was felling a bit dejected wondering about his family, of how they were coping. Was the baby growing did young Harry look like his Daddy, was Peggy coping without him did she miss him. He would write to her later that night that was if he could tear himself away from Pamela his feelings for her grew stronger day by day and he felt ashamed of himself but he was powerless to stop. It was probably a case of Pamela was here and Peggy wasn't, and he was a male after all with powerful urges. However things were not running smoothly, since their last encounter when she had run off and left him standing Pamela had become aloof and hardly acknowledged him at all. Harry felt that she was playing hard to get and he wished that she would stop the silly game, but if the truth be known she just wanted to be left alone and try to get over her feelings for him. If he kept up the pressure she was afraid that her resolve would crumble and she would be back in his arms, the place where she really wanted to be more than anywhere else in the world. The truth was that he was a married man with a baby and it was wrong to want him, of all the hundreds of men on the base she had to fall for him. Pamela cursed her luck and tried to get on with her everyday life as best she could, no-one knew what tomorrow had in store for them and while she was a little afraid it was also exciting to be involved with the war effort. There was a very handsome officer who had made it very clear that he was just waiting for the nod from her, she would give him that nod and maybe he could make her forget Harry. The more she thought about it the better it felt, so she got one of her friends who knew how she felt about Harry to make a date with him. Quite quickly the date was made and before she had time to back down she found herself dressed in her best bib and tucker, and with the help of her friends almost frog-marched to meet him. Sebastian greeted her warmly and quickly put her at ease he was a real gentleman and she felt comfortable and relaxed in his company, it was obvious from the start that he came from a long line of military men and wanted nothing more than to follow family tradition. He didn't make her pulse race but he was nice to be with nice in every way, and he was smitten with Pamela and he didn't try to conceal it. At the end of the night when he escorted her back to her quarters he asked her if she would attend the Saturday night dance at the officers mess with him, she quickly accepted. Expecting a crushing embrace she was somewhat taken aback when he leaned forward and lightly brushed her cheek with his lips, thanking her for her excellent company he bade her goodnight. Pamela stood there in the moonlight wondering perhaps if he didn't like her very much, all the men she had ever known couldn't wait to kiss her passionately at the end of every date. Yet this seamed different it felt right and in spite of herself and her thoughts of Harry she really wanted to see Sebastian again, and Saturday couldn't come soon enough.

Harry was fuming he had been told about the date between Pamela and the Officer, well if that's what she wants good luck to her he muttered to himself. He knew that he couldn't offer her anything only a hell of a lot of lovemaking, of which he would have liked to have participated in. His thoughts at every waking moment were of the two of them in bed always in the throes of passion, locked together lunging clinging, body fluids squelching embarrassingly but not to enough to put them off. This was what he wanted more than anything, but would it ever happen and how was he going to stop the longing he groaned in utter misery.

Peggy would have found a way to deal with him had she known but thankfully she didn't and hopefully never would, life went on normally for everyone and time seemed to fly by. Weeks turned into months and the war that they had been expecting didn't seem to materialise, there were no bombs dropped on them no-one had invaded there shores or held them at gunpoint. Which was a blessing when all was said and done.

Mary was preparing for bed when she had a sudden sharp pain in her belly which doubled her up, she knew that she was due to have her baby at anytime but she dismissed it as bellyache. Because she didn't want the baby, it hadn't died like she had hoped but maybe it would be born dead then her problem would be solved. However everything was prepared just in case, the family interest was very evident still and she couldn't let them know how she still felt after all these months. The pretence had to be there as she met up with neighbours and the like, 'won't be long now I bet tha'll be glad when thee babbies here'. That was what she had to put up with every day, she had to smile and feign happiness and longing for the tiny tot she loathed and despised. Thankfully her workmates at the shed had made a collection for her and with the money had bought every garment and aid that she could ever need for a new-born child, she had washed the dozens of nappies and hung them on the line and when she had aired them in front of the fire and they were soft and warm on folding and she could smell them she wept. It could all have been so different if only she had kept her legs closed, but all the if only's in the world couldn't change things. Life would never be the same again and she would have to put up with it, and if her baby was born deformed which she was sure it would be then she would have to look after it that would be her punishment.

The pain didn't go away and by morning she was sure that she would die, and when Jean called round at half past eight and let herself in with the key that she had insisted on keeping Mary was squealing in agony. After checking on her sister Jean scurried of to find the midwife, then when she had tracked her down she took Elizabeth Jean to stay with Joyce Hibbert for however long it took Mary to have her baby. Jean knew that her little one would be safe and well looked after so she would have no worries there and she could concentrate on her sister, back at Mary's there were kettles to be boiled cotton wool laid out with a clean bowl and plenty of towels. Mary was screaming blue murder and Jean was already worn out with running up and down the stairs, she held her sisters hand as contraction after contraction ripped through her belly. When Mary let rip with a string of obscenities Jean had to make allowances for her, she well remembered her own labour it wasn't easy to deal with and the pain was terrific at times, however Mary was sure that she was going to die and the baby was according to her already dead and good riddance too. Jean shuddered and hushed her sister and taking her by the shoulders shouted at her to remember that the midwife was on her way, and if she came out with that kind of talk in front of her there would be hell to pay. We have got to spend the rest of our lives here she told her and if you carry on like this we shall become outcasts no-one will ever speak to us again, and don't forget that Brian will get to hear of it too and his Mother and the rest of his family.

This seemed to do the trick and Mary quietened down a little, the pains were getting even stronger and Jean was almost at the end of her tether. "Where the hell is that bloody midwife," she shouted more in fear than anything else. Whatever could she do Mary's eyes were wild and red rimmed and Jean thought that she might peg out if someone didn't come soon, she had been in labour for an awful long time. In answer to her prayers someone was running up the stairs and young Winnie appeared at the bedroom door, Winnie was the midwife's assistant and Jean was thanking God for her appearance. She was only young but strong and capable sprang to mind quickly weighing up the situation she gesticulated for Jean to go and make them all a cup of tea, and Jean couldn't get down the stairs fast enough. When she returned with the cups of tea she asked where Mrs Darnel was, Winnie assured her that she would be along presently and not to worry Mary wasn't fully dilated it would be a while yet. "I've gin her a painkiller to settle her a bit," she told Jean and she dipped a flannel in cold water and laid it across Mary's feverish brow. "It wont be long now Mary," she whispered to her hoping to calm her but the impending birth was scarring Mary to death. Why didn't they bugger off and leave her alone she thought standing there bloody gawpin at her arse every two minutes, was now't sacred. When Winnie had appeared with the shaving kit and had started to hack of her pubic hairs it was all Mary could do to stop herself from attacking the young lass, she wanted to launch herself at her in a rugby style tackle and wrestle her to the ground.

After another three hours when Mary was about to slash her wrists, Mary Darnel the midwife appeared. Mary radiated calmness and tranquillity, she had that certain something that put her patients at ease and they relaxed a little more in her presence. "Well we have two Mary's here," she beamed. "Not virgins though," laughed Winnie. Even the pregnant Mary couldn't help but laugh at this, "well we two might not be but I don't really know about you." "The amount of lads that follow you around well who can say," Winnie pretended to be outraged at the suggestion and winked at Mary Bailey. They then proceeded to check that everything was going along smoothly with their patient and once more an inspection was made of her undercarriage, the pain had moved to Mary's back and she was just about at the end of her tether. Nurse Mary clucked and tutted to her and turning her over gently massaged her aching back, "it won't be long now Mary your almost fully dilated" she told her. Then proceeded to tie two towels one each side of the bed posts, guiding Mary's hands to them she told her to pull on them when the time came. Mary had seen this procedure many times with different members of the family over the years, so she knew what to expect.

Jean was still sitting downstairs trying to drown out the sound of Mary's moaning and weeping, the labour had gone on for much longer than hers and she grew afraid for her sister. Would the baby be alright or born dead as her sister had hoped and prayed for, Jeans heart went out to Mary why had this happened to her what had gone so wrong. Mary had always been such a loving girl caring for others helpful and kind, but not now she was rude quarrelsome even hateful at times and she wished her baby dead. Jean hoped with all her heart that Mary wouldn't blurt out her secret to the midwife when she was in the throes of pain, Nurse Darnel was the soul of discretion but Winnie was another matter. Although she was a lovely girl she liked a good gossip and nothing would stop her from telling Mary's story, she would have a field day with it and who could blame her. Jean was thankful that Mary Darnel was attending her sister she was a really nice woman, she had come from Norfolk a couple of years ago to nurse her sister who was dying of cancer, her husband dying of the same decease the year before leaving her bereft. Her two babies had been stillborn so she knew the pain of childbirth and the aftermath, so with nothing to go back for she had stayed on to live with her sister's husband and three children. Gossips said that the couple slept together but they couldn't prove it, in fact Mary wished that it were true there was nothing she wanted more than to be in her brother-in-laws bed making love to him night after night. However he didn't see her in that light she was the sister of his beloved wife and was to be treated with respect, although if he could have read her mind things might have been different.

The factory hooter sounded out dinner time and the workers spewed out rushing and bustling about their business, most would be shopping for the evening meal something filling for the husband and kids. Buy it then scuttle home and prepare it quickly, shove it into the oven on a low heat and leave for the rest of the day. Mostly it would be meat and potato pie or stew, a casserole if they were lucky. Then it would be a race back to work and on with the afternoon graft, with thoughts of getting the huge pile of washing done and dried and then have to stand for hours and iron it. This all to be done in-between the days work and seeing to the large brood, and trying to keep the men folk happy.

Big Jim Moore was feeling very happy and wondered why he hadn't moved Meg in long ago, she was perfect for him and she was good with the kids too good really what they needed was a swift punce up the arse. She had his blessing to crack them one anytime she wanted, but she preferred to mother them and they were beginning to respond to her after a very shaky start. They had tried it on at the start but Meg was so warm and loving that they all melted under her gaze, all they had ever been short of was a bit of love and kindness and it looked like they were going to get some at long last. Jim was getting ready for his afternoon shift at the foundry and fancied a bit of loving himself before he left, as he drew Meg to him there came an almighty banging on the front door. Jim let out a string of bad language and Meg chastised him for it, "I canna answer'th door wi this." he told her pointing to his quite visible erection, Meg tittered and ushered him into the parlour while she answered the door.

On the doorstep stood the local Bobby, and Meg was quite taken aback to say the least.

"Is Jim about," he enquired. "Come in officer" answered Meg and shouted for Jim, she was feeling very nervous something must have happened to one off the children. Jim didn't appear so Meg ushered the policeman into the parlour where Jim was sat with a newspaper on his lap hiding the obvious, the sight of the officer soon dampened his ardour and he jumped up demanding to know what the matter was. The Policeman cleared his throat, "well Jim its about Ginny." He looked across at Meg indicating that he might not want her present, "Meg can stay there's nowt to hide" muttered Jim. "Right oh then" the Policeman answered and added, "well I have to inform you that Miss Ginny Wilkinson was found dead recently." At this both Jim and Meg turned pale, "dead" gasped Jim "How." The policeman went on to tell them the date and time of Ginny's demise but not the cause, adding "My Inspector would like you to call in at the station this afternoon just to tie up a few loose ends." He added, he bade them good afternoon then he left leaving the bewildered pair to wonder at Ginny's fate. Jim was too shocked to speak and sank down on the settle in utter bewilderment, Meg put the kettle on and began to weep a little for Ginny but mostly thankful that Jim's kids were safe and well.

After a few moments Jim stood up and followed Meg into the kitchen, where he could see that she was preparing a brew of tea. " Dunna make one fer me lass I'd best get off to'th nick and find out what's gone on," he reached for his coat and work bag and said that he would carry on straight to work or he would be late for his shift. Meg hugged him tight to her breast and told him not to worry, you havn't done anything wrong she told him. Jim trudged up the road deep in thought what the bloody hell was going on, fair enough he had wanted rid of Ginny she had become a pain in the arse but dead he could'nt imagine it. He could picture her oozing sex appeal what a bloody waste he thought she really had been good in bed, in no time at all he was entering the local nick and was aware that beady eyes were watching him along the high street. He almost laughed out loud at the thought of his neighbours; they would be having a bloody field day wondering why the Police had been to his door. Curtains would be twitching all day long, the poor buggers wouldn't be able to leave there windows in case they missed something.

Jim asked for the inspector and was ushered into his office pretty quickly, he was a rugged man mean looking with eyes that bored right down into your soul. Jim held out his hand to shake but the officer ignored it, ignorant bastard thought Jim and sat down before the man asked him to not giving a shit if he was supposed to or not. The Inspector droned on and on before finally telling Jim that Ginny had been found dead in a boarding house just a week after she had left Bridgevale, she was in Edinburgh searching for some family members. Septicaemia was the cause of her death and the full results of the post mortem would be sent to them as soon as possible, he then went on to ask Jim if he knew anything about events leading up to her illness. Jim was aghast what the bloody hell did he know about septi-whatsit, he'd never heard of it, "she didn'a get the bugger off me that's for sure." Hollered Jim raising himself up to his full height, the Inspector hastily assured him that he wasn't being accused of anything. Then told him to calm down explaining that septicaemia wasn't contagious, adding it wasn't something you could catch from someone else like measles or the like.

This seemed to calm Jim down and the officer went on to explain as best he could about Ginny's condition, when Jim told him about Ginny falling to the floor and being in pain quite often they got a picture of how things were. Also how it had all started on her return from Haverfordwest, the police Inspector mulled this over and wrote a few notes down. "I'll get on to the police there," he told Jim see if they knew anything about Miss Wilkinson. "From what I gather she was no shrinking violet," he added. Jim stood up to leave and this time the policeman shook his hand and thanked him for his time, well thought Jim the police weren't to bad after all he laughed to himself him having a good word to say about the law. What next he would be selling tickets for the police ball, he shouldn't be laughing really poor Ginny was dead and it wasn't funny and his thoughts remained of her for the rest of the day at work. One or two of his fellow workers nudged and winked behind his back wondering what the police had wanted him for, not one of them dared to ask him outright and risk a smack in the mouth.

Over at Mary's house little was happening, the labour seemed to go on for ever and the poor girl was at her wits end. The midwife tut tutted and Jean ran about making comforting sounds, Mary told them to piss off and leave her and the baby to die and the women shuddered at her rantings. Jean tried to make excuses for her it was the pain that was all, and reminiscences of her labour were aired for the tenth time that day. Nurse Darnell gave her another internal and Mary squealed with pain and longed for oblivion, the midwife and her assistant exchanged glances and wondered why Mary was behaving in this way. Every woman in childbirth knew only to well the pain and suffering they had to endure, but also that they would hold a precious child in there arms. Even if money was tight and the old man was out spending what little there was, there was something wonderful about the birth of a child and almost all were welcome. Just a few like Maggie Scully and the late Sally Moore were the exception, and today Mary joined them in this category. Suddenly Mary began to push and squealed out loud, the Nurse told her to pant like a dog and not to push down just yet. Mary was quickly turned over onto her side the Nurse told her that she would be more comfortable that way, but Mary wondered if the woman had gone completely barmy because if was even more painful than on her back.

Mary continued to scream and holler at the top of her lungs until the baby gushed forth in the midst of a tidal wave, and was only inches away from the edge of the bed before being grabbed by a very shocked Midwife. Mary was still clinging to the towels at each side of the bedposts, squealing for all she was worth not realising that the baby had arrived. Jean shook her roughly and told her to stop it, "look the baby is here Mary." Jean told her, Mary stopped hollering but didn't make any attempt to look at the baby. Nurse Darnell took the baby over to the washbasin and gave it a lick and a promise, she didn't believe in bathing a new-born baby until the day after birth. Wrapping baby Bailey up in a fluffy white towel she offered it to Mary, but Mary turned away and closed her eyes. "You have a beautiful baby girl Mary," she told her but the young woman wasn't interested. Jean held her arms out and took the newly born off the Midwife, her eyes pleading to the woman for understanding. "Well" exclaimed Jean in total disbelief as she gazed at the new born, "she is absolutely beautiful. Jean had fully expected the baby to be ugly like its father, but no she had the most beautiful face that Jean had ever seen on a baby. Her eyes were like deep blue pools with the longest darkest lashes Jean had ever seen, she didn't cry just looked around. Jean held her close to her bosom and wished with all her heart that she was hers, and made up her mind there and then that if Mary didn't take to her little girl then she would bring her up as her very own.

Long after the midwife and her assistant had left and Aunty Ada had been and gone, promising to look after Jeans little one to give Arthur a break. Jean took the still peaceful baby over to Mary and forced her to look at her child, "tha'l av'ta feed er our Mary "she told her and dropping the baby into Mary's reluctant arms she scurried off down the stairs to make a cup of tea. The little one yawned and stretched and almost fell out of Mary's arms, and gave a little cry of alarm. Mary looked quickly at the child and couldn't believe what she saw, she had expected her to look like Tom

Scully but she didn't Jean was right she was beautiful. What a little angel she was absolutely wonderful, and Mary examined her closely looking for any defects but there were non.

By the time Jean returned Mary had her baby suckling at her breast like she was born to it, "Jean isn't she beautiful" asked a happy contented Mary. When she had feed and winded her baby and changed her nappy she laid her down to sleep, then the realisation set in. The tears the self loathing the disgust at what she had tried to do to her innocent beautiful child, Jean reassured her as best she could but it took many hours before she calmed down and promised that from now on she would be the best Mother in the whole wide world. Arthur came round to sit with Mary so that Jean could go home and get some sleep, the poor man sat throughout the long night gazing at the sleeping Mary and her baby wishing that they belonged to him. Arthur nursed the baby when she became a little fractious in the night and kissed her tiny forehead and warm pink cheeks, and he watched in wonder and longing as Mary pulled out her large breast swollen with milk and guided the baby's mouth to its ripe nipple. Arthur's stomach churned in knots and he ached to caress the swollen breast and suck its rounded nipple, he thanked the lamplight for masking his tears and had to tear himself away from the sight of Mother and child at feeding time. "The Nurse'l be err in a bit lass so I'll wait down yonder" pointing to the stairs, "Arthur dunna go yet," "tell me what tha thinks of'th baby dust'tha think err's pretty." "Lass that little'n is the prettiest baby that I've ever sen," "apart from me'own." Added the embarrassed Arthur going redder by the second, "she looks like a little angel." He stood there gazing down at the Mother and child wishing that they were his very own, but it wasn't to be a he let out a huge sigh. Arthur almost jumped out of his skin as Mary shouted out "Angel I'll call err Angel," "Arthur ow does Angel Bailey sound to thee." "Well I dunna know lass," replied a puzzled Arthur "I've non eard on a little'n wi'th name Angel afore." "Well I dunna care Arthur I think it's perfect so Angel it is an that's that," He could see that her mind was made up and she wouldn't be budged so her bade her tarra and went off down the stairs. Thankful of the chance to get away from the sight of those enormous breasts and hide his embarrassing longing for her,

Mary was happy to be left alone with her tiny offspring and she marvelled at her perfection. How on earth could she emerge unscathed after all that she had done to herself, she was a little miracle and no mistake and Mary thanked God for the umpteenth time that morning. Now she had a lifetime to make amends and she would do so, her lifestyle would change she would pick up where she left off before the dreadful Tom Scully.

making damned sure that nothing like that ever happened again, and she gazed at her beautiful child suckling contented at her breast and swore that she would be the best cared for child in the whole wide world. Brian' she had almost forgotten about him, she would make sure that he never found out not to ease her own conscience, he didn't need to know it would hurt him too much.

A letter would be sent off to him as soon as possible and a photograph would have to be taken too, she would ask her brother Joe or maybe Teddy he was very artistic he would know what to do. They would be calling round anytime today as soon as they heard the news about the birth, she coloured up thinking about Aunty Ada but she knew that wild horses wouldn't drag the story out of her. Then her thoughts turned to her Mother and her beloved Cammy and she wept till her heart felt broken in two, Cammy would have loved baby Angel and perhaps she might have had a baby of her own with the handsome Finton. Perhaps she would use the name Cameo as Angels second name, Angel Cameo Bailey it sounded very posh and she hoped that people wouldn't ridicule it anyway she liked it so that was all that mattered in the long run. There would be no visit from her Dad he never bothered with any of them, and she wasn't worried about that he'd never been much of a Father anyway. As long as the kids came round she would be happy, let that old bugger stew in his juice and sod him.

The Midwife appeared at the bedroom door and wished her a good morning, thankful to see her with the baby at her breast. Throughout the labour she had shown signs that she didn't want the child at all, and Mary Darnell had been very worried indeed. However the sight of Mother and child before her today told a different story, so perhaps it was the painful labour and nothing more than that thank goodness.

Greeting Mary she relieved her of her baby and proceeded to bath her and put on clean clothes as Mary watched, and ached to do it all herself thinking her child's head would fall off with the rough handling from the nurse. Then when baby was put down for a nap it was Mary's turn to be washed and changed, then she had to rub lanolin into her nipples to stop them from getting sore. The smell of it was horrible and Mary feared that her child would throw up at the taste of it, she hoped that it wouldn't be necessary to do it every day and as soon as the nurse had gone downstairs she wiped the lanolin off with her handkerchief. Just as she lay back to have a little nap heavy footsteps thundered up the stairs, "co'ee art'th decent" it was Aunty Ada, she swept into the room like an express train her widows weeds wafting behind her. Mary was gathered up into her heaving bosom and almost suffocated in her bear hug, the tears gushed forth and cry's of anguish uttered. How many times Ada said how much Uncle Ted would have loved the tiny bundle Mary lost count off, when the tears had dried up Ada asked if Mary had chosen a name or was she still thinking about it. In fact, she was quite surprised to see Mary had taken to her baby after the things that she had stated when she was carrying. "Dunna thee laugh Aunty dost'thear," answered Mary I want no skittin. Ada puffed out her chest "me skittin IL'ave thee know," Mary stopped her in her tracks before she could recite the Gettisburgh address. "Ow dust'tha like Angel" she asked, Ada was a little taken aback. "What di'th say" she enquired, "Angel Cameo Bailey." Answered Mary, Ada was speechless for once in her life. Mary's eyes filled with tears, but Ada was quick to reassure her. "Nay lass I'm non sayin as how I dunna like it, just that I've never erd of'th name afore." Mary was warmed by this response and the tears dried quickly as she explained to her Aunty that it was an unusual name, and did not Ada think that her baby looked just like a little angel.

Ada had to tread very carefully and weigh her words so as not to upset Mary, she agreed that Angel was a very beautiful name once you got used to it. However, the Cameo bit well she had to be very tactful now, and she explained to Mary that having Cameo for a second name meant that no one else in the family could use it. Ada then added that perhaps one day when Lizzie was wed that she might want to use the name herself when she had children, as she had stated many times. Now it was up to Mary she could please herself have the two names if she so wished, but she would have to think about it at length. Also not to let on to the kids until she had fully made up her mind, the two of them continued to bill and coo over the baby and Ada had to admit that Mary's first born was indeed the most beautiful baby she had ever seen. When she thought about the real Father well her whole body shuddered and she thrust him to the back of her mind as quickly as she could, it was time to feed the baby and the nurse ushered Ada out of the bedroom. As she left she found a few more tears to shed, and going down the steep staircase Mary could here her Aunt sniffling and farting on every step which made Mary almost hysterical with laughter.

Lizzie and the boys called just before tea full of excitement, they had gathered a few flowers on the way. Mary eyed the lupines remembering the host of wiggies usually within and sent Joe back down the stairs with them to be left on the kitchen sink, Lizzie was transfixed with the baby and when Mary let her hold her she was beside herself with joy. When Lizzie asked for the baby's name Mary told her Angel but left out the Cameo bit she did not know why, it just seemed right. Lizzie was made up with it, "oh our

Mary it's reet gradly I've ner'erd on it afore but err does look like a little Angel." The boys had a hold and each one nuzzled her to them in turn, all agreeing that they had the most beautiful niece in the whole wide world. The nurse came up to tell Mary that it was time for the baby's feed so the kids trooped out reluctantly, they were to embarrassed to stay and watch anyway but assured her that they would be back soon. When they reached home Meg wanted to hear all about little Angel, but was quickly shut up by Jim. Meg was fuming about this and later when the kids were in bed, she let Jim know clearly how despicable she thought he had acted.

"They are all your family Jim each and everyone and you can start and act civil to them all or I'm off," she told him and then stormed off to bed leaving him to ponder over it. Jim was not used to being on the receiving end and was quite taken aback, he thought about lashing out with his fists but somehow he just couldn't do it. He didn't want to hit Meg or hurt her in any way and as soon as she was gone he wanted to be with her, so off he went to bed stripping naked he climbed in beside her and pulled her around to face him. Meg tried to resist him but he was strong, as he pressed his body closely to hers she could feel his urgent need of her and was just about to draw away from him. Jim felt this and pulled her even closer and as he prepared to mount her he whispered huskily "I'll try Meggy I'll try," this was enough for Meg and she surrendered to him with all her being "God I love thee Jim Moore" she gasped as waves of longing swept over her and she abandoned herself to his lovemaking.

Next morning a very happy Meg asked Lizzie if she thought if might be alright if she bought something for the baby, as she didn't want to get on the wrong side of the family and do anything that would upset them. Lizzie thought it best to ask Aunty Ada and she offered to do it before she went to school, Meg was very pleased with this and could not wait to know the outcome. Perhaps it would be all right maybe she would be able to see the baby, then again maybe not she was an interloper after all and had been carrying on with Jim before his wife had died. She would wait and see hope for the best that was all she could do really; she loved the children and wanted desperately for them to like her. They had not had very much love that she knew but it had not affected them as far as she could tell, they were thoughtful and kind with one another. Meg had told Jim that she intended to make the home life better for the children, and that she didn't want them to cook and clean anymore. Jim had told her she was soft and she must make them do their share in the house, but she was adamant that those days were over as far as she was concerned. The house was quiet when all had left for work or school and she sang as she polished and cleaned, she was happy there she was happier than she had been for a very long time.

Ada wasn't very pleased about the request from Lizzie about Meg, and let her know in no uncertain terms. "By ek lass tha'll be bringin tuth'a bugger back and av er visit next," and she threw her arms up in the air in mock despair. "I canna bring Ginny back er's dead," answered Lizzie to a shocked Ada. "what doe'th mean er's dead" demanded Ada looking bewildered, Lizzie looked uneasy and hung her head not knowing what to say. "Come on girl out wi'it," demanded a very puzzled Ada. "Tha must'na say owt to Dad or he'll skin me alive," answered Lizzie. Then went on to tell Ada what they had overheard their Father and Meg talking about one night, about Ginny being found dead and the police calling round to tell Jim about it. Ada was shocked to the core she hadn't liked the hussy but she didn't wish her dead, "well I never" exclaimed Ada "did they say ow she died." Lizzie shook her head, "but me Dad telt Meg it were summat that appened in Lan bloody ethli". Ada tried not to laugh at Lizzie but tut tutted about her language, "Now now Lizzie we'll ave less of that sort'a talk dust tha err." Lizzie bade her Aunty tarra and was of before she got into any more trouble, school was calling and she didn't want to be late.

Ada wondered what had happened to the strumpet Ginny; she would pluck up courage and ask Jim Moore about it. Oh but she couldn't not without getting Lizzie into trouble, she really hadn't liked the woman she was a bad'n and no mistake. However there must be family who would miss her somewhere, and she found herself feeling sorry for the late Ginny Wilkinson. They were all someone's children there Mothers must have loved them, and Meg she didn't seem to be as bad as Ginny the children actually liked her. Perhaps she wasn't that bad if she was going to be an asset to the kids then maybe Ada should meet her halfway, she would visit and then maybe just maybe she would change her mind. She scolded herself as she went about her chores, thar't getting soft in thee old age Ada whatever would her Ted have thought. The tears that were never far away began to fall and Ada sat and wept buckets for the man that she missed so much, how would she ever get over his loss the answer was she never would. Ada then had a brainwave she would bake a batch of bread and take some round for the kids, that way she would have a chance to observe Meg see what she was like then she could take it from there. By eck Ada thar't a wily owd bugger she tittered to herself, they would ave to get up early to get one over on her.

With the fresh baked bread packed into her basket Ada waddled up the street panting and puffing with every stride, now and then someone would stop and ask after her welfare. Everyone of them remarked on the wonderful aroma coming from the basket, Ada loved a gossip with her neighbours and took her time to reach her late sisters home. Pulling herself up to her full five feet nothing Ada pounded on the door she hadn't meant to knock so hard and felt a little foolish, it was answered quickly by a startled Meg wondering what was going on. Seeing the portly Ada standing there was enough to send her dashing for cover, but she managed a feeble hello and held the door open for Ada to enter. Ada stood on the doorstep not knowing what to say, but as Meg walked back into the house she had to follow. "I've just brought some bread fer'th children, I wer bakin an thought the'd like some." Huffing and puffing she laid the large basket on the table, her eyes swept the parlour and she couldn't help but notice how tidy it was in fact it was spotless.

This pleased Ada she couldn't bare untidiness or sloth, Meg was trembling in her shoes she was an interloper in this woman's sisters home. "Wilt tha ave a cuppa tea Missis Harris," she asked. Ada answered that she didn't want to put Meg to any trouble, but she didn't attempt to leave so Meg put the kettle on the fire to boil. "Sit thee down Mrs Harris," said Meg almost adding take the weight off thee feet but thought better of it on looking at the portly Ada. "My that bread smells right good Mrs Harris," added Meg "I canna bake bread it allis falls flat and goes as ard as lead." She told Ada, and Ada went on to tell her that it wasn't easy to bake a good batch, it took years of practice and promised her a recipe to lend. Meg passed Ada a cup of tea her hand shaking so much the cup rattled a tune in the saucer, by eck thought Ada errs feered to death on me and in spite of everything she felt a warmth towards the other woman. Ada decided to ask Meg about Ginny telling her there were rumours going round the village, When Meg told her of the police visit and her death from septicaemia Ada was aghast. "Well I never did," she said "whoever would have thought it."

As Ada sat and talked to Meg she began to feel comfortable and welcome there, and in spite of herself found herself telling Meg all kinds of stories about the family. Meg listened with interest but was unable to keep the feeling of guilt out of her mind, after all she had been seeing Jim Moore when his wife was still alive and no excuse in the world could alter that. As she went on about Ted and Cammy the tears inevitably followed, Meg felt for the woman and would have liked to comfort her but her guilt wouldn't let her and she just sat and watched. They had another cup of tea and Ada changed the subject to the birth of little Angel, and told Meg that it would be very nice of her to make the baby something.

The back door opened suddenly and Jim Moore appeared making both the woman jump in surprise, he was aghast to see Ada sitting there and waited for the icy blast but non came. Ada leapt to her feet declaring is that the time realising that she had been there for two hours, it had gone so quickly she couldn't believe it. Thanking Meg for the tea she added I'll bring that bread recipe round and she was gone much to Jim's amusement, and he stood and laughed out loud.

"By gum what were all that about then," Jim wanted to know. Meg blustered and stammered and got on with her chores, but Jim gathered her up in his arms and made her aware of his need for her too. He liked this shift work where he was home at two in the afternoon; it gave him time to be alone with Meg before the kids came home from school. They ran up the stairs laughing and giggling like a couple of teenagers, afterwards Jim would want to know why Ada had paid them a visit.

As Ada trundled back down the cobbled street she realised that she had left her basket behind, but decided that she wouldn't go back for it just yet she would leave it for a while. In spite of herself she had enjoyed herself in Megs company, the young girl was warm and likeable and for the life of her she couldn't understand what she saw in the detestable Jim Moore. However the house was clean and tidy warm and welcoming for the children, a good smell of cooking coming from the kitchen yes things were looking better. Ada decided that she would keep her eye on things just in case if was a new broom so to speak, but she had a good feeling about Meg and she hoped that she was right those kids deserved better.

Early next morning Meg was at Ada's door with the basket, "I thought tha might need it for thee shopin." Ada was rather pleased and thanked her, "come in an av'e a cuppa." Added Ada and explained to Meg how she didn't go shopping very early anymore as she found it difficult with her bad legs to get about the same.

In no time at all Meg had Ada writing out a shopping list and promising to do the shopping for her, this pleased Ada very much as the thought of heaving round all the shops filled her with dread these days.

However she wouldn't be won over right away she would observe, keep her council and see how things developed. There was a cuppa waiting in the pot on her return from the shops and Meg was glad of it, and as she drank it she told Ada of her longing for children. Ada asked her age and Meg told her that she was twenty six and had never been married, explaining that she had looked after her elderly parents until their deaths some two years before. They hadn't wanted children and she was a shock to them coming into the world when her Mother was almost fifty, they hadn't saved for a rainy day and didn't think that they would have anyone to leave there money to so they spent it. They enjoying a comfortable lifestyle but when the end came, the house was rented and the landlord told her she would have to leave he wanted to sell it. The furniture didn't raise very much and the money her parents left just about paid for their funerals, just weeks apart. It was as if they didn't want to live without each other, so Meg was left alone without family or money. Having met up with Ginny Wilkinson briefly in a pub where she had gone to drown her sorrows, the latter told her that she was welcome to join her in Bridgevale there was a room next door to her for rent and a barmaids job if she wanted it.

The rest was history and she stayed clear from any mention of Jim Moore and his longsuffering wife Sally, having listened to Megs story Ada felt quite sorry for the lass and although she was no angel she had looked after her old Mum and Dad. In Ada's eyes that was a good thing she had just fallen on hard times, she shut her eyes to thoughts of them together in bed and shook her head a few times tut tutting. Meg then made her exit but not before she asked Ada the time and date of baby Angel's arrival, she would make something she declared then she was off. Ada stood at the front door and watched her departure, and in spite of everything she couldn't help but like the girl. Gazing skywards she hoped that her Sal wouldn't be looking down disapprovingly at her, Ted wouldn't he knew that she had the family's best interests at heart.

A few days later there was a gift from Meg she had bought a child's plate and around the edge she had painted the details and name of the child, read Angel Bailey born June 24th 1940 at 4-32pm. It was beautifully done and Mary was thrilled with it even if her Father's bit on the side had made it, at least she had made an effort so she couldn't be all bad. Ada went on to tell her about the talks she'd had with Meg and that in spite of everything she couldn't help but like the woman, the kids also sang her praises of her so Mary told Lizzie to bring Meg round to see the new baby. After all thought Mary she's no worse than me, and I don't want to be shunned by every one.

The war didn't seem to effect the villagers very much, large city's had been bombed and many people killed but life in Bridgevale went on as usual the days turned into months and months into years. People went about there business as usual and then things started to happen, lots of local men were posted overseas and the womenfolk held the fort doing all the things that their men folk had always done. By December 1942 things were hotting up and rations were getting more scarce, Jean and Mary were gathering provisions together for a New Years Eve party. Everyone was joining in to make it a splendid do, the children were excited and running about squealing in anticipation. Tilly offered to take them for a walk while preparations were underway, so donning their winter coats and scarves plus gloves off they trooped.

Tilly and Sally Victoria now aged six, Elizabeth Jean five, little Harry aged three, he was tucked up in his bassinet. Sally Victoria was allowed to push him at a steady pace, and last but by no means least there was Angel. Mary's treasured and adored little two year old, the light of her life. They set of down the cobbled street and after many cry's of ducks please from the children they headed for the canal towpath, it was bitterly cold and the water was frozen over solid Tilly hoped that the local children would keep off it there was always a danger lurking there. The cold didn’t seem to bother the children they didn't seem to mind at all as they shouted and laughed every inch of the way. "Have we brought any bread Aunty Tilly," Sally Vicky wanted to know. Tilly had to admit that she had forgotten because she hadn't known what there destination would be when they set off, however she assured them that the ducks would still come over to them bread or no bread. Sure enough when they reached the canal banks the ducks came waddling over the ice towards them making a heck of a racket, they were so noisy that Harry began to cry in fear of them. The others tried to reassure him that they wouldn't harm him, but it was no use he roared even louder.

"Tha want's shut thee noisy buggers up" shouted a woman's voice, "canna a body ave a bloody bit o peace an quiet fer God's sake." Tilly looked over to see that it was Polly Simmons sat on the wall looking angry and belligerent, "sorry" she started to say but Polly turned away intent on snubbing her. There wasn't much that she could do except take the children further down the canal away from the offending ducks, so off they trundled and seeing the feathered pets disappearing into the distance Angel began to whimper. Huge tears welled in her eyes "duck duck" she chanted over and over "duck duck, there wasn't a lot that Tilly could do only reassure Angel that they would see the duck ducks again in a moment or two. Fancy that misery guts Polly Simmons behaving like that, and her language in front of the children it just wasn't right. Tilly would have words with her one of these days when she was without the children, mind you it was only to be expected from someone who got rid of babies for a living she wasn't human thought Tilly.

Looking down on her charges she thanked God for not letting Polly get hold of any of her family, they were all so precious. Gazing at the beautiful little Angel with her golden curls and those eyes huge blue pools filled with tears, how would Mary have coped without her she had been so ill whilst carrying that the family had feared for her well being. "We'll come again later on my precious," she whispered to the weeping child and hugged her close. That seemed to do the trick and Angel was back to her old self giggling and laughing with delight as they trundled down the towpath, The tears had dried for Harry too and he had promptly dropped off to sleep, that made it easier for Tilly and she began to relax a little more and talk to the girls about her walks when she was young.

Jim's next leave would be months away so she would have nothing to look forward to except his letters of course which were few and far between these days, but she understood that his duty was to his country and he had a difficult and dangerous job to do. Thinking about Jim only made her miss him more and brought the tears to her eyes, what would he be doing on New Years Eve she wondered it upset her to think about him perhaps dancing close to some shapely female so she had to put him to the back of her mind for a while and concentrate on the family.

On the way back along the canal towpath one of the bargee men jumped down from his craft and called hello to the children, he was a scruffy chap but nice and friendly and Tilly didn't feel threatened by him. The children laughed along with him and he showed them how to call the ducks over, he made a silly quacking sound and lo and behold the ducks for miles around flapped and paddled over to where the children waited shrieking with delight. They had never seen so many before and they loved it but Tilly was a little alarmed afraid that the children might get harmed in some way, the bargee laughed at her apparent fear and told her not to worry. "They're more afeered on us than toother way round missis," he laughed. "Ast tha sin'th size on them to us wer'n like giants too'th poor buggers." He roared with laughter again displaying a mouthful of brown and rotten teeth, and Tilly felt nauseous at the sight of them. Remembering the gleam of her darling Jim's smile, o'h how she wished that he was here with her.

"Come on lets get home and ready fer'th party," she called and shunted the children along the path away from the man. He'd have them there all day long if she didn't do something about it, as they went scuttling along the bank he called out to Tilly. "A party can anybody come e'h lass," Tilly was mortified and shouted back quickly "it's only fer'th family mister tarra now." he said something in reply but she couldn't hear him for the quacking of the ducks, cheeky bugger she thought to herself tryin to invite himself to the do tonight he would probably have brought along his woman and many brats. Angel had begun to cry and shouted duck ducks over and over again, Tilly promised that they would see the ducks again later on. Angel was normally so well behaved it wasn't like her to go on about something, it was just that she loved the ducks so much. Tilly bent down to kiss her tear stained little face and soothe her promising that they would be back, she was glad when they reached home and she could hand the children over to their own mothers and have a cuddle with her own dearest Sally Victoria,

Mary demanded to know why her baby was so upset and Tilly had to go over the story about the ducks, and she left the two together and went home to get changed for the New Years Eve party. Mary bathed her precious child and dressed her in her new party frock made by Meg with loving care; it had large pockets so that she could put her little dollies in them when she went for a walk. Mary brushed her golden curls until they gleamed tied in the pretty bows, pulled, and teased until she looked perfect. Black patent shoes and white cotton socks came next then she was ready with plenty of time to spare, with many don't get dirty cries ringing in her ears. All Angel was interested in was when would she be able to see the duck ducks again and went on and on about them until Mary was almost driven mad and shouted at her not to mention them again.

The family were holding the party at big Jim's house, his Meg had turned out to be an absolute treasure after the dreadful but deceased Ginny who's death still remained a mystery. Jim had mellowed a lot with time and he didn't want to get on the wrong footing with Meg, not when there seemed a likelihood of him being called up to fight for his country.

Everyone was gathered at the family home and the party was in full swing, when Mary noticed that Angel was nowhere to be seen. The other children were quizzed about her whereabouts but they did not know, however they had noticed that she had been filling her pockets with crusts from the table all evening. The house was searched from top to bottom but she could not be found, then someone called out that the back door was not shut to properly and they all spilled out on to the yard. The gate was open and Angel was gone, Mary began to shout hysterically and the others tried to reassure her as best they could. Aunty Ada would be left in charge of the other children and the rest of them would split up and search the area, Ada began to weep whilst chomping on a giant sized portion of pork pie almost choking with each mouthful. It had been baked that very afternoon and was still hot, with juice running down her chin Ada looked a picture nothing got in the way of food where she was concerned. Tilly had decided to look towards the canal end of the town just in case Angel had decided to look for the duck's, she shuddered all over hoping and praying that she was wrong. Tilly ran like the wind towards the canal and was almost there when she came across Polly Simmons, "Hast tha bin down to'th canal Polly," she asked. Polly looked at her with contempt spat on the ground and walked away, what the bloody hell's up with her thought Tilly why was she so horrid towards her. "Have you seen a little girl," she shouted not to be put of. Polly didn't answer her but began to cackle in a most horrible way sending shivers down Tilly's spine, Polly almost fell over in her fit of laughter and Tilly couldn't understand her at all.

When she reached the widest part of the canal she saw a tiny figure in the middle of the frozen water, her heart skipped a beat oh lord what should she do. None of the others were around so she gingerly lowered herself onto the ice wondering how angel had got there, she must have jumped down and would probably have hurt herself too unless that harridan Polly had helped her. No she mustn't think like that no one would put a little child on the ice at night time and go off and leave her, she called out to Angel to come to her. The little girl called out duck duck and squealed with delight, Tilly called out more urgently and something in her tone set Angel off in floods of tears. Tilly then tried to soothe her but it only made the little one worse and she began to squeal feeling frightened for the first time, the ice creaked under Tilly's feet and she wanted to jump back onto the banking but Angel was stuck in the middle and wouldn't move. There was nothing left to do only go to her, but young Jim's words were ringing in her ears from that afternoon a couple of years ago about someone will die in there mark my words and fear gripped her very vitals.

Tilly trembled from head to foot as she gingerly made her way across the ice, she had never felt so afraid and her legs were almost turned to jelly but she had to go on. Angel was almost hysterical by this time and Tilly wanted to shout out at her to shut up, as she drew nearer to the little child she called shush to her putting her fingers to her lips to indicate this. Angel began to cry mama and her little body convulsed with fear, when she had gotten a little nearer Tilly called to the youngster to come to her and held out her arms. Angel then proceeded to run to her and Tilly felt the ice vibrate under her feet, how could she tell a two year old not to run it was impossible under the circumstances. Tilly bent down to sweep the little girl in her arms and held her close to her bosom for a few seconds, that was the worst part over now there was just the return, as she held the weeping shivering child in her arms she prayed that someone would arrive and help them. As she turned to walk off the ice she froze with fear as it cracked beneath her feet, at that very moment someone shouted to her it was her father-in-law Jim. Thank God, she thought now we'll be safe, but then suddenly the ice gave way under her and the two of them plunged down into the black frozen waters beneath.

Jim Moore watched in horror as the pair disappeared and he screamed out to them to hang on, but on to what he didn't know. He tried to walk on the ice towards them but It gave way under his weight and he had to scramble to safety, he began to holler at the top of his voice and soon people came running but it was to late and nothing could be done.

They were found the next morning by the police frogman diving team, Tilly first of all and much later little Angel both of them black with mud and slime. The little ones golden curls no longer a joy to behold, the family were in a state of shock and the New Years celebrations forgotten by each and every one. Doctor Hallam had been called out to give Mary an injection to put her to sleep as the family feared for her sanity, and he also had to attend Ada as she suffered a slight stroke brought on by the shock. Almost the whole village rallied round the family and wondered how much one family should have to suffer it seemed that they were cursed somehow.

Jean waited nervously for the train to arrive at the station, no one else felt that they could face young Jim at the moment. Brian had been posted overseas and hadn't yet heard about the tragic happenings. Jean was always left with the worst jobs to do and she was fast getting fed up with it all, why me she told herself. What would she say to Jim, how on earth could she comfort him. Before she could answer herself the huge steam train thundered down the track hissing and hooting as it approached the platform, Jean shrank back into the shadows praying that her brother would not alight. However the Gods as usual were not on her side and the figure of her Brother came slowly into view, Jean took one look at him and her heart skipped a beat. "Jim" she called "oh Jim" their eyes met and huge tears began to flow. Jean ran to him and held him in her arms as his body convulsed with sobs the like of which she had never seen before; gently she led him out of the station and down the road. People stopped and stared but had only sorrow for the poor young man, Jean decided to take him to Ada's that would be best she would know how to deal with him. Once there she left him with Ada whilst she put on the kettle for a cup of tea, Ada tut tutted and fussed around him and after a while he composed himself and began to talk about the dreadful happenings. At breaking point he told them that Tilly was going to announce to them as the New Year rang in that she was expecting there longed for second child, so that meant that there had been three lives lost not two on that dreadful night. Jean was bereft at this news and they sobbed together the three of them their hearts broken for Jim wondering how much more they could take. Jean then decided to leave him with Ada in order to collect Sally Victoria whom she had left with her Arthur and Elizabeth Jean, it would be good for the child to be with her father after all that she had been through. Ada did her best to console Jim but he was absolutely bereft, however he did try his hardest knowing that his dearest Aunt had suffered a stroke and had to be very careful. Ada went off to make them another cup of tea and Jim picked up the paper that she had been reading when they had arrived, he was not reading it just glancing through. When suddenly a picture caught his eye and he took in every detail of it. The picture was of Coral and her young son James Mathew Spencer Her husband was now an eminent Member of Parliament, but the boy was not a Spencer at all Jim's blood ran cold, "My son that's my son" he whispered and he cried out with grief and pain. Ada ran in from the kitchen at his cries and she was just in time to see him throw the paper down onto the floor and rush out of the house, Ada wondered what he had witnessed in the paper it must be something to do with the drowning she scanned the paper wondering what she had missed. There was nothing then she caught the eye of the little boy with his Mother, an ex RAF girl latterly stationed at Biggin Hill. There was something about the child but Ada couldn't put her finger on it, why had Jim run out of the house what was going on.

Two coffins stood on trestles in the parlour at Tilly and young Jim's house, one large size and the other a tiny white one. They were covered with flowers and the perfume filled the entire room, young Jim Moore knelt at his wife's casket and sobbed as if his heart would break. "Forgive me Tilly please forgive me," he repeated over and over again "I didn'a mean it I didn'a mean to do it." "Dunna leave me Tilly please," it went on and on and Lizzie was wondering what to do for the best. People were gathering for the funeral and no one could get any sense out of Jim, Lizzie felt anger at Jim at God at everyone "what a bloody life" she thought and tomorrow would be her first day at the mill.

Printed in the United Kingdom
by Lightning Source UK Ltd.
104184UKS00001BA/16

9 781845 490171